UNQUIET SPIRITS

Unquiet Spirits

A SHERLOCK HOLMES ADVENTURE

BONNIE MacBIRD

COLLINS
CRIME
CLUB

HarperCollins
PUBLISHERS
Since 1817

COLLINS CRIME CLUB

An imprint of HarperCollins*Publishers*
1 London Bridge Street
London SE1 9GF
www.harpercollins.co.uk

Published by HarperCollins*Publishers* 2017
1

Copyright © Bonnie MacBird 2017
All rights reserved.

Drop Cap design © Mark Mázers 2017

Bonnie MacBird asserts the moral right
to be identified as the author of this work.

A catalogue record for this book
is available from the British Library

Hardcover: 978-0-00-812971-2
Paperback: 978-0-00-812972-9

Set in Sabon by Palimpsest Book Production Ltd, Falkirk, Stirlingshire.

Printed and bound in Great Britain by Clays Ltd, St Ives plc

Find out more about HarperCollins and the environment at
www.harpercollins.co.uk/green

For Rosemary and Mac

Contents

PART SEVEN – THE POUR

Preface

Several years ago, while researching at the Wellcome Library, I chanced upon something extraordinary – an antique hand-written manuscript tied to the back of a yellowed 1880s treatise on cocaine. It was an undiscovered manuscript by Dr John H. Watson, featuring his friend, Sherlock Holmes, published in 2015 as *Art in the Blood*.

But what happened last year exceeded even this remarkable occurrence. An employee at the British Library whom I shall call Lidia (not her real name) found *Art in the Blood* in her local bookshop, and upon reading it was struck by the poignancy of Watson's manuscript surfacing so long after the fact.

It triggered something in her mind and shortly afterwards, I received a phone call in my newly rented flat in Marylebone. This was curious, as our number there is unlisted. She identified herself as 'someone who works at the British Library' but would not give her name, and wanted to meet me at Notes, a small café next door to the London Coliseum.

She refused to give me any information about the purpose of this meeting, saying only that it would be of great interest to me.

I could not resist the mystery. I showed up early and took comfort in a cappuccino, watching the pouring rain outside. Eventually a woman arrived, dressed as she had told me she would be with a silk gardenia pinned on the lapel of a long, black military-style coat. A pair of very dark sunglasses and a black wig added to her somewhat theatrical demeanour.

She carried a large nylon satchel, zipped at the top. It was heavy, and the sharp outlines of something rectangular were visible within. 'Lidia' then sat down, and in deference to her privacy I will not reveal all she told me. But inside her bag was a battered metal container that had come from the British Library's older location in the Rotunda of the British Museum many years ago. It had somehow been neglected in the transfer to the new building and had languished within a stained cardboard box in a basement corner for some years.

It was an old, beaten up thing made of tin and was stuck shut. She pried it open gently with the help of a nail file.

Certainly you are ahead of me now.

Within that metal box was a treasure trove of notebooks and loose pages in the careful hand of Dr John H. Watson. You can well imagine my shock and joy. Setting my cappuccino safely to the side, I pulled out a thick, loosely tied bundle from the top. It had been alternatively titled 'The Ghost of Atholmere', 'Still Waters' and 'The Spirit that

Moved Us' but all of these had been crossed out, leaving the title of *Unquiet Spirits*.

Like the previous manuscript, this, too, had faded with time, and a number of pages were so smeared from moisture and mildew that I could make out only partial sentences. In bringing this tale to light, I would have to make educated guesses on those pages. I hope then, that the reader will pardon me for any errors.

She left the box in its satchel in my care, wishing me to bring the contents to publication as I had my previous find. As she stood to go, I wanted to thank her. But she held up a black-gloved hand. 'Consider it a gift to those celebrants of rational thinking, the Sherlock Holmes admirers of the world,' said she. She never did give me her name, and while I could have ferreted it out in the manner of a certain gentleman, I decided best to let it lie.

I later wondered if she had actually read the entire story that was the first to emerge from that treasured box. But let me not spoil it for you.

And so, courtesy of the mysterious 'Lidia', and in memory of the two men I admire most, I turn you over to Dr John Watson for – *Unquiet Spirits*.

—Bonnie MacBird
London, December 2016

PART ONE

A SPIRITED LASS

'Oh, what a tangled web we weave . . . when first
we practise to deceive'
—Sir Walter Scott

CHAPTER 1

Stillness

s a doctor, I have never believed in ghosts, at least not the visible kind. I will admit I have even mocked those who were taken in by vaporous apparitions impersonating the dead, conjured by 'mediums' and designed to titillate the gullible.

My friend Sherlock Holmes stood even firmer on the topic. As a man who relied on solid evidence and scientific reasoning, he saw no proof of their existence. And to speak frankly, to a detective, ghosts fulfil no purpose. Without a corporeal perpetrator, justice cannot be served.

But hard on the heels of the diabolical and terrifying affair of 'The Hound of the Baskervilles' which I recount elsewhere, our disbelief in the supernatural was put to a terrifying test. One might always expect my friend's rational and scientific approach to triumph, yet some aspects of the strange and weird tale I call *Unquiet Spirits* defy explanation, and there are pieces of this puzzle that trouble me to this day.

Holmes forbade publication of these events until fifty years after his death, and I believe his reasons were due less to any momentary lapse on the subject of ghosts than they were to the revelation of facts concerning Holmes's last days at university. Thus I defer to my friend's wishes, and hope those who are reading this account at some unknown future date will understand and grant us both the benefit of a kindly regard on the actions we took – and did not take – in Scotland, in the winter of 1889.

It had been a year filled with remarkable adventures for us, culminating in the recent terrifying encounter with the Baskervilles and the aforementioned spectral hound. Back in London afterwards, with the great metropolis bustling about us in the noisy pursuit of commerce, progress, science, and industry, the dark occurrences of Dartmoor seemed a distant nightmare.

It was a late afternoon in December, and the coldest winter of recent memory was full upon us. A dense white fog and the promise of snow had settled over the streets of London, the chill penetrating to the bone.

Mary had been called away once again to a friend's sickbed, and without her wifely comforts, I did not hesitate to return to visit my singular friend in our old haunts at 221B Baker Street, now occupied by him alone.

My overcoat hung dripping in its usual place, and as I stood in our formerly shared quarters awaiting the appearance of Holmes, I thought fondly of my first days in this room. Just prior to first encountering Holmes, I had been in a sorry state. Discharged from the army, alone in London and short of funds, my nerves and health had been shattered by my recent service in Afghanistan. Of that ghastly campaign and its consequences, I have written elsewhere.

The lingering effects of my wartime experiences had been threatening to get the better of me. But my new life with Holmes had sent those demons hurtling back into darkness.

I stood, taking in the familiar sights – the homely clutter, Holmes's Stradivarius carelessly deposited in a corner, the alphabetised notebooks and files cramming the bookshelves – and found myself wondering about Holmes's own past. Despite our friendship, he had shared little of his early life with me.

Yet I was certain Holmes had ghosts of his own.

In Paris the previous year the remarkable French artist Lautrec had called my friend 'a haunted man.' But then, artists see things that others do not. The rest of us require more time.

A loud, clanking noise drew me from my reverie. Off to one side, on Holmes's chemistry table, a complex apparatus of tubes and flasks steamed and bubbled, shuddering in some kind of effort. I approached to examine it.

'Watson! How good of you to stop in!' exclaimed the familiar voice, and I turned to see the thin figure of my friend bounding into the room in a burst of energy. He clapped me on the back with enthusiasm, drawing me away from the equipment and towards my old chair.

'Sit, Watson! Give me a moment.' He moved to the chemistry equipment and tightened a small clamp. The rattling subsided. Gratified by the result, he favoured me with a smile, then dropped into his usual chair opposite mine. Despite his typical pallor, he seemed unusually happy and relaxed, his tousled hair and purple dressing gown giving him a distinctly Bohemian look.

Holmes rooted for his pipe on a cluttered table nearby, stuck it in his mouth and lit it, tossing the match aside. It landed, still smouldering, on a stack of newspapers.

'Are you well past our ghostly adventure, Watson?' he asked with a grin. 'Not still suffering from nightmares?' A tiny thread of smoke arose from the newspapers.

'Holmes—'

'Admit it, Watson, you thought briefly that the Hound was of a supernatural sort, did you not?' he chided.

'You know that as a man of science, I do not believe in ghosts.' I paused. 'But I do believe in hauntings.' A wisp of pale smoke rose from the floor next to his chair. 'Look to your right, Holmes.'

'Is there a dastardly memory in corporeal form there, Watson, waiting to attack?'

'No but there is a stack of newspapers about to give you a bit of trouble.'

He turned to look, and in a quick move, snatched up the smouldering papers and flicked them into the grate. He turned to me with a smile. 'Hauntings? Then you do believe!'

'You misunderstand me. I am speaking of ghosts from our past, memories that will not let us go.'

'Come, come, Watson!'

'Surely you understand. I refer to things not said or left

undone, of accidents, violence, deaths, people we might have helped, those we have lost. Vivid images of such things can flash before us, and these unbidden images act upon our nervous systems as though they were real.'

Holmes snorted. 'Watson, I disagree. We are the masters of our own minds, or can be so with effort.'

'If only that were true,' said I, thinking not only of my wartime memories but of Holmes's own frequent descents into depression.

The clanking from his chemistry table resumed, loudly.

'What the devil *is* that?' I demanded.

He did not answer but instead jumped, gazelle-like, over a stack of books to the chemistry apparatus where he tightened another small clamp. The clatter lessened and he looked up with a smile, before once again sinking back into the chair opposite mine.

'Holmes, you are leaping about the room as though nothing had happened a year ago. Only last month you were still limping. How on earth did you manage such a full recovery?'

The grievous injuries he had suffered in Lancashire the previous December in the adventure I had named *Art in the Blood* had plagued him throughout 1889, and even in Dartmoor only weeks earlier. But he had forbidden me to mention his infirmity in my later recounting of the next several cases. Had I described him as 'limping about with a cane' (as in fact he was, at least part of the time) his reputation would have clearly suffered.

But now any trace of such an impediment was gone.

He leaned back in his chair, lighting his pipe anew. 'Work!

Work is the best tonic for a man such as myself. And we have been blessed with some pretty little problems of late.' He flung the match carefully into the fire.

'Yes, but in the last month?'

'I employed a certain amount of mind over matter,' said he. 'But ultimately, it was physical training. Boxing, my boy, is one of the most strenuous forms of exercise, for the lower as well as upper extremities. Only a dancer uses the legs with more intensity than a boxer.'

'Perhaps joining the *corps de ballet* at Covent Garden was out of the question, then?' I offered, amused at the mental image of Holmes gliding smoothly among dozens of lovely ballerinas.

Holmes laughed as he drew his dressing gown closer around his thin frame. Despite the blaze, a deep chill crept in from outside. A sudden sharp draught from behind the drawn curtains made me shiver. The window must have been left open, and I got up to close it.

'Do not trouble yourself, Watson,' said Holmes. 'It is just a small break in the pane. Leave it.'

Ignoring him, I crumpled a newspaper to stuff into the gap and drawing back the curtain I saw to my surprise – a bullet hole!

'Good God, Holmes, someone has taken a shot at you!'

'Or Mrs Hudson.'

'Ridiculous! What are you doing about it?'

'The situation is in hand. Look down at the street. It is entirely safe, I assure you. What do you see across and two doorways to the right?'

I pulled back the curtain and peered down into the growing darkness. There, blurred by the snowfall, two doors down and receding, spectre-like into the recesses of an unlit doorway, stood a large, hulking figure.

'That is a rather dangerous looking fellow,' I commented.

'Yes. What can you deduce by looking at him?'

The details were hard to make out. The man was wide and muscular, wrapped up in a long, somewhat frayed black greatcoat, a battered blue cap pulled low over his face. A strong, bare chin protruded, his mouth twisted in what looked like a permanent sneer.

'Bad sort of fellow, perhaps of the criminal class. His hands are in his pockets, possibly concealing something,' Here I broke off, moving back from the window. 'Might he not shoot again?'

'Ah, Watson. You score on several counts. His name is Butterby. He is indeed carrying a gun, although something more important is concealed. He is dressed to hide the fact that he is a policeman.'

'A policeman!'

'Yes, and, in a sense, he is rather "bad". That is to say, he is among the worst policemen in an unremarkable lot. Even Lestrade thinks him stupid. Imagine.'

I laughed.

'But he is enough to frighten away my would-be murderer, who is himself a rank amateur. So bravo, Watson, you improve.'

I cleared my throat. 'A rank amateur, you say? Yet with excellent aim. Who, then?'

'An old acquaintance with a grudge, but I tell you, the situation is handled,' he said. Then noticing my worried face, he chuckled. 'Really, Watson. Your concern is touching, but misplaced. The mere presence of our friend below will end the matter.'

I was not convinced and would try again on this subject later. 'Where is the brandy?' I said, moving to the sideboard looking for the familiar crystal decanter.

I found the vessel behind a stack of books. It was empty.

'I am sorry, Watson, there is no brandy to be had,' said he. 'The shops are barren except for a few outside my budget. You have heard of the problems with the vineyards in France? I have been studying the subject. But I can offer you this.'

From next to him on a side table, he lifted a beaker of clear liquid. He poured a very small amount into each of two glasses. 'Try it,' he said, with a smile.

I took the glass and sniffed. I felt a sudden clearing of my sinus cavities and a burning in the back of my head.

'Good God, Holmes, this smells lethal!'

'I assure you it is not. Give it a try. Here, I will drink with you.' He raised his glass for a toast. 'Count of three. One. Two—'

On three we both gulped the liquid down. I erupted into such a fit of coughing and tearing of the eyes that I did not notice whether my companion did or not. When it subsided, I looked up to find he had tears streaming down his reddened face and was laughing and coughing in equal measure.

'What is this stuff?' I sputtered, wiping myself with a handkerchief.

'Raw spirits. Distilled pure whisky, but before the ageing which renders it mellow. I diluted it with water, but clearly not enough.'

He held up a small booklet, entitled *The Complete Practical Distiller*.

'That was a rather mean trick.'

'Forgive me, my dear fellow. All in the name of science.'

A sharp pop and a sudden loud hiss emanated from the chemistry table. I glanced back at the complex system of flasks, copper containers and tubing.

Holmes normally employed a small spirit lamp to heat his chemicals, but I now noticed a very bright flame arising from a Bunsen burner which was connected by a length of rubber tubing to the wall. Over this was suspended a small, riveted copper kettle in a strange teardrop shape, one end drooping into a line which proceeded through valves and tubes into various looped and coiled copper configurations, complex and confusing, and—

'Holmes!' I cried. 'That is a miniature still!'

'Ah, Watson, you improve. Decidedly.'

'But you have tapped into the gas line! Why? Is that not dangerous?'

'I needed a higher temperature. And, no, it is not dangerous when you take the precaution of—'

The noise had increased. The entire apparatus began to vibrate. The copper kettle and odd configuration of tubes and beakers rattled and shook. One clamp came loose and clattered off the table to the floor. A tube shook free and several drops of liquid arced into the air.

'Holmes—!' I began, but he was up and out of his chair, bounding across the room when a sudden small explosion blew the lid off the copper vessel, broke three glass tubes and an adjacent beaker, and sent a spray of foul smelling liquid up the nearby wall and across a row of books. A flame erupted underneath it.

We shouted simultaneously and in a flash he was upon the equipment, dousing the fire with a large, wet blanket pulled from a bucket he had evidently placed nearby in anticipation of such a possibility. The blanket slid down among the broken pieces. The flame went out and there was silence except for a low sizzle.

The room now reeked of raw alcohol, and a dark, burnt smell. A slow drip fell from the table to the carpet.

Mrs Hudson's familiar sharp knock sounded at the door. 'Mr Holmes? Dr Watson?' she called out. 'A young lady is here to see you.'

Holmes and I looked at each other like two schoolboys caught smoking. As one, we leapt to tidy the room. Holmes flung a second wet cloth sloppily over the steaming mess in the corner while I used a newspaper to whisk some broken glass and other bits under an adjacent desk.

I threw open the window to let out the hideous odour and in a moment we were back in our chairs, another log tossed onto the fire.

'Show her in, by all means, Mrs Hudson,' shouted Holmes.

He picked up his cold pipe and assumed an insouciant air. I was less quick to compose myself and was still sitting on the edge of my chair when the door opened.

CHAPTER 2

Isla

'rs Isla McLaren of Braedern,' announced Mrs Hudson.

Into the room stepped a vibrant young woman of about twenty-eight, exquisitely poised, small and delicate in stature. I was struck immediately by her beauty and graceful deportment but equally by the keen intelligence radiating from her regard. She was elegantly clothed in a deep purple travelling costume of rich wool, trimmed with small touches of tartan, gold and lace about the throat.

Her luxurious hair was brown with glints of copper, and her eyes a startling blue-green behind small gold spectacles. She removed these, took in the room, the mess, the smell and the two of us in one penetrating and amused glance. I immediately thought of a barrister assessing an opponent.

'Oh, my,' she said, sniffing the air.

A strong, rank odour emanated from the contraption, the newspapers and wet cloth on the chemistry table. This mess continued to hiss and clank intermittently.

I rose quickly to greet her. Holmes remained seated, staring at her in a curious manner.

'Madam, welcome. Let me close the window. It is so cold,' I offered, moving towards it.

'Leave it,' commanded Holmes, stopping me in my tracks. 'Do come in, Mrs McLaren, and be seated.'

The lady hesitated and suppressed a cough. 'Some air is welcome. Well, Mr Holmes, how clearly you have been described in the newspapers. And you must be Dr Watson.' Her accent carried a hint of the soft lilt of the Highlands, but modified by a fine education. I liked her immediately.

Holmes appraised her coolly. 'Do sit down, Mrs McLaren, and state your case. And please, be succinct. I am very busy at the moment.' He waved a hand, indicating the settee before us. I knew for a fact that Holmes had no case at present.

The lady smiled. 'Yes, I see that you are very busy.'

'Welcome, madam,' I repeated, mystified by my friend's unaccountable rudeness and attempting to mitigate it. 'We are at your service.'

'Let me come straight to the point,' said she, now seated before us. 'I live in Scotland, in the Highlands to be more precise, at Braedern Castle, residence of Sir Robert McLaren, the laird of Braedern.'

'McLaren of Braedern. Yes, I know that name,' said Holmes arising languidly with a slow stretch and then in a sudden movement vaulting over the back of his low chair as if on springs. Arriving at the bookcase, he ran his finger along several volumes of his filed notes, pulled down one and rifled through it.

'Ah, McLaren. Whisky baron. Member of Parliament. Working at the time of this article to establish business in London. Effectively, it appears. A Tory. Unusual for a Scot. Widower. Late wife very wealthy. And, ah, yes. Go on.'

He returned with the file and draped himself once more in the chair.

'Yes,' she said. 'He is my father-in-law.'

'Obviously. It says here a daughter who did not survive infancy, and three sons.'

'You are not *au courant*. Two sons survive. The eldest, Donal, died three years ago, killed during the siege of Khartoum.'

'You are married to one of the remaining sons. Not Charles, the current eldest, but Alistair, the younger.'

Mrs McLaren smiled. 'That is correct, Mr Holmes. And how did you deduce this?'

I did not like Holmes's regard. 'Madam, how can we help you?' I said.

But the lady persisted. 'Mr Holmes?' she wondered.

'It is obvious. Your ring. Lady McLaren's famous amethyst and emerald engagement ring – I have a clipping here on its history – matches your dress perfectly and would surely be on your hand if you had married the elder son. The rest of your jewellery is quite modest. Therefore the younger son.'

The lady put a hand to her small gold brooch from which dangled a charm. Along with a simple wedding band

16

and gold earrings this was the sum total of her jewellery. She smiled.

'Regarding my jewellery, perhaps I am simply not in the habit of overt display, Mr Holmes. Rather like yourself.' Her eyes flicked to his dressing gown.

'Nevertheless?' Holmes said. She remained silent. Her silence was a tacit acknowledgment. He smiled to himself, then he got up and moved back to the fireplace, making rather a fuss over his pipe. It struck me that she simultaneously disturbed him in some way, and at the same time incited those tendencies which I can only describe as showing off.

'I have come to London to attend the opera, see my dressmaker, and to do a little Christmas shopping,' she began. 'While I was here, I thought—'

'On second thought, I have heard enough, Mrs McLaren.'

'Good grief, Holmes! Madam, I beg your forgiveness,' said I. 'Please do relate your concerns. We are all ears.'

Before she could answer, Holmes barked out, 'Your husband either is, or you imagine he is, having an affair. I do not deal in marital squabbles. Kindly close the door behind you.' He moved sharply away to a bookcase and stood there, his back to her.

She remained seated.

Holmes paused and turned around. 'Really, madam, I beg you. What would your family think of this visit?'

'It matters little what my family might think of my visit. I am quite on my own in this matter. Your opinions, while incorrect, are of moderate interest. Do enlighten me as to your train of thought.'

17

She had opened Pandora's box. 'Madam, mine are not opinions, but facts,' he began in his didactic manner.

'Go on,' said she.

'Holmes!'

'If you insist. You have recently lost weight. For you, this may be considered beneficial. I observe that your dress has been taken in by a less than professional hand. However, something has changed. You have had your hair elaborately done and now are buying new clothes. The latest fashions are little valued in the Highlands, rather the opposite, and it is too cold for most of them. You are either having an affair here – but not likely as you are wearing your wedding ring – or trying to remake yourself to be more attractive to your husband. The jewellery I have explained. Now please, go away.'

'You are wrong on several counts, Mr Holmes, but right on two,' said she. 'I do wish to make myself as attractive as possible. For women, it is sadly our main, although transient, source of power. Perhaps that may change some day. And yes, Alistair is my husband.'

Holmes sighed. 'Of course.'

'However I have not lost weight, this dress has always been too large, and I have fashioned my hair myself. I shall take both errors as compliments.'

Holmes nodded curtly.

'Why, Mr Holmes, do you have such disdain for women? And what is that smell? Never mind. I wish to get to business. I am here to consult you on a case. I see that you are a bit low on funds, so perhaps you had better hear me out.'

Holmes exhaled sharply. 'Pray be brief, then, madam. What exactly is puzzling you?'

'One moment, Mrs McLaren,' said I. 'What makes you think Mr Holmes is in need of funds? Surely you are aware of several of our recent cases which have reached the news.'

'Yes, and I do look forward to your full accounts of them, Dr Watson.'

Just then a sharp noise came from under the wet cloth and it suddenly slid off Holmes's chemistry table. Holmes leapt to replace the blanket over the crude homemade still but not before the lady had a clear look.

'An experiment,' said Holmes sharply. 'Will you not tell us your problem?'

She appraised him with cool eyes. 'In a moment, sir. First I will answer Dr Watson. I see clearly that Mr Holmes requires cash. He has recently had his boots resoled instead of buying new. His hair is badly in need of a barber's attentions. And his waistcoat, trousers, and dressing gown should be laundered, and soon. This does not fit with your description of Mr Holmes. He is either despondent or conserving money. His spirit bottles on the sideboard are empty, and he is rather ridiculously attempting to refill them with homemade spirits. Therefore the latter, most likely.'

'It is a chemical experiment,' snapped Holmes. 'If you require my assistance, please state your case now.'

Isla McLaren reclined in her chair and flashed a small smile at me.

'There have been a series of strange incidents in and around Braedern Castle,' said she. 'I cannot connect them and yet I feel somehow they are linked. I also sense a growing danger. Braedern Castle, as you may know if it appears in your files Mr Holmes, is reputed to be haunted.'

'Every castle in Scotland is said to be haunted. You Scots are very fond of your ghosts and your faeries.'

'I did not say that *I* thought that ghosts were at work. Quite a few of my fellow Scots demonstrate the capacity for rational thought, Mr Holmes. For instance, James Clerk Maxwell, James Watt, Mary Somerville . . .'

'Yes, yes, the namesake of your college at Oxford. I see the charm dangling from your brooch, Mrs McLaren.'

Oxford! Isla McLaren grew in stature before my eyes. Somerville College for women was highly regarded, and the young ladies who attended were thought to be among the brightest in the Empire.

'As I was saying, our small country has contributed a disproportionate number of geniuses in mathematics, medicine and engineering.'

Holmes at last took a seat and faced her, his aspect suddenly altered. 'I cannot contradict you, Mrs McLaren,' he said. 'Forgive me. Let us address your problem.'

Mrs McLaren took a deep breath and regarded my friend for a moment, as if trying to decide something. 'There have been a series of curious events at Braedern. Perhaps the strangest is this. Not long ago, a young parlour maid disappeared from the estate under unusual circumstances.'

'Go on,' said Holmes, as he opened and once again began to flip through the file.

'Fiona Paisley is her name. She was a very visible member of staff, quite beautiful, with flame red hair nearly to her waist.'

'Is? Was? Be clear, Mrs McLaren. Where is she now?'

'Back at work, but—'

'Continue. An attractive servant disappeared briefly but has returned. What is the mystery?'

'She did not simply return. She arrived in a basket, bound, drugged, and with her beautiful hair cut off down to the scalp.'

This had at last piqued Holmes's interest.

'Start from the beginning. Tell me of the girl, and the dates of these events.'

'Fiona disappeared last Friday. She returned two days later, three days ago.'

'Why did you wait to consult me?'

'Allow me to tell you this in my own way, Mr Holmes.'

Holmes sighed, and waved her to continue.

'Fiona was flirtatious and forward, quite charming in her way. She had many admirers. Every man in the estate remarked upon her. We thought at first she had run off with someone until the servants appealed to the laird *en masse*, insisting that she had been kidnapped.'

'Why?'

'No one else was missing. She would not have run off alone. And then her shoe was found near the garden behind the kitchen. A search party was sent out, but discovered nothing else.'

'But she has returned. What was her story? Did she not see her attacker?'

'No. She could offer no clues.'

Holmes sighed and rose to find another cigarette on the mantle. He lit the cigarette casually. 'Very well. Every man in the estate noticed her. Might your husband have done so?'

'"Every" means "every".'

'Then you suspect an affair? Perhaps retribution? Is it possible that you or another woman in the house felt threatened by the girl?'

'Why would I have come to you if I were the perpetrator?'

'Mrs McLaren, believe me, it has been tried. Let us be frank. There is a certain degree of conceit in your self-presentation.'

'I would describe it as confidence, not conceit. Will you hear me out, or is your need to put me in my place so much greater than your professional courtesy? Or, perhaps more apropos to you, your *curiosity*?'

To his credit, my friend received the reprimand with grace. 'Forgive me. Pray continue, Mrs McLaren. The shoe that was found near the garden. Was there no sign of a struggle, nothing beyond the one object?'

'None. I made enquiries and undertook a physical search of my own, but her room yielded nothing and the area where the shoe was found was by then so trampled that it was impossible to learn anything.'

'Do you mean you played at detective work yourself, Mrs McLaren? Would not a call to the police have been in order?'

'I think not, Mr Holmes. Dr Watson has made clear in his narrative your opinion of most police detective work.

Our local constable is derelict in his duty. He is, quite frankly, a drunk. The laird refused to call him in.'

'Yet I hardly think an untrained amateur such as yourself would be—'

I shot a warning glance at my friend. He was, I felt being unduly harsh. This woman had set something off in him I did not understand.

Isla McLaren was unfazed. 'It is Fiona's own story that concerns me. She was frightened beyond words. She was taken at night and there was a heavy mist. She saw nothing.'

'Yes, well, what then?'

'She awoke in a cold damp place, on what felt like a stone floor with some straw laid atop, apparently for meagre comfort. She was bound tightly but with padded ropes, and with her eyes covered. She had a terrible headache.'

Holmes had returned to his chair, and was now listening eagerly. 'Chloroform, then. Easily obtained. Effective, if crude. Next?'

'Someone who never spoke a word to her stole in and proceeded to cut off her hair with what felt like a very sharp knife. It was done carefully and she had the impression that the person was arranging the locks of hair beside her in some way. Possibly to keep it.'

Holmes exhaled and leaned back. 'But not harmed otherwise?'

'Not a bruise upon her. However, for a woman, her hair—'

'Yes, yes, of course. It does grow back. Who discovered the basket?'

'The second footman who was leaving to post some letters.'

'Is that all? Where is the girl now?'

'At home, but unable to work. She is beside herself. Fiona was superstitious before, and her friends have tried to convince her the kidnapping was the work of something supernatural.'

'Why on earth?'

'The attack was so silent. She neither saw nor heard anyone approach.'

Holmes leaned back in his chair and closed his eyes. He did not move for several seconds.

'Mrs McLaren, tell me more of the girl, her character, her reputation.'

'Fiona has, or had before her abduction, a sparkling demeanour, flirtatious and flighty. She is no scholar, though canny. She has been unable to learn to read, but enjoys attention and is straightforward about it. I really do not dislike the girl at all, in fact I quite like her. She is, without the slightest effort, a magnet for male attention. I have not bothered to track her own affections or actions, but I wager that there could be any number of men or women who might be jealous of the attention she receives.'

'You imply much, but can you confirm any specific affairs? A husband's attraction to a pretty servant would certainly trouble most women, Mrs McLaren. Even you.'

'I am not most women, Mr Holmes. But I think Fiona's attractions may be beside the point. I think her desecration is the beginning of a larger threat, as described in the note.'

'You have a note? Why withhold it? Let me see it!' Holmes was irritated.

She withdrew a crumpled piece of paper from her handbag. He squinted at it, then thrust it at me. 'Here, read this, Watson.'

I did so, aloud.

'The crowning glory sever'd from the rest.
But only hair and n'er a foot nor toe
The victim or her kin ha'e fouled the nest
And 'tis likely best that she should go
If you heed not this warning and persist
In bedding sichan beauties as yon lass
You may lose something which will be more miss'd
And what you feart the most will come to pass
So at your peril gae about your lives
But notice what and whom you haud most dear
And mind your interests, no less your wives
For if unguarded, may soon disappear
You hae been warned and this should not deny
If tragedies befall you, blame not I.

—A true friend to the McLarens'

'Hmmm' said Holmes. 'This ghost is an amateur poet. A schoolboy Shakespearean sonnet, if not a particularly brilliant one. Scots dialect. Paper common in Scotland and all through the north, calligraphic nib on the pen. Letters formed precisely as if copied from a manual, therefore the writer – who is energetic, note the upstrokes – was disguising his or her handwriting, which is only prudent. While this is marginally interesting, Mrs McLaren, I still believe this to be a domestic issue. Look to whoever was 'bedding' the lass, and whoever may be discomfited by this.'

Mrs McLaren drew herself up. 'I consider what happened an act of violence, Mr Holmes. And the note indicates trouble to come. But I sense that you—'

'Mrs McLaren. I do not take on cases before there is an actual reason. While the events are somewhat unusual, and certainly cruel, I do not share your degree of alarm. Unless of course, you feel personally threatened in some way? Do you?'

'I do not.'

'Madam, then this case is not within my purview. It appears to be a common domestic intrigue, although with *outré* elements. Good day.'

Holmes leaned back in his chair and stubbed out his cigarette. But Isla McLaren was not to be put off so easily. She took a deep breath and pressed on. 'Mr Holmes, I have come to you for help,' she said. 'Braedern is said to be haunted. There have been unexplained deaths. I have a growing sense of unease which I cannot dispel.'

'Ghosts again! All right, what unexplained deaths?'

'Ten years ago, the Lady McLaren, mother of the three sons we discussed, went out in a wild, stormy night to supervise the delivery of a foal which proved to be a false alarm. When she tried to return to the castle, she was locked out and could not enter. She froze to death.'

'Was there an official investigation? Or did you, Mrs McLaren, play detective?'

'Mr Holmes, you mock me. Obviously this was before my time, and yes, the police investigated. When Lady McLaren died, some of the servants first saw tracks in the snow indicating someone had tried to enter on the ground floor in several places, broke one window, but could not breach the shutters. Her frozen body was found later, and the laird was inconsolable.'

'No bell was rung? How was it that no one inside was alerted?' asked Holmes.

'The bell apparently malfunctioned. I know no more.'

'A very cold case, and likely an accident. Why bring this up now?'

'Since that time her spirit is said to haunt the East Tower – a malevolent spirit that causes harm,' said the lady.

Holmes sighed.

'What kind of harm, Mrs McLaren?' I asked.

'A servant fell down the stairs to his death last year – pushed, it is said, by this ghost. A child, you see, disappeared from that hall years earlier.'

'Hmmm, that would be . . . the laird's only daughter, Anne. Aged two years and nine months,' murmured Holmes.

'None of the servants will enter after dark, now, and I fear—'

'You do not seem the type to believe in ghosts. What precisely do you want of me, Mrs McLaren?'

'Perhaps you could investigate and prove that there is nothing—'

Holmes waved this thought away. Mrs McLaren steeled herself and changed course. It would be hard to dissuade this woman, and I admired her fortitude, though I wondered at her persistence. The lady was intriguing.

'Mr Holmes, ours is a complex family. McLaren whisky is renowned but within the family there is dissension over control. Rivalries.'

'I have heard of your whisky,' said I, warmly. '"McLaren Top" is quite good, I am told.'

'Yes. Just last year it was adopted as "the whisky of choice" by the Langham Hotel, among others. There is a great deal of money at stake. We could be considered for a Royal Warrant, but plagued as we are by these legends and fears . . .'

Holmes sighed. He opened his eyes and gazed fixedly upon the lady.

'A missing girl who is no longer missing. A note in rhyme with the vaguest of threats. Accidental deaths. Ghosts. And now rivalry among brothers. You are scraping an empty barrel, I sense. Madam, there is nothing for me here. Please close the door as you depart.'

But Mrs McLaren was not finished. 'Mr Holmes, yesterday I found this in the garden shed.' She reached into her handbag and withdrew a stick of dynamite and a long fuse.

We froze and I heard a sharp intake of air from my friend.

'Careful with that, Mrs McLaren!' said Holmes. 'Hand it to me, please.'

She made no move to do so, but placing it in her lap, instead withdrew a cigarette from her reticule, and before we could stop her, extracted a vesta from a silver case and lit it.

We both shouted and leapt from our chairs, and Holmes managed to snatch the dynamite away. He pulled back from her and stood a moment, holding it stiffly in the air, uncertain, as any step away from her and her lit match would draw him nearer the fire, or nearer the chemistry table which still sizzled quietly under its moist covering.

'Relax, gentlemen. It is a dummy. I checked. There is no nitroglycerin in this room – unless it is your own.' The lady smiled sweetly at us.

Holmes glowered at her.

'You must admit, it captured your attention,' said she, lighting her cigarette. She inhaled and blew several small circles towards the ceiling, peering upward through them to view my companion with laughing eyes. 'As it did mine.'

CHAPTER 3

Rejection

olmes sighed, sniffed, then examined the dynamite stick. Satisfied, he flung it on a side table.

'Mrs McLaren, you have made your point, albeit more theatrically than necessary. What is so funny, Doctor?'

I shrugged and he continued.

'Dynamite is the classic tool of the railway builder, the miner, and the anarchist. These appear to be Nobel's latest type, made in their Scottish factory. What do you think these were doing in this form, wrapped as though filled, and yet not? Dummies, you say. And where exactly did you find them?'

Mrs McLaren smiled. 'I have no idea. I found these two dummies, and a cache of what I believe were filled sticks in a tool shed in the back of the kitchen garden. And as to your other question, I have only to guess.'

'Please do not. Guessing is for amateurs. Is there anyone in your family connected to the Scots Separatist movement?

To the Russian Revolution? To French anarchists?' He paused. 'To the women's suffrage movement?'

'You have covered a great deal of territory, Mr Holmes. I myself support women's right to vote as any clear thinker must. But I am not a radical. As to the rest, I could not be certain. Politics are not the primary subject at our family gatherings.'

'What is, then?'

'Money, Mr Holmes. The whisky business. Techniques of distillation, ponies, hunting, local gossip – and ghosts.'

Holmes sighed. 'Dynamite is used in clearing lands for new buildings, is it not? And has your distillery been recently enlarged? Is there not a logical reason for dynamite to be present for these uses?'

'Well, yes,' said the lady. 'But I wonder about the dummies.'

Silence. Small sounds came from the chemistry table. Holmes's knee vibrated in impatience.

'Madam,' he said after a moment. 'There are many hints of mystery in your various stories, and yet I am afraid I do not see a case for me. Dr Watson will show you out.'

I will admit my astonishment at this. I thought there was quite enough intrigue presented for several cases! But even more puzzling was Holmes's rudeness to the lady. While he could on occasion display insensitivity, he was usually the soul of courtesy, especially where women were concerned.

Mrs McLaren stood abruptly and I rose with her. 'I can find my way out, Dr Watson,' she said. She then turned to my companion.

'I am afraid I have wasted your time,' said the lady. 'And my own.'

Mrs McLaren took her leave, and as soon as the front door closed behind her downstairs, I could not contain myself. 'Holmes! Why do you hesitate? There is so much of interest here! And Mrs McLaren—'

'What? A servant girl has her hair shorn, servants fear ghosts, and some empty dynamite sticks may or may not have been found in a garden shed? By the way, those were not created as dummies. Someone had removed the cordite, for whatever reason. I suspect the lady herself did so, then brought these along to bring out if her other stories failed to get my attention.'

'Holmes, that is an outrageous notion!'

He shrugged. 'Do you not think her capable?'

'That is beside the point! She seems far too intelligent and level-headed to resort to such trickery. Did you not find her story, indeed the lady herself, intriguing?'

'No, *you* found her intriguing. I find her—'

'Utterly fascinating.'

'—provocative. Really, Watson, you must raise your sights.'

'Provocative is not a bad beginning for a case, Holmes.'

'I have decided and that is that. Besides, Mycroft has something for me and I am to meet him in the morning. Would you care to join us? It will most certainly be more interesting than the McLaren imbroglio.'

'Yes, I will come, Holmes. Though I do not understand this decision. Ah, it is freezing in here now.'

As I moved to close the damaged window, I stole a glance outside. The snow was coming down hard now and the air was growing opaque. But across the way, I saw something that made me stop short.

'Hullo! Your man is in trouble down there!'

In the deepening shadows, the hulking Butterby was struggling with a tall, well-dressed stranger, who wielded his walking stick like a club. The attacker was clearly at an advantage, and suddenly struck the larger man in the face. Butterby fell back into the shadows.

Holmes bounded to the window, took one glance and ran for the door shouting, 'Stay here! On *no account* come down. Do as I say!'

In a moment I saw him dash into the snow *sans* overcoat and dodge the traffic, across Baker Street to where Butterby had arisen and was now locked in combat with his attacker. From the distance I could only discern a gentleman of about our own age, who was fighting with a particularly vicious energy. Butterby was taking a beating as Holmes ran towards them.

But the attacker sensed his approach, broke free from Butterby and whirling at the last instant aimed a fierce blow at Holmes with his walking stick, striking his shin with a crack I could hear from across the street. Holmes shouted and went down. Two pedestrians nearby fled.

I was down the stairs and into the street without a thought.

By the time I reached the trio, Holmes had regained his footing, and the three were struggling on the slippery pavement, the snow swirling wildly about them. Butterby fell and the attacker turned his attention full on Holmes.

But perceiving my approach and sensing the odds were no longer in his favour, the assailant broke free and started to flee, his camel hair coat billowing behind him. Fate, however, intervened and he suddenly slipped on the icy pavement and fell, striking his head against the base of a lamp post as he went down.

He lay still. We stood gasping, Butterby still splayed on the curb next to us, holding his head.

'Are you all right, Holmes?' I shouted over the rising wind.

'Yes, see to that man, Watson,' Holmes replied, helping Butterby up.

I turned to the downed attacker. His was a handsome face, chiselled and refined. The eyes remained closed and he was still. I knelt, checking his pulse and his pupils, They were not dilated, a good sign. The wind continued to whip snow around us in a flurry. Holmes and I were without our coats.

'Get him inside,' I shouted. Holmes hesitated for only a moment, but then nodded.

With Butterby's clumsy help, the three of us managed to transport the fellow up to our sitting room, and minutes later, the mysterious attacker was stretched out unconscious on our settee, his hands secured behind him with Butterby's handcuffs. Holmes grabbed a second pair of cuffs from the mantle and secured his feet to one leg of the settee. I was shivering from my brief exposure to the elements but applied myself to examine the man further. I placed a pillow to raise his head where it had tilted back over the edge of the settee.

My patient was a tall, well-built fellow. His coat was of the finest Savile Row tailoring, now dirtied and torn from the fight. He had suffered a nasty cut on the forehead, and remained unconscious, but his pulse was strong and regular, his breathing normal. I called down to Mrs Hudson for hot water and towels and blotted the wound with a clean handkerchief and some of Holmes's clear spirits.

A silent and glowering Butterby stood like a plinth in the corner of the room. Melting snow dripped from him, splashing lightly onto the rug. He held a dirty handkerchief to a bleeding cut on his cheek and grimaced. I handed him a clean one. Holmes looked up and, finally noticing him, suggested he fetch Lestrade and be quick about it.

'Right-o, then,' Butterby grunted, and lumbered off. Holmes shook his head in annoyance.

Our man on the sofa was struggling to regain consciousness. He groaned and his eyes rolled upwards in their sockets, closed, and opened again. I turned to my friend.

Holmes was pale with exertion and cold, snow still visible on his hair and the shoulders of his dressing gown. He rubbed his shin and grimaced.

'Are you all right, Holmes?' I asked again.

'It is just a bruise. Our man here has been in training since last we met. I underestimated him. What is the damage?'

'You know him, then?'

'The damage, Watson?'

35

'He will live. I would ask for brandy, but—'

'Here, give him some of this. My best whisky, though he hardly merits it.' He handed over a bottle. McLaren Top!

I held the drink to the assailant's lips, supporting his head. He squinted and took in his surroundings and then suddenly jerked his limbs only to discover his restraints. With a splutter he pulled away from the drink, but clipped it with his chin and several drops spilled over his damaged coat.

He shook his head to focus and suddenly noticed Holmes standing above him. He emitted a deep-throated cry and jolted violently towards me. Struggling against his bonds he began making a series of strange, garbled sounds.

'Now that is a waste of perfectly good Scotch, St John,' said Holmes. 'Not to mention you have further damaged your rather fine coat. I see you have retained your excellent taste in tailoring.'

'How do you know this man?' I asked.

'It is a very long story,' said my friend, his voice strained.

Another set of unintelligible sounds emerged from the fellow. Turning to stare at him I discovered why. As he continued to make noises, I remarked in horror that the man had lost his tongue! The wound was not recent. There was not a trace of blood, just a dark space where a tongue would rest.

St John glowered.

Holmes turned to me. 'This is Mr Orville St John. A distinguished member of the St Johns of Northumberland, titled landowners, enormously wealthy from their logging endeavours. We were undergraduates together at Camford. Shall I tell Dr Watson what happened there, St John?'

The man said nothing.

'I shall presume that was a yes. Mr St John and an equally well-placed friend, both of whom enjoyed great prestige at Camford, took top honors in mathematics and chemistry, until I arrived upon the scene and began to prevail. A prize or two, the favour of a famous professor, and suddenly I was, to them, some kind of nemesis, an object of both envy and derision.'

I noticed St John staring with vehement anger at my friend.

'They began a campaign to drive me from the University.' Holmes's tone was matter of fact, even light, but the tension in his face spoke of more behind the words. 'He attempted to persuade students and faculty alike that I had harmed his dog, and had blown up a laboratory deliberately. My position was precarious. Not only did I lose the few friends I had – well, not that popularity was ever my goal—'

On the couch, St John snorted.

'I very much doubt they got the better of you,' said I.

St John grunted loudly.

'You would be wrong, Watson. Of course he could speak then. In fact, St John was President of the Union and a champion debater. His nickname was "The Silver Tongue" and he managed by dint of his extraordinary powers of persuasion to turn an entire college and most of the dons against me.'

Holmes paused, remembering. 'Eventually I was sent down. Although at that point I had lost the will for . . . other reasons. In any case, Watson, there is my reason for leaving the University, sitting before you in all his glory.'

I was sure that there was much more to this story. St John stared at Holmes, unblinking and cold. Holmes turned to face him, all pretence of humour gone. The hatred between the two was palpable, an electric current travelling through the air.

'You were very persuasive, St John,' said he.

I had long wondered about the reason that Holmes had left university without taking his degree. This seemed an incomplete explanation. I pulled him aside, behind St John, where our captive could not see us. I indicated the tongue, with a gesture demanding an explanation. Holmes just shook his head, 'Later,' he mouthed.

There was a noise on the stairs and Mrs Hudson showed in Lestrade and two deputies. The wiry little inspector was as usual, full of energy. 'Mr Holmes!' he cried.

'Ah, Lestrade, I see Butterby has succeeded in something at last,' said Holmes. 'He has delivered you in a timely fashion. In a moment I would like you to remove this man, Mr Orville St John.'

'Ah, a gentleman, he appears, but without manners. To gaol then, Mr Holmes? Butterby claims assault and battery. Him as well as you, and the good doctor,' said Lestrade, with relish.

'One moment if you please, Inspector.'

Turning to St John, Holmes said the following slowly

and carefully. 'St John, you are now known in these parts and have tried to kill me three times in the last six days.'

Holmes leaned in and removed a revolver from St John's outer coat pocket. The man inhaled sharply as Holmes opened it, checking the bullets. He handed it to Lestrade. 'Recently fired, and the calibre and make will match, no doubt, this bullet found in my wall over there.'

He pointed and I discerned a new bullet hole in the wall, just under my picture of General Gordon.

'Attempted murder, then, as well!' said the policeman.

'Patience,' said Holmes, and turned again to the man restrained before us. 'I am going to make you an offer for your freedom, St John. If you agree to my terms, I will not press charges. And Lestrade, I ask that you convince Butterby to drop his charges as well. Release this gentleman's ankles, would you please, Doctor.' He handed me the keys to his cuffs. 'And you his hands, Butterby.'

As he was freed from his restraints, St John looked pointedly away, rubbing his wrists. I was unable to read his reaction to these last words. Holmes continued.

'What is so completely odd, St John, is why now? What has sent you here?' He leaned forward.

St John turned away again coldly. Holmes sighed. 'You must let this vendetta go. You know that I am not guilty of that which you accuse me. In your heart of hearts, you know this.'

St John remained inscrutable. I scanned his motionless face but read no sign of the man relenting.

'Once again, in front of witnesses, can you let this

vendetta go? If so, then you walk away a free man. If not, it will be to gaol with you, where I will ensure you stay a very long time.' Holmes then made several strange gestures in the air with his hands. I recognized the motions as French sign language used by the deaf or mute, but had no clue to the meaning.

St John hesitated, and a torrent of emotions passed over his face as he clearly fought to regain control. He made a brief reply in sign language.

'Fine then, St John, but consider this. If you do not desist, although I am not a vindictive man, you will leave me no choice. I will investigate your personal business, and create as much difficulty as I can for your family. You will bring trouble down on all you love. Do you agree to let this go once and for all?'

St John closed his eyes for a moment, then opening them, he stared fiercely at my friend, then nodded in assent.

'I need your word.'

'Let him say it, Mr Holmes,' said Lestrade.

Holmes shot a glance at Lestrade. 'He is mute.' He turned to glare at St John. The man hesitated, then finally, an affirmative 'Uh huh' came from him.

'That will suffice. Gentlemen. I now formally drop my charges against Mr St John for his attempts on my life. For the time being.' Turning back to St John he said, 'Take care that you keep your vow. Do you understand me?'

St John slowly raised his eyes to meet Holmes's. There was a cold rage, now, in that look. The man was ready to kill Holmes, of that I was sure. And yet my friend seemed eager to let him go.

St John nodded one more time.

'Escort Mr St John back to the Langham Hotel, please.'

St John started at this.

'Yes, I know your hotel, and a great deal more,' Holmes said. Then, to Lestrade, 'It is a lodging well suited to this gentleman's means and style. He lives on a grand estate just outside Edinburgh, and he is the respected owner and editor of St John and Wilkins, a major publishing house. He has three small children, a growing business, a loving wife, and a brother in delicate health. He has much to lose.'

St John stood, and as he did, one of Lestrade's deputies approached and took him by the arm, and they moved to the door. As he stood in the doorframe, St John turned to Holmes and elaborated some complex thought with sign language, ending with an aggressive gesture.

Holmes clearly received the message. He sighed and shook his head.

The men departed, Butterby with them.

Lestrade shook his head. 'Well, Mr Holmes, I have seen some strange things in these rooms, but that gentleman is surely one of the strangest. I do not have a good feeling about your letting him go like that.'

'Nor do I, Holmes,' said I. 'I think you are making a mistake.'

My friend stood peering into the fire. 'Gentlemen. I am very tired suddenly and need to rest. If you will excuse me, please. Good evening, Lestrade. Watson, would you be so good as to meet me at the Diogenes Club at 9.30 tomorrow morning.' He shrugged. 'Or stay, if you like. Your old room is probably habitable.'

Without a further word, he retired to his bedroom and shut the door. As soon as he did so, I realized that I had meant to have a look at the leg where St John had struck him. But he would not be disturbed now. I turned to Lestrade, who was now staring curiously at the still gurgling chemistry mess in the corner.

'What on earth is that, if you do not mind my asking?' he said.

'I promise you I have not the faintest notion, Inspector.'

'You must have a very forgiving landlady,' observed the little man tartly. On cue, the saintly Mrs Hudson appeared with his hat, coat and umbrella.

'Good evening, Inspector Lestrade,' I said.

As he left, Mrs Hudson sniffed the foetid air and took in the chemistry disaster. 'Mr Holmes?' she enquired.

'He is resting,' said I.

'I shouldn't wonder,' she said. 'I shall bring you both some warm soup. Will you be staying, Doctor?'

'My room—'

'It has been made up fresh as Mr Holmes requested.'

I smiled. Had Holmes known that Mary was not home and would not miss me? It should not have surprised me. But meanwhile, the weather had grown increasingly inclement.

'Thank you, Mrs Hudson. I will stay.' In truth, I felt uneasy at the recent events. Until I was sure that this St

John had been dissuaded from his mission, Holmes might well make use of my help.

Thus I decided to stay the night and accompany my friend in the morning to see his brother, Mycroft Holmes. As it turned out, it was lucky that I did.

CHAPTER 4

Brothers

n route through snowy Regent Street to Mycroft the following morning, I found myself puzzling over both Holmes's rejection of Isla McLaren's case and his handling of the treacherous Orville St John incident. But my friend was in an impatient mood, his black kid-gloved fingers drumming restlessly upon his knee. He refused to be drawn into a discussion of either. I persisted on the St John issue and at last he said, 'Mr St John will not trouble me again. He is particularly protective of his family and my bluff will suffice. He – why do you look at me that way? Surely, Watson, you cannot imagine that I would forcibly cut a man's tongue from his head for any reason on earth!'

The thought had in fact occurred to me. 'Well, not a live one, at any rate. But how did it happen?'

'It was the act of a madman, a mutual acquaintance, Watson, who has since passed on to meet his Maker.'

'Strange. But why does this St John think *you* were responsible? And why attack you now?'

'Certainly some recent event has served to reanimate his rage. Perhaps a letter. I intend to find out. In any case, it is complicated, and long past. Leave it, I say.' His tone brooked no argument and I knew it was useless to pursue for the moment. We soon pulled up in front of the Diogenes Club.

'I shall pay,' I offered, in an attempt at *détente*. Perhaps Mrs McLaren had been right and he was in need of cash. I fished in my own pocket.

'I have it, Watson. You are a bit short of funds yourself.'

It was regrettably true! My practice had suffered recently when a doctor of considerable charm and a decade more experience had hung his brass plate two doors down from my own. But how could he know?

'What herculean efforts you make to keep track of my personal affairs!' I exclaimed as we entered the august precincts of the Diogenes. 'Perhaps better spent elsewhere!'

'Very little effort at all,' said he, 'Watson, you are an open book.'

'Well, you are wrong about that,' I insisted.

Soon afterwards were seated in the Stranger's Room at the Diogenes, awaiting Mycroft Holmes.

The antique globes in their familiar place, the bookshelves filled with leatherbound volumes, the large window onto Pall Mall – all was as it had been before. While the club's peculiar regulars must have chosen it for its rules of silence, I found the place oppressive.

The Stranger's Room was the only place in this eccentric institution where one was allowed to speak. Eventually Mycroft Holmes sailed in as a stately battleship through calm waters to sit before us. Mycroft was over six feet tall, and unlike his brother, very wide in girth. He carried a leather dossier in one enormous hand. He smiled in his particular mirthless way, and then he and my friend exchanged the usual pleasantries characteristic of the Holmes brothers, that is to say, none at all.

Coffee was served. The clink of china and silver was hushed in the room.

'How is England doing?' asked Holmes finally.

'We are well,' said Mycroft. 'Considering.'

Holmes leaned back in his chair, a twitching knee giving away his impatience. Mycroft eyed his younger brother with a kind of concerned disapproval. 'But you, Sherlock, must watch your finances. I have mentioned this before.'

'Mycroft!' exclaimed Holmes.

'Little brother, you are an open book.'

I cleared my throat to cover a laugh, and Holmes shot me a look. 'What is it you want, Mycroft? Trouble in France I hear?'

'Precipitous. The threat of war. You have heard of the phylloxera epidemic? It is not a virus, but a little parasite, it seems, and it is destroying the vineyards of France. Their wine production is down some seventy-five per cent in recent years. Dead brown vines everywhere. A good, cheap table wine is impossible to come by, and the better brandies, too. An absolute disaster for the French, and keenly felt.'

'Come now, Mycroft . . . war?' said Holmes.

'There are those highly placed in France who feel the debacle was deliberately engineered. And by Perfidious Albion, no less.'

'Blaming the epidemic on Britain!' exclaimed Holmes. 'Is such a thing possible?' He smiled. 'Or is this merely a question of French sour grapes?'

'Who knows?' said Mycroft. 'But, a highly placed gentleman, one Philippe Reynaud is leading the charge. He is *Le Sous Secrétaire d'État à l'Agriculture*. Reynaud thinks the Scots are behind it. Or at the very least, prolonging it.'

'The Scots!' I exclaimed. 'Why, they have long been allies of the French.'

Mycroft gave me a withering glance.

'Which Scots? And why particularly?' asked Holmes, then had a sudden thought. 'Oh. Whisky, of course.'

'Three Scottish families are singled out and under suspicion. One may interest you particularly, the McLarens. It is in the report,' said Mycroft, indicating a dossier which he had tossed on the table between them. The name struck me but Holmes gave nothing away. Mycroft turned to me. 'Numerous entrepreneurial types including the McLarens, James Buchanan, and others have been laying siege to London clubs and restaurants, aggressively promoting their 'uisge beatha' or 'water of life' – that is the Scots' Gaelic term – as the new social drink to be enjoyed in finer society. The fact that spirits, such as brandy, cognac and wine have grown costly and scarce has helped them tremendously.'

'Oh yes! I particularly like Buchanan's new Black and White—' I began.

'The fortunes of these companies are rising,' interrupted Mycroft. 'Not just in London but internationally. The French are talking of trade sanctions, and a couple of militant specimens, including this Reynaud, have pushed for a more aggressive response.'

'War over drinks?' I exclaimed. 'Ludicrous.'

'It is an entire industry, and war has been declared for less, Watson. The French vineyards are closely tied to French identity,' said Holmes.

'Yes, they are quite heated on the subject,' said Mycroft. 'Cigarette?'

Holmes took a cigarette from Mycroft's case and lit it.

Mycroft sighed. 'These ideas have been gaining purchase, and that is why I have called you in, Sherlock.'

'What of research?' asked Holmes. 'Is there no potential remedy in sight for the scourge?'

'The leading viticultural researcher is in Montpellier, Dr Paul-Édouard Janvier. He is said to be close to a solution. But, and here is where you come in, dear brother, he has been receiving death threats, and this Reynaud insists they come from Scotland.'

'What has been done so far?'

'France has put its "best man" on the case to protect Dr Janvier and discover the source of the threats, but Dr Janvier has taken a dislike to the gentleman in question and I can't say I blame him. I know the man; he is an irritant, and, based on his past history, I would not put it past him to exacerbate the situation.'

Holmes was smiling at this. 'France's "best man" you say? An irritant? This sounds like someone we know.'

'Yes.'

The brothers exchanged a look of amusement.

'Who is—wait!' I suddenly guessed the identity of this this unnamed man. 'Can it be Jean Vidocq?' I blurted out. Their silence was confirmation.

The scoundrel! We had had some unfortunate dealings with the famous French detective last year. Vidocq was a dangerous charmer who saw himself as Holmes's rival. The man had not only attacked me physically but had complicated our case involving a certain French singer and her missing child. This same man claimed to be a descendant of the famous Eugène François Vidocq who founded the *Sûreté* nearly eighty years ago. But the connection was spurious – the real Vidocq had no known descendants. Despite his questionable character, Jean Vidocq was not without considerable skills, and was frequently consulted by the French government.

'What exactly do you wish me to do?' asked Holmes.

'Three things. First, meet Dr Paul-Édouard Janvier, and let me know the status of his research. How close is he to a cure for the mite? The second is to discover and neutralise whoever is threatening the man and his work – if these threats are indeed genuine.'

'Why would they not be genuine?' asked Holmes.

Mycroft shrugged. 'Attention. Sympathy. Who knows?

But if the threats to Dr Janvier are real, and they have been perpetrated by a Briton, then detain that gentleman with the utmost discretion and notify me. The Foreign Office and I shall handle it from there.'

'And if there is a villain, and he or she is not British?' asked Holmes.

'Well, then best to leave it. I shall pass on the information.'

Holmes stopped smiling and sat back in his chair.

'Protect Britain, that is your only interest? Not this man, or the crisis itself? No, Mycroft,' he said. 'I will not undertake this.'

Mycroft seemed not to have heard. 'And the third task: extricate Jean Vidocq from this situation, the sooner the better. This man Janvier, who is something of a genius, may well be in danger. Vidocq only complicates things and is unlikely to be protecting him.'

Holmes said nothing.

'As for the three Scottish families I mentioned, at the top of the list are the McLarens. You improve at concealment, Sherlock. I mentioned them before, and you revealed nothing, but in fact, you had a visit from the younger daughter-in-law yesterday. Most convenient.'

Holmes set his coffee cup in its saucer abruptly, 'Stop having me watched, Mycroft.'

'You may one day be thankful.'

'Yet you missed the recent attempts on my life.'

'Not very effective, was he? Need I say more?'

Holmes said nothing.

'The McLaren family is or will be en route shortly to the South of France where they winter each year in the vicinity of Nice. This year it is the new Grand Hôtel du Cap Eden Roc in Antibes. Did your client fail to mention this? I wonder why she came to see you? It is a curious coincidence.'

'She came on another matter. a domestic intrigue. And she is not my client, as I turned down the case.'

'Dear me! If you are declining cases left and right, how wrong I was to imagine you in straitened circumstances, dear brother.'

Holmes actually turned scarlet at this jab.

'In any case, you are free to travel,' Mycroft said.

'No, Mycroft. Watson, call for our coats, please.'

I stood.

'Our Monsieur Reynaud fears that an attack on Dr Janvier is imminent. It seems precisely your kind of case, Sherlock. Protect an innocent who advances science.' Mycroft stubbed out his cigarette and sipped his coffee. He smiled kindly at his brother. I immediately thought of a mongoose.

'I said no.' Holmes leaned forward, stubbing his own cigarette into the ashtray in the centre of the table. Without shifting position, and with a dexterity I could scarcely credit, Mycroft suddenly thrust his arm forward and clapped his large hand over Holmes's long thin one, slamming it into the ashtray and onto the still smouldering cigarette. And there he held it. I could not believe what I was seeing.

51

His hand unmoving, Mycroft's voice remained warm and friendly. 'Consider the plight of this man, Dr Janvier, Sherlock. He is brilliant, a genius with few friends. A naïf in a certain way. But his work is vital, with economic and political repercussions. I assure you, no British official wishes him dead.'

He continued to hold his hand clamped over Holmes's. My friend indicated nothing, but I could see the sweat beading on his brow. With a sudden move, I took up the coffee pot and poured a small splash of hot coffee on Mycroft's hand. With a cry he released Holmes and the two sprung back from the table, each cradling an injured hand.

'So sorry, gentlemen,' I said. 'As long as we are discussing saving wine and Western civilization, might we not be a little more civilized ourselves?' I said.

'And there is my point, Sherlock. Paul-Édouard Janvier has no Watson. Do this for me, will you not, little brother? You are uniquely suited. England will thank you. I will thank you, and a certain august personage at Windsor will certainly be grateful.'

From his pocket Mycroft now withdrew a large, thick envelope and placed it on the table. 'You will be needing an advance, of course. Report to me daily on your progress.'

Holmes stared at the envelope in disdain. But he then looked away thoughtfully, and to my surprise, reconsidered.

'I will do it, Mycroft, for this man Dr Janvier. But not for you,' said Holmes. He reached down and flicked the envelope back across the table to Mycroft. 'Keep your advance. Pay me when the case is closed.'

Mycroft smiled and sat down, delicately wiping the coffee from his hand with a white linen napkin. 'Dr Watson, you have been little challenged of late. Might you break free from the marital bonds to accompany my brother on a trip to the Riviera?'

Little challenged! Had I been watched as well? Holmes glanced my way with a nod of encouragement. 'This can be arranged,' said I. 'My dear Mary has some obligations herself, you see, as she has to—'

'Capital! The 4.15 from Waterloo, the day after tomorrow,' said Mycroft. 'Tickets, and a packet of information will be at Baker Street within the hour. You may change your mind later about the advance, Sherlock. Meanwhile, enjoy the South of France. The sunshine will do you both good.'

He glanced in my direction. 'But do stay away from the casino, Dr Watson.'

I could feel my cheeks colouring at this comment. 'I have given up gambling,' I said.

'Not at all,' said both brothers simultaneously.

'Good day, gentlemen,' said Mycroft.

I will admit to a curious, if not longing glance at that thick envelope as we departed.

Back on the street my friend was in a dark humour. The snow was coming down in a fury now, and I looked about for a cab.

'Your brother is mad,' I remarked. 'And you are not far behind.'

'No, Watson. He is just a type you have not encountered.

He is . . . effective. But I am generally ahead of him, and will be quicker next time.'

Quicker? What kind of family spawned these two?

'Why did you not take the money?' I asked.

'I dislike taking payment in advance,' said he. 'It changes the equation.'

But in this he was inconsistent, as in so many things. At last I spotted a free cab. I would use my last coins if need be to get out of this weather. Holmes preferred to walk, and as the cab departed I looked back to see his thin, lone figure vanish in the swirling snow. Whatever awaited us in the South of France, it would include sunshine. Of that, and only that, I was certain.

CHAPTER 5

Nice

s Mycroft had decreed, Holmes and I began our journey two days later. Passing through Dover, we traversed the channel and our train wended its way south through France. Holmes buried himself obsessively in notes and newspaper clippings on the phylloxera epidemic, and the Scottish families named as suspects in the threats to Dr Paul-Édouard Janvier. I, on the other hand, could not help but wonder about Mrs Isla McLaren, and her curious tale. That the McLarens featured in two cases presented to Holmes within twenty-four hours intrigued me. But Holmes was not willing to converse, and so I passed the time buried in Mary Shelley's intriguing novel inspired by Galvani's electrical experimentation. We thus passed the journey in companionable silence.

Our route took us through the Loire valley where Holmes disembarked unexpectedly at the city of Tours. 'I have arranged to meet with someone who may assist us in this case,' he explained 'Would you be so good, Watson, as to carry on to Nice and attempt to make contact with Isla McLaren?'

'Certainly, Holmes. But why?'

'In light of the suspicions about the McLarens and the threats to Dr Janvier, the coincidence of her recent visit grows even more curious.'

'What do you want me to do?'

'If she still wishes to engage me, perhaps you might get her to invite us to dine with her family. If not, I will think of something.'

I still did not fully understand his motive but I will admit that the prospect of seeing this fascinating young woman as a client was intriguing. 'Shall I wander, then, by the Grand Hôtel du Cap?' I asked.

'No. It is in a secluded location, and our contact must appear to be serendipitous. I have it from a reliable source that the lady walks daily along the Promenade des Anglais and enjoys shopping in Nice. I suggest you frequent the Promenade and keep an eye peeled. I will follow later and will step in if needed.' He smiled at me. 'Though with your wide-ranging experience with the fair sex, I hardly doubt you will be successful.'

'I am married now, Holmes,' I said with a bit of pique.

'You needn't remind me.'

There were worse assignments, certainly, and I carried on with enthusiasm, despite Holmes's curt refusal to elaborate further on his own immediate plans. He did, however, specify a hotel in Nice where we would be lodged for free, he said, due to his special relationship with the hotel detective. That was a relief as I had little money with me.

Arriving in the bright sunshine of Nice, my spirits lifted. It was a welcome change from the relentless grey and dismal snow of London. During my short ride from the station, I was struck by the difference in the air – the tang of fresh ocean breezes blended with warm smells of garlic, flowers and baking bread.

I soon arrived at the Hôtel Du Beau Soleil. The ivory stone façade, which sparkled in the sun, promised glamour, but inside, the dim and faded lobby with its scuffed marble floors and drooping ferns spoke of better days. My hopes plummeted further when I opened the door to the one room allotted to us both. It was a cramped, dingy space with two single beds, hard and uninviting. To make matters worse, the single window opened over the rubbish bins, their ripe odour quite pungent. I slammed it shut.

This was not quite the holiday glamour I had anticipated.

Holmes had said the hotel detective might consult him on one or two issues in exchange for free lodging. He should only get half an issue for this sorry room, I thought. However I had a mission to accomplish, and soon wandered several blocks down towards the seaside, and the famous Promenade des Anglais.

What a sight! A vivid azure sky topped a deep turquoise ocean. Palm trees and bright flowers competed with the equally colourful frocks of a number of very attractive ladies. Below me, extending out at the end of a long pier stood one of Nice's famed casinos, its exotic Byzantine architecture evoking something between a Russian Orthodox church and a carnival.

Nearby, children devoured fruit ices, and the rich scent of coffee enticed me to purchase a hot cup from a small stand. The air was cooler than I had thought, but the sun warmed the skin. It was an instant balm to my spirits, and I felt myself begin to relax.

I had a twinge of regret that Mary was not with me here to enjoy this beautiful city. She had loved Brighton and longed for another restorative, peaceful sojourn together. The seaside was her preference, calm and soothing. But my gaze returned to the casino, and I could not help but feel a small thrill of anticipation. Perhaps I might have time to slip away and try my hand at baccarat, if a few extra francs came my way.

But finding Isla McLaren was my goal, and I spent the next hour or two walking, wondering where might be the best place to spot my quarry. Eventually I grew discouraged and stopped at another stand, considering a second coffee.

I felt a sudden tap on my shoulder. I turned and there stood the lady herself! She was attired for a holiday in a fetching navy and white striped dress with a matching parasol and hat. Her skin and hair were glowing in the slanted sunlight of late afternoon.

'Dr Watson, what a pleasant surprise!' she exclaimed, examining me with her forthright and penetrating gaze. 'I hardly expected to find you in Nice.'

'Nor I you,' I lied. 'How lovely to see you here, Mrs McLaren. Are you wintering here by chance? It is wonderful to escape the snow, is it not?'

'We are, and yes, it is, Dr Watson, though I doubt *you* are here for a holiday. Mr Holmes seems hardly the type.' She looked around me. 'He is here with you, is he not?'

'Er, yes, in Nice.'

'Are you following us?'

'Why do you think that? You did not tell us you would be here.'

'Do not be coy, Dr Watson. Mr Holmes has his methods, you write about them. If he wished to know where I had gone, he would easily find out. Let me see. If you are not following us, you two must be on a case. No doubt something more compelling than my own sad story of the sheared little parlour maid?'

'You look quite lovely, by the way. Your hat—'

'All right, then, Doctor.' She fingered her velvet hat with its jaunty white ostrich feather, and smiled, coquettishly. 'Thank you, kind sir. My hat is French, bought only this morning. They do these *chapeaux* only too well.'

She dropped the act and took my arm. 'Now, do you mind? There is news about Fiona. I should like to bring you up to date. Shall we stroll?'

'Why, yes,' said I. 'If Mr McLaren would not object.'

'He is not the jealous type.'

She took my arm and we sauntered along the Promenade. The sun gave Mrs McLaren's chestnut hair bright copper highlights, and the frames of her small gold spectacles glinted as she spoke. I wondered anew why Holmes had turned her away so abruptly.

'I shall come straight to the point,' said the lady. 'When I returned to Scotland from London, I found that Fiona had disappeared again and no one knew where she had gone. The laird hesitated to leave for France yesterday with mystery hanging in the air, but then a note was found. She seems to have eloped with the groundsman's son.'

Eloped. 'Well that is certainly good news,' I said.

'The family is greatly relieved. Fiona had been so upset by what had happened to her that she could not function. Though we may never know what precisely did happen.'

'Well, then, it was certainly a domestic intrigue, as Holmes surmised. What brings you to Nice?'

'I told you, Dr Watson. We winter here in the South of France.'

'Yes, but I mean specifically here, in Nice, today. The Grand Hôtel du Cap is more than an hour from here.'

She stopped walking and just stared at me. Her voice turned icy. 'Then Mr Holmes *is* tracking the family. How do you know we are staying at the Grand Hôtel du Cap?'

'Well, the Grand Hôtel du Cap . . . I just presumed you would be in the best hotel in the area,' said I, realising my gaffe.

She looked unconvinced. I knew I was in trouble and went on the offensive. 'Well, I might then ask you how you managed to discover me here, on the Promenade? That is certainly serendipitous.'

'In fact, it was exactly that, Dr Watson. I came in for

some shopping. You see?' She opened a large canvas bag she had been carrying which contained some brightly embroidered linens, and then tapped her new hat. 'We have only just arrived and it is always how I spend my first day.'

As Holmes had said, of course. 'Forgive me,' I said.

'Forgiven,' she said with a smile, taking my arm. We resumed our walk. 'Though I do not give up easily, Dr Watson. I know full well that the McLarens are under a cloud of suspicion of having to do with the phylloxera epidemic and some vague threats to the research. I do not see it myself. The laird is not the warmest of men but he is not an evil man. His elder son, Charles, has not the courage or brains to have engineered such a thing, which began some years ago, anyway, and my Alistair thinks the notion of the epidemic being man-made is foolish and impossible. Nevertheless we have been questioned and I would not be surprised if your Mr Holmes was sent to investigate us.'

This young woman was making me nervous, and I am not a nervous man. The McLarens were most certainly on Holmes's agenda.

'No, he has been sent on another matter,' I said, thinking that investigating Vidocq made this at least partly true. 'Would you care for a fruit ice?'

'Dr Watson, you are a very poor liar.'

I said nothing.

'I noticed a book on phylloxera on his table in Baker Street. The research on this pest is centred in Montpellier. When do you plan to visit?' The lady stood looking at me, her blue and white dress now billowing in the sea breeze. She held on to her feathered hat with one hand and smiled at me.

'The wind is coming up, madam, perhaps it would be best if—'

'That is all right. Let me help you. Dr Watson. I would wager my last shilling that you are here on the business of the French wine industry. What you fail to understand is that I am on your side. I brought the dynamite to you, did I not? If there is something amiss in my family, I am as interested as you or Mr Holmes to discover it.'

'I really do not know what to say, Mrs McLaren.'

'I will make sure you and Mr Holmes are invited to dine with us at the Grand Hôtel du Cap. It is a stunning hotel, and as you said, the best in the area. You will at least be certain of a wonderful dinner.'

My luck was changing. 'Well, perhaps—'

'Where are you staying?'

'The Beau Soleil, here in Nice.'

'Hmm, I have not heard of it. Dr Watson, will you hail me a cab, please? It is growing chilly and I should like to return to my hotel. You can expect an invitation soon.' Stepping into the street, I easily procured a cab for her, and as she mounted it, she turned and gave me a small wave.

How very curious, I thought. If it were not so illogical, I might entertain the thought that she was pursuing us, or Holmes, for some unfathomable reason. But the wind had picked up, and I was dressed lightly. I shivered and turned back to the Beau Soleil.

Some hours later, after a fitful nap and dinner in the modest hotel restaurant, I returned to the room to find Holmes stretched out, catlike on one of the wretched beds.

'Ah, Watson. I see from your expression that you have been successful,' he cried. 'And so have I. Your news first!'

'Yes, I found the lady almost immediately, or rather she found me,' I said. 'She had her shopping with her. But she seemed to suspect that we are on the trail of her family regarding this vineyard problem! Why she could possibly—'

'Watson, Mrs McLaren is observant. Remember that she espied the miniature still on my table in Baker Street and likely the phylloxera materials as well. It is not a very far leap to infer my involvement.'

'I suppose. Holmes, let us leave this room and take some air.'

In a few moments we were on a rooftop terrace with glasses of Pernod. There was almost a view of the ocean, if somewhat marred by intervening buildings in various stages of disrepair. Ours was not precisely a first-class hotel.

'If only I had known of the suspicions surrounding the McLarens, I might have taken Isla McLaren's case then,' said Holmes. 'No matter, I shall take her case now.'

'Too late. The maid Fiona seems to have eloped with the groundsman's son. There was a note.'

'A shame. I could have used that as our entry point—'

'In any case, Holmes, Mrs McLaren said we would be invited to dinner. Just as you had hoped.'

Holmes reacted strangely to this. 'This is rather more

convenient than it should be. And yet I do not believe in coincidences. I wonder about her agenda.'

'She did know that her family is suspected of interference in the phylloxera research.'

Holmes started at this. 'Interesting. I am surprised she did not mention it in Baker Street.'

'But what of your detour in Tours? Did you accomplish what you hoped?'

Holmes's meeting, as it turned out, had been with a man we knew from an earlier case. This supremely wealthy and powerful gentleman had, since our dealings with him, bought a château and vineyard in the Loire Valley, in order to be nearer a certain French singer of our acquaintance with whom he was most painfully in love. Her name was Cherie Cerise, or Mademoiselle Emmeline La Victoire, as we had known her.

'This man happens to be a close friend of Philippe Reynaud. They were old Etonians together. Alas he could offer no insight into Reynaud's suspicion of the British but something else of use came of the meeting!'

'What was that?'

'He was absolutely shocked when I told him that Jean Vidocq had been hired by his friend Reynaud to protect the French researcher.'

'Why would he care about this?'

'Because this same Vidocq has developed into a nemesis. Do you remember the friction between them on our case last year? They continue to be rivals in love for the French chanteuse.'

This fit exactly with my impression of Jean Vidocq. 'I see,' said I. 'But . . . how do you intend to use this?' I wondered. 'I mean, given that "domestics" as you call them do not fall in your purview.'

'Ah, Watson, you chastise. Vidocq's role in this phylloxera scandal is precipitously attached now to his private romantic life.' Holmes laughed. 'I can ensure his dismissal from that post if I can prove the affair.'

The winter sun had dropped low in the sky and dark gold bands of light played across the table and the nearby patrons.

'Did this man you refuse to name know that his friend Reynaud had hired Vidocq?'

Holmes smiled impishly. 'Now he does.'

Holmes was ever a master of the long game. But the short-term concerns fell to me. 'Order some food, Holmes. The omelette is quite good I am told.'

'Nothing, thank you.'

'Well I see you have leverage now over Vidocq, if indeed he is romancing Mlle La Victoire.'

'It is as likely as the sun rising tomorrow.'

'But is there any chance that Vidocq is actually fulfilling his role? That he is actually protecting Dr Janvier from a very real threat?'

'That is the far more important question, Watson, and takes precedence.'

He looked out at the sliver of ocean thoughtfully. The slanted rays of the setting sun highlighted his London pallor and he looked rather more like a figure at Madame Tussaud's than was healthy. As usual while on a case, he had eaten nothing.

'Shall we take a stroll?' I offered. 'Perhaps some dinner?'

'Not for me, Watson. Go ahead. I have more reading to do before meeting with Dr Paul-Édouard Janvier. We leave tomorrow on a very early train for Montpellier.'

CHAPTER 6

Docteur Janvier

omorrow came after what seemed only minutes of rest in our ghastly room, I was rudely awakened by Holmes shaking my shoulder.

'Come Watson, we must be on the 4.30 train.'

I stumbled groggily into my clothes, and we set out in the predawn hours for the station. Hurriedly gulping down a hot coffee before boarding, I then tried to read a small Montpellier guidebook but soon dozed. Once again, I felt Holmes's hand on my shoulder, jostling me awake. We had arrived in Montpellier, a small medieval city renowned for its scientific research. I yawned in anticipation of a long day discussing the vineyard scourge. But fate held something quite different in store.

We disembarked just before noon at the Gare de Montpellier and made our way north through the dusty streets to the Place de la Comédie. The weather had warmed since the day before, and the bright Mediterranean sun glowed on the golden brown sides of the crumbling and picturesque ruins that formed the Citadel, once an 11th-century fort. Despite its look of antiquity, this city had developed over the years into a kind of Mecca for scientists.

We were to meet Dr Paul-Édouard Janvier at La Coloumbe, a café on the main square, and we immediately spotted our quarry from a photograph provided by Mycroft Holmes. Seated at an outdoor table, the renowned horticultural scientist and leading investigator in the vineyard scourge, Dr Janvier was younger than I had anticipated, in his mid-thirties. Black-haired and intense, he sported an impressive, curled moustache and a lightweight suit of linen, appropriate here even in December.

Janvier gazed out at the passers-by, drumming his long thin fingers in a manner not unlike Holmes. He seemed lost in thought.

'*Docteur Janvier?*' said Holmes, approaching the man. '*Je suis Sherlock Holmes, et voici Docteur Watson, mon collègue.*'

Rising to shake our hands, the gentleman replied in perfect, mildly accented English, 'Gentlemen, welcome. I have received a letter of introduction and know why you are here. But I have not much time. Please let us order our lunch and we shall discuss what you will.' We took our places. Holmes positioned himself to look out at the square.

'I prefer to speak English, if you do not mind,' said Janvier. 'I have recently been abroad in America, where few speak my language.'

I squinted in the bright sun at the menu as Holmes

entered straight into the subject at hand. 'Dr Janvier, as my speciality is crime, and not viticulture, I shall begin with the question of your security. I understand you have received threatening letters?'

'I received a letter that you would come. Are you a threat?'

Holmes laughed. I was less sure of the joke.

'Perhaps you are not aware of Mr Holmes's successes in criminal investigations?' I said. 'He is a well-respected—'

'Humour, Dr Watson. Of course, I am well aware,' the scientist remarked.

'The letters, then?' asked Holmes. 'How many?'

'Two. No, three.'

'Might I see them?'

'I have thrown them away.' At Holmes's surprise, he continued. 'I consider them irrelevant. Gentlemen, try our version of Salade Niçoise. Here, let us order our lunch.' He signalled a waiter.

'Dr Janvier, your government feels you have been legitimately threatened and, through an intermediary, has asked me to offer my services. I presume you showed the letters to someone.'

'I did.'

'And then you destroyed them?'

'The entire matter has served only to waste my time. The only outcome of this threat is that I have been distracted and delayed by the man sent to protect me. Really, sir, I do not take them at face value. It is my choice to ignore the matter.'

As did Holmes with Orville St John, I thought.

'Perhaps that is best decided by a detective, Dr Janvier. Can you tell me more of these letters? Were they all written by the same hand? In English, by chance?' asked Holmes.

'In English, yes. But first things first, Mr Holmes, let us order our food. We are in France, after all. Ah, here is the waiter!' Janvier, in the manner of many of his countrymen, would not be rushed. He ordered our lunch and, of course, some wine.

'A good *Château Des Flaugergues*, from very nearby. Since the 17th century! The one I have ordered comes from before the phylloxera.'

'What did the letters say?' persisted Holmes. 'Certainly enough to have the government wish to send someone to investigate?'

'Mr Holmes, have you never been frustrated by those who claim to share your goals and yet impede your work? That is how I feel about my government. Everyone is concerned about my safety, and yet so slow to understand the results of my research. They are impatient for completion. They do not understand how research works!'

'Yes, yes, I sympathize,' said Holmes.

'I imagine you can. I have read Dr Watson's account.'

The wine arrived and now Janvier busied himself with tasting and approving the precious liquid. It was clear he did not wish to discuss the letters. I took a sip of the wine. Even to my relatively untutored palate, it was truly delicious. Holmes's glass remained untouched, and I could sense his growing impatience.

But at Janvier's urging, he took a sip. 'Yes, a splendid vintage,' my friend conceded. 'We shall return to these letters. Regarding your research, Dr Janvier, how close are you to a cure?'

Janvier immediately warmed to this question. 'Ah! To understand this,' said the scientist, 'you must understand the phylloxera itself. Let me give you some background.'

Dr Janvier then proceeded to regale us with far more than I ever wanted to know on the subject of the phylloxera plague that was destroying the vineyards, how it affected the roots, how American wine varieties seemed immune, and how a search for resistant rootstock version that would thrive in the limestone of French soils was being sought.

Meanwhile our rather large and complicated salads arrived, filled with a variety of olives, seafood, and vegetables. Mounds of vegetation are generally not my choice of a meal, but this was surprisingly good, and some minutes later I was fishing for any stray olives that might have escaped my fork, when Janvier's description became particularly detailed about the tiny worm-like parasites and their effects on the roots of the vines. His words were so graphic that I could suddenly stomach no more of the leafy greens I faced.

Holmes ate and drank very little but as the meal progressed remained on alert, glancing frequently at our fellow diners, and those passing through the square. This had not escaped Janvier.

'Mr Holmes,' said he, pushing away his empty plate, 'you may relax your hawk-like vigilance. I do not believe these threats, and even if I did, I would certainly feel safe in public nevertheless.' He took a sip of wine.

The waiter cleared our plates, including Holmes's full one.

'Dr Janvier, please allow me to decide whether or not there is a threat. I am perhaps more accustomed to these things.' Holmes looked to his salad but the plate was gone. He threw down his napkin in annoyance. 'What is the status of your research currently?' he asked.

'The vintners distrust science, and gaining their cooperation has been challenging.'

'That is a shame,' said I. 'Surely you can educate them to—'

'No, they are a superstitious lot. Many persist in their magical thinking.' The scientist offered a hint of a smile from underneath his enormous moustache.

'What do you mean by that curious term?' asked Holmes.

'Well, some believe that burying poisonous toads near the roots of the afflicted vines will scare away the evil spirits! Others imagine that the measurements of their casks must match the golden mean, or that magnetic forces under the ground should dictate the layout of their plantings. Ludicrous!' He looked around for the waiter. '*Garçon! Du café, s'il vous plaît!*'

'Frustrating, I am sure. Dr Janvier, are you aware that the French government suspects intentional sabotage?' asked Holmes.

'Pah!' exclaimed the scientist. 'They are idiots.' Janvier sounded more and more like Holmes in one of his disputatious moods.

'A certain Monsieur Reynaud of your government thinks one of my countrymen was at fault,' said the detective.

'Well, that is so.'

Holmes looked up in surprise. 'What?'

'I am fairly certain that a British horticulturalist brought it in on a cutting from America.'

'Indeed!' said Holmes. 'Whom do you suspect?'

'I know the man and he is innocent. It was accidental, a mistake anyone could make. Well, I would not. But it is remarkably easy to do, and probably would have happened sooner or later.'

Holmes pressed Janvier on this topic, but he would say no more.

Over coffee moments later, the scientist lit up a cigarette. 'Mr Holmes, if it were sabotage, what motive would the British have for this? You are one of the largest importers of our wines, cognac and brandy. Britain would suffer from the loss.'

'Yes, but our whisky business is profiting wildly just now,' I said. 'Some say—'

'Watson!'

'I have heard,' said Janvier. 'They suspect the Scots. Or some particular Scots, I do not know. I have seen no evidence. But Mr Holmes, consider the mechanics of such a plot. It is impractical, uncontrollable. Only a madman or anarchist would attempt to make such an obtuse statement in this way.'

'But to stop your work? That might be useful. Let us return to those letters,' said Holmes.

Janvier shrugged. 'Mr Holmes, let me ask you this. Have you ever received vague threats from someone who seems, well, deranged? And did you alter your course because of it?'

I cleared my throat.

Holmes shook his head in irritation. 'I take your point. But crime is my business and I am accustomed to receiving threats. Please tell me everything you remember about the letters.'

'I can tell you only this,' said the scientist, 'All three were in English, anonymous, and all three on the kind of cheap paper that is available in hundreds of places all over France. The first was written in ordinary black ink, with an aged but costly pen with a flexible nib, the other in a slightly more expensive blue ink but a similar pen. And the third, in black ink like the first, on the back of a postcard with a cheap pen.'

I began to realize the remarkable similarity of the two men sitting at the table with me.

'Was the handwriting male or female?' asked Holmes.

'Male, for all three, I would say. Educated. There were, however two curious things.'

'What were those?'

'Well, I noted that while my initial impression was that the hands were different, upon a closer look, it became apparent that they were actually written by the same person.'

'And how did you—'

'The looped "t"s,' said Janvier.

'Of course. That must have been a relief,' remarked Holmes with a smile.

'Just so.'

Both men sipped their coffee in contemplation of the brief exchange.

'Wait?' I asked. 'Why did that relieve you, sir?' I wondered.

'The single writer clearly wanted Dr Janvier to think that the opposition to his work was more widespread, Watson. But it was only one person,' said Holmes.

Janvier nodded. Of course, now it was obvious.

'Dr Janvier, the question of the hour. What did the letters say?' asked Holmes.

'That I must stop my work or suffer dire consequences. The exact threat was vague. Flowery. The phylloxera was God-sent, or something, and that evil would befall me if I interfered with God's will. Both me and also my family. But of course, I am unmarried and have no children. They also mentioned that objections to my work were rampant and in persisting, I risked awakening "a sleeping giant", and my work would go "up in smoke".'

'A sleeping giant? Up in smoke?'

'The exact words. And that is all. Would you care for some dessert?' asked Janvier. He indicated a nearby cart on which were arrayed a tempting selection of *tartes*.

'No, but a visit to your laboratory would be in order. I am still concerned for your security,' said Holmes.

'My pleasure, Mr Holmes.'

After a brief walk through the narrow streets of this hilly

town, during which I had difficulty keeping up with my long-legged companions in the hot afternoon sun, and directly after eating a full meal, we arrived at *l'École Nationale d'Agriculture de Montpellier*.

We passed several low buildings in a compound with numerous garden plots, all planted with vines, which were carefully labelled and divided by string. A collection of broad, straw sun hats rested on poles throughout, evidently abandoned there by the workers at lunchtime.

We entered one of the buildings and made our way down a long hallway. The building was strangely deserted. 'Where is everyone?' I asked Holmes in a low voice.

'We are in France, Watson.' he whispered. 'Lunch!'

But Janvier apparently possessed similarly acute hearing. He laughed. 'Yes! Meals happen, as you say, like clockwork. In our country, we are quite sensible about refreshing mind and body. We lunched intentionally early as I wished to keep your laboratory visit private.'

'I see no security measures here, Dr Janvier. Anyone could enter, and tamper with your work,' said Holmes.

'They would have to understand it to do so. Everything is done in duplicate, or triplicate, and meticulously recorded,' Janvier smiled. 'I am not concerned,' said he, waving a hand.

'What of this man they have sent to look after you – Jean Vidocq, what has he done?'

'Yes. Ah, you know him, do you? At least Dr Watson does. Your face tells me all, Doctor. Mr Holmes, you have the gift of obfuscation but your friend here is an open book.'

I began to think I should place obfuscation on my list of attributes to cultivate.

'This Vidocq, then—'

'Irritating man. He does nothing but fan the flames of fear among my researchers. He comes and goes. I should like to be rid of him.'

'I can well imagine,' I said.

'Whenever he is here, he attempts to worry me and my researchers with concocted scenarios. I regret burning the letters, Mr Holmes. But that man Vidocq is such a pest. He exaggerates the danger. I wanted him gone and so I scorned the entire idea of any threat and burned them in front of him. He was as angry as you are!'

'Indeed. How close are you to a solution to the phylloxera epidemic, Dr Janvier?'

'Very close.'

'Is that so? Who knows this?' asked Holmes.

'Any number of people, in the government and elsewhere.'

'What is it?'

'Grafts and hybridization show promise. But at present, we have taken several batches to maturity, and they adversely affect the flavour.'

'Then you have not found the solution. Although as you near it, you may be in more danger.'

We had rounded a corner and now progressed down another long corridor, this with doors open to reveal laboratories, their rich wood cabinets and slate-topped counters gleaming from the afternoon sun slanting in the windows.

'We may have been looking at the wrong question' said

Holmes. 'Might there be a more personal motive to stop your work? Have you any rivals who wish to take credit? Anyone you have specifically angered? Anyone who comes to mind that would profit directly and personally from *your* cure not being advanced?'

Janvier paused midstride and turned to us. We stopped.

'And there you have me, Mr Holmes. No. My first thought was that someone deeply invested in wines that rival the French might profit. The Americans. The Germans, perhaps the Italians. But I think not. The Americans have been helpful, and the Germans and Italians now face the same plague, though to a lesser degree. Regarding jealous colleagues, I think not. This particular problem has united the larger research community to a remarkable degree.'

'And still Britain may be suspect,' said Holmes. 'As Watson mentioned, our whisky business is said to be growing in leaps and bounds.'

'I think as a scientist does. Instinct is perhaps as important in my work as observation and logic. And my instinct tells me this disaster is an accident and nothing more.'

Holmes nodded. 'I wonder, could this divisive theory then originate from someone who profits from a deterioration of Franco-British relations?'

'There you exceed my expertise, Mr Holmes,' said Janvier. He turned and placed a hand on a single, closed door at the end of the hall. It was locked and he felt in his pocket for the keys.

'Back to the letters, Dr Janvier,' said Holmes. 'You

mentioned there were two curious things. What was the second?'

Finding the key, Janvier unlocked the door. It swung open with a bang and both Holmes and I jumped, primed for what, I am not sure. What we saw was a complete surprise.

The room stood vast and empty, a laboratory like the others, but this one was not only devoid of people but of equipment as well. Bright sunshine flooded in from an expanse of windows, and dust motes floated over barren zinc lab tables. Along one end of the room were a row of cardboard boxes, from which protruded various pieces of equipment.

'Ah, *mon Dieu!*' said Janvier with an embarrassed laugh. 'How could I have forgotten! We moved our laboratory to larger quarters in another building only yesterday. I was so engrossed in my story that it completely escaped my mind. We must go to another building!' He strode through the laboratory to the other end. 'Follow me, please. It is a shorter way out.'

'You were about to mention the second curious thing, Dr Janvier?' said Holmes.

Janvier unlocked a door at the other end of the deserted lab and we entered a small decoratively tiled antechamber where a set of double doors led outside. They, too, were locked. He withdrew another set of keys from his pocket and began to unlock them. As he flung the double doors open wide the brilliant sunlight blinded us momentarily. He turned, silhouetted in the bright rectangle.

'Ah, yes. The last one was in rhyme,' said he.

But before this fact could yield further thought, there was a sudden deafening roar and the sound of splintering glass. The entryway in which we were standing blew outwards into rubble. In a kind of slow motion the air turned a solid white and I felt myself propelled forwards through the air like a rag doll.

We were buried in an avalanche of bricks, mortar, plaster and dust. I was conscious only of white everywhere and a single thought: Janvier was wrong. And then blackness.

PART TWO

GETTING AHEAD

'If you can keep your head when all about you are
losing theirs . . .'
—Rudyard Kipling

PART TWO

CHAPTER 7

Vidocq

I must have lain there a moment or two, perhaps even a minute, as the roar echoed in my head, a temporary deafness and blindness robbing me of action. The sounds of gunfire and shouts resounded and echoed through my brain, and then receded into silence. The battlefield.

Was I dead?

Wiping my eyes, I blinked out the dust, and rolled over onto my side. I opened my eyes to see the octagonal red tiles of the hallway in which I lay. Not Afghanistan. Not the battlefield. Montpellier.

I felt a sudden stab in my bicep, and sitting up, I noticed a long shard of glass was embedded in my sleeve. Light streamed in from above and I looked up, noticing a shattered clerestory window.

France. Janvier's lab. An explosion.

I lurched to my feet, head clearing.

Janvier, who had been before us, had received a small

cut over his eye. But he now stood, apparently otherwise unharmed, though a bit stunned. He vigorously brushed the dust from his own clothing.

'Your forehead,' I said. 'It is bleeding.'

'Thank you, Doctor,' said he. He drew out a handkerchief and pressed it to his cut forehead. 'I am all right,' he said. 'And you, Dr Watson? You look as though you had seen a ghost.'

I gently extracted the piece of glass. No large patch of blood; it was merely a scratch. 'I am fine.' I turned to look for Holmes. I could not see him, but nearby a wall had collapsed. My heart began to race. He had been right behind me. Had he made it through the door?

'Holmes?' I cried moving towards a mound of rubble, terrified at what I might find there.

'Look!' shouted Janvier. 'He has gone back inside!' The Frenchman pointed behind us into the damaged laboratory, where in the heavy layer of dust I saw a disturbed area where Holmes had fallen, and then footprints heading directly back inside towards the site of the explosion.

'Holmes!' I shouted again, peering into the room. I started after him.

'Careful!' Janvier cried. 'There could be a second bomb!'

But I was already halfway across the room. Nearer the site of the explosion white dust filled the air.

I paused, now enveloped in a miasma of white and having lost view of the footprints, which vanished below me into the floating cloud. I squinted and bent down, trying to locate them. After some moments, I finally found them and proceeded slowly forward into the impenetrable whiteness.

A ghostly apparition, covered from head to foot in plaster, emerged from the fog. It was Holmes. In his hand he held something wrapped in a handkerchief. I heaved a sigh of relief.

'All is well, Watson,' said he.

'Thank God. Did you find anything?' I asked.

He nodded as Janvier came up behind me. The Frenchman fanned the air and coughed. 'Outside, gentlemen, please!'

We made our way out of the building, and across a courtyard I could see a crowd of people gathering and pointing. I heard whistles and shouts and the clanging bells of the French police growing nearer.

'Tell me what you found, Mr Holmes?' urged Janvier.

'Whoever did this has made his escape,' said the detective. 'However the explosion is a large one at the back of that room near the sinks. Dynamite. A second stick had been lit but I found it and managed to stop it before it ignited.' He held up the offending item, and then placed it in his pocket.

'You are mad, Holmes,' said I. 'You could have been blown to pieces.'

He smiled and shrugged.

I looked back at the swirling dust. 'We should check for injured people!'

'I did. There was no one.'

Bonnie MacBird

Janvier placed a hand on my arm. 'No one was there. As I said, our work was transferred yesterday to a larger building. And everyone is eating their lunch.'

'But you are different, Dr Janvier. Do you not occasionally work during lunch?' asked Holmes.

'True. Perhaps it is the American influence.'

'But to the point. The timing of this – might you have been the direct target?' asked Holmes.

Janvier paused. He and Holmes stared at each other intently for a moment. I had the impression that both were sifting the information and perhaps coming to some kind of joint conclusion.

'Not likely,' said Janvier. 'The mistaken laboratory. The timing of the detonation.'

'I concur. A message. Not intended to kill,' agreed Holmes. 'But dangerous nonetheless.' He withdrew the stick of dynamite from his pocket, using his handkerchief to do so. It was a few inches long, wrapped in brown paper with a label. The fuse was blackened. 'Made by Nobel, in Scotland. The best for the task that can be found anywhere. You are very lucky, even so.'

It was exactly like the dynamite that Isla McLaren had so casually displayed at 221B.

'Holmes! That is the same—'

'I know,' said Holmes. He turned to Janvier. 'The letters threatened you to stop or your work would "go up in smoke" I believe you said.'

The scientist looked down at the ground 'But they will have to kill me first.'

'Do not tempt fate, Docteur. I suggest you post a guard at all times.'

A police commissionaire rushed up to us, bristling with urgency. His blond hair was clipped short, and he was bronzed so deeply from the Mediterranean sun that he appeared almost metallic. Holmes and Janvier answered a few quick questions in French, and after a few minutes the man retreated and headed back to the site of the explosion. His accent was indecipherable and I had understood nothing.

'Might you translate, for my colleague?' said Holmes.

Janvier laughed, with a tinge of bitterness. 'He attempted to apologize to me. When the letters first arrived, the director of the lab showed them to the police. They dismissed the threats as I did, but for a different reason. They thought I was simply trying to draw attention to myself!'

Holmes snorted. Janvier continued. 'Idiots. But it alerted someone in the Chamber of Deputies, and their response was to send that horrible . . . *et voici* . . . here he is now. Excuse me for a moment.' He moved quickly away to speak to two worried assistants.

A dark figure slowly approached us from the other side of the courtyard, emerging from behind the building which had suffered the blast. He was silhouetted against the bright sunlight and at first I could not make out who it was. The swagger, however, was striking.

'Sherlock Holmes!' exclaimed the familiar, French-accented voice. He passed out of the bright light, and into view. It was the disreputable Jean Vidocq himself.

In contrast to our dishevelled and whitened state, the tall, handsome Frenchman was the picture of elegance. He strode forward with a smile, impeccable as always in a well-tailored frock coat and jaunty cravat.

The man was a rakish charmer, to whom women seemed drawn as by a magnetic force. He was insufferable. In fact, I still felt the occasional pain in my back directly due to our contretemps at the Louvre last year. The man had knocked me down a flight of steps.

'You!' I said.

Vidocq responded with a cocky grin. But as he approached, Sherlock Holmes surprised me in the extreme. He rushed to embrace this rogue.

'Jean Vidocq! *Bienvenue!* I am so happy to see you here!' he gushed, clasping the Frenchman to his bosom, kissing him on both cheeks in the French manner of greeting.

Vidocq, equally surprised, recoiled and backed away in disgust, frantically brushing at the white plaster dust, which Holmes with his embrace had deposited on his pristine frock coat. Holmes hid a quick smile.

'*Mon Dieu!* What the hell is the matter with you, Holmes? Is it the cocaine?' exclaimed Vidocq.

'*Ah, non, non!*' said Holmes. '*C'est trop de soleil!*'

Too much sun? Holmes was inventive today. Janvier looked on in confusion.

'Ah, so sorry,' said Holmes, apparently recovering. 'It is the shock also. Vidocq, my old friend!'

Turning from Holmes with a look of doubt, Vidocq focused on his fellow Frenchman. 'Dr Janvier? *Ça va?*' he asked. What followed was a rapid exchange in French, of which I only understood that he was ascertaining that the famous scientist was unharmed. Satisfied, he turned to us.

'Well, Monsieur Holmes, what an interesting coincidence. And Doctor Wilson, I believe it is.'

'You know my name, Monsieur Verdun!' said I.

Vidocq was taken aback. 'Ah, yes, Dr Watson, forgive me. It slipped my mind. How very strange to find you both here at this precise moment. Where were you exactly when the bomb went off?'

Holmes smiled. With a grand gesture he indicated our plaster-covered selves. In fact, we were so whitened by the dust as to look like madcap bakers in a comedy turn at the Gaieties.

Vidocq eyed us with derision. 'A little close for comfort, *n'est-ce pas*? But again, why are you here, in the *laboratoire*? It is lunchtime.'

'Indeed. One might ask the same of you, Vidocq,' said Holmes brushing the white powder and bits of plaster from his own coat.

'Police business.'

'Excellent timing! Or are you simply prescient?' asked Holmes.

'Dr Janvier has received death threats. I have been sent by the government to investigate and protect. Your presence here is suspicious.'

Holmes laughed. 'You will get nowhere with this line of thinking, Vidocq,' said Holmes.

Dr Janvier now returned and Vidocq turned to the scientist with an expansive smile. 'Ah, Dr Janvier. So very happy that you are unharmed!' he gushed, grasping Janvier's arm in what I thought was an overly familiar gesture. 'It was thanks to God that—'

'It was luck or miscalculation on the part of the bomber, M. Vidocq, nothing more. If you will excuse me,' the scientist said, breaking free and turning pointedly to us. 'Gentlemen, my staff return from lunch and I must reassure my colleagues. I believe you have learned all I can tell you now. I will see that you receive a copy of my paper on the phylloxera on your way out.' He started to leave but turned back. 'And I shall take your advice, Mr Holmes. We will take more care.'

He strode off, brushing at his clothes. We stood facing Vidocq.

The Frenchman's pretence at charm dropped like a curtain. He advanced on us with a frown. 'Holmes, I will not have you meddling in this affair. I am hired by the French government to protect this man. In fact, we have every reason to suspect British hands in these threats and . . . well, here you are. I should have you arrested.'

'You are joking!' I said.

Holmes shot me a warning look. 'Vidocq, I do not know what your game is here, but assuredly it is financially driven. Your altruism is never what it seems.'

'Speaking of finances, my dear friend, I understand you are currently lodging at the laughable Hôtel Du Beau Soleil. How difficult it must be to attempt to command the world stage from such undignified surroundings.'

Somehow he seemed to know of our hotel misadventures in Nice. My surprise at this must have shown on my face. Vidocq laughed.

'Not only M. Holmes keep the track of his special friends, Doctor.'

'Vidocq, I suggest that you stay out of our way on this and on all matters,' said Holmes.

'Or what?' replied Vidocq with a sneer.

'Or I shall make your latest indiscretion known.'

'And what indiscretion is that?'

'Ah, then you admit to more than one.' Holmes smiled as he reached into his pocket and removed a train ticket which he held aloft. The Frenchman gasped and patted his waistcoat, discovering he had been neatly pick-pocketed. Furious, he snatched at it, but Holmes pulled the ticket away and waved it in the air. 'Paris–Nice, only yesterday,' said my companion.

I could not help but laugh. Holmes enjoyed my amusement and Vidocq's discomfort perhaps more than was polite. 'Ah, Paris, the city of light. And of love,' said he. 'You have no doubt enjoyed yourself there, Vidocq, in a particularly close encounter.'

'*Ce n'est rien!*' snarled the Frenchman. 'I have been in Paris. The rest is wild conjecture, Holmes.'

Holmes paused. He sniffed the air pointedly.

A maelstrom of expressions crossed Vidocq's face. And then he understood.

'Ah, *Mon Dieu*. Remind me to keep my distance.'

I was still in the dark. Holmes turned to me. 'Our friend's

frock coat collar is quite redolent of a certain perfume. Jicky, you remember, Watson?'

'That proves nothing,' said Vidocq. 'That scent has taken Paris by storm. Many men and many women wear it.'

'Really. And am I to conclude from your collar that you have been embracing many men and many women all over the City of Light? Random individuals, no doubt, and at considerable length?'

Vidocq shrugged.

'No, the evidence, while circumstantial, I agree, is suggestive. We both know that Jicky is the signature scent of a certain Mademoiselle Emmeline La Victoire.'

Vidocq smirked. 'In France this is hardly a scandal.'

'Perhaps you do not know that the lady is engaged. Her fiancé is as well connected in France as he is in England. The gentleman is a schoolboy friend of M. Reynaud, who is, I believe, your current employer.'

Vidocq's smile fell away and he stepped back in surprise.

'A word to this fine man and your lucrative connections will vanish,' said Holmes. 'May I suggest you drop both your affair, and the dangerous game you are playing here, lest I find it necessary to intrude on your own personal liberties?'

Vidocq's retort was interrupted by the bronzed French policeman, who cut through a gathering crowd to stand with us. He spoke sharply in French, but Vidocq held up a hand.

Holmes smiled and leaned forward. 'Oh, and you are careless, Vidocq,' he whispered. 'Your coat pocket? The right one. Here, let me.'

His arm flashed forward and he pulled a stick of dyna-mite from Vidocq's pocket. The policeman started, and turned to Vidocq, grasped him suddenly by the arm, and called out for reinforcements.

As several gendarmes ran forward to assist, Vidocq shook his head in annoyance.

Holmes smiled, turned on his heel, and despite his ludi-crous white countenance managed a dignified exit. I paused only a moment longer to enjoy Vidocq's discomfiture, gave him a small salute, and followed my friend.

The level of Holmes's research never failed to surprise me. But then, it has always been a hallmark of his methods.

Our return train to Nice that afternoon was less than pleasant. Unable to remove the dust fully from our clothing, we were forced to travel in the baggage car, seated on boxes covered with sheets and warned severely not to get our dusty selves on anything else.

As the purser slammed the door shut behind us Holmes looked at me and burst out laughing. 'Watson, you look like a man who has been frustrated by an encounter with the pastry dough.'

'Holmes, this trip has been something of a disappoint-ment. As despicable as Jean Vidocq is, I am appalled that you would stoop to planting evidence on him. It strikes me as beneath you.'

Holmes looked at me strangely. 'How could you think so, Watson?' He took his handkerchief, and reached into his pocket and withdrew the stick of dynamite. 'Notice this was lit, and put out. That one had not been. Had we not been here, he would have set off a third. Really, Watson, you must sharpen your skills.'

'But why would Vidocq himself set off the explosions?'

'Many reasons. Primarily it ensures his job, and probably raises his fee.'

'But might he not continue with this plan?'

'He would not dare to do so right at present. We are not finished on this count, however.'

'He exceeds even my low opinion of him. I apologize, Holmes.' I eyed the stick of dynamite. 'Is that safe?'

'Reasonably so. It takes a detonator to set these off. That is Nobel's contribution to the art of explosives. There is a binding agent with the nitroglycerin which—'

'Really, I do not care to know. But why is it here? Why did you not hand it over to the police?'

'I will test it myself for fingerprints. The bronzed fellow we met in Montpellier is in Vidocq's pocket.'

'I thought he was arresting Vidocq!'

'They wished it to appear so. The fellow did not know I speak fluent French. Even their fast-paced argot.'

'Argot?'

'Slang.'

'And if the fingerprints are Vidocq's . . .'

'I am certain they will prove to be so. This will show he is behind, or at least complicit with the threats to Docteur Janvier. Mycroft will have what he needs, and Monsieur Reynaud, through our old friend in Tours, will most certainly relieve Vidocq of his exalted position. The universe will align, Watson, providing science prevails. Those finger-prints will be key.'

'Are they admissible in court?'

'They will certainly be so in the future, but sadly not at present. The die will be cast, however, and Monsieur Reynaud will play his part, I am sure of it. Vidocq will get his just desserts.'

We were silent for a time as the train rumbled on. It was hot in the car, with no windows to relieve us. I wiped my sweating brow with my handkerchief, and it came away filthy.

'There is something troubling me,' said I. 'Mycroft—'

Holmes sighed. 'I intended to help the British government all along, Watson. Mycroft had been imploring me for some time. You saw that I had been studying the subject.'

'But then why the little dance with your brother? Why refuse his advance?'

'A useless gesture, Watson, I will admit. It is difficult to erase old patterns. You would not understand.'

'Yes, well why let some ghost of your past—'

'Watson! This from a man whose own ghosts wake him shouting in the night.'

'Lingering effects from battle are well known, Holmes! You are squabbling with an older brother. Why? Did he steal your toast and marmalade as a child?'

I expected a sharp retort, but instead Holmes was silent for a moment. 'You misjudge me, again,' he said quietly. 'Watson, there are those rare people who elicit behaviour from us that others may not. Let me suggest that you were one man on the battlefield, another with your patients, a third altogether with Mary and perhaps a fourth in my company, for example?'

'No, Holmes. I am always myself. Well, perhaps I smoke less around Mary.'

He smiled at this.

'But whatever the situation, I try always to be the best man I can be.'

He paused.

'Of course you do, and how well you succeed. My apologies, Watson.'

As we spent an uncomfortable six hours on the train I ruminated that it would take effort to continue being the best man that I could. But I was determined to stay the course.

CHAPTER 8

Ahead of the Game

n the following day, the expected dinner invitation arrived, not from Isla McLaren, but from Laird Robert McLaren himself, and at five minutes past seven our carriage, fees charged to our hotel, pulled up at the Grand Hôtel du Cap in nearby Antibes. I was never particularly comfortable in my formal attire, though Holmes seemed quite at ease. The letter was flattering and had indicated that the laird wished to make use of Holmes's 'renowned skills'. It would be a case, we presumed.

'Whatever the task may be, Watson, we must stay on our guard. The McLarens are not yet entirely cleared of any connection to that bombing, and may in fact wish to draw us into their fold for their own reasons.'

'Surely they can intend no violence at this dinner.'

'Unlikely. But you have your Webley with you?'

I nodded.

The Grand Hôtel du Cap was a far cry from the Beau Soleil. Ensconced in a wooded hill overlooking a brilliant blue sea and a rocky beach, the building arose like a tiered pink bride's cake from among the olive and cypress trees.

The lobby was gleaming marble, with velvet benches and liveried porters swarming around the richly attired guests. Everything and everyone conveyed a look of polished ease. The concierge waved a hand and a page ushered us down a long hallway past magnificent views of the ocean to gilded doors leading to a private dining room.

Seated there was our party, already assembled. There were five people: three gentlemen and two ladies, one with her back to the door. Expensive tailoring, tartan details in the waistcoats of the gentlemen, glittering gowns on the ladies, and an overall impression of immense wealth worn with casual ease made up my immediate impression.

At the head of the table, a large man in his fifties rose to greet us. 'Welcome Mr Sherlock Holmes, and Dr John Watson,' he boomed in a deep voice, with a strong Scots brogue. A mane of dark, greying curls surrounded a handsome face, now creased with a warm smile. 'You are guests of the Clan McLaren, and I am Sir Robert McLaren, Laird of Braedern.'

Holmes nodded his head in acknowledgement.

'Sir, we thank you,' I said.

'My sons, Charles and Alistair,' said the laird, indicating the two younger men with a sweep of his hand.

The two arose and nodded a greeting. Both were tall and robust, wide-shouldered and dark-haired. The elder had bushy eyebrows which gave him an angry demeanour.

The younger had a high forehead and a permanent look of arch incredulity.

'My daughter-in-law, Catherine, wife of Charles.' A blonde lady in a glittering pale blue gown looked up demurely at us over a glass of champagne. She nodded a wan greeting.

'And my younger daughter-in-law—'

'Mrs Isla McLaren,' said Holmes in a flat voice. 'Wife of Alistair.'

Something passed over the laird's face but he recovered in an instant. 'You have met then?'

Before Holmes could answer, Isla McLaren interjected. 'As I said, Father, I chanced upon Dr Watson in Nice, and recognized him from a newspaper photograph. I failed to mention that we spoke briefly. I am sure he told Mr Holmes about it. Did you not, Dr Watson?'

I nodded. I was not accustomed to prevarication on short notice. I could feel Holmes's eyes upon me.

Isla McLaren smiled warmly at us both. She was radiant in a deep purple beaded evening dress, and even with her small gold spectacles, stood out from the group as an early blooming iris might in a spring green garden. She coughed softly, while very subtly putting a finger to her lips. She wished us to be silent about our previous meeting.

Holmes exhaled.

'Do come and sit down, gentlemen,' said the laird. 'It is our winter holiday and we are celebrating, as we do every year, this time at the Grand Hôtel du Cap. Your reputation is known, Mr Holmes. It was Isla who prevailed upon me to invite you tonight.'

He winked at her and I suddenly guessed that this canny gentleman might very well be aware of his daughter-in-law's previous visit to us in Baker Street.

'In any case, she suggested we would enjoy meeting you,' said the laird.

He then indicated two empty seats at the table, next to one another at the far end, facing him and the rest of the group. I moved to my chair, but Holmes remained just inside the door.

I could sense my friend evaluating this and weighing his choices. 'Is this a social occasion then?' he asked. 'I understood there was something you wished to discuss.'

The laird smiled. 'In time. The first order of business is to join us in this wonderful place for dinner. The cuisine here is worth its fine reputation.' His tone changed. 'Do be seated.' It was almost a command.

I was surprised to see Holmes acquiesce. Thirty minutes later we were well into a vast dinner with multiple courses of unusual fish, chicken, and beef dishes, seasoned with the bright flavours of the South, solicitous French waiters hovering at our elbows. Holmes said little but I conversed slightly with each person in turn and as the meal progressed, I took to examining them furtively, wondering what Holmes would deduce from each.

To the laird's left, his elder daughter-in-law, Catherine, was an elegant woman of erect posture and initially rigid bearing, blonde-haired and beautiful, if slightly vacant. She struck me as a person who was holding something back, and I noted that as the dinner progressed, she ate but little, yet consumed glass after glass of wine. Every so often a tiny grimace passed over her, as if she were in pain. As the evening wore on, she grew ever more limp and unfocused.

Between Catherine and myself sat the younger son, Alistair, husband of our would-be client. I would not have put this man as Isla McLaren's husband. Alistair resembled his father and brother physically, tall and muscular, but his sharp features and sarcastic wit, tinged with a combative tone, made me uneasy. Holmes sat beside me, the two of us opposite the laird.

Next to Holmes sat the largest man in the room, elder son Charles, red of cheek and athletic but with beetle brows overhanging strangely watery eyes and a nervous habit of glancing furtively around the table when he felt no one was looking. He was immense, and I could picture him hurtling cabers at a Scottish festival. He and his brother Alistair never addressed nor looked at each other. Their mutual dislike was clear.

Between Charles and the laird sat the intriguing Isla McLaren. A serene presence, she was careful not to regard Holmes or myself with anything resembling familiarity. Intelligence radiated from her, not in words, which were few, but in her subtly amused reactions to the conversation around her, which ranged in topics from the Universal Exposition in Paris, which the family had visited earlier, to the opening of the Moulin Rouge, and Nelly Bly's attempt to duplicate Jules Verne's round the world trip in eighty days.

101

Just prior to dessert, more champagne was brought in and placed in iced silver urns at intervals around the table. The laird held his hand over his flute, however, as he evidently had a different idea and whispered something to the server. In a moment a cart was wheeled in containing several hand-labelled bottles. The laird had brought with him several choice examples of McLaren whisky, of varying vintages and finishes.

He passed small glasses around, leaving the expensive champagne untouched. With each sample he held forth on the warm smokiness of one, and the toffee and chocolate notes of another.

I tried each, and rolling the amber liquid around my tongue, was able to discern something of what he described. They were stronger than my usual Black and White, and yet delicious in an aggressive, though very seductive fashion. I felt warmed and strangely relaxed.

I could well understand the developing preference for whisky. And I was surprised to learn that it was as nuanced and different as the much-vaunted French brandies.

Holmes did not partake, despite the laird's urging. This might have been taken as an insult, I decided, and gave him an encouraging look. He remained inscrutable, but did ask one or two questions about the production and sales. Charles, the eldest son, answered with considerable pride.

A final sample was poured, darker, with a reddish tone. It had been retained for last. It had a strange, musky taste but was rich and complex. Not smoky, the laird explained, although some whiskies tasted of the peat burned in their making. But this was different. Whether it was the Highland waters, the particular old oak casks in which the spirit had been matured, or simply a bit of magic, this 'edition' was clearly the whisky on which the family would base their fortune. The laird and his sons savoured the few drops as if it were liquid gold. Not only was this the 'Special Edition' but it was from the laird's favourite cask, number 51.

'Each whisky has its own personality,' said the laird. 'This special is the one that will put Braedern permanently on the map. None can surpass it.'

'We will aim for a very select market,' said Charles.

'An exclusive one,' said the laird. 'But business later, Charles. And now are we ready, ladies and gentlemen, for the evening amusement?'

'Pray, not a singer,' whispered Holmes to me, while pretending to pick up his napkin.

Coffee was served, and the laird requested that dessert be held for a few minutes. This rather ebullient gentleman clearly had something on his mind. He struck his glass with his spoon and the table hushed.

'As you may have guessed, Mr Holmes, you have been invited here for a reason. Isla has spoken to me of your many accomplishments, and has made me aware of your powers.' He held up a copy of *Beeton's Christmas Annual* from two years before. The preparation inherent in this startled me, as my first writings of Holmes first appeared there.

'When she mentioned you were here, nearby in Nice, the idea came to mind.'

'Sir, I am at your service,' said Holmes. 'But I am not usually consulted in such a public forum. May I suggest we withdraw somewhere more discreet to discuss whatever case you may wish to lay before me?'

The laird burst out in a huge booming laugh, and was joined by the other men at the table. Catherine McLaren yawned. Isla McLaren, oddly, was staring down at her plate in embarrassment.

'Case, Mr Holmes? There is no case. But, I have been impressed in reading of your uncanny ability to discern facts about those you meet, by observing how they part their hair, the trim of their moustaches, and the like. It is almost supernatural, I am told. And as you know, we Scots enjoy the supernatural. Or some of us do.'

Holmes stiffened. A tiny blossom of worry appeared in my mind.

'My skills are quite of the natural type,' said he. 'There is nothing supernatural about them. If there is no case, perhaps there is a mystery of sorts. Some problem that may be troubling you or your family?'

There was an awkward pause.

'Mr Holmes, on our last trip to the South of France, we had a different entertainment for each night of our stay. A lovely violinist. A singer. A fortune teller. And a sleight-of-hand artist. Three were excellent, though the singer was a bit of a novice.'

There was a rather fawning murmur of agreement from the group. Isla McLaren would not meet my eyes. The laird continued. 'Although we live far from London, we are yet a family of sophisticated tastes. We have exhausted the entertainment in the immediate vicinity. This year I have decided to be more selective. It is my view that your analysis of each person at this table could be both illuminating and entertaining. I challenge you to give me some secret about each person here. And it will probably be the best amusement we have ever had in the South of France.'

I felt my face colour. Sherlock Holmes was being asked to be the evening's entertainment. I cringed, thinking of my role in setting up this fiasco.

I could sense Holmes had gone very still beside me.

'It cannot be done, Father,' said Charles, the eldest, sourly. 'He has only just met us.'

'What is the point?' asked his blonde wife, a small bead of sweat appearing on her brow. She dabbed at it with a napkin.

'A jolly idea,' said Alistair, with a touch of belligerence. 'I like it.'

Holmes turned to me and smiled like a friendly executioner. 'What an interesting notion, Watson!' He then turned to the laird. 'Sir, you compliment me greatly. But I must decline this kind offer as, frankly, it would be nothing short of embarrassing to your family. If you will excuse us, please.' He rose to go. I rose with him.

'But, Mr Holmes, do stay. Consider it not the price of your dinner, I would never be so bold, but merely the polite request of one who admires you.' The laird could not have been more charming. Yet somehow I knew that underneath he was well aware of his insult. There appeared to be a double meaning in everything the man said. The evening grew more curious.

Isla McLaren burst out 'Sir Robert! I would never have recommended Mr Holmes for anything like this. He is a professional, not a travelling player. Really, sir, you insult our guests.'

'No insult at all. Sit down, Mr Holmes. And Dr Watson. I have something which may attract your interest.' He snapped his fingers.

Charles McLaren at once stood up and took from his pocket a small leather bag held closed by two drawstrings. He loosened the top and poured out a small pile of what looked like at least fifty gold sovereigns on the table before Holmes. They glittered in the candlelight, a tempting mound of freedom and luxury. But at such a cost to Holmes's pride. I glanced at him.

Holmes, whom I thought to know so well, was ever a surprise. A slow smile spread across his face. I had seen it before, after solving a crime and just before confronting the perpetrator. It did not bode well for this overbearing laird. I felt a prickle of incipient amusement.

'Ah, the laird is most convincing,' said he. He turned to Charles who loomed next to him. Despite his very fine clothes the man had an aura of violence. 'Sit down, Chimney, for I perceive that is your nickname. Before your bad back has you limping from the room, exchange seats with your brother and take the hand of your wife, who may very well learn to love you again. Although some effort will be necessary to forgive your philandering.'

There was an audible gasp from those around the table. Isla McLaren coughed to stifle a laugh. The laird stared at Holmes in some confusion.

'Well, your method bears some explanation,' said the laird. 'But you may very well have hit the nail on the head. Has he, Charles?' Charles said nothing but reddened. Poor Catherine looked down at her lap and I felt a pang of sympathy for her. Alistair offered Charles his seat with a flourish and the elder brother duly changed places and sat, glowering.

The laird laughed, although with some discomfort. 'Well, then, you have just given us confirmation, son. You must learn discretion.' He turned to Holmes. 'And how did you come to this theory? Pardon us, Catherine.'

'They are not theories,' began Holmes. 'They are—'

'I am no philanderer!' exclaimed 'Chimney'. He turned to Holmes in a fury, and pounded his fist on the table, making the silverware jump. 'Be damned man, I will not have my name besmirched.'

'I am merely acting at your father's behest,' said Holmes quietly.

'Hmph. I see that you are right,' said the laird. 'Charles, you reveal yourself piteously. Get control. Mr Holmes, I demand to know your reasoning. What are the clues?'

'Perhaps it would be best—'

'Sir, I insist.'

Holmes shrugged, and then turned on his considerable charm. The malice beneath it was obvious to me but masked, I hoped, to others. I glanced at Isla McLaren. Her look of alarm told me I was mistaken. At least one other saw what was ahead.

'It was quite simple. Obvious, really,' said Holmes. He turned back to Charles. 'Your wife called you by your nickname earlier when you arose to speak to that waiter. Softly, but I heard it. Your shifting in your chair, obvious discomfort, and the placement of a small pillow to support your lumbar region – none of the rest of the chairs has one – and your particular manner of eyeing the flaxen-haired young woman pouring coffee, and your wife's observation of this tells me what I need to know. Perhaps your back condition is not due to riding horses, but some other strain. You must take care. And then, the gambling—'

His furious wife stifled a gasp. Holmes turned to her. 'By the way, you, my dear lady, must see a doctor and soon. The slight palsy in your hand and your pale face indicate lead poisoning. It could be the use of an inauspicious cosmetic, and made all the worse by drink. Perhaps Doctor Watson could be of service.'

The laird shifted in his chair. 'Catherine, see to it, my dear. I will not have you failing when the McLaren clan needs wee ones for our future. We look to you and Isla for an heir. Get yourself in hand.'

He then turned to Holmes. 'Well, I do not quite know what to say. But that is simple observation, after all. Anyone might have noticed these things.'

'But anyone did not,' said Holmes. 'My methods always seem trivial when explained. If you wish me to continue, I will not offer further explanation.'

'But then where is the fun?' asked the laird.

'Indeed I do not know,' said Holmes.

'You are a charlatan!' said the eldest brother. He turned to his father. 'There's no magic here. He has investigated us beforehand; I am sure of it. That I gambled before is well known, but those days are past. He has simply read things and now is making up stories!'

Alistair turned towards us. 'Hmm. It is true that you are gratuitously insulting. What is your game?'

He turned a fierce stare upon my friend.

'No agenda, gentlemen,' said Holmes, lightly. 'Recall that it was the laird who invited us here. As to reading, yes, of course I have read up on all the great families of Britain. I make it my business to know those who play a role in business and society.'

And crime, I was thinking. Although I wondered if Holmes had taken more interest in Isla McLaren's story than I originally suspected. Might our two days' delay have given him time to research this family?

'Father,' said Isla, 'this is a dangerous recreation. I recommend we instead ask Mr Holmes or Dr Watson to entertain us with an account of one of their more interesting cases.'

'Aye!' chorused everyone at the table.

The decision rested with the patriarch, who clearly ruled his extended family with a velvet-clad iron hand. Suddenly he threw back his head and laughed. 'All right then. Enough. The purse is yours, Mr Holmes.'

Holmes stood up. I joined him and began to gather the sovereigns into their little suede bag. The laird smiled at me.

'At least one of you has sense,' he said. 'And I apologize to you. You were doing nothing more than obliging my request. Please stay for dessert.'

But Holmes remained standing as I leaned across him to pick up the last of the prize. 'Thank you, no,' he said. 'Come, Watson. And thank you, your Lordship for a most interesting evening,' he added with a straight face and nod of his head.

Holmes signalled to one of the waiters for our coats. As he did so, a large platter was brought in with much fanfare. It was covered with a silver dome, and this dome was tied onto the platter with a copious amount of ribbon looped into a frothy bow on top, in which fresh flowers were arranged. Flowers were also strewn around the plate rim.

An envelope rested on the front of the dome and the entire thing was placed before the laird.

The headwaiter bowed. 'A gift. Dessert, sir.'

He withdrew. The laird stared at the thing for a moment. Whatever this dessert was, it had been chilled, as condensation appeared on the silver dome. 'Something frozen, then! What do you think?'

'A *bombe*!' said Charles.

At my confused look, Isla McLaren offered. 'It is a frozen ice cream dessert, Dr Watson, in a round shape. Very popular here in France.'

There was nervous laughter. Holmes and I exchanged a glance.

'Yes, ice cream, and delicious. Sit down, gentlemen, please, and enjoy it with us,' said the laird with a smile that must have melted many a female heart. 'No more games.'

I glanced at the younger Mrs McLaren. Her look silently beseeched us to stay.

I tugged at Holmes's elbow and he flashed me an angry look. 'Come on, Holmes, be a sport.' I whispered and sat down. He remained standing. But now he was staring at the platter in a curious manner.

'Did that come from the kitchen?' he asked suddenly. But the waiter had retreated and no reply was forthcoming.

'Wait, the note! Who sent it?' The laird opened the envelope and shrugged.

'Empty,' said he, waving it aloft. He tossed it aside, took up his knife, and flicked it through the ribbons. 'Chocolate, then? Or strawberry?' he mused.

'Leave it!' shouted Holmes.

But the laird ignored him and lifted off the dome. A round, snow-white object lay on the platter. It was covered with a light layer of frost that caught the light in a shimmer.

Something strange, not ice cream.

And then I recognized it. It was, God help us, a frozen, human head.

There was a moment of dead silence.

'Fiona?' said the laird in a small voice.

A scream went up around the room. Both sons leapt to their feet, and Charles's wife Catherine pitched forward onto the table in a dead faint. Isla McLaren sat stunned.

The laird dropped the dome with a clatter onto the floor and stared at the head before him. He had gone as white as the frozen orb. I was transfixed in horror at the awful thing.

The head lolled on the platter, suddenly revealing the young face. It was deathly pale, ice crystals in the red eyelashes, the beautiful features frozen in open-mouthed astonishment. The head was completely bald, snow tipped, ethereal.

Isla McLaren leaned in for a closer look and stifled a gasp. She turned beseeching eyes to us. 'Mr Holmes!' she cried. 'It is Fiona!'

I turned to my friend. Like a hawk on a promontory who has finally spotted its prey he stood charged and unmoving, every cell aquiver with attention. All eyes went to him.

'No one move,' commanded Sherlock Holmes.

CHAPTER 9

The Staff of Death

ll eyes were on the detective as he approached the platter. He removed his magnifying glass and with the detachment so characteristic of him in such moments, began to inspect the frozen monstrosity close up, moving in to get a better look. The room was silent except for stifled murmurs of panic. Charles stood, his hand covering his mouth to suppress vomiting. Alistair gently helped Catherine to sit up in her chair, his own face a mask of revulsion.

'Holmes,' I said.

He glanced up at me and I gestured to the waiting group. An overturned water glass dripped onto the floor in a steady rhythm. A clock over the fireplace ticked loudly. Every face was ashen and tinged with revulsion. Charles McLaren gagged and turned away. The laird was vibrating with shock. Holmes shrugged and looked back down at the hideous apparition.

'Laird McLaren,' said Holmes. 'Please send the ladies to their rooms.'

The laird seized control of himself and he and Alistair gently guided the two women towards the exit. His younger daughter-in-law paused at the door. 'I should like to remain,' said she.

'I know, my dear,' said the laird, and seemed to consider this briefly. 'But no, Isla,' he said. 'Help Catherine, if you would. Waiter!' He signalled to a waiter hovering in the hallway. 'Escort the ladies to their rooms, please.' He closed the door behind them. Only the men remained. I studied each in turn. Charles coughed, fighting the urge to vomit. Alistair was grim, shaking his head slowly back and forth as if in denial. Holmes continued to examine the frozen object, now picking up a large serving fork and moving it gently. It rolled nause-atingly on the platter. 'Doctor?' he said. I joined him. He handed me the glass.

Despite my years on the battlefield, I shivered in revulsion. Close up, the ghastly white globe with its lifeless eyes and melting frost was unworldly, unreal, and utterly terrifying. Death in itself is only natural, but this death was anything but.

Strangely, there were burn marks on the severed edges of the neck. From heat or cold I could not tell. I turned the head over. It appeared to be frozen solid. I pressed the skin on the face, directly under the left eye. It was just beginning to defrost and gave to my pressure only slightly, but felt deeply frozen just below the surface.

The room remained silent. Time stood still. Bile rose in my gorge. I called upon my training and steeled myself to examine it further. But in its present state, and disembodied, there was little I could tell.

The lips were parted and I attempted to view the tongue. Holmes stared at me, waiting. So did everyone at the table. I shook my head, not wanting to say more in company.

As I continued my careful examination of the head, Holmes asked of the laird, 'You can confirm the identity of this unfortunate young person?'

'It is Fiona Paisley. A young servant at our estate,' said the laird in a strangled voice. 'Isla was correct.'

'You are certain?' asked Holmes. I glanced up and he was taking in the group with that particular piercing regard. He was searching for a reaction, of that I was certain.

'Of course it is she. It could be no other! We all know her!' cried Charles.

'Mr Holmes! I wish you to investigate this matter,' said the laird. He paused, struggling to control his emotions, and clearly unused to the need to apologize. 'I did not mean to make light of your gifts. Sir, will you take this case?'

Holmes waivered. But, to give him credit, for only an instant. 'I will investigate the delivery of the remains here tonight. It will have to be done in concert with the local police. As to the rest, I will give you my answer in the morning.'

The laird nodded. 'Gentlemen, give Mr Holmes your full cooperation.'

'I do not wish to remain in the room with that gruesome

relic,' said Alistair. 'The head was brought here while we were all at table. It was not one of us, clearly!'

'It is true,' said the laird in a choked voice. 'Perhaps it would be best if we all returned to our rooms. The shock—'

Holmes abruptly pocketed his glass. 'Gentlemen, no. I will follow up in the kitchen while the trail may still be warm. But I ask you to wait here while I do so.'

The laird began to object but Holmes silenced him with a finger to his lips. 'Sit,' he commanded. 'All of you. And do not leave this room. That is, if you would like this case solved.'

'I will not remain in the room with . . . with—!' cried Charles, looking at his father.

But just then the doors burst open and four French policemen ran into the room, led by a tall and mousta-chioed officer. Isla McLaren stood behind them in the hall.

'Ah, Inspector Grégoire!' exclaimed Holmes, recognising the man in charge. 'How quick you are!'

Holmes moved to block the view of the grisly platter from the inspector.

'Monsieur Sherlock Holmes! I remember you well, sir. The contretemps with the Venetian and his lapdog!'

'A trifle, Grégoire, and some time ago,' said Holmes, modestly.

'I have not forgotten and must thank you again.' The Frenchman clicked his heels and bowed.

'It was nothing. But how is it that you are here, just

now?' Holmes eyed the row of policemen, the three underlings now lined up behind Grégoire.

'We are summoned for a theft in the kitchen. But this lady, she says there is something, a murder—' He indicated Isla McLaren, still lingering in the hall, her keen interest evident.

Holmes sighed. I am sure he had hoped for a little more time before the police arrived. 'Here is the problem,' said he, stepping aside to provide a clear view of the head on its silver platter.

'*Ah, alors!*' said Grégoire. He stepped over to regard the head, removed a monocle from his waistcoat pocket and leaned in for a closer look. He grew pale.

The laird, seeing his daughter-in-law hovering in the doorway, ushered her out with a whispered remonstrance and closed it after her.

Grégoire touched the poor victim's face gently. '*Mon Dieu!*' he said. '*Elle est gelée!*'

'Frozen, yes, Inspector Grégoire,' said Holmes.

Recovering, the policeman smiled up at Holmes. 'Monsieur, how is it that you are so often at the scene of the most interesting, well, events? Please, if you will excuse us.'

Grégoire waved his hand and barked a command. Two underlings seized the platter, and carried it off, both holding the grim artefact at arms' length, and in doing so, nearly allowing it to roll off onto the floor. '*Attention!*' he cried.

There was a murmur of revulsion in the room.

All this might have been comic had it not been so tragically bizarre. Grégoire reiterated Holmes's request for them all to remain and the third policeman was posted at the door.

Holmes and Grégoire next slipped out and I glimpsed them through the doorway having an intense interchange. Whatever was said, Holmes seemed to have prevailed, for in a moment he returned to the doorway and waved for me to follow him.

Once beyond the McLarens' earshot, Holmes explained. 'Vidocq is not the only one with friends in the South. I have been given unofficial leave to conduct our own inquiry. To the kitchen, quickly! I would like to stay ahead of the police. Grégoire is to retain everyone at the table until our return. I have given instructions to them to keep the head frozen.'

'It is remarkable that they are here, now.' I said.

'Yes, that theft in the kitchen! It must relate.'

'But four of them?'

'Watson, use your imagination. What policeman would not like to visit the kitchen of the Grand Hôtel du Cap? It is surprising that the entire department did not heed the call.'

As we hurried down the corridor towards the kitchen, we came upon Isla McLaren heading back in our direction.

'Where are you going, Mrs McLaren?'

'Back to the dining room.'

'You cannot be helpful there,' said Holmes.

'Then where can I be? To you, perhaps? I will do anything to help you discover who killed Fiona.'

Holmes sighed with impatience.

'Seriously, I implore you, sir. A murder has been committed.'

'Are you quite sure, Mrs McLaren? Despite the grisly and theatrical presentation, do you *know* it was murder?'

'Are you joking, Mr Holmes?'

'No. Consider suicide. She was an emotional young woman, recently shamed and terrified. Might she have killed herself?'

'And then cut off her own head?'

'Of course not. Perhaps some enterprising villain found the body and decided to use it for his own purposes. Many things are possible.'

'Mr Holmes, you insult me.'

'All that I say is possible. If you will excuse us—'

'Fiona would never have killed herself!'

'People may surprise one on that account,' said Holmes.

I remember at the time thinking this was a peculiar theory and I wondered why it had arisen at that moment. The lady said nothing, but stared at Holmes with intensity.

Holmes shrugged. 'All right, unlikely then. Do you know who the culprit is?'

'If I knew I would surely say it. Again, sir, can I help?'

Holmes considered a moment. 'Stay here, in the hall. The police are questioning the men. If, afterwards, you can discourage any of them who may attempt to leave the room—'

'I can have no effect if they choose to leave.'

'Understood. Then follow them and determine where they go if not straight to their rooms.'

'If I may split myself into three, I suppose that might be possible.'

Holmes smiled. 'You will think of something,' said he. 'Faint, perhaps?'

I thought I saw the glimmer of a smile from Isla McLaren. An unusual girl, I thought. On this note we left her and proceeded to the kitchen.

Over the next hour, Holmes quickly interviewed every member of the staff in the chain of the receipt, transport and delivery of the head to the dining room. Working backwards from the moment the head was served, Holmes discovered the young waiter had touched the platter only briefly, and had it directly from the chef.

Entering the kitchen, we found it buzzing with whispered gossip and excited theories. Holmes approached the chef, Gaston Peringes, a rotund Frenchman of about forty-five, who was perspiring madly as he tried to rein in the chaos around him.

'Is there somewhere more private to talk?' asked Holmes.

In a moment we were inside a small pantry next to the kitchen, the door closed behind us. It was dusty and close, and I began to perspire immediately. Holmes had begun without preamble, placing the man in a defensive position.

'No, it was not normal, not normal at all,' cried Peringes in a theatrical whisper. 'I am not in the habit of serving food that did not come from my own kitchen.'

'Of course not,' said Holmes reasonably. 'Then why this time?'

The chef shrugged and cleared his throat, tossing his head in a gesture that flung droplets of sweat nearby. I felt a sudden lurch at the thought of the meal I had just eaten. He was now in a frenzy of explanation. 'I take great pride in my desserts,' he continued. 'For example my meringue with the cherries, and the cream, with *vanille*, just a touch of *vanille*, the special one, you see—'

'M. Peringes! Please! What happened?' said Holmes.

The door clicked open and a tall, cadaverous Spaniard poked his head inside. 'You received a note,' he stated. 'I believe it was thrown away. Minot is looking for it now.'

Were we being overheard? The chef barked out a furious barrage of French and the taller man retreated with a sour look.

Recovering, Peringes attempted a smile. 'All of this, so extraordinary! *Vraiment!* But due to a stupid error on the part of my sous chef, the soufflé that I had planned, for which I am justly famous, had collapsed just prior to the dessert's arrival. This gift and its timing were fortuitous in the extreme. And so I sent out this dessert—'

The tall Spaniard poked his head in again. 'The soufflé, she was good. You threw away—'

The chef screamed at him a rapid invective that I could not understand. The Spaniard retreated and the chef slammed the door, pushing it a second time to make sure it was closed. '*Mon Dieu*, one has the privacy of the market-place here!'

'Yes, well,' said Holmes. 'May I compliment you on your English. Where is this sous chef now?'

Chef Peringes looked distinctly uncomfortable.

'Who knows? I fired him when the dessert, she is ruined.'

Holmes stared at the man with his penetrating gaze.

'His name?'

'Er, Bernard.'

Holmes paused. 'There is no Bernard,' he said. 'Your staff will agree, no?' Holmes opened the door but the chef quickly pulled it shut.

Holmes continued. 'You responded to a note, anonymous, yes?' The chef was the picture of guilt. 'Ah yes, then you threw out your failed soufflé, and sent out this gift, without checking it.'

A small rivulet of sweat now dripped down the chef's face and he mopped at it with a towel hanging from his waist.

'The presentation, the bow, was clearly professional,' snorted Peringes. 'And time was of the essence. The soufflé was not one of my best. But I added the flowers to the gift.'

'What was the content of the note that accompanied this gift? Let me see it.'

The chef turned a slow, dark red. 'A little . . . a little money was there.'

'How much?'

Peringes shrugged as if it hardly mattered.

'*How much?*'

'I do not remember.'

A small boy appeared at the door. It was apparently Minot, with a grease-stained note, picked from the trash. 'Sixty francs,' said the boy handing over the note. 'You were angry because it said sixty but there was only fifty.'

Holmes snatched the note and examined it.

The chef was mortified.

'You called the police,' said Minot helpfully.

The chef began to shout at the boy in rapid, colloquial French. Minot backed away in fear as the man picked up a rolling pin and advanced on him. Holmes stopped the man with a hand to the arm.

'Who delivered this note?'

'How do I know?' shouted the chef. 'Probably it came to the concierge.'

The Spaniard, who had stepped in front of Minot to protect him, nodded at us. 'Pierre Mathurin. In the lobby.'

Holmes released the chef, handed me the note, and took off at a run. We left the kitchen in chaos.

By contrast, the lobby was a calm oasis, bathed as it was in fresh sea breezes and lit by generous electric lights. There we found the concierge Mathurin, a handsome man with a smile that could melt the frown from the most travel-weary guest. While strained, he was yet the picture of grace under pressure.

The French police ran past us like ants to and from an anthill, and two of them slowly conveyed the horrific platter towards the entrance, its ghoulish contents now covered with a white tablecloth. Mathurin smoothly guided two

123

nervous guests standing in the lobby away from the policemen, indicating the bar just beyond.

On spying us, he attempted to usher us there as well, but at Holmes's brief explanation, he invited us instead into a small adjacent office, and closed the door.

'Mr Holmes, we are lucky for your presence. Inspector Grégoire has told me of your reputation,' he said. 'We must keep as much from the guests as we can. *Quelle horreur!* Some of them are rather elderly. And all of them *très, très* respectable, you understand.' Beneath his practiced manners Mathurin struck me as not only a kind man, but an honest one.

His story matched that of the chef. The covered platter was delivered in exactly the state in which it had been presented, beribboned and resting in a box, by a cab driver named Jean-Jacques whom he knew well. There had been a sizable tip for the concierge and the simple instructions to deliver the note and platter to the chef. There was a second envelope for the chef.

'And you did not think to examine this gift?' asked Holmes.

'Alas, I did not. If only. But Monsieur, many guests here receive gifts – food, flowers, theatre tickets. Not usually a head. It would be indiscreet to examine each item that arrives.'

'This cab driver; can you summon him, please?'

'Sir, I have done so already. He should be here in a moment. I presume you wish to speak to him before the police do?'

If a talent for anticipating needs is the hallmark of a good hotel man, Mathurin was a genius at his profession.

Minutes later a man of forty, sleepy and dishevelled, arrived. Mathurin clapped him on the back and drew him forward to meet us. He evidently had been roused from his bed, and apologized to the concierge.

'This is Jean-Jacques. He is an honest man. I know him well,' said Mathurin. There was an easy familiarity between them.

Holmes asked him how the 'gift' had arrived in his possession, where and from whom.

'The train station! I came directly!' the man called Jean-Jacques exclaimed. 'It was a gift of food, no? It had not been ruined by delay, surely? It was cold, very cold! I received it less than twenty minutes before I deliver! I came directly! *Rapidement!*'

Mathurin patted the cabbie's arm. 'Peace, Jean-Jacques,' said he. Then, to Holmes, 'If I may?'

Holmes nodded his assent and under the gentle questioning of the concierge, we learned that Jean-Jacques had been hired at the railway station by a stranger wearing what seemed to him to be an obvious disguise.

'Details, man. And tell me your words and his, exactly as you remember them,' said Holmes.

'This man ask me do I speak the English,' replied Jean-Jacques. 'I reply that yes, I do. He then say he has job for me.'

'Strange, no?' said Holmes.

'At this point I am suspicion!'

'Suspicious. Hmm. But not reluctant?' said Holmes.

The cabdriver shrugged. 'I ask him "what kind of job?" I am no criminal. Once, you see, someone ask me to take a very young girl—'

'Yes. But never mind this. What was the reply?'

'He say, I have a gift that must be delivered *toute de suite* to the Grand Hôtel du Cap. It is food and will be ruined if not . . . if not to remain very cold, but . . . what an idiot, I am thinking. "I have no cold box," I tell this man. He annoy me. He look very strange.'

'Strange, how?' asked Holmes.

'Comme dans une pièce de théâtre!'

'What do you mean "like in a play"?'

'Stupid, I think. So then I ask, "Why you wear this false beard and glasses?" And a wig, he wear a long, dark wig.'

'You actually said this?' I exclaimed.

'Jean-Jacques has always spoken his mind,' said Mathurin.

'Your brother is in the wrong business,' said Holmes with a smile to the concierge. He turned back to the cabbie. 'Consider applying to the *Sûreté.*'

Mathurin was startled. 'How do you know he is my brother?'

'Family resemblance. The nose. Continue, please.'

'This man he laugh. "It is the special surprise," he say,' said Jean-Jacques.

'His accent? Foreign?'

'He is from your island. I do not know. English? Scottish? He give me a great deal of money. And three envelopes. One for Pierre, here. One for the chef and one for the man to get this gift. A Sir Robert McLaren who is having the dinner party at that very moment, he say. "Time is very important. Hurry!"'

And it was there the trail ran cold. The box had been cardboard, and ruined by the dampness of condensation. The note from the kitchen was written in block printing and revealed nothing of use to Holmes, although he kept it. There was no more information to be gleaned and it appeared to both Holmes and myself that it was a simple matter of the hotel staff being bought that enabled the passage of the heinous gift to our table.

As we made our way back from the lobby to the dining room I asked Holmes his thoughts. He paused before two large windows looking out towards the moonlit ocean below us. It was a magnificent view, an expensive one, and yet it offered little comfort at the moment.

'We have made only limited progress,' he said. 'The head came down on a later train than the family. It is likely that it was severed and frozen elsewhere. This was a well-planned and effective gesture, but to what purpose, I cannot say.'

'But where is the rest of the body, Holmes?'

'Indeed that is the question, Watson. Most likely it is still in Scotland. Consider how much simpler it would be to transport only the head.'

'Then you think she was killed near home and the head brought down on the train?'

'We have not enough data to theorize, but that seems the most likely scenario. Come, my dear fellow, back to the McLarens.'

CHAPTER 10

Unwelcome Help

e arrived at the private dining room after an absence of a little over an hour. To Holmes's dismay the door stood open and the room was empty. Only Inspector Grégoire remained, and after a brief word with this gentleman in the corridor, Holmes rejoined me, closing the door behind him. Isla McLaren was nowhere to be found.

I regarded the table, which had not yet been cleared. Napkins were thrown onto empty dessert plates, and two chairs had been overturned by hasty departures. The many candles in the two candelabra in the centre of the table, left alight, now guttered. A wave of exhaustion overcame me and I sat. Holmes paced in front of the large windows, lost in thought.

'The police, as I expected, gleaned nothing from the family,' said he after a moment. 'They refused to be interviewed and returned to their rooms. And they depart for Scotland in the morning.'

'Surely you did not expect them to wait here for us to return?' I asked.

'I had hoped.'

'Where next, Holmes? Shall we interview each in his room?'

'I doubt they will cooperate. The chase is over for this evening,' he remarked, continuing to pace. I turned back to the view. The flickering candles were reflected faintly in the large windows. Below us the Mediterranean flashed silver in the moonlight.

'What of the man who brought the head in on the train?'

'Grégoire has sent officers to inquire at all the local train stations. Of course the villain or his messenger will have changed his disguise and be long gone by now.'

'What then, Holmes? Some coffee, perhaps?' It was now after midnight and we had yet to return to Nice. I had begun to flag. At least the gold sovereigns would see us home in comfort.

But Holmes continued, on fire with this *outré* mystery.

'You saw the reaction at the table, Watson. I am quite sure there was genuine grief from the laird, and possibly Charles as well,' he said. 'But the precise nature of their affection for the victim has yet to be determined.'

'Holmes, you cannot think that the laird could have been in love with the girl?'

'I must remain impartial. The head was sent as a message for someone in the room. Most probably the intended recipient is a man.'

Mrs McLaren's words about Fiona filtered up to my

consciousness for the first time since the head had made its shocking appearance.

'Holmes, I do not understand why you refused Isla McLaren's offer. She seems a very astute young woman, and may offer insight into the family.'

'I did not refuse, but rather set her on a somewhat mundane task. She is quite underfoot.' Holmes stopped pacing and turned to look at me with a small smile. 'You are attracted to Mrs McLaren the younger. Now, that, dear Watson, is unworthy of you, married as you both are.'

I flushed uncomfortably. 'Not attracted. Intrigued. Respectful. And yes, I do like her,' said I. 'I sense a young woman of intelligence and spirit.'

'Let us remain impartial. No one at this point is above suspicion.'

'But our own client—'

'She is not our client,' said Holmes. 'Laird Robert is, if I proceed with the case.'

'But I am on your side, Mr Holmes,' said a female voice behind us. We turned to see the lady in question, who had opened the door noiselessly and now stood just inside the room. 'Thank you, Dr Watson, for your kind remarks,' said the lady. She smiled, then turned to Holmes. 'But "Mrs McLaren the younger" has a somewhat gothic ring, do you not think?'

'What have you found out, madam?' said he, with more than a tinge of irritation.

'I followed your instructions, more or less, Mr Holmes. Fainting was not in my character and would not have been believed, creative as that suggestion was. So instead I followed them to their rooms sequentially in the order of my own suspicions. I began with Charles and Catherine, listened at their door and can tell you that these two began a row about his indiscretion. Next I listened at the laird's and, I am sad to report, he sobbed himself to sleep, or so it sounded. My own Alistair retired immediately and slept, as he always does, without sound.'

'He did not await your own return?' asked Holmes, one eyebrow raised. 'And why is that?'

'Alistair and I keep different hours. He is used to retiring well in advance of my own bedtime.'

'Where would he assume you were tonight, then?' asked Holmes.

'He would neither assume nor care. I am accustomed to taking a stroll in the evenings when we visit here. It settles my mind, and gives me time to think. As I said, it would not be unusual. Alistair always retires before me.'

'Even after the shocking events of this evening?'

'Even then.'

There was a pause. I will admit to a fleeting curiosity about the state of their marriage. Isla McLaren slowly walked to the table and sat down across from me. It was as though she presumed to join our team. Behind me Holmes remained standing and cleared his throat. I sensed his sudden unease.

'And so, gentlemen, what are the results of your inquiries?' she asked.

'Mrs McLaren, that is of no concern of yours,' said

Holmes. 'I shall give my report to the laird. And to the French police.'

'Holmes!' I said. 'Madam, forgive us. We are greatly fatigued.'

But she seemed unaffected by my friend's inexplicable rudeness. 'The police are back with the concierge now,' said the lady. 'Presumably they will follow your own path of inquiry, in their clumsy fashion. I have thought of something that may help.'

'We would be most appreciative,' said I. 'Would you care for some coffee?'

'No, thank you,' said she. 'Eventually I hope to sleep. But I cannot until I have had my say. While I am saddened by Fiona's death, it did not surprise me. The bizarre display of this evening, however, is another matter. This has to do with what I spoke to you about in Baker Street. Thank you, by the way, for not giving away our little secret.'

'Your ruse was pointless. The laird was aware of your indiscretion,' said Holmes.

'He misses little,' she said with a sigh. 'I had hoped—'

'Yet he did not predict the arrival of this singular dessert,' said Holmes acidly. 'What can you offer us that may help, Mrs McLaren?'

She appeared not to hear. 'Are you certain that Fiona was murdered elsewhere?' she asked, looking at me pointedly.

'Much is unclear,' I said. 'I could not ascertain the time of death as the head was frozen.'

'A pathologist will examine the head tonight, and will

determine what he can. Now, madam, how long had the lady been missing from the estate?' asked Holmes, seizing control of our wild conjectures.

'Since Tuesday.'

'And she eloped, it is said, with the groundsman's son?' pressed Holmes.

'Upon reflection, she must not have done so,' said the lady.

'Why not?' he asked.

'Because he is, or was, incapable of such that we saw here tonight. That is what I wished to tell you. The boy is simple. But then how could her head have arrived in Nice, Mr Holmes? Could she have travelled here alive, and accompanied by her murderer?'

'How does this eliminate the boy with whom she ran away?' said Holmes. 'Murders have been committed by people of impaired abilities before.' He turned to me. 'How long would it take to freeze a head all the way through, Watson?'

'At least two days, I suppose. Longer, perhaps.'

He nodded, then resumed pacing in front of the windows.

Isla McLaren stared at my friend with keen interest. Suddenly she rose from her seat and approached Holmes. She placed her hand gently upon his sleeve. He started and stepped away from her.

'Mr Holmes, will you commit to this case and come to Braedern? I am sure the answer awaits us there. This is an act of pure evil and cunning villainy. There is no one more suited than yourself to help us.'

'Mrs McLaren! I will take this case. But you must leave detection to the professionals!' he said.

Before she could reply, I stepped towards her and took her arm, guiding her gently to the door. 'Mrs McLaren, do understand that we have your best interests at heart,' I said gently. 'Whoever is behind this may begin to resent your curiosity. But we will come, won't we, Holmes?'

There was silence. Isla McLaren stared frankly at Holmes, awaiting his answer.

He nodded once.

'You are a cold man, Mr Holmes,' she said, finally. 'But I do look forward to seeing you soon. We are booked on the Train Bleu tomorrow. I shall see you at the station in Nice. Good evening.' She swept from the room.

Holmes and I stood silent for a moment. He approached the door and looked into the hall, then closed it behind him. 'Just making sure she has actually left.' He smiled and fished in his pocket for a cigarette. I lit it for him. I noticed that his action had caused the corner of an envelope to protrude from that same pocket.

'To Scotland, then, tomorrow?' I asked. 'And what is that in your pocket?'

'Of course, Watson.' He ignored my question, and nodded, inhaling with satisfaction. 'Now give me those sovereigns and let us return to Nice.'

We made our way to the front portico of the hotel, Holmes stopping once more to confer with Inspector Grégoire and to arrange for the head to be returned to us at our hotel by morning.

135

As we awaited a carriage, I turned to Holmes. 'You seem to have a marked aversion to Isla McLaren which I do not understand.'

'She is irritating, that is all. The sovereigns, please. They are, after all, my earnings.'

I pointed at his pocket once again.

'Oh, this,' he said, pulling out the envelope as if he had forgotten it was there. 'Wired by Mycroft today for the work in Montpellier.'

Despite my fatigue and the horrors of the evening, a flood of relief came over me. We were free at last. But then . . . 'Holmes! At dinner you could easily have walked away!' I said. 'You did not need these sovereigns.' I patted my jacket, still heavy with those painful earnings.

'That is true, Watson. But we would have missed all the fun.'

'Fun! Remind me never to play you at cards.'

'I do not gamble – at least not at the game tables. Watson, stay away from that casino. In fact, give me those sovereigns now.'

'No.'

'Yes.'

'No.'

We left the Grand Hôtel du Cap in adamant, if childish disagreement on the matter.

CHAPTER 11

A Fleeting Pleasure

 knew, of course, from the moment of the grisly unveiling that there was never a doubt that Holmes would take the case. I had one small regret in leaving Nice. I had not had the time to explore the casino. But more important matters took precedence. We were off to discover the monster who had murdered and beheaded a beautiful young woman. At the Gare de Nice the next morning, we made our way to the platform designated for the illustrious Train Bleu, a glamourous conveyance I had seen advertised on many a colourful poster. A porter followed along, with our few meagre bags, save for one notable exception.

I was carrying one quite heavy and bulky carpetbag, containing the sorry evidence of the case on which we were embarking. The head had been delivered to us earlier, as prearranged by Holmes. I had organised the conveyance that very morning with the help of a butcher whom I had found two blocks from the Beau Soleil. Butchers, I reasoned, must have the means to keep their wares fresh while transporting them to luxury hotels and restaurants in the heat of the Côte D'Azur summers.

The device consisted of a waterproof metal box sitting within a larger metal box lined with ice, placed inside a leather container with the name of the butcher inscribed on it. To disguise this, I had placed the leather container inside an innocuous, if bulky carpetbag purchased at a street market near our hotel. All in all, a good solution for the ghastly problem, I felt.

As this was a first-class train, I was certain to be able to procure additional ice along the way.

Upon seeing my solution, Holmes deemed it ingenious and probably similar to whatever means the murderer, or the murderer's emissary, must have used to get the head down here, though secretively, no doubt. He had arranged with Mycroft for the legal transport of our grim package.

We made our way down the platform, passing the famous dark blue cars with their elegant gold lettering. I was struck by the opulent clothing and jewellery of our fellow travellers. Expensive perfume lingered in the air, and the glitter of diamonds flashed in the oblique morning light of the train station. Porters scurried while nannies attended scrubbed and velvet-clad children, mostly British, and already complaining about the heat, and being shuttled about like puppets.

I sighed, feeling at last that Holmes and I would enjoy a touch of luxury. But it never once left my mind that I was bearing the gruesome remains of a victim for whom justice was so urgently required.

The bag was heavy, and as I shifted it to the other hand, I did so gently. I shuddered to think that anyone on the platform would suspect the contents.

Isla McLaren, in a smart green travelling costume and what was undoubtedly another French hat with a silk robin perched upon it, was standing in one of the windows of a first-class wagon-lit. As we passed it, she called out to us.

'Mr Holmes! Doctor Watson! Enjoy your journey. Meet me in the dining car for lunch at noon, please?' Holmes growled under his breath, and moved along. I waved and smiled. She indicated my case with a questioning look. I nodded and she shivered and withdrew.

As Holmes ascended to the car, he turned to help me heft the heavy bag in after him. Just as I began to hand it up, a sudden shrill whistle caught our attention.

Four French policemen ran in our direction full tilt down the platform. I looked past us to see what could be the disturbance, but without preamble, one knocked me aside, two pulled Holmes from the steps and seized the carpetbag, while the fourth clapped handcuffs on us both.

A small scream came from two ladies nearby. Like noisy geese rushing for breadcrumbs, a crowd ignited by *schadenfreude* instantly appeared to witness the fascinating spectacle of two well-dressed gentlemen being handcuffed and led roughly away.

'Thank goodness!'

'The ruffians!'

'Criminals by the look of them!'

In twenty minutes we were seated on a hard bench at

the police station, still in irons, with our luggage surrounding us, including the grisly package. To his credit, Holmes attempted to warn them of its contents.

But they had been told what we were carrying and undaunted, one policeman was determined to open it. As the inner box was unlocked, a stout policeman behind him fainted, landing with a soft thud on the floor. A flurry of reactions ensued. Holmes spoke in rushed French. I caught next to nothing except 'investigation' and the name of Holmes's contact, Inspector Grégoire.

Eventually, we were freed from the handcuffs, and pushed into a dank cell with two long, narrow benches and a tiny, barred window high up on one wall. A tray was inserted under the door with water, two pieces of bread and one slice of mouldy cheese, evidently to share between us for some time to come.

At least we were alone. I rubbed my bruised wrists. 'Well, what is the story, Holmes?'

'The police chief was tipped off about our grisly package. He imagines we are two thieving murderers travelling with stolen body parts.'

'Shades of Burke and Hare, then?' I asked. 'Surely the truth will come out. I heard you tell them to contact Grégoire. But who on earth would have devised such a thing?'

Holmes was looking past me through the bars to the corridor. I turned, and lounging there was the implacable and smiling Jean Vidocq.

Of course.

'*Bonsoir, mes amis*,' said he. 'I see you are enjoying the fine cuisine of our French hospitality. What a shame you were unable to travel on the famous train! It is such a pleasure. I have done so many times myself.'

He inspected his manicured nails casually, and then picked an invisible piece of lint off his expensive frock coat.

'*Alors*, it is so dirty in here!'

'Do any of your compatriots know your real name, Vidocq? Or do they all swallow your tale of being related to the great Eugène Vidocq?' asked Holmes.

'But it is true; I am his great-grandson.'

'And Watson here is a morganatic Duke, aren't you, Watson?'

'I am. You may address me as "Your Grace."'

Vidocq snorted.

'You know this will easily be cleared up, Vidocq,' said Holmes. 'Unlike your own situation.'

'Perhaps,' said the Frenchman. 'But in the meantime, I am, how do you say, welcoming what providence provides. Enjoy your stay.'

He departed.

I sighed. 'How did he know of the head?'

'Ah, Watson. Police contacts are a requirement of our profession. No doubt one of Grégoire's men is in his employ.' Holmes sighed. 'We must be patient on the matter of Vidocq. He has more friends in the police force than I do here. My evidence is circumstantial at best until I can link his finger-prints absolutely to the dynamite I kept from exploding at the laboratory.'

'Where is it now, by the way?' I asked, suddenly worried about its fate in our luggage, now upstairs with the French police. We could all be dead in moments.

'I removed the cordite from it in Montpellier. The empty shell is in my valise.'

'Can they do that with fingerprints? Compare them, I mean, with any certainty without the suspect to provide a live one?'

'The technique is in its infancy, and as I said before the results will not yet stand up in court. But if the dynamite has enough of a print extant, and the police upstairs do not handle it, I can compare the prints with Vidocq's previous prints. I believe they will match, and we will have our man.'

'His previous prints?'

'I have examples, which rest in my files at Baker Street, along with many dozens of others.'

Of course he did. Presumably he had begun this collection after my marriage, for I had never seen them.

Holmes stretched out on his bench. It was too short for his tall frame, and his feet hung off the edge.

'Holmes, there is something troubling me. Simply ensuring his job for the French government does not feel like enough of a reason for Vidocq's extreme actions. Surely there is some other reason to risk setting off explosives?'

'Your instinct is correct, Watson. Money plays a role. It is his *modus operandi* to play both ends against the middle.'

'But what is "the other end"?'

'I believe that some deluded miscreant actually does want

Docteur Janvier's work to be stopped and is paying Vidocq to frighten off the scientist. Vidocq is making it look like he is carrying out these acts – but without actually harming Docteur Janvier or his work.'

'Bombing where no one is present! Yes, now I see. Diabolical!'

'And yet still rather dangerous. I suspect the McLarens, quite frankly. The coincidence of their arrival here is too great. They have the resources to pay Vidocq, and they were at the top of Mycroft's short list of suspicious persons.'

'How will you prove this?'

'Well, first I need proof that the McLarens are involved. We are being handed a golden opportunity to find it.'

It occurred to me that Holmes's mind must work like an enormous chessboard with hundreds of pieces, fanning out in all directions to distant horizons. It was difficult to keep up with his strategies, but I had learned over time to trust them. 'You are positively Machiavellian, Holmes.'

'The long game, Watson.'

By the next morning, the interventions of Mycroft Holmes via wire and Grégoire in person had evidently provided enough explanation to satisfy the aggressive police who held us, and after dawn we were released into a small back street and the brisk air of the early morning.

At last, with our precious cargo restored to us, and plenty of fresh ice, we caught the fastest train we could take back to Paris, and from thence to London, and then Scotland. I slept as we rolled through France, but I recall Holmes staring morosely out the window as I dozed off, and he was in exactly the same position when I awoke some hours later.

We were in London by the next morning and at Victoria, Holmes and I disembarked, taking a cab to Euston where we were to catch The Caledonian to Scotland. Holmes had wisely had some of his warm clothes and some files and study materials delivered to him at the station. I longed to return home for a short embrace and some warm clothes but had failed to plan. I did, however, send word of our plans to Mary.

The train pulled out of Euston and we were shortly northbound.

Holmes next plunged into his reading on the whisky and wine industries, as well as the agony columns he had recently missed, and would not be interrupted. Mary Shelley's novel no longer suited my current mood as I cringed at the notion of galvanic stimulation bestowing movement on the contents of the container on the floor between us. I switched instead to a fanciful Jules Verne, napping intermittently, as our train steamed northward. It was not until we were an hour away from Edinburgh, that gothic and mysterious city, that Holmes roused himself from his studies.

'I will disembark in Edinburgh, Watson, as I have arranged with a man there to examine the head for the cause of death.'

'At the University? A medical man?'

'You may know him. Doctor Aden Fleming.'

'I have heard the name.'

'I would like you to carry on to Aberdeen, Watson.'

144

Aberdeen was the gateway to the portion of the highlands, and Braedern castle lay due west, near Balmoral.

'Holmes, I should prefer to accompany you. I was in Edinburgh for a time during my medical studies. I know the city.'

'You are worried about our tongueless friend, Mr St John,' said he.

Holmes's attacker in London, I confess, did still give me pause. 'Well, yes, a little. I am not convinced his "vendetta" as you call it, is over.'

'Watson, I say it is.'

'Your cavalier disregard for your own—'

'I will stay well away from Mr St John. I know the city myself, even though I was but fifteen when I—' Noticing my sudden look of interest, he cut himself off. 'Never mind, Watson. Carry on to Aberdeen. Gather what information you can about the McLaren family, their estate, the family business. Any gossip, family lore. Take a room somewhere, leave word at the station, and I will join you in the morning.'

'Fifteen? Were you studying then? In Edinburgh?'

Holmes had long kept his early life in the shadows, and while it was not in my nature to pry, it was ever a source of puzzlement. For some reason I felt this Scottish connection deserved attention. He pretended not to hear my question and instead rifled through the package Wiggins had delivered, took out Janvier's article and became engrossed in it.

'Holmes? Did you attend school in Edinburgh?'

He was annoyed. 'It is not important.'

'Is that where you met St John?'

'No, Watson, I met him later, at Camford. Do not worry about St John. I told you I shall avoid him easily.'

'Then *how do you know Edinburgh?*'

He sighed. 'Watson, you are a dog with a bone. I attended school at Fettes for a year. Does that satisfy you?'

Fettes! The little I knew of that institution did not fit with the man before me. Fettes was a Foundation school, created primarily to educate abandoned boys, founded less than twenty years earlier. It had a reputation for extreme austerity and a very vigorous team sports programme. Had Holmes been orphaned? Certainly no parent would have chosen it for the kind of boy he must have been.

'I cannot picture you at Fettes.'

'Pray do not. It was one year only. And you are correct; it was not exactly suitable.' He glanced up at me and smiled. 'However, ultimately it served me well. I learned to box.'

The Caledonian slowed into the approach to Waverley Station in Edinburgh, the great rock of the Castle rising above us in eerie, snow-dusted splendour. Holmes assembled his belongings and finally our grisly package.

I was relieved to be free of that tragic memento of our time in Nice, but despite Holmes's dismissive response to my warning, or perhaps because of it, my mind was not at ease. I was not afraid for myself, certainly. But the strange sequence of events that we had just experienced did not fit into any pattern I could yet discern, and yet something told me that much of what had gone on was somehow connected.

As he pushed aside the door to our compartment he

turned and said, 'Watson, do suspend your worries for now. Reason dictates that we have not enough data to make theories, and the case of this tragic girl promises to be complex. I will find you tomorrow.'

But we admonished each other to take care, and frankly, that was unnerving in itself.

PART THREE

NORTHERN MISTS

'When death's dark stream I ferry o'er
A time that surely shall come
In Heaven itself I'll ask no more
Than just a Highland welcome'
                                    —Robert Burns

CHAPTER 12

Arthur

fter another twelve hours I disembarked in Aberdeen, into air so frigid that my breath threw white clouds ahead of me, and I shivered uncontrollably in my light woollen suit. I was dressed, after all, for the South of France, and had packed sparsely for only a couple of days in a distinctly different climate.

I sought relief and hired a small room at an inn not far from the station. But my intended chamber had only just been vacated and as I waited, I took a seat in the inn's crowded pub. A group of locals across the room who were singing to a fiddle were perhaps more irritating than picturesque. I was in no mood for festivity but recalled Holmes's request to gather what gossip I could.

Soon a robust young serving girl brought me a steaming bowl of the local venison stew and I attempted unsuccessfully to engage a table of nearby diners on the subject of the McLarens. A few locals eyed me suspiciously, and laughed when I asked them about Braedern.

As my stomach filled and my equilibrium returned, I decided to find a clothing shop and provision myself with attire more suitable to the climate. Perhaps I would have better luck engaging with someone in the shop.

The innkeeper had churlishly refused to store my valise, and so I ventured, weighed down by the case, out into the streets. Outside it seemed midnight, though it was now just late afternoon. Gaslights along the street were yellow orbs in the swirling darkness, the wind damp from the ocean. A light snow was falling, and the pavements, while swept free of snow, were dangerously icy.

In due course I found a small haberdashery. The proprietor had just turned his sign and was locking the door. I approached and put my face up to the glass, and smiled at him hopefully.

The man, sharp faced and wary, with a smartly trimmed moustache and sideburns but a wild fury of red hair sprouting from the top of his head, mouthed the word 'Nae!' With a flick of his wrist, he indicated I should be about my business. I gestured in supplication. Getting no response, I pulled out a gold sovereign.

He immediately unlocked the door and beckoned me in. I explained that I was a traveller, called suddenly to the Highlands.

'Sassenach!' he said in mock disgust. 'You'll nae be takin' my time for naught. Is that all ye have, then?' he indicated my lightweight suit and thin, travelling mackintosh. 'What were ye thinking, man?'

'I came from the South of France, and had nae, I mean

no, time to pack,' I explained, immediately regretting my volubility. No one need know the details of my business.

The proprietor, who soon introduced himself as MacAuliffe, appraised me with the practised eye of the experienced clothier. 'A winter suit. An ulster. Detachable cape. Some gaiters, a hat, and some boots, I would wager. Gloves. Have you nae warm undergarments? Two sets in wool, then. A warm knit. Not even a scarf, man?'

'None,' said I.

He quickly took my measurements and bustled around the shop gathering an array of ready-to-wear clothing. In three quarters of an hour, under his expert eye, I found myself kitted out with a remarkably flattering and comfortable set of garments, muted green and brown tweeds, a cloud soft cashmere cravat, and a very handsome shooting cap which would become my favourite ever after. In spite of our inauspicious start, this visit had turned out well. I was filled with renewed cheer.

As I looked over the bill, I reflected that the man's careful, skilled attention and relaxed manner might indicate an open door.

'I am off tomorrow to the Castle Braedern,' said I. 'Do you know it?'

He stiffened. 'Ye've been invited?' he asked.

'A shooting party,' I added lamely. 'This weekend. I understand they are good people there.'

The man stared at me. 'Shooting, you say? In this weather? And sae urgent ye canna pack your bag properly?'

'Well, the invitation came late. And I am to see to one

153

of the ladies there. I am a medical man as well.' Good God, what had prompted me to say all this?

MacAuliffe stood back and stared at me with eyes gone bright with suspicion, and something else. Fear?

'Ye had better watch yourself, Sassenach. 'Tis not a place for a casual visit. There's nae one of us in this city who would be sleeping there of our own accord.'

I said nothing but reached down to unlatch my valise and retrieve the sovereigns.

'Unless ye perhaps be a hunter of ghaists?' he added.

Ghaists? 'Do you mean ghosts, sir?' I wondered. I was definitely no longer in London.

'Aye. Are you fully kitted out, man? I suggest one thing mair – a good hunting knife, like this one here.'

He held one out, and I could see immediately it was no ordinary knife. It was foldable, a jack-knife, but larger than usual. It had a distinctive handle of horn, inlaid with a silver Celtic design and an amber jewel in the centre. Its keen blade gleamed in the gaslight, and was sharp from the tip back an inch or so, then serrated. An unusual and beautifully crafted item. But I did not anticipate an immediate use for it.

'No, thank you,' said I. Buried deep in my bag was my revolver, and this I deemed sufficient protection. 'What did you mean, ghosts?'

'Many a tale is tellt about Braedern. The family is cursed, some say. A bairn vanished there long ago. A girl of only two or three. And the lady of the house, ne'er the same after that. 'Till she, too, died. A sad, sad, story.'

'What was the lady's name? I should hate to put a foot wrong.'

'You will be finding out soon enough. But take heed. The ghaists, we understaun, are nae so friendly.'

'Very well, I thank you, sir, for the excellent provisions here.'

'Are ye sure about the knife, man? You're gaeing into the Highlands after all. It can be useful, in sae many ways. And look here, it folds, sae nice and neat.' He folded the knife in on itself. It was now compact enough for a pocket.

'It is almost as though you would like to be rid of it!' I laughed.

His face darkened. 'What makes you say that?'

I shrugged. 'Nothing really. But I can't take it, I have spent enough. Thank you.'

He shrugged and busied himself with wrapping up my purchases in brown paper and securing them with string. 'The distillery, at least, will be a fine destination. A remarkable whisky, McLaren Top. And the laird has made even the unwelcome welcome there.'

'What do you mean?'

'He has hired the unhirable, has the laird. Men, some of them crippled, missing limbs, blinded, half-witted, harmed by the wars, by accident, by life. He gies them help, and puts them to work in the distillery, each to his own ability. It is a fine thing he does.'

'That sounds very charitable.'

'Aye, that it is. And we in Aberdeen are grateful. Ach, these desperate men! Some went to war and returned to find their tenancies gone, victims of the clearances, and sheep grazing now where once they tended fields. What the landlords didnae realize was the anger. A whole population thrown away like rubbish. Now so many up to nae good with now't to dream of and work for. It has brought madness into the land.'

'So these are clearance victims who work the distillery? People whose land was taken?'

'More are war veterans, as I said. Some with both war and clearance to mar their lives. But the laird has given, some say eighty men, work and hope. And the whisky, 'tis the finest in the land, if ye go by what is written.'

'I shall be sure to sample it.'

He completed wrapping my clothes into a neat package tied up with string. 'But hear me, man, be careful there, if you value your safety.'

I nodded. 'Thank you. I will be off then!'

Later, as I finally settled in my little room above the pub, I stumbled about in the near darkness, as only one meagre candle had been furnished for my use in this rustic lodging. I opened my package to remove and store my new things in my valise, and to lay out warm clothes for the morning.

There, buried between the new woollens and tweeds something glinted in the dim light. I reached in and pulled it out.

It was the shiny steel edge of the folded hunting knife I had been offered earlier by MacAuliffe.

But why? I took it up and snapped open the blade, holding it up to the light of that single candle. It was indeed a beauty, the delicate design at odds with the fearsome blade, and I wondered at the generosity of the gift.

I looked closer. The candle guttered and the flickering light reflected on the polished steel, giving a sensation of movement. I shivered, and blinked my eyes to clear the vision.

I must have been more exhausted than I had realized. Holmes would surely have laughed had he been with me. I quickly folded the knife and hid it in my valise.

Collapsing on the bed, I fell into a heavy sleep immediately. I dreamed I was King Arthur and before me was Excalibur, though looking like my new jack-knife, and buried in the stone. I grasped it with two hands and pulled. Try as I might, the blade would not come free.

CHAPTER 13

Braedern

awoke just before dawn the next morning drenched in sweat despite the damp chill in the room. A serving girl brought me hot water and I quickly washed and shaved and donned some of my new, warmer clothes. Stowing my shaving kit in my valise, I caught the gleam of the knife and without a thought tossed it into my trousers pocket. Abruptly I realized I had forgotten to leave word of my lodgings for Holmes and would need to return to the station.

With the smell of strong coffee wafting from the inn's pub below, I made my way downstairs in eager search of a quick breakfast. I had no sooner sat down before a large dish of porridge when I became aware of a shadow looming over the table from behind me.

Holmes! He stood smiling down at me, dressed for the Scottish weather in his familiar tweed ulster and travelling ear-flapped cap, a suitcase in hand.

'Holmes!' I cried, 'You found me! I am so sorry, I forgot to leave word.'

'Watson, my dear fellow, you leave quite a footprint behind you,' said he. Setting the case down, he removed his outer garments and sat before me, ordering nothing but a cup of black coffee.

'I see you managed to equip yourself for this visit,' he said, eyeing my clothes.

'Yes, a Mr MacAuliffe has furnished me nicely and – for some reason – he saw fit to give me this.' I withdrew the beautiful knife and lay it on the table. Holmes stared at it in surprise.

'That is a bonnie thing! The clothier gave you this? Why?'

'Yes, it did strike me as odd. He seemed to be a bit worried about my going to Braedern. Said none in Aberdeen would stay overnight in the castle. Haunted, can you believe?' In the morning breakfast room, with the sun pouring through the leaded window, it all seemed rather silly.

'Well, a knife would do little against a ghost, Watson,' said Holmes with a smile. 'You do, however, have your Webley on hand, do you not, in case we encounter any living enemies?'

'Always. Was your visit with Dr Fleming fruitful?'

'Yes. But he has more to study. His initial theory is that death resulted from a brain haemorrhage under a flat, wide, eggshell crack to the occipital portion of the skull, as from a fall. Decapitation was probably post mortem, and done with a serrated blade, with the edges then burned, presumably to hide this. But he will be investigating further to confirm the cause of death, and I hope to hear from him in a day or so.'

159

We set out on a train journey of several hours westward towards Ballater and thence travelled by carriage to Braedern Castle.

As promised, there had been heavy snowfall during the night, which slowed our journey but made it all the more beautiful. It was a crystalline morning, the sky a deep blue, and the temperature down considerably from the day before.

The tracks ran along the valley of the Dee, passing the Catholic College of Blair, into rolling countryside, blanketed in snow and heavily wooded in areas, passing numerous glittering streams, croft houses with smoke arising from chimneys, small villages and various farm vehicles creaking over icy, rutted side roads. I caught a glimpse of Drum Castle and other ancient structures. Behind the nearby hills were smaller mountains – the so-called 'Caledonian Alps.' I was struck by the brilliant cold light and a sense of wildness that is not found in the southern regions of Britain. The Scottish Highlands have always been described as mystical and so they appeared to me as we made our way towards our remote destination.

Holmes, rarely moved by country scenery, ignored the sights, taking far more interest in the details of what MacAuliffe had told me of the legendary hauntings at Braedern, and especially of the laird's hiring the 'unhirable.'

'Where does he find these men, I wonder?' mused Holmes.

I knew, and told him. There were organizations in London who dealt with returning veterans damaged by the war and who had no means of sustenance. I reminded him that I had been in a sorry state myself when I arrived in London before we had met. But there were men far worse off than I. I had declined these same services when offered, but some unfortunates had no choice.

At last, after alighting at Ballater, we were conveyed by private coach another ten miles to the Castle Braedern, arriving in the early afternoon. The medieval castle stood on a hill, a monumental stone structure which had been added onto many times over the years. It had evolved as an uneven rectangle, with two wide round turrets and two quatrefoils taking up the four corners. An enormous wooden gate stood open, affording a glimpse of the courtyard within.

Beyond the castle and down the hill, at the side of the quickly flowing river, stood a large group of buildings, from one to three storeys high, one of which was topped with an odd, pagoda-like structure. Behind these lay a cluster of modest brick residences. Grazing fields and barns took up another area to the east, along with what looked like a reservoir.

'A remarkable estate,' I said.

'The laird is one of the wealthiest men in the country, Watson.'

I was taken aback. Their stay at in Antibes, their clothes, and their casual change of holiday plans had left a clear impression of ease, but their holdings were impressive nonetheless.

'How wealthy, Holmes, do you know?'

'Their fortunes were built on land, water rights, and steel, but whisky is the laird's passion. They could buy the Grand Hôtel du Cap if they so chose to do so.'

'Well, they certainly thought they could buy you.'

'All in service of my plan,' said Holmes. The carriage turned and approached the massive open gate, entering a large courtyard paved in rough stones. Within were several carriages of various sizes, and some rougher wagons as well with a number of grooms handling the horses. The driver pulled up to a gothic arched main entrance We were greeted by a footman, who immediately fetched the butler, a taciturn, balding man.

We entered a reception hall, which was enormous, freezing cold and empty. A wide stone staircase led steeply upwards.

The butler signalled and two tall footmen approached. They looked like wrestlers so muscled and rough were they. 'Your weapons, please,' demanded the butler as two men stepped forward to receive them.

Holmes and I exchanged a glance. 'Ah, yes,' said Holmes. 'An old Highland custom, guests are to leave their weapons at the door. That did not go well for Duncan, did it? Well, I have nothing. Only my wits, which I am told, may have a rather cutting edge. And Watson here, well, you have what, that penknife?'

Did he mean the jack-knife given me in Aberdeen?

'You peeled an orange on the train?' prompted Holmes. 'Remember?'

'Ah, yes,' I said and fumbled for the small, dull little knife that I usually carried.

The butler stared at me suspiciously. 'It will be returned to you,' said he. 'But certainly Mr Holmes carries a weapon of some sort? You are in a dangerous business, are you not, sir?'

Holmes turned an icy glare to his interlocutor. 'My business is none of yours. And no, I have nothing further.'

'The laird awaits you this way, sir,' said the butler, indicating a passageway to the right. Holmes swept past the butler and directly through the two footmen who stepped aside to let him pass.

Handing the butler my penknife with a look I hoped was more remonstrative than worried, I followed Holmes, secure in the knowledge that I had both a Webley and the strange Scottish knife I had been given secreted about my person. I was already leery of Scottish customs.

We soon found ourselves in the Great Hall, a strange and cavernous combination of medieval pageantry and modern convenience. It was two stories tall, with gothic arches leading in various directions, and stone walls decorated with an array of Scottish weaponry and heraldic banners. Beams of light crisscrossed the ornate tile floor, augmented by modern electrical lighting fixtures spilling small pools of light at regular intervals along the walls and on various carved tables around the perimeter.

Isla McLaren and Sir Robert stood on a rich Turkish rug before a large roaring fireplace. The mantel was taller than a man's head, and carved with either writhing or dancing figures, I could not discern.

The lady, upon spotting us, cried out in joy and rushed forward. 'At last you are here, Mr Holmes and Dr Watson. I am so very glad! These are troubled times.'

The laird stepped forward with a look I could not read. Pain, certainly, was part of it. 'I am relieved that you are here, gentlemen. I am sorry to have left France so suddenly. Your telegram arrived this morning, only a few hours before yourselves. I apologize for not having sent my carriage to the station.'

'Let us commence the inquiry into the late parlour maid's demise,' asked Holmes. 'The longer we wait, the colder the trail.'

'Immediately,' agreed the laird. 'I will have your things brought to your rooms in the East Tower. My daughter-in-law is perhaps your most ardent admirer, Mr Holmes. She has convinced me that no one is more qualified than yourself to deal with your vexing problem.'

'Good, then let us begin, Sir Robert,' said Holmes. 'What have the police been told?'

The laird looked past us to where the footmen stood with our luggage. 'What has become of the . . . do you have with you the—'

'The girl's partial remains are with a forensic medical expert in Edinburgh. I should have more information soon from him. And now, Sir Robert, the police?'

The laird and Isla McLaren exchanged a look.

'I have not brought them in on the matter.'

'And why is that?'

'Mr Holmes,' said the lady. 'Sir Robert knows of my earlier visit to you.'

'That was apparent before,' said Holmes with irritation. 'The point, madam?'

'Isla expressed to you her low opinion of the local constabulary. They were unable, for example, to find the culprit for a small matter of theft a month or so ago, and so bungled the attempt and irritated my workers that I was forced to ban them from the property.'

Holmes's eyebrow shot up.

'Come now, Mr Holmes. My reading tells me you do not have the highest opinion of your own police in London,' said the laird.

'They must be notified, however, and present at the arrest.'

'I appreciate your confidence that the culprit will be found. However, I am accustomed to handling things on my own,' said the laird.

'I will not be party to vigilante justice, Sir Robert,' said Holmes. 'My work serves the law.'

Except when it does not, I thought. There had been occasions where Holmes had served as judge and jury on those guilty parties whom he confronted at the end of a case. However, he was never led by feelings of retribution or revenge. He was more likely to let someone go free if he felt they would be of no future harm. The chance of this happening in these circumstances was nil.

'Oh, no, you misunderstand me!' said the laird. 'I mean to have the culprit arrested and dealt with by the law. I simply do not want the idiots who are our local police interfering in your work. Mr Holmes, I refuse to involve them just yet. Those are the conditions of your employment here. And now, as to the matter of a fee—'

'I am not employed, I consult, Sir Robert, at my own

discretion and using the methods I prefer. I will do my best to find your culprit. In terms of a fee, you may reward me commensurately at the end, as you see fit. But delaying official police notification may cast suspicion on you and your family.'

The laird paused. He and his daughter-in-law exchanged a look. The wisdom of Holmes's words was not lost on them.

'A compromise, then,' said the laird. 'I give you three days to solve this mystery. At the end of this I will call in the police, or another detective as I see fit. I mean to see this solved, and you have my word that I intend the culprit to receive due process of law. And Mr Holmes, I am sure you will find it easier to make your inquiries unencumbered by the bumbling local police.'

It was Holmes's turn to pause. 'Agreed,' said he, finally. 'I will begin by interviewing each of the family members in their private quarters, as soon as possible, without preamble, and preferably before any cleaning takes place.'

The laird nodded. 'As you wish. However, you should know that a very thorough housecleaning was undertaken by the staff upon our departure for France. It is our custom at this time of year.'

'That is unfortunate,' said Holmes. 'Let us proceed at once.'

The butler was then dispatched to release our coachman and oversee our luggage delivery.

Our things were brought in, and led by a stoop-shouldered old servant introduced as Mungo, we were led to the East

Tower. I reflected on Holmes' insistence on seeing each family member's private quarters. He would no doubt infer a great deal from the details there. I smiled inwardly at the thought of what one might erroneously infer from Holmes' own messy abode, or indeed my own, now festooned with flowers and doilies by my wife.

In this remote corner of the castle, daylight seemed a treasured resource to be sparingly allotted. Our route took us up steep circular stone stairs, worn by the ages and lit with few windows. We then entered a long dark hallway, where a lavatory entrance facing a narrow window was pointed out down at the end of the hall. The latest of modern plumbing had been installed over the remnants of a medieval latrine, we were told, as they had been throughout the living quarters of the large castle. No expense had been spared.

The lighting in the hallway was extremely dim. The newest electric fixtures or bright gaslights had shone in previous rooms we had seen, but only candles and oil lamps were in evidence here.

We were given two near but not adjoining rooms with heavy wooden doors that must have dated back at least two or three centuries. The bedrooms were comfortable enough, with carved wooden bedsteads and walls hung densely with tapestries against the frigid air. But here, too, there was a lack of modern lighting.

There was no time to linger in these rooms to unpack or explore, for Holmes was eager to begin the investigation. We returned to the Great Hall, where Holmes informed the laird he would begin with him.

The laird agreed to this, and to being first, but then Holmes surprised us both.

'Laird Robert, I should like to begin with a quick tour of your distillery, and interview you initially there.' The laird acquiesced and stepped away to call for horses to be readied.

'Why the distillery, Holmes?' I whispered.

'We have met the family. I must determine the scope of our search for suspects. If there are more there, I should like to know it now.'

The three of us bundled up against the bitter cold and left the castle for the courtyard, where the laird called for horses.

CHAPTER 14

The Highland Magic

e headed down a steep hill towards what was, for the laird, the heart and soul of his property, the McLaren Distillery. The buildings were somewhat farther away than they appeared. Though only mid-afternoon, it was already quite dark. Our horses picked their way along the icy path, while the laird gestured towards a large body of water off to the right. It was rectangular, and clearly devised by human hands.

'The reservoir,' he said. 'Built by my grandfather in 1823. Our water is one of the secrets of our whisky. It originates in the mountains up yonder, passes through rock and bramble, peat fields and rich earth, acquiring its unique Highland flavour, before it arrives here.'

'It is a considerable feat of engineering, then,' said Holmes.

'We are well supplied but quality is as important as quantity. Not all water has the special ingredient.'

'What ingredient is that?'

The laird turned to us. 'The Highland magic,' he said, and winked.

The subject of whisky, his great passion, apparently drew the laird from his grief. Like Holmes, this man's immersion in work was all consuming.

We dismounted in front of an arched entrance to a large complex of unusually varied buildings. Entering a cobbled courtyard, I noted that some of the buildings were in decorative brick, some ancient and picturesque in stone, and others in cold, modern concrete. The three-storey tower with its pagoda-like top was, I learned, designed to draw and expel the kiln smoke.

The laird explained that power had recently been converted from waterwheel to steam engines. The noise from these was audible across the snow-covered courtyard in which we now stood.

'I would like a brief tour, if you would, Sir Robert, then is there an office where we may speak privately?' said Holmes.

'Certainly, Mr Holmes.'

The laird was more than happy with this brief distraction from the tragedy.

'The Highland magic is far more than the water, gentlemen,' said he as he led us through a warren of buildings. 'Each step of the way combines artistry with the latest engineering. We have increased our production to 750,000 gallons a year in the last two years alone. Follow me.'

We passed through many and varied buildings with rooms large and small. There were steep wooden staircases, slick with moisture, and circular steel ones, ladders and platforms and overlooks, lifts and pulleys, and elevators, each with a distinct purpose and design. The laird pointed out the kiln that dried the damp malt. Men in rolled-up shirtsleeves, their muscles gleaming with sweat, shovelled masses of combustibles into roaring furnaces, serving both the drying rooms and the steam engines. Although fragrant, the peat smoke made it difficult to breathe. But Holmes, I observed, was more interested in the men working there than in the process itself.

It was a particularly rough-looking and strange crew of men who toiled at the McLaren Distillery. I reflected on the fact that I have been fortunate never to have laboured in an industrial setting such as this. As we passed through the malting floor, a milling area, then a grain elevator, and kiln, I was struck by the immense physical effort, but also by the many perils to life and limb – not only the kilns but the grinding machines which could suck a man in to a horrific death with the careless catch of a sleeve.

We crossed a courtyard and entered the distillery itself, coming first into the mash house. Warm and humid, the room was dominated by a large, riveted cast-iron vessel with a copper canopy. Sir Robert slid a section of this aside to reveal what looked like a steaming vat of porridge.

'This is the mash tun,' he said. 'Alistair has been experimenting with the dimensions and temperatures. Here, the ground, malted barley, called "grist" is steeped three times in increasingly hot water. This converts the starch in the malt into sugars, which dissolve into the hot water.'

Stepping around a guard rail, Holmes and I peered into the vessel, which was about ten feet deep, filled just over halfway high with the grey, gluey mush. Below us were a rather alarming set of slowly turning steel rakes, at least five feet in diameter. These resembled nothing so much as the metallic appendages of some winged dinosaur, keeping the 'pot stirred' by clawing relentlessly through the steeping mash. The steady, deep huff of the steam engine which powered these rakes, along with the sounds of splashing through the viscous liquid echoed through the large room. To be caught in one of those would be a fearsome way to depart this earth.

I had the sudden sense of being watched and looked up to remark upon two workers who stared at us with unmistakeable malevolence. They turned quickly away. A shout from another direction drew our attention to two rough and angry-looking men engaged in a tense conversation before a complex set of gauges. A third man approached them carrying a long section of pipe. To my physician's eye, his lopsided gait and grimace spoke of grievous prior injury.

The conversation grew heated, and the third man flung his pipe to the ground, where it came close to hitting one of first two. They nearly came to blows.

The laird stopped and shouted above the cacophony. 'Joey, separate them!' A fourth man, equally large, and with facial scarring just visible above a scarf tied over his nose and mouth, emerged from behind a second tank and stepped into the fray, with a quick wave to his employer. In an instant he had subdued the aggressor by twisting his arm behind his back and forcing him to his knees.

The laird moved us quickly away from the scene. 'We are having trouble maintaining water temperature in the tank. Some of the newest equipment seems to be faulty.'

'You are having more trouble than that,' remarked Holmes.

The laird said nothing, but led us out of the room and on a circuitous route to our next destination.

'Something is not quite right here,' I whispered to Holmes while we were out of earshot.

He nodded. 'Clearly, Watson.'

Entering another room, we found ourselves on a platform looking down at several huge wooden vats the laird referred to as 'washbacks' reeking with the strong beer-like odour of fermentation. They too were covered as these fumes were strong enough to render one unconscious with prolonged contact. Men worked on the platform where we stood, adjusting the temperature, checking progress. A cold draught made me shiver and I noticed a door open on the floor one storey below us.

Holmes noticed my discomfort and smiled. 'Be grateful for the fresh air, Watson. Carbon dioxide is a by-product of fermentation and, since it is heavier than air, has collected down there.'

'Precisely,' said the laird. 'Linger there at your peril.'

'Has anyone been asphyxiated?' asked Holmes.

The laird avoided a direct answer. 'I have an excellent safety record.'

We entered a back staircase down to a lower level.

'I cannot help but notice, Laird Robert, your crew is a rough lot. How many of these men were rescued from, shall we say, questionable circumstances?' asked Holmes.

'What do you mean, Mr Holmes? These are veterans. Dr Watson here knows how difficult it can be to return from war. There is a period of adjustment. Fifty of our seventy men are those who have been given a new start.' said Robert McLaren.

The laird's familiarity with me was disconcerting, although of course it was all in *Beeton's Christmas Annual*. And it was true; I knew well the despair of the forcibly retired soldier. It was only fate that delivered me to 221B and not a life of grinding penury. Perhaps I had been too harsh in assessing these men.

'It is more than that. I sense a criminal element here, Sir Robert,' said Holmes.

'You witnessed a rare moment, Mr Holmes. A minor disagreement.'

'Then why do two of your overseers carry pistols?'

I had not noticed this.

'You interpret wrongly. There are few problems,' said the laird. 'These men are grateful.'

'I would wager that some have police records,' said Holmes. 'Sir Robert, it has been my experience that once one has crossed the line to criminal behaviour, the way back can be hard to find, and regular employment may not be sufficient.'

'My late wife would find you a harsh judge. It was she,

God rest her soul, who convinced me to give the most desperate of men a chance of redemption. Where is your charity?'

The laird stepped away before Holmes could answer. But I bristled at the insinuation. Holmes was a most charitable man, but he knew danger when he saw it.

At last we arrived at the heart of the distillery, the room containing the stills themselves. These were fantastic constructions, enormous, two-storey versions of the tiny still I had seen at 221B.

These riveted copper dinosaurs were shaped like metallic tulip bulbs, swelled wide at the bottom, studded with rivets and narrowing into long pipes at the top which then bent sideways. As the liquids passed through them, their surfaces became hot and dangerous. They brought to mind fantastic diving bells or space ships from a Jules Verne novel.

'We put our liquid, which is clear in colour at this point, through the distilling process more than once. It is the second time that produces the whisky. But not all the liquid makes it into the casks. The first stuff, the foreshot is too strong, then comes the "heart" which is the usable stuff, followed by the "feints" and "spent lees". It is my foreman – using a combination of artistic taste and pure science, you'll appreciate that, Mr Holmes – who makes the choice by smell, by clarity, by instinct, and by this instrumentation here.'

He then pointed out an elaborate, beautiful glass and brass box with precise measuring equipment inside. 'This is called the spirit safe. There the precise level of alcohol is measured as there are strict legal requirements.'

'Sir Robert, I have seen enough,' said Holmes suddenly. 'Let us return to the subject of your men. In the problem of your murdered parlour maid, it seems an entire crew of suspects tend to your business here.'

'No. Her killer is not one of these men.'

'How can you be sure?'

'I have taken great care to separate the distillery workers from my family and those who attend the estate. My foreman has put into place a number of precautions. The dormitories are patrolled. The castle is locked like a fortress at night. No, you may rest assured it is not one of these men.'

Holmes stared at him, one eyebrow raised. He was clearly not convinced.

The laird paused thoughtfully. 'Follow me, gentlemen. Mr Holmes, now that we are away from the house, it is time for me to be more frank with you. There is something I wish to tell you without risk of being overheard.'

We moved to Sir Robert's private office, a small room set in an upstairs portion of the distillery, and behind two sets of doors. Quiet and warm, it was panelled, with a fire, a desk, a paraffin lamp, and a row of decanters. We sat at a table near the fire, and the laird moved to the decanters. He hesitated, then held one up, offering it. Holmes waved him off impatiently. 'Please, sir?' he said. 'You had something to tell us, Laird Robert?'

The older man hesitated, then took a breath and began.

'My son Charles, you see, was attracted to Fiona, and possibly Alistair was, as well. Charles, as you have noted, Mr Holmes, has shown a certain lack of restraint, and, well, my boys were already at loggerheads over control of the business and I feared this rivalry would make it worse.'

'Might you consider one son more likely than the other to murder the girl?'

'Neither, sir! Both have tempers. And yet I cannot imagine it.'

'Charles is estranged from his wife, Catherine, is he not? This much I have seen for myself.'

The laird looked off a moment, as if lost in thought. He turned back to Holmes. 'Yes, and his many dalliances with girls below stairs were known. Yet . . . I cannot conceive of Charles behind such an act.'

'His wife Catherine is impaired by drink and has reason for jealousy. What of your younger son and his wife?'

'Alistair, oh no! His temper is short, but there is a basic goodness in Alistair that would make him an unlikely villain. No, I think not.'

'Jealousy can twist a man.' said I.

'Yet he is quite complacent where his wife is concerned,' remarked Holmes. 'Isla McLaren is a very independent young woman, it seems.'

'Yes and it is a shame. Alistair ignores her at his peril, I tell him. She is a treasure, my Isla,' said the laird.

'And what of Isla herself? Jealous, perhaps?' asked Holmes.

'I would say she is above such a feeling. My daughter-in-law shows a refined nature and advanced intellect. If she were a man, the business would be hers.'

I glanced at Holmes. He appeared unmoved by this assessment.

'It is said that Fiona was one to stir the pot, presumably below stairs as well. What of the other servants?'

The laird paused. 'She flirted with them all. Or at least three of whom I am aware. I allowed it because a marriage to one of them, I thought, would end my worries.'

'What worries? Affairs between servants and masters, this is common, is it not?'

The laird was a rabbit in a trap, casting his eyes about for an escape. 'The real problem, Mr Holmes lay with my two sons. I had to . . . I had to stop this, before . . .' He covered his eyes in an emotional gesture that seemed strangely out of character. Recovering instantly, he turned to us with sudden ferocity. 'What I am about to relate to you now, is not to leave this room. Do you swear? Because if it does, heaven help you both.'

'Laird McLaren,' retorted Holmes, 'if I am to continue, you must refrain from making casual threats.'

The laird immediately realized his mistake. 'Yes, of course. But I require the utmost discretion.'

'That is understood. Now, if you please, Sir Robert, let us get to the heart of the matter. You were responsible for the girl's abduction, were you not?'

It was all I could do to suppress a gasp.

The laird froze. There was a long silence. Yes,' he said finally. 'I was. How did you know?'

'I can well imagine the motive; I need to understand the details. Did you kidnap the girl yourself? And cut off all her hair?' said Holmes.

A flicker of remorse passed over the man's face.

'Not precisely,' said he. 'Rather, I commissioned the act. For her own good, of course.'

'Commissioned? We shall get to that in a moment. Why was it "for her own good"? Was she in some danger?'

'Well, I, yes, danger.'

'From whom? Again, is one of your sons inclined to violence?'

'No, it was not that. Well, not directly—'

'What then?'

'I needed to prevent an unthinkable turn of events—'

'Whatever is unthinkable, as you say, surely worse has happened. How did you intend this act to protect the girl?'

'I had hoped to frighten the girl off.'

'And the hair?'

'I thought to make her less attractive to . . . her admirers.'

'And why was this so important to you?'

'It—'

Holmes leaned in towards the laird. 'Because this young girl was *very* important to you, was she not? Almost as important to you as the sons you were also protecting.'

Protecting from what? I was not following this conversation.

The laird understood my friend perfectly. 'Your reputation is indeed merited, Mr Holmes. Yes, the girl was very important to me.'

'But why?' I exclaimed. 'And why would you damage her so?'

'It was an impermanent gesture, no lasting harm done!' said the laird.

Holmes stared coldly at the man. 'There is a simple explanation, Watson,' said he. 'Shall I give it, or will you, Sir Robert?'

The man held his gaze, and then suddenly looked away.

'Ah, it is to me, then,' said Holmes. 'The young woman was your illegitimate daughter. Am I correct?'

'Your daughter!' I exclaimed.

The laird did not move, but dropped his eyes. 'Yes,' he said softly. 'Fiona is – was – my daughter.' A tear fell from one eye, and he wiped it away quickly.

I could not help but feel a wave of revulsion. To frighten and shame a young girl in this way to protect his sons from inadvertent incest was unthinkable.

'Why did you not simply send her away?' asked Holmes.

'I promised her late mother I would personally look after the child and provide for her myself. Braedern is a safe haven for many.'

'Unless they are kidnapped and shorn, or murdered,' said I.

'Dr Watson! Mr Holmes, I had no idea . . . the murder . . . I am not responsible! Gentlemen! I am a tolerant man, and a generous employer. Ask anyone. That one of my . . . that this should have happened—'

'Did Fiona know you were her father?' asked Holmes.

'No. She was told her father died when she was an infant. I could not trust her with the secret of her birth.'

'Of course not. She might have laid claim to a part of your estate.'

'Mr Holmes, you continue to misjudge me! It was the

promise to her mother that bound me. That I would care for the girl personally.'

'Presumably, that promise extends to her funeral,' said Holmes. 'Why did you not confide in your sons?'

The laird's face contorted in pain. 'To admit to adultery would have destroyed the family. They hold the memory of their dear late mother as a saint.'

'Yes, well, blocked at every turn,' said Holmes, the note of sarcasm evident, at least, to me.

'Mr Holmes, please. I made efforts. Many times. I sent Fiona away to school, despite the other servants' jealousy. She failed, I tried again, and again she failed. The girl was ineducable. The letters all went backwards, she said, and she could learn to neither read nor write. In desperation I sent her to work at the MacElheny estate, twenty-five miles to the south. They returned her in a week. No one could handle her.'

'Then what?'

'She grew even more forward with the men of the estate. She was also highly superstitious. We have troubles with that here. The servants all believe in ghosts, and I have had the devil of a time getting them to tend to certain areas of the castle. Fiona loved the drama. She told many a wild ghost tale and enjoyed the effects. Among the servants, this was like throwing kerosene on a simmering flame. She had everyone in a turmoil, from my sons to my lowliest scullery maid.'

'So you decided to frighten Fiona into submission?'

'As a last resort, you see, having exhausted all other options, I thought of the plan. But oh, I never imagined—'

'You had your daughter abducted and shamed. In desperation, you say?'

'Mr Holmes, I sense your disdain. But sir, you have no idea of the depths of my remorse. I have made a terrible mistake.'

'For which your child has paid with her life.'

The laird flushed with rage and for a brief moment I thought he might strike Holmes. But his face contorted strangely as a second emotion swept over him. He closed his eyes as if to blink back tears and emitted a painful sigh.

Holmes and I exchanged a look.

In a moment, the laird composed himself. 'Find who killed Fiona, Mr Holmes. And I will make you wealthy beyond your wildest dreams.'

'I do not dream wildly, Sir Robert,' said Holmes. 'But I am here to find the killer. Now, tell me about her disappearance. I understand you received a note from her saying she eloped. Are you sure the note was her writing?'

'I am sure! The backwards letters. It was her writing.'

'And she said she eloped with the groundsman's son? Is this something you believed?'

'Yes. Yes, it was. Iain Moray. That boy loved her since childhood.'

'Where is this note now?'

'It is here.' The laird rose, and unlocked a small drawer in a desk under the window. He handed a sheet of foolscap to Holmes. The detective studied it for a moment then handed it to me. It was hastily written, with many letters backwards. Clearly an uneducated hand. I pocketed it.

'You are sure it is Fiona's hand?' asked Holmes.

The laird nodded sadly. 'Unmistakable.'

'Whom did you hire to carry out this abduction?' said Holmes.

The laird hesitated.

'Perhaps it was he who later returned to kill the girl,' I prompted.

The laird shook his head violently. 'Never. On that fact you may be reassured. I hired the strongest, most loyal, most calm and wise man on the estate. A man of utmost integrity and to whom, if only he were my son and not my employee, I would gladly give the running of the business.'

'Who is this sterling character?' drawled Holmes.

'My right-hand man. Third generation distillery foreman for McLaren whisky. From a long line of coopers, they come. And no better man to have at the helm. I hired Mr Cameron Coupe.'

On cue, as he must have been listening just outside, a man opened the door and stepped into the room.

CHAPTER 15

Cameron Coupe

o say Coupe was a man with presence would be to understate the impression he made. Well over six feet tall, powerfully built and remarkably handsome, he was a man of about our own age, with curling black hair and penetrating dark eyes. He was attired simply, in a white collarless shirt and vest and worn moleskin breeches, with tall waterproof boots and a worn but well-tailored tweed jacket. A silver watch fob was just visible above a pocket. He conveyed a quiet confidence that more often accompanies men of privilege.

'Gentlemen, this is Cameron Coupe, my right hand, manager of the estate and Master Distiller. Cameron's father, and his father before him held the same position.'

Coupe nodded a greeting. The man was polite, but hardly subservient.

'Cameron here is my intimate confidant, and the only man on the estate who knows Fiona's parentage. As I mentioned, Mr Holmes, it was he whom I commissioned to carry out the—' Here he hesitated.

'—abduction,' supplied Holmes.

'Yes. And the rest. But neither Cameron nor I killed the girl. We are eager for you to reveal the true culprit, Mr Holmes.'

Holmes was busy lighting his pipe. He shrugged and glanced up at the estate manager with what I knew to be feigned indifference.

Coupe met Holmes's gaze with frank openness, his confidence unshaken. If he was guilty, he gave no hint of it. 'Sir, I was told you wish to speak to me,' said Coupe, affably. 'What might I do for you?' His accent conveyed some years at university, at least to my ear.

Holmes turned to the laird. 'If you will excuse us, Sir Robert' said he. 'May we interview Mr Coupe alone? We could then continue our conversation later in your private quarters, as we discussed.'

The laird paused then stood abruptly. 'Later, at my own convenience,' he said, somewhat discomfited by the dismissal. He exited in haste, causing his man to step aside.

'Pray be seated, Mr Coupe,' said Holmes. The man hesitated at the door as if deciding whether to comply or not.

'What would you gentlemen like to know?' asked Cameron Coupe. This was the voice of a man who commanded others. 'I am, as you have heard, bound to help you in any way I can. But I am busy with work just now, so I would appreciate this being brief, sirs.'

'We will take the time we need and no less, Mr Coupe,'

said Holmes sharply. 'As a kidnapper, you are on tenuous ground legally, and I think you know that.' He pointed at the chair.

Coupe paused, considered, then relaxed into a smile and joined us at the table. His large figure dwarfed the small wooden furniture, and as he leaned forward onto the table he presented an intimidating presence, the shock of wild hair tumbling forward on his forehead. His bright, dark eyes confronted us without any trace of fear, though with a certain amount of humour.

Holmes, by contrast, leaned back lazily in his own chair, as if indifferent to the conversation. Once again he busied himself with his pipe. I knew this posture well, and it usually reflected the opposite state of mind. Inside, at this moment he would be like a polar bear fishing at a hole in the ice, perfectly still, taught with anticipation, and keenly attuned to the slightest ripple.

'Describe the kidnapping, where you took the girl, what you did exactly, and how you returned her,' said he, carelessly.

'First let me say, sir, I meant no harm to the girl. I took special pains, was gentle, and—'

'Forego the apologies and give me the details.'

The large man paused, struggling with his anger. He then proceeded to give his account calmly and in detail, showing himself to be an intelligent and observant man, not without sympathy for his young victim. Despite his precautions not to harm her, he freely admitted that the experience frightened her terribly.

'The problem, you see, was that she must not catch a glimpse of me, or, well, you understand. Knowing well the patterns of the estate, I disguised myself in a dark cloak with a hood, and surprised her in a rear yard by the kitchen, at a time when others were occupied. It was there that I took her, by means of throwing a blanket over her, gently of course, and I made a few ghostly noises and the like to frighten her. "Woo. Oooo".' He smiled at the memory.

Neither Holmes nor I found this amusing. 'Why the noises?' said Holmes.

'I thought that impersonating a ghost might make her more pliable.'

'A believer, then?'

'Fiona could be peculiar on the subject of ghosts. She frequently mocked her fellow servants who were believers in the spirit world, you see, but in her heart of hearts she was afraid, that I knew. All the servants believe in ghosts.'

'To be sure.' said the detective. Holmes was clearly goading the man. Coupe did not rise to the bait.

'But she struggled wildly, and so I had to render her unconscious so as not to hurt her, using—'

'Chloroform,' said Holmes. 'That was ghostly of you. How is it that you are acquainted with this substance?'

'We have a stable. Champion ponies, has the laird. The veterinarian uses it,' said Coupe.

'Did he show you how much to use, and how to administer it?' asked Holmes quickly. 'It is quite dangerous.'

'No, sir. This had to be done in secret.'

'Then how did you know?'

187

'I read, sir.'

'Of course you do. Now do something for me.' Holmes pulled out a small notebook and his mechanical pencil and laid them on the table before Coupe. 'Write your name here. Then print your name below. Then write my name. Then write a line of poetry.'

The man looked puzzled but obliged. I noted a certain effort to his actions, and the writing went slowly. After a moment he looked up. 'I can think of no poem. Can you give me a line?'

'Alack! What poverty my Muse brings forth,' said Holmes dryly.

Coupe stiffened. 'You mock me, sir.'

'Not at all. Shakespeare. Sonnet 103.'

Coupe wrote it out, gave the notebook back to Holmes. My friend pocketed it without looking at it.

'Describe what else happened,' said he.

'Well, once she was sleeping, I had a second task. The laird asked me to cut the lass's hair off, and I did so, leaving enough to look decent, and placed her on a bed of straw in one of the underground holding cells.'

'What cells?' asked Holmes.

'Under the castle, from the days when the lairds of Braedern held local assizes here. In any case I also put on some blankets so that she should not catch cold, and the laird came down to check that she was all right.'

'Did she see him then?'

'No, she was still asleep.'

'Unconscious. What happened next?'

'The laird, he was not satisfied, and asked me to take it further. Cut off all her hair. Shave her.'

'Why?'

'I do not know. Presumably so the effect would last longer. It felt like a cruel thing to do, but the laird, he is not a cruel man. I believe he thought to make her un-attractive. For the reasons you have already learned, that is for her own protection.'

'An unusual solution,' said Holmes.

Coupe did not reply. He pushed a dark lock of hair from his forehead in an angry gesture.

'Did you sense there could be another motive? Any other reason for this strange action? Punitive, perhaps.'

The man's voice grew louder. 'I do not question the laird. He is a man of impeccable reputation.'

'And yet, there remain some doubts surrounding the death of his wife,' said Holmes.

Coupe sprang to his feet and loomed over the table at Holmes. My hand went automatically to my pocket, where my Webley resided.

'Do not say that,' said Coupe, vehemently. 'The laird loved her truly, and mourns her death every day.' Here the man paused and his look grew darker. 'If you be thinking ill of him, sir, it would be wrong of you to accept his hospitality, and this case, and I suggest you make your way off.'

Holmes laughed. 'Really now, Mr Coupe, you overreach yourself. We are not here as guests, and I feel no compunc-tion to act as one. I have been asked here to solve a murder.

It is my job to suspect everyone. Besides, the tale you now tell is hardly flattering to your employer.'

Coupe was breathing heavily.

'Sit down, Mr Coupe. Let us continue. It is Sir Robert's request.'

Coupe hesitated and then grudgingly complied.

'Now, Mr Coupe, how did the poem come to be attached to the laundry basket in which the girl was returned?'

'Poem, Mr Holmes? I do not know what you are talking about.'

Holmes stared hard at Coupe, and a tense silence ensued for several seconds. Coupe returned the stare, unblinking.

'Perhaps I am mistaken. Tell me the circumstances of her return,' said Holmes at last.

'I used a basket, a very big one, the gardener uses it for cuttings, and put her in it, with the blankets and all, and brought it to the main entrance in the dead of night.'

'"The dead of night"?' said Holmes. 'Pray, what time might that be?'

'I would guess around two in the morning.'

'Alone? It would have been rather unwieldy for one person.'

'I am a strong man.'

'I see. And you added no note?'

'Yes, there was a note, which the laird directed me to write.'

'If you would kindly be more descriptive in your answers, we could complete our task more quickly,' said Holmes.

'The note he asked me to write was this: "No man shall

touch this lass until she regain her full complement of crowning glory. Or the spirits will wreak havoc upon the house.'"

But what was this? Isla had read us a poem that had supposedly been delivered with the girl in the basket. Holmes and I exchanged a quick glance.

'A threat of supernatural harm. If you do not believe in spirits, why did the laird expect his presumably educated sons to do so?' asked Holmes.

Cameron Coupe let out a large, booming laugh. He relaxed into his chair. 'A good question, sir. If it is not telling tales out of school, I should say the entire family believes in ghosts. Though well they hide it.'

Holmes said nothing.

'But why cut off her hair?' I asked.

'It that not obvious, gentlemen? He thought to keep his boys from dallying with the girl. It made her, well, less enticing,' said Coupe. He flushed uncomfortably as he spoke.

'For a time, perhaps. And what followed? Did you participate in any further ghostly games to keep the various participants in this little drama in line?' asked Holmes.

'I did not, sir.'

'Were you never attracted to the lass yourself?' Holmes asked.

'No,' said Coupe, a little too quickly. 'I was immune.'

'How was that?'

'The girl did not appeal to me, sir.'

'And where were you during the past four days?' asked Holmes.

'Here, on the property. We were installing a new hot water tank in the mash house, and I took some deliveries of new equipment. Then I attended a distiller's meeting in Aberdeen.'

'And someone can vouch for your presence here as well as there?'

'Twenty people can do so, Mr Holmes.'

Holmes nodded. 'Did you believe she had eloped, then?'

'I had no reason to disbelieve it. Except for perhaps the young man in question. He seemed, well, he was, or rather is a handsome and strong lad, gentle in nature. But not right in the head, and he longed for the girl in a most inappropriate and obvious manner.'

'Did you believe she ran off with this boy?'

'I did, and I still do,' said Coupe, firmly.

'And then he killed her?'

'That I would be loath to say.'

Holmes stood to leave and I did as well. 'One more thing, Mr Coupe,' said Holmes. 'Are you married?'

'I am not,' he replied. I could feel his eyes upon us as we left the room.

CHAPTER 16

The Groundsman's Sons

t was already near dark when we left to visit the groundsman, one Ualan Moray. Holmes decided to continue with the laird later. We asked and were directed to a small cottage some quarter of a mile to the east of the castle. The man was out, but another son, a small boy of ten or so, was there alone, tending to a large pot of soup. At Holmes's request, he ran to fetch his father.

We awaited him in the single large room of this stone cottage, simply furnished, and with the man's own double bed and two smaller, stacked beds visible behind a make-shift curtain. Soon he arrived, a man of fifty, weather-beaten, with the large, gnarled hands of a hard-working outdoorsman who had touched earth, stone, and wood for years. His small green eyes were bloodshot and squinting, his manner subdued. He wore layers of rough woollen cloth, with a leather vest over the top, and a pair of thick leather gloves clipped to a heavy belt. Holmes gave him our names. He took us in with a sweeping glance and let out a long sigh. 'I am Ualan Moray. What do you need?' he asked.

Holmes told him he was there to investigate the death of Fiona Paisley, and the father bade his boy make us tea. After taking our winter garments, the child did so and then retired out of sight. As we three sat by the fire nursing cups of the strong brew, the old man said the laird had instructed everyone on his staff to cooperate with Sherlock Holmes.

But it was hard for him to speak. Grief coloured his every movement. Holmes began gently but his initial questions about the man's son, Iain, were met with silence. Moray at last admitted that his son Iain had disappeared, along with Fiona, on the day her letter had arrived saying she had eloped. And then the poor man stopped, staring into the fire, unable to proceed.

'Mr Moray, I know that this is a difficult task,' said Holmes carefully. 'But I must persist if this mystery is to be solved.'

Ualan Moray looked up at Holmes. Slowly and with deliberation, the man tipped a splash of whisky from a flask into each of our cups, drank his cup to the bottom, and refilled it. Only then did he open up.

'I will tell you the story. But the ending you must tell me. I fear it, I say. I fear it.'

'Let me hear, Mr Moray, and I will see if I can help you. What was the relationship exactly between your son and the parlour maid Fiona Paisley? Can you say?'

'Ach, that lass. Fiona and my son, Iain, were very close since they were wee bairns. Like brother and sister. Played together. Only it changed when they got older. Not right away . . .' He drifted off.

'But over time, then?' prompted Holmes.

'The girls, they are older first, see. She grew into a beauty, sae bonnie and fresh. She had the beautiful red hair, like a waterfall a'fire.'

'I understand,' said Holmes. 'You said the friendship changed?'

'Two years ago. Iain, he was seventeen. But Iain . . . he . . . Iain has always been young. He . . .'

'He was stupid, Faither,' said the child from a corner of the room. I had not noticed him there. 'He went and got hisself killed.'

The old man stiffened and turned to his son. 'Get back to your room, Calum. Do it, now.' The boy sniffed and moved behind the curtain. He would still be listening, of that I was sure.

'She weren't a cruel lass, but she teased him, did Fiona. Not mean at first, but Iain didnae understand. He was simple, you see.'

'Simple? Do you mean he was slow? Unusually so?' asked Holmes, with a gentleness I would not have anticipated.

The man nodded. 'Aye. His mother, bless her heart, said the faeries must'a dropped him on his head one night while we were sleeping. He wisnae normal.'

'Can you tell me more? Was he ever violent? Did he hurt things?' asked Holmes.

'My Iain? Never. Gentle as a lamb. He loved all things, and all people. But most of all, he loved Fiona. He took to following her like a lost puppy.'

'How did Fiona respond?'

'The girl was friendly, then of a sudden went cold. Happened o'ernight. She told him to stay away, she didnae want to play anymore. She didnae want to be followed.'

'What did Iain do then?'

'He stopped following her.'

'Are you sure of that?' asked Holmes. 'If he loved her—'

'Well, he could no longer. She went away somewhere, to school, I think. But then she came back. She were angrier then and wilder. Something changed. She shouted at my Iain.'

'What then?'

'Iain wis broken-hearted.'

'Angry at her?'

'Nay! He wisnae that kind, I tell you. It went into melancholy. He moved slowly. I couldnae hardly get him out o'bed i' the morning.'

'Then Fiona was kidnapped,' prompted Holmes.

'Aye. And Iain was mad with worry. He began tae look for Fiona. He lookit everywhere he knew she might hide.'

'How did he know? You said he did not follow her.'

'Nae, from before. The two of them as bairns, they hid all the time. All those places.'

'Do you know those places?'

'Only a few.'

'I knows 'em,' said the boy, emerging from behind the curtain.

'Excellent, young man! Calum, is it?' said Holmes before his father could rebuke the boy. 'Perhaps you'll show me.' He turned back to the groundsman. 'Is there any dynamite on the property?'

This sharp detour from Fiona's case took me by surprise.

'Nay,' said the groundsman, exactly as the boy said, 'Aye!'

'Faither, 'tis in the little room,' said the boy.

'And how d'ye ken that!' exclaimed his father. The boy shrugged.

'What little room?' asked Holmes of the boy.

'Ah, well, it is not meant for all to know,' interrupted the father. 'We hae some dynamite. I keep it in a little locked room in the back of the garden shed. Where the expensive tools are kept. Where no one is to enter,' he said pointedly at the boy.

'Obviously entirely secure,' said Holmes with one of his mirthless smiles. We exchanged a glance. Isla McLaren had discovered this 'secret' cache as well. 'And the purpose of these explosives?'

'We used it last year. We cleared an area to build housing for the new men. We expanded the distillery, you see—'

'Yes, you have many new hires, I understand. An interesting crew.'

'That is not for me to say, sir.' We could see a shudder of disgust. At least one member of this estate did not think of the laird's charitable hiring policy as benign.

'What of these newer distillery workers? Could any of them have harboured ill feelings towards Fiona?'

'Perhaps, sir, but they are much separate from the castle. I doubt that even that daring girl would hae gone there. My Iain would hae noticed this and stopped her. He would hae told me.'

Holmes considered this. 'Back to the explosives, then. You keep this dynamite around, on hand as it were?' he asked.

'We may hae use for it in the future. And it is safe. Nobel's newest—'

'Yes I know all about that kind. It will not explode from mere movement. Yet precautions must be taken. Is it kept in a fireproof box? Where, exactly?'

'Little danger, Mr Holmes. That shed is damp and canna catch on fire. Or no' easily. The dynamite is in a metal box. Protected. The laird is very strict on the matter, sir.'

'Good. Now, what can you tell me of the laird's late wife?'

'The Lady Elizabeth?' Ualan Moray looked confused. Holmes nodded in encouragement.

'A sad tale there,' said Moray. 'She was a fine lady. 'Tis she that now wanders the East Tower. 'Twas the nursery at one time, from which her wee daughter Anne disappeared. She's no' a happy spirit, and wanders there at nights.'

'Her ghost, yes, we have heard,' said Holmes. 'What a tragedy!'

'Lockit out by chance on a winter nicht. She froze to death.'

'How is it possible no one heard the lady try to enter?'

''Tis a mystery, sir. But the laird recently had the castle secured. It wisnae long after he had brought a' the . . . veterans and . . . others . . . to work here.'

'New locks. I see. Who saw the body? Who found her? Any of the staff?'

'The laird, as I understand it found her. He woudnae let a soul touch her. Carried her in himself. She is buried in the back garden, near the East Tower.'

'Where we are staying, Holmes,' I said.

'She chose the place long before. To be near if little Anne were to return, it is said.'

'Odd. As groundsman, was it you that dug the grave?'

'I expected to sir, but no. The family did it, privately.'

'You are sure she is dead, then?' I asked. Holmes frowned at me.

'Her ghaist is the proof, sir.'

Holmes sighed. 'There are no ghosts.'

'Perhaps no' in London. Here things are different, Mr Holmes. But please, sir, my son. I must know about Iain.'

'Yes. Let us return to Iain. Please describe him to me.'

'He were—he is—twenty but looks younger. Light hair, blue eyes. About the height of your friend, here, but bigger in the shoulders, and shorter legs like myself. But strong, my Iain was. Is.'

'Good. Thank you, Mr Moray. I shall do my best.' Holmes stood up and I joined him.

'Calum, their coats!' the man called out. The boy came forward laden with our things.

'Mmm. It seems to me that you could keep a better eye on young Calum, here, sir,' said Holmes, retrieving his blue scarf and untangling it from his coat. 'How old are you, boy? Ten, I would wager?'

'Aye,' said Calum.

'Not an age to be playing with dynamite.'

The boy nodded, and handed us the rest of our outerwear.

The groundsman shrugged. 'C'mere, son,' said he, taking the small boy by the waist and drawing him in close. 'Listen to the man, then, Calum. Stay clear of the shed.' Turning to us, he added, 'He is all I have got.'

'We do not know that yet.' I offered.

'One more thing, Mr Moray,' said Holmes, now tying his scarf. 'When Fiona and Iain supposedly ran away to get married, what did you think had happened?' asked Holmes.

'I thought maybe she ran away and he followed. But never did I think they were married.'

'You were not worried then?' asked Holmes, donning his ear-flapped cap.

'Aye, worried. My Iain hasnae the experience of the wider world. We didna know where they went.'

'And now . . .'

'The girl is deid and my boy missing. Please, Mr Holmes. I hae nae money and I ken you are here on the business of Fiona. But please, find my son.'

His voice caught. I knew the grief was real.

Holmes shrugged on his long tweed coat. 'Thank you, Mr Moray. You have given me much to consider. I intend to get to the bottom of this mystery.'

The groundsman closed his eyes. ''Twas not Iain that killed Fiona,' said he. A tear leaked from one eye and he brushed it away with a rough hand.

Holmes turned to the boy. 'And you, son? What do you think?'

Calum threw his arms around his father and looked up to meet Holmes's gaze. 'Nay. Not Iain. My brother wisnae . . . he wisnae smart. But he was kind. He was always kind to me.'

'You are lucky to have such an older brother,' said Holmes.

'He protected me.'

Holmes knelt before the boy.

'From what?' he asked, his voice gentle. I was always surprised at the rapport Holmes had with children.

'Anything. Everything.'

'Like what?'

'Scary men who work here. Wolves. Faeries. Falling down. Anything. I love my brother. Can you find him, Mr Holmes?'

'I will try.' Holmes patted the boy on the shoulder, rose and turned to the father. 'Mr Moray, I do not think Iain had anything to do with Fiona's death. But I have just begun, and there is much to discover.' He paused, searching the groundsman's face. 'Was there something else?' The man nodded.

'There was jealousy, if I may say so, sir, a great deal.'

'Jealousy? Among the family? The servants?'

'Both, sir. You would think the family would be above it. But—nae, I speak out of turn.'

'Do continue, Mr Moray. Your thoughts are most welcome.' Holmes and I stood bundled, ready to depart. But I knew he would not leave without following up this statement.

Ualan Moray shifted uncomfortably.

'If you must know, I always thought that Mrs McLaren was a one. Fiona, she talked about how much the lady hated her. Laughed about it, she did. But I told her to watch herself. Something were not right with that woman.'

'Ah, it is Isla McLaren to whom you refer?' asked Holmes. I thought this question a touch too eager.

'No, the elder Mrs McLaren. Catherine,' said Mr Moray. 'But I shouldnae say a word, sir, I am not there to see.'

Holmes nodded and I will admit to a moment of relief.

'Find my son, Mr Sherlock Holmes. Find Iain, please.'

As we trudged our way through the snow to the castle, a wind had picked up. 'Sad story,' I said. 'But what an interesting child, that Calum! And then, of course, Isla McLaren found that dynamite, too.'

'Yes, for a secret room, it is not very secret, is it? Yet, I am sure the groundsman was telling the truth about his son. Iain did not kill Fiona.'

'But he had motive. The girl had spurned him.'

'Yes, but cut off her head and bring it to the South of France? He did not make the delivery, that is for sure. He was not the man our French cabby described. This reeks of subtle planning. No, I think not, Watson. But he had some role in this little tragedy, of that I am certain.'

'I fear we will not find him,' said I.

'Ah. And I fear we will,' said Sherlock Holmes. 'I fear it very much, for Ualan Moray's sake.'

CHAPTER 17

Catherine

ur next interview, by chance, was with Catherine McLaren, Charles's wife. As we made our way back to the castle, Holmes said that he thought the lady was clearly an alcoholic, and as such too disorganised to plot or carry out such a heinous crime, but that perhaps we might still learn something of use from her.

'Though I doubt she will reveal much to me now,' he admitted, 'after my unfortunate revelations about her husband at the hotel in Antibes. I may have need of your charms, Watson.'

Holmes rarely misjudged a response, but here he had. The lady not only seemed to have forgiven him, but began the interview as though she had altogether forgotten his embarrassing assertions in France. Or perhaps she was thankful that he had drawn her father-in-law's attention to Charles's wayward affections.

We were seated by the fire in her heavily gilded and

overheated suite of rooms in the West Tower. Scattered throughout the salon were numerous embroidered pillows. On the walls hung several unremarkable land-scape paintings in ornate frames, and a bright floral embroidery project draped, unfinished, over the arm of a chair. Under the window stood a row of crystal decanters of whisky.

The lady sat before us, bizarrely coquettish if not inap-propriate in a scanty green silk gown, over which had been thrown a gold housecoat embroidered in gilt thread. Her blonde curls tumbled girlishly around her shoulders, a look more suited for an intimate encounter than for a formal interview. The fact that the meeting had been prearranged made her choice of attire all the more disconcerting.

All three of us held cut crystal glasses of whisky. The lady sipped from hers continuously throughout the inter-view. I felt the situation was awkward in the extreme, although Holmes proceeded as if nothing were amiss.

'Mrs McLaren,' he began, 'perhaps you can help us in the matter of the unfortunate Fiona Paisley. Can you tell us anything about this young woman?'

'I had very little contact with the girl, Mr Holmes. You should ask my husband about her.'

Holmes nodded, and appeared to sip his whisky, allowing silence to fill the space. Holmes rarely touched alcohol while on a case, and I was fairly certain he was not doing so now.

'Charles and I see little of each other recently,' the lady allowed.

'That is a shame,' said Holmes. 'Your husband was much affected by what happened in Antibes.'

'Were we not all affected, sir? I mean, my God, that poor girl.' She closed her eyes and took another swallow of the amber liquid. A moment passed and she took another.

'Madam, I could not help but notice that you and your husband, if you will pardon my indiscretion . . .'

'Yes, you are indiscreet,' said Mrs McLaren, an odd smile on her lips. Her mood seemed to flit from one extreme to another. Her smile dropped away. 'And yes, he and I, well, he has moved his rooms far from mine, and is now in the North Tower, where he knows I will not venture.'

'And why would you not venture there, madam?' asked Holmes.

'The ghost.' She took a long drink, draining her glass. 'He knows me well. The ghost. I will not go there. He sometimes visits here. But—'

'The ghost, madam?' pressed Holmes, ever so gently.

She eyed him with the sudden suspicion of the inebriated. Then just as abruptly she dropped this attitude, her eyes scanning the room as if in search of support. They alighted on her whisky decanters and she rose to refill her glass, holding up the crystal decanter to offer us each more. We declined, having barely yet tasted our own.

She refilled her own glass, then sat again before us and sighed deeply. 'Only *I* have seen Charles's ghost. *Everyone* has seen the ghost in the East Wing where you stay. You must take care.'

'Madam, thank you, we have been warned. But of this other ghost?' said Holmes.

'A servant died near your rooms, you know. Fell down the stairwell.' She leaned to her right towards a small marble-topped table which rested next to her chair. On it were three cloisonné vases, each containing a sprig of rosemary. She took two sprigs out, and held them up. 'Rosemary,' said she, handing one to each of us.

Her hand lingered on Holmes's own as she gave it to him. He flinched almost imperceptibly.

Catherine laughed. 'Really, Mr Holmes. There is something of the schoolboy about you. Take it.'

He waved the offering away and stood up. 'Excuse me, madam. Rosemary does not agree with me.' Nor do ghosts, I thought. As he moved away, he threw me a frowning glance that I understood only too well.

'Madam, thank you,' I said, and pocketed both Holmes's and my own small gifts. 'Rosemary for remembrance?' I asked, hoping to distract. A vision of daft Ophelia came to mind.

'No! Rosemary protects against ghosts,' said Catherine McLaren. 'They think me mad. But it has been a tradition at Braedern for a hundred years.' She took another drink, emptying the second glass. She held it aloft. 'Pour me another, Mr Holmes, while you are standing.'

To my surprise, Holmes brought the decanter back with him, filling her glass and unnecessarily adding more to each of our own. I wondered at the wisdom of this, but the lady seemed mollified. She raised her glass to us in a toast, and we followed suit.

'Carry that with you at all times,' she admonished, pointing at the rosemary which now protruded jauntily from my pocket.

'Mrs McLaren, we will take care, I assure you,' said Holmes, resuming his seat facing the lady. 'But of this ghost in Charles's rooms – does it not frighten Charles as well?'

'Charles claims never to have seen a ghost in his rooms. He calls me mad! I am not! But the ghost in his room – she is young, and female – serves him well. It keeps his wife away. I will never venture . . .' Mrs McLaren's eyes closed, she swayed slightly in her chair, and I put out a hand to steady her. The lady turned her full attention to me. 'Doctor Watson, you will understand. You have a great sympathy for the ladies, or so I observe. Charles and I—he used to take me everywhere. To London. To Pa—to Paris sometimes to view the collections. I—we— . . .' Her voice caught and a tear rolled down her pale cheek.

Instantly Holmes pulled a handkerchief from his pocket and offered it to her.

'Mrs McLaren, it is inconceivable to me that he would wish to distance himself from you,' said Holmes, the soul of sympathy.

I had removed my handkerchief to offer it as well, but it went unremarked and I mopped my own forehead instead. The fire was stifling, and I perspired in my winter woollens, made worse by the warming effect of that same fine whisky she had pressed upon us.

The lady dabbed at her eyes. 'I am sure he wished to

spend more time with Fiona, and others. Oh, Mr Holmes, you were right about Charles in Antibes. But I am right about the ghosts. I know you do not believe. But—'

'If madam will allow me to continue,' said Holmes in his most conciliatory of tones. 'You are a very observant lady. I wonder if perhaps you may in fact be the most observant member of the family? Who had reason to hate Fiona Paisley?'

The most observant? Why did he flatter her so, I wondered.

'I had reason! But I would never hurt the girl. At first I was angry but with Charles, all things pass. And yes, I am observant. Why, yes. Yes, I am!' Her words were slurred, and she struggled to focus as she addressed Holmes. 'I observe that you are nervous in my presence. That you are drinking nothing. Is it my deshabille? Is it simply that I am a woman? Well, no matter. I observe that you, sir, are in need of some work.'

Holmes cleared his throat but did not respond to this odd comment. Instead, he smiled at her in his friendliest manner. 'Why do you think Fiona was interested in your husband? I would be extremely grateful to hear your thoughts, Mrs McLaren.'

'Hmm. Conquest? Amusement? Fiona Paisley was a forward girl . . . but what a terrible end.' Catherine McLaren's words were slurred. 'She . . . her head . . . Laird Robert, he was the most upset of all the family, did you not think?' Holmes nodded. 'It was someone who hated the laird. Hated Sir Robert. Thass what I think.'

'I quite agree, madam.'

She began to ramble. 'But who might have done, well, that could be a lot of people. But, no. Most of them are dead.' She leaned back against the cushions. 'Perhaps Charles did it.' Her head lolled back and she closed her eyes. Her dressing gown gaped ominously.

Holmes shot me a look of mock horror. 'Really madam! Your own husband? Has he reason to hate his father?'

She spoke with her eyes closed. 'Yes and no. But if he killed her, no good reason, really. Act of in—of sudden agg— anger, not planned. That little trumpe—rum —scallop probably demanded something. They were together, yes of course, I knew. Yes, that sounds right. It might have been him.'

'So you think she may have been killed by Charles? A sudden act, before you left for France, then?'

She answered without opening her eyes. 'It is possible. He is an impala . . . imply . . . he just acts.'

'Impulsive. I see. And yet it took a lot of planning to freeze her head and send it down to the South of France. Cutting off a head is not a casual act.'

She murmured in the affirmative. Suddenly she sat forward and her eyes flew open. 'Have you seen his rooms?'

'Not yet,' said Holmes. 'Why?'

She giggled. I will admit a deep sense of unease at this woman and her chaotic demeanour. Holmes, however, seemed quite focused on her.

'Watch yourselves, there!' she said. Her head went back

and her eyes shut once more. I took the whisky glass from her limp hand from which it threatened to fall.

'Charles seemed as shocked as anyone. It is the motive and method for the beheading that puzzles me most,' said Holmes.

She continued to talk from behind closed eyes. 'Charles does not have the backbuh . . . back break . . . stomach for that,' she said. 'Someone else, p'rhaps. Coupe? That terribly handsome man? He wanted Charles's job. Everyone wants something here.' She opened her eyes and peered blearily at Holmes. 'Oh, you tire me enormously. You are very thin. Go away.' She waved us off.

I will admit to a pang of guilt as we descended the tower back towards the Great Hall. 'My God, Holmes, do you think it is safe to leave her in such a state? And you encouraged the lady!'

'She would be in precisely the same state with or without our visit, Watson.'

'I suppose so. But her theories were so preposterous. She was so drunk it is hard to give credence—'

'*In vino veritas*, Watson. When spirits rob a person of inhibition, it is often the case that the truth spills forth.'

'Do you mean about Charles? About Coupe?'

'Well, what else could I mean?' he said testily. 'I think the lady spoke what is, to her, the truth. And I did not lie about her gift of observation. It is often the most observant who find the need to soften the harshness of reality with artificial means.'

As Holmes himself did, with morphine or cocaine, I

thought. He was now walking so fast, I nearly had to break into a run. 'What is the hurry?' I called out.

If I did not know Holmes as well as I did, I might have thought that Catherine McLaren's more personal comments had stung him. *In vino veritas.*

CHAPTER 18

Charles

oon after, Charles McLaren met us in the front hallway of the building, as we were warned that his rooms were difficult to find. Located, as his wife had told us, in the North Tower, they sat at some distance from hers, and quite close to his father's quarters. They had been formerly his mother's private rooms.

Like his brother and father, Charles was tall and powerfully built. His dark, curly auburn hair was worn unfashionably long in the style of our fathers' era. A thick moustache and wild eyebrows gave him a bear-like appearance. The dazzling smile he bestowed upon us could not hide the hostility and arrogance simmering beneath the surface. While he was dressed impeccably in modern attire, there was something warrior-like about Charles's demeanour, as if the ghost of a tartan kilt flapped about his legs, and a spear lay hidden somewhere nearby.

And, as Mrs McLaren had just suggested, there hung the means of beheading a person several times over. Indeed, a formidable collection of antique weapons did line the walls of his luxurious chambers, including any number of knives and swords, shields, a gigantic crossbow and other military relics of both recent and distant origin. And of course, there was the requisite collection of decanters waiting on a sideboard.

Whisky glasses in hand, we soon stood near a fireplace, above which was festooned a bizarre, complex array of stag antlers and more hunting knives. Holmes had begun the interview by effusively complimenting the man on his recent success in expanding the McLaren whisky business.

'It is true!' exclaimed Charles. 'I have done what few could have done. I have gone up against the mighty Buchanan in London to secure some of the more lucrative contracts in the city. And I have doubled our production, without sacrificing quality, I may add. We have gone from being merely a source whisky for the insipid blends of our southern counterparts to producing the best self whisky in the world, if not *yet* the best selling – in my humble opinion, of course. We will shortly unveil our coup de grace, McLaren Garnet, and we expect with this remarkable new whisky to achieve no less than a warrant to supply the Royal Household.'

Humility clearly had no place in this man's worldview. But a Royal Warrant! Every distillery in Scotland must covet that distinction on their labels.

'Laird Robert must be pleased with your accomplishments,' said Holmes.

'I know my father thinks I am doing a better job than Donal ever would have done. There is no question, none could do it better.'

'He compliments you on this?'

'Well, not aloud. It is not our way. But I am aware of his feelings of pride.'

Holmes took out his pipe and felt absentmindedly in his pockets for tobacco. 'Of course, your brother Alistair has been of some help to you, has he not, in some way or other?' I became aware that he had launched into the guise of fumbling, an effective ruse I had witnessed in the past.

'Ha! Alistair may tell you so. But it was I who demanded the increase in output and even suggested its method. My younger brother lacks imagination and flair. He is like a plough horse, strong enough to hoe the rows, or tweak the distillery with his minor inventions, but he is so consumed with detail that he little sees the importance of big ideas.'

'A curious metaphor,' said Holmes, finally arriving at the package of shag in his pocket. He began to stuff the bowl of his pipe. At Charles's frown, he added, 'Do you mind?' asked he, distractedly.

Charles shook his head impatiently. 'If you must. Continue.'

Holmes managed to drop some shag onto the carpet. 'Ah! Sorry.' He stooped to gather it up, bumping into a nearby table as he did so, setting an ornate lamp asway and some papers tumbling to the ground. 'Careful!' Charles quickly grasped the lamp, a rather garish stained glass affair, and kept it from falling. Holmes fumbled with the papers,

215

replaced them on the table with an awkward smile and continued to feel in his pocket for matches.

'Devil take it. My apologies. Have you a match, Watson?' Holmes then smiled at Charles McLaren. 'And your wife, Mrs McLaren, has she long had trouble with the drink?'

The man's face darkened. He took a sip of his own whisky. 'Of what relevance is this question?'

'I do not know what is relevant until I view everything,' said Holmes. 'Pray be patient, and tell me of your wife, please.'

Charles grunted, refilled his glass and took a large sip. I handed Holmes my matches.

'Catherine was a fair young lass with great promise, socially, when I married her. Her problems with the drink, come, I think, from her mother's side, as does her ridiculous belief in ghosts. Ach, the woman is a loss.'

'You no longer take her to London, do you?' asked Holmes as he now fumbled awkwardly to light his pipe.

'Social life is very important in London if one is to get ahead, but of course you understand that, as a man about town yourself.'

I coughed, and Holmes shot me a severe look. I cleared my throat.

'My Cathy was an asset when I first began, beautiful as she was, but as the drink began to take hold this asset became a liability. If she were a man, I would have fired her. As it was, I merely left her here.'

Holmes nodded. 'I have observed her difficulties.'

'The drinking is a weakness, certainly, but with support some have overcome the curse,' I said.

Charles turned a cold stare upon me. 'And who are you to judge me? The woman has a defect in her construction that I cannot influence. Have you ever attempted to wean someone from destructive, habitual comforts?'

How little you know, I thought, but said nothing.

Holmes began to pace, growing in concentration. 'How long have you been in these rooms?' he asked.

'Not long, a few months perhaps.'

'You have an impressive collection,' said Holmes, waving absentmindedly towards the gleaming weaponry.

I recognized several claymores and what I thought might be a halberd. 'What is this one?' I wondered, pointing to a kind of axe with a hook on the back, and long pieces of metal extending along the sides down from the blade onto one third of the shaft.

'That is a Lochaber axe, Watson,' said Holmes.

Charles smiled. 'Well done, Mr Holmes. And a keen piece of weaponry she is. Gets them coming and going. And clever, these long pieces of metal, down the sides,' he said, with pride.

'Langets, I believe they are called,' said Holmes. 'Prevents the head from being cut off.'

'The head?' I stammered, aghast.

'Of the weapon, Watson,' smiled Holmes.

'Exactly. You know your Scottish weaponry,' said Charles, reaching for the dastardly object. 'Want to heft her?' Holmes shook his head and Charles replaced it easily on the wall. 'How is it that you know this detail?' Charles persisted. I was wondering the same thing myself.

'I attended school briefly in Edinburgh,' said Holmes.
Ah, of course.

'Where?' asked Charles.

Holmes sighed. 'Fettes. But that is neither here nor there.'

'An acquaintance went to Fettes,' said Charles. 'Rigorous place. Not for the faint of heart. Made men of boys, they say. You do not seem the type, Mr Holmes, no insult intended. I thought it was mainly Foundation pupils.'

'Not entirely,' said Holmes. 'Beautiful claymore,' he remarked, indicating another fierce weapon. 'But let us continue, Mr McLaren, with the subject at hand. What exactly was your relationship with Fiona Paisley?'

'She was beautiful and forward, and pressed herself upon every male member of the household,' he murmured, taking a long sip of his drink. He smacked his lips, a most unpleasant sound.

'Pressed herself?'

'Flirted, Mr Holmes. A crafty girl. Many of us fell under her spell.'

'And did you press back?' Holmes asked.

'Do not be vulgar, sir. The girl offered herself, if not directly, then indirectly, by her manner, her words, the way she dressed. As I have mentioned, my marriage bed is a cold one. If I dallied with her, or with anyone for that matter, nary a soul could blame me. I will tell you this, though, I did not kill the girl.'

'Did I suggest you did?'

'I tell you I did not.'

'Who do you think did?'

'I have my theories.'

'May I hear them?' said Holmes.

'My wife is both jealous and vindictive. She is my first thought. But she has not the nerve, nor the organisation to do so. And then, of course, Cameron Coupe. He thought to be put in charge of the distillery instead of myself.'

'Did he then? He presumed he might take precedence over a family member?'

'Who knows? Although it could very well be my brother, Alistair. He is, shall we say, less noticed by the ladies, and is sorely jealous of me. I believe he may be the only male to have been turned down by that feisty little minx.'

I shuddered at his words. No respect for the dead here.

'It seems you have no theory, after all, Mr McLaren,' remarked Holmes. 'You say Alistair is not beloved of the ladies?'

Charles shrugged dismissively. I thought briefly of Alistair's beautiful and intelligent wife Isla and wondered at this man's deluded thinking.

'Perhaps he is jealous because you have the running of the business?' Holmes said.

'Yes. Alistair, too, assumed it would go to him.'

'Why? You are the elder.'

'He has made a study of our business since childhood, and further with organic chemistry at University. He fancies himself both an engineer, and a master of all pertaining to the making of whisky. Tries to invent things.'

'I see. That explains a certain resentment. But in regards to Fiona, is he not happily married?'

'Happily!' Charles bellowed a laugh. 'To that usurping harpie?'

'Isla McLaren? What do you mean?'

'Well, have you not noticed? She presumes to have the intelligence and judgement of a man, and will not hesitate to let you know at every turn. She is tiresome in the extreme. The more fool my brother for marrying her.'

'And was Alistair dallying with Fiona?' asked Holmes.

'Perhaps not. But I am sure he made the attempt to "scale her ramparts".'

'How can you be sure?'

'I caught them once, whispering together in the halls one night. Alistair was attempting to force his attentions on her. She, in turn, was fending him off.'

If what the man said were true, I felt a pang of concern for Isla McLaren.

'*En flagrante*, then? You would think Alistair would choose his time and place with more discretion,' said Holmes.

Charles laughed. 'My brother lacks finesse.'

'Do you think the same person who kidnapped Fiona and cut off her hair was the one who killed her?'

'I have no idea. Why not?'

'Well, the first was clearly a warning, a shot fired across the bow,' said Holmes. 'The second act smacks of retribution.'

'I suppose if you put it that way,' said Charles.

'Otherwise why not simply kill her the first time?'

'I have no idea. Mr Holmes, this interview tires me. I do not know who killed the girl, and while what happened in the Hôtel du Cap was shocking, frankly her story interests me very little.'

'Your response when the head was revealed indicates otherwise, Mr McLaren.'

'Well, it was repulsive, that is all.'

'You had feelings for this girl,' Holmes stated with some force.

'No, I—'

'Do not lie to me, Mr McLaren. It is obvious.'

'You are seeing things that are not there. Rather like my wife, Mr Holmes. Do you see apparitions in the night? They are often visible in the East Tower where you are staying.' Charles's tone was mocking.

'You do not believe in ghosts, Mr McLaren?'

'Pah! Old wives' tales. It is a country filled with ghosts if you listen to the uneducated.'

'I see you keep rosemary by your bed,' said Holmes nodding towards the open doorway into Charles's bedchamber.

'My wife puts it there.'

'She comes into your rooms, and places it there?'

'Well, no. I do not allow her in here. And she is afraid. A servant does it for her.'

'I see. And you leave it?'

'I like the scent.'

'Mmm. Your wife cares for you. Looks after you, does she? Despite being spurned from your company?' persisted Holmes.

'Well if you must insist on this indiscretion, Mr Holmes, I visit her occasionally. It is an arrangement that suits me well. I am a busy man but I make time for her even so. And this, despite her despicable habit.'

His own row of decanters gleamed in the light from an electric sconce. The master of a distillery denigrating his own wife for drink seemed the height of hypocrisy to me. I set my empty glass on the table.

Shortly after, the interview concluded and we made our way back to the Great Hall. We were alone in the cavernous space. We stood near the large stone fireplace where we first saw Mrs Isla McLaren and the laird upon our arrival. The dwindling fire gave out a faint warmth.

'I like Charles McLaren not at all,' I said.

'Nor I,' said Holmes.

'What did you find there?' I asked. 'Something on the table?'

Holmes smiled and took from his pocket a folded pamphlet. It was a monograph on the new forms of dynamite, published by the Nobel company. On it were some handwritten notes.

'Could these be Dr Janvier's looped "t"s?' mused Holmes. At my puzzled look, he reminded me of the threatening missives that Dr Paul-Édouard Janvier had received in Montpellier – and the single detail of handwriting that he could recall – the one that assured him that all the letters were from the same individual.

'Those threats could have come from Charles, then,' I said.

'They may well have, but without the originals to compare, I cannot be sure. Watson, these waters grow ever deeper. The degree of obfuscation in this family exceeds even my expectations.'

CHAPTER 19

The Laird's Sanctum

s we pondered our next interview, a liveried servant arrived to bid us to the laird's chambers to complete our interview with our host and client. We duly made our way to the South Tower.

Laird Robert's quarters displayed a subtle wealth beyond all the others. The stone walls had been covered alternately by carved wood panels and medieval tapestries. The combination of electric lights, which seemed to have been laid on randomly throughout the castle twinkled here, and a blazing fire and silver candelabra added a warm glow. Thick oriental carpets hushed our footfalls.

On a side table near a window were the ever-present whisky decanters. The room conveyed immense wealth, taste, and masculinity untempered by the soft touch of a woman. There was a peculiar lack of personal items – no books, pictures, stationery.

The laird emerged from his bedroom, now in evening attire. He seemed distracted.

'Have a seat, gentlemen, but we must be efficient. I will not be joining you at dinner. I am called away suddenly this evening, to Balmoral. It is an hour from here and I must leave shortly.'

'The royal residence!' said Holmes. 'That is propitious!'

The laird nodded. 'The invitation is sudden, but long awaited. I feel certain that if I can manage to get one of the family, or at least the Master of the Queen's Cellars or the Lord Chamberlain, to visit and taste, the Royal Warrant will be ours.'

'Yes, Charles alluded to your hopes riding on the McLaren Garnet,' said Holmes.

'There is no finer whisky.'

'Then you are pleased with Charles's management of the business?'

The laird had poured us each a dram without enquiring whether we wanted any. He handed them to us and took a chair opposite ours next to the fire. I took a small sip. This was the fourth interview with whisky. A wave of sleepiness washed over me and I put the glass down. I can normally drink with any man but even I had begun to feel outmatched.

The laird sighed. 'Charles has obtained some lucrative contracts, and a certain presence in London. However he lacks judgement at times and is unaware of his own failings.'

'And what might those be?'

'They are legion. For one, he has not the technical skills.'

'And the younger, Alistair? Does he possess those skills?'

'He does. He has doubled our production in the last two years.'

225

Holmes and I exchanged a glance. Charles had neatly taken the credit for that.

'And yet you awarded the stewardship to Charles?' said Holmes.

The laird took a sip of whisky. I could see that the subject was an uncomfortable one for him.

'Alistair, despite his gifts, lacks finesse.'

'But paired with his highly intelligent wife?' prompted Holmes.

'Isla is impressive, I will agree. But I am of the opinion that women are not capable of running a business.'

'Really?' said Holmes. 'I understand that Cardhu distillery in Speyside is doing well, with a Mrs Elisabeth Cummings at the helm since her husband died.'

'You are well informed. But she is the exception to the rule.'

Holmes rose from his chair and, abandoning his libation, began to wander the room, idly, it seemed. The laird, however, was no fool. By now he understood the detective seldom did anything without a reason.

'What interests you there, Mr Holmes?'

Holmes now stood over a table on which large blueprints had been spread, and was glancing at them with casual interest.

'I see you are planning an expansion of the distillery,' he murmured.

'I am. It is hardly a secret. Why?'

'Will you be using dynamite to prepare the grounds, to level part of it perhaps?'

'It is rocky land. Dynamite is a necessity.'

'That explains it!' exclaimed Holmes, straightening. 'I am so relieved.'

'What do you mean?'

'There is a large cache of dynamite in a secret, locked room of your garden shed. I say "secret" in jest, as any number of people here know about it.'

'What? I—well of course we keep it on hand. I shall look into its security. But why exactly does this *relieve* you Mr Holmes?'

'It relieves me that you have good reason for its presence. Were you aware that during your family's stay at the Hôtel du Cap, a large explosion occurred in Montpellier?'

'No, I was not.'

'The laboratory of the French horticulturalist, Paul-Édouard Janvier, was bombed. He is the leading researcher in his field. Fortunately, no one was hurt.'

'And why is this of relevance to me?'

Holmes eyed the laird with a cold stare, one eyebrow raised. 'You are surely aware of Dr Janvier, and his work combating the phylloxera epidemic. You are also no doubt aware of the suspicion with which the French government regards the British on this matter, and in particular three families, of which the McLarens take precedence.'

'This means nothing to me,' said the laird. 'Why would I—'

'Please do not waste my time, Sir Robert. I know you have been questioned on the matter. Dr Janvier has been receiving threatening letters. The device used recently was

227

the same make and type as your dynamite. This is a very new product from Nobel. It has extremely limited distribution at this point. Charles had a monograph about this dynamite in his room. In fact, your son—'

'We use dynamite in construction, as I have just explained.'

'As to the bombing in Montpellier, your family have motive, and were nearby when it occurred.'

'That is hardly compelling evidence, Mr Holmes. Circumstantial, I believe you call it.'

'True,' said Holmes. He continued to stare at the laird.

The older man finished his whisky and put down the glass abruptly. 'Let me elucidate. Yes, the troubles with the French wine industry have opened the door to the expansion of Scottish whisky markets. But as for someone here causing the phylloxera disaster? Impractical, if not impossible. Surely you agree?'

'I do,' said Holmes. 'But delaying the cure might well help to extend your business development.'

'It seems a foolhardy venture, Mr Holmes. Do I look like a foolish man to you?'

'You do not. Nevertheless, this must be examined. Even your daughter-in-law Isla is alert to these implications.'

'I cannot control what the French think! Or my daughter-in-law either.'

I suppressed a laugh, and the smallest smile passed over Holmes's face, then was gone.

The laird did not share in our amusement. 'I can assure you I had nothing to do with this incident, nor can I imagine

Charles doing so. I would not risk my reputation or my family with such a cowardly act.'

'Well, that is good to hear. No reason to worry about this particular dynamite then,' said Holmes. 'Nor the threatening notes that have been received by Dr Janvier.'

'Nor those, either. May I suggest that you confine yourself to the case for which you were hired, Mr Holmes. Find out who killed Fiona and sent her . . . sent her . . .'

'Sir Robert, I will do whatever necessary in order to understand what happened to Miss Paisley. The appearance of her head on a platter at the hotel is, I admit, still opaque to the light of reason. Now, if you do not mind, as I said I would need to, I will examine your bedchamber.'

'I must depart soon, Mr Holmes. Please do so in haste.'

The second room was only slightly smaller than the first. It held thick velvet curtains lined with a tartan wool and an ornate bedstead, with a gilded picture frame above the bed containing a sweeping Highland landscape.

Once again, there were few personal touches. My eyes landed at last on a small silver frame set on the nightstand. I picked it up. It was a daguerreotype of a young man who sported a profusion of dark hair, a pronounced chin, and a bold, uncompromising stare.

It could well have been the laird himself as a young man. I handed it to Holmes who regarded it with interest.

'Donal,' said the laird quietly. 'My eldest. Lost at Khartoum.'

'Ah,' said Holmes. 'And so buried there, I assume?'

There was a pause. 'No bodies were recovered,' said the laird simply.

'I presume Donal attended university before his army service?'

'Why, Camford, the same as yourself, Mr Holmes. Though Donal was older. Perhaps you met there?'

'No,' said Holmes. He did not bother to conceal his own irritation. 'You have researched me, I see.'

'It is my way, Mr Holmes. I understood you left under something of a cloud of controversy.' The laird's dark eyes bored into my friend with an icy concentration. I was surprised that anyone had heard of this besides myself, and even I had learned of it only recently.

Holmes took no notice. 'Back to Donal, if you would,' said he. 'This portrait on your nightstand speaks of deep affection.'

'I will admit it, Donal was my favourite. One wishes not to have preferences but it is unavoidable. It was Donal who most resembled me. He did have a temper, but in spite of this it was he who was best suited to carry on the business of this estate. I had high hopes for the boy.'

'I recall reading about that temper,' said Holmes. 'A newspaper in Aberdeen reported that he once beat a servant.'

'Insolent fellow, he baited my boy and had it coming. But still, inappropriate. Had Donal lived, time would have mellowed him.'

'That report said the man was "nearly beaten to death".'

'That was grossly exaggerated.' In a brusque move, the

laird retrieved the picture from Holmes and replaced it on his nightstand. 'I put Donal's indiscretions down to youthful vociferousness and energy. That is all.'

'If Donal was intended by you to take over the distillery, how did he end up in the army, if I may be so bold?' asked Holmes.

The man looked down at the floor a moment. 'It was to remove him from some small troubles caused by another. A few years after Camford. I used my influence to get him a commission in the Guards. It was intended to be a more of a ceremonial posting, you understand, for two or three years. To my surprise he seemed to take to the life, and chose to stay on . . . and it ended in tragedy.' The laird consulted his pocket watch. 'But let us attend to the matter in hand, Mr Holmes.'

Holmes sighed, then moved from the bedside to a window, drew the curtain and looked out. 'The weather has taken a nasty turn.' He let the curtain fall and turned back to our host. I expected him to terminate the interview. But instead, he started on an entirely new tack.

'And your late wife Elizabeth? She was a beautiful woman by all accounts,' said he.

'Aye,' said the laird, his voice dropping to a whisper. 'That she was. But what do the late members of my family have to do with the present issue?'

'And yet there are no portraits of her here, in your room. Nor of your daughter, Anne.'

The laird flushed slowly to the roots of his hair. His face reflected a changing parade of strong emotions. He turned

231

abruptly from us and strode to a second window, looking out at the gathering storm.

'Mr Holmes. There are things I simply do not wish to contemplate on a daily basis. The death of my wife is one. And little Anne—'

'I am told she disappeared from the nursery one night as a young child.'

'Not quite three years old. One moment she was asleep in her bed. The next, gone. The nurse was beside herself with guilt over it.'

'A search was undertaken?'

'For days.'

'Could the child have wandered off? Are there wells?'

'She was but three. Every avenue was searched, every possibility examined. And no, no wells.'

'There was no note, no ransom demand?'

'None. Elizabeth was . . . she was inconsolable. Returned every evening to check on her remaining children after that and remained through the night. A thorough investigation proved fruitless. Our little daughter simply vanished.'

'Perhaps it was a kidnapping gone wrong. Had you received threats?'

'None. I cannot bear the thought of harm having come to the child. I hold the fond hope that she was kidnapped and lives on. Healthy. Happy. Somewhere. I had the nursery redone to accommodate guests after my wife's death and moved the boys to their own rooms, elsewhere.'

'And so you choose to expunge the memory of your wife and daughter by removing all traces of them?'

'I do not see how his can relate to the case.'

'Humour me, sir.'

'Those memories are tinged with pain, Mr Holmes. Have you no ghosts from your past that you wish to keep separate from your present?'

'Do you believe in actual ghosts, Laird McLaren? Ones who roam the halls?' asked Holmes, avoiding the question put to him.

'Why? Of course not.'

'What of the sightings of your late wife in the East Wing? It is said her unquiet spirit returns with a vengeance. Why?'

'The servants will believe any nonsense.'

'But why would she be vengeful?'

'I suppose they think she seeks to understand Anne's disappearance. She was angry at the time and felt it had not been sufficiently investigated. I assure you it was.'

'But what of her own death some time later? She was locked out on a freezing night?' asked Holmes.

'It was an accident. A tragedy I must live with for the rest of my life. The outer doors had only recently been secured, the bell malfunctioned, and no one heard her attempts to enter.'

'So we are told. What of her own people? Were there no questions asked?'

The laird sighed. 'Mr Holmes, you torture me unnecessarily. My wife had no family of her own. Elizabeth was orphaned by then. No siblings. The police ruling was clear; death by misadventure. I fail to understand your reasoning at this juncture. I must bring this interview to a close or

233

risk being late. If there are more questions, you may find me tomorrow.'

Holmes nodded, but made no move to leave. Outside the drumming of what sounded like hail had begun to fall on the stone battlements and, presumably, the gargoyles that I had noticed adorning the outside of this area of the castle. A sudden wind blew one of the windows open, and the heavy velvet draperies swayed inward into the room.

The laird moved to the window and bolted it. 'Ah. My wife would have taken that as a sign.'

'And you perceive it as what?' said Holmes.

'The weather,' said the laird. 'Now, gentlemen, supper will be served soon, and I must make haste.'

CHAPTER 20

Reviewing the Situation

ome fifteen minutes later I was alone in my room dressing for dinner, with a vow to drink no more whisky that night, when I heard Holmes's familiar sharp rap on my door. He entered, glanced at my formal attire, and smiled. He was wearing his dressing gown and slippers, pipe in hand.

'Holmes!' I cried. 'We are expected in ten minutes for supper!'

'Please convey my apologies, Watson. I am going to remain in my room to think. I have sent down for some soup. You can say I am feeling unwell. But do keep your eyes and ears open.'

'*Are* you feeling unwell?' I asked.

'Only fatigued. And I have much to ponder.' As I continued to dress, he perched himself on a large armchair by the fire and stared into the flames, his legs drawn in close, his pipe glowing. It was a posture I had seen before and I knew it signalled a serious session of brain-work.

'Holmes,' said I, struggling with my tie as I peered into a veined and silvered antique mirror which reflected only a blur, 'What I cannot understand is the motive behind sending Fiona's head to the South of France. It seems that several people had reason to wish the girl dead, but why go to the bizarre lengths of transporting it there?'

'Agreed. It is most puzzling. Such an act speaks of deep-seated hatred. It was meant to stun, to hurt, to wound someone on the receiving end. The act was cold and calculating; it took much planning and complex execution.'

'Perhaps if we could find the messenger—'

'I think not, Watson. It was most likely a hired hand, possibly unconnected to anyone else in this drama, and the disguise and the cold trail leave us few options to pursue. I wager the deliverer did not know the exact contents of the package.'

'Yet he knew to keep it cold.' I could not see to make the tie behave and squinted into the mirror.

'Yes, but that could be explained, a perishable comestible for example. In any case, it would have been delivered to the family as a gift, and the bribes ensured a reasonable chance of it arriving as intended. Expensive luxuries are often sent to hotels of that kind. We are seeking someone with a long simmering animosity, and a sadistic nature. Our investigation thus far has disclosed a nest of vipers, of jealousies and intrigue here at Braedern. Fiona's head was a message intended for someone in the family. Consider their reactions.'

'Well, it was shocking enough to horrify everyone, Holmes.'

'Yes. But I thought that the laird was most seriously wounded. And now that his paternity is confirmed – I will admit that it was an immediate theory of mine – he was clearly the most affected there. Many have reason to hate him. First there is his mysteriously departed wife. Can we be sure there are none who wish to avenge her? Both sons feel out of favour. Then there is Cameron Coupe, who by all accounts should have the running of the place – and who apparently thought little or nothing of kidnapping and shaving the girl.'

'But even the laird himself is not free of suspicion,' said I. 'Could he not have planned all of this to rid himself of an inconvenient daughter, and at the same time pin it on another person who might be giving him trouble?'

'Bravo, Watson, your theories improve. It is possible, but if so, he is a remarkable actor. Did you notice that he was not surprised that threatening notes had been sent to Dr Janvier? How would he know this? But I digress. On the subject of Fiona, we cannot discount him yet, but my instincts run counter to this theory. We must also look at the persons least affected by the head.'

My bow tie eluded my efforts a third time. 'Devil take it, Holmes. Tie this for me, will you? It is difficult to see in here.'

He got up, squinted, and moved me into better light. As he managed the recalcitrant tie for me, I realized how dim the room was. The corners were shrouded in darkness, and while electric light had been laid in various parts of the castle, it apparently had not in this tower.

Hail continued to rattle on the exterior of the castle, the wind moaned outside and with the draught, various candles around the room flickered and the curtains moved on the wall. I shuddered.

Holmes chuckled. 'Steady, Watson.'

'Merely a draught. A chill.'

He patted me on the arm and resumed his seat by the fire. I continued with my cufflinks.

'There was one person who reacted least to the delivery of the head, Watson, surely you noticed this?'

'Isla McLaren, do you mean? I would not describe her as having had no reaction. I looked to her immediately and I would be prepared to swear that it came as a severe and horrifying surprise.'

'Yes, followed, however by a remarkably quick recovery.'

'True, but what would be her motive? Holmes, I cannot believe—'

'We should not eliminate anyone at this point. Think, Watson.'

I pondered this. I liked Isla McLaren and had been impressed by her intelligence, humour and desire to help. But I knew that this perhaps clouded my thinking on the matter. I tried to apply Holmes's pragmatic approach to this question.

'Hmm. It is hard to imagine. Perhaps if she could somehow pin this on Charles and have him removed from his position, her husband Alistair might be given the running of the distillery?'

'Possibly. What else? Never be satisfied with only one theory, Watson.'

'I do not know, then! Jealousy, perhaps? I do not sense it from her, though.'

A sudden draught extinguished the candle next to Holmes and he was now silhouetted by the fire. He remained silent.

'All right. I do have another theory,' I offered. 'Could this . . . no, that is a preposterous idea.'

'Relight the candles, would you? Go ahead, speak it. While you may not glow brightly yourself, Watson, our conversations do occasionally serve to illuminate my own processes.'

I sighed and lit a match. He had made a similar remark during our Dartmoor adventure, but I decided to focus on the faint compliment behind the sentiment. 'Well, here is an alternate motive,' said I, 'one that paid off handsomely. What if the entire reason was to get *you* to come to Braedern?'

Holmes swivelled to face me in surprise.

'It certainly worked,' I added.

He took his pipe from his mouth and saluted me with it. 'Why, you are absolutely correct, Watson!'

I smiled.

'It *is* a preposterous idea.'

Just as he said this, the candles on the table next to him blew out again, and the room was plunged into total darkness.

PART FOUR

A CHILL DESCENDS

'But do none of us believe in ghosts? If this question be read at noon-day, when every little corner, nook, and hole is penetrated with the insolent light – at such a time derision is seated on the features of my reader. But let it be twelve at night in a lone house . . .'

—Mary Shelley

CHAPTER 21

Dinner

he dining room of the castle was adjacent to the Great Hall. It, too, was a gothic stone wonder, the walls dotted with a combination of massive oil paintings of moody Scottish landscapes, mounted animal heads, and fanciful brass electrical lighting sconces, all turned down low so that the primary sources of light were the multiple silver candelabra down the centre of a long table. Seven places had been set at one end.

The polished dark wood floor was laid over with an expensive tartan rug in muted colours. Ever since the Queen had established her residence at Balmoral and publicly embraced all things Scottish, the use of Highland motifs had come into vogue. Even in Scotland, apparently.

Isla came up behind me as I took in the room.

'Are you enjoying our Highland hospitality, Doctor?' she asked.

'I have had little time to do so,' I said. 'We have been hard at work since we arrived.'

'So I have heard. I have been awaiting my turn to be interrogated by The Great Detective. I confess I am surprised you did not question me first.'

'It is not up to me. However I know Mr Holmes is looking forward to speaking with you.' In fact he had expressed the opposite to me, earlier.

'Dr Watson, I do think that I could be of help to you.'

'And I agree,' I said with a smile.

The lady looked past me to the Great Hall.

'Where is he, by the way?'

'I am afraid he is indisposed, Mrs McLaren.'

She stared into my eyes with that disconcerting penetration. 'Nothing serious, I hope?'

'Not at all, madam. Perhaps he will join us for coffee later.' I knew that this was unlikely.

'Hmm,' she said, and took her seat at the table, allowing me to hold out her chair.

The various family members took their places one by one. I was directed to a seat between Charles and Alistair McLaren. Facing me were Isla McLaren and her sister-in-law Catherine, with a seat left vacant between them for Holmes.

I passed along Holmes's regrets which were met with a snort by Charles, and a knowing smile from Alistair. It was my first glimpse of the younger brother since the South of France. His supercilious attitude had not shifted at all. While his intelligence was in evidence, and a sharp contrast to his brother, his arrogant expression never seemed to waiver.

Holmes had evidently been positioned so that they could

observe him. But once I had given his apologies, I was moved to his chair and my old place setting was swiftly removed.

The laird's ornately carved seat at the head of the table, however, remained empty, yet with its place set. Was it possible that the household did not know of his trip to Balmoral? Several servants stood at attention along the wall, awaiting signal to begin. It was at this point that I realized Holmes and I had not stopped for lunch.

Charles gave the servants the signal, and announced 'Sir Robert will not be joining us tonight. He has been called to Balmoral for a meeting with the Lord Chamberlain.' Murmurs of pleased surprise came from the ladies. I sensed Alistair already knew.

'Charles!' said Catherine to her husband. 'Is a Royal Warrant at last under consideration?'

Charles flashed her a look of annoyance. 'It is. And, if all goes well, the family will accept our invitation to sample the new McLaren Garnet. It was intended as a 21 year but has matured beautifully at 18.'

'Congratulations,' said I.

'Or at least casks 12, 51, 253, 647, and 895 have done so,' remarked Alistair. At my puzzled look, he turned to me. 'Those are our samplers. I have detected a larger than usual inconsistency in this edition.'

'How can there be a difference among the casks of a single edition of whisky?' I wondered.

'Many variables. An accident of wood, previous contents, amount of charring inside the cask, position in the maturation warehouse, small variations in the distilling process, any number of things may affect flavour.'

'Then how do you sell a—what do you call an unblended whisky?'

'A "self whisky" is our term.'

'How do you create a run of "self whisky" with any consistency?'

'At the end of maturation, we vat them all together before bottling,' said Alistair.

'And flavourings can be added,' said Charles.

Alistair snorted in disgust. 'Not if I have any say.'

'In any case, it is superlative,' said Charles with evident pride.

'Do not take credit, brother. It was put to cask when we were in school. And the decision has been the laird's, along with Coupe. Our foreman has a remarkable nose,' said Alistair. Charles bristled at his brother's remarks.

'Until now, McLaren whisky has met with indifference from the Royal Household,' said Isla McLaren.

'That is an exaggeration, dear wife. This is an honour sought by every distillery in Scotland. We are merely in a very long queue,' said Alistair.

'Few distilleries are so near Balmoral geographically,' said she. 'We are quite convenient to supply them.'

'Yes, but Royal Lochnagar is even closer and already has the Queen's favour. In any case,' said Alistair, 'the laird has at last received an invitation to a meeting tonight. It is an important first step and bodes well for McLaren whisky. I propose a toast.' He raised a glass.

'No, that is to *me*, dear brother.' Charles stood and raised his glass. 'A toast to McLaren whisky, our father, and royal connections.'

The meal proceeded with desultory conversation about the weather, the prize horses owned by the laird, some technical aspects of the distillery, and the results of some local archery contest. The evening was relieved only by an extraordinarily delicious dinner featuring Scottish salmon, venison, a variety of vegetables and a potato dish with local cheese. I focused on that more pleasant aspect of the evening, as each time I tried to engage the ladies on a topic I was overridden by one of the brothers, who vied with each other continually for dominance in the conversation.

At last we adjourned to an adjacent small salon, lit by a cheery fireplace and featuring a piano. The ladies were incited to perform, and Isla went first, playing a lively polonaise with admirable musicality. Catherine followed with a lamentable and piteous German song, sung in a voice that could etch glass.

I fortified myself by sampling the various whiskies on hand. But the other two men continued to converse in a corner during this appalling demonstration, an act of rudeness that only inflamed my irritation with them. This left Isla McLaren and myself to feign interest and give the poor creature some token applause at the end of her piteous warbling.

At last Catherine abandoned the piano and picked up some needlework and a large glass of whisky, sitting herself across the room, nearer the men. With a gesture, her sister-in-law beckoned me away from the salon and into the Great Hall where she took my arm and drew close.

'Mrs McLaren!' said I. 'Perhaps we should rejoin—'

'Oh, do be sensible, Dr Watson. My need to speak to you is not personal.'

'Of course not. Forgive me.'

'Listen. I have canvassed the servants about Fiona's disappearance. There is something strange there. When Fiona eloped, she left all her belongings behind, in her room that she shared with another young parlour maid, Gillian, who relates that shortly after Fiona left, Cameron Coupe entered the room and gathered up all her things.'

'She told you this?'

'Yes. This is why you need me to help you. Fiona and Gillian were close. They had a kind of pact, or so says Gillian. If either of them married and left the estate, they had promised some of their treasured belongings to each other. When she told Coupe of this, crying of course, Coupe apparently asked her what Fiona had promised her and kindly gave her those items. But what was strange was that Fiona had said nothing to Gillian about eloping.'

'What did Gillian have to say about Fiona's kidnapping? The hair?'

'She refused to elaborate, saying only that Fiona was deeply distraught and was determined to find out who had done this. Cameron Coupe had agreed to help her, but had made no progress.'

Coupe, of course, had performed the deeds himself.

'This is strange news indeed. Do you know what items he allowed the girl to retain?'

'Some trinkets and a Bible is all she said. Fiona possessed little of value.'

'Thank you, Mrs McLaren. I will relate all you say to Mr Holmes.'

She smiled ruefully. 'Please ask him to include me in the investigation, Dr Watson.'

'I will make sure to mention it. But Mrs McLaren, Mr Holmes has his own way of working. There are times when even I am in the dark as to his processes.'

'They would be clear to a mind accustomed to logic,' said she crisply. Then, seeing that I might have taken this amiss, she added, 'Forgive me, Dr Watson. I meant no aspersion.'

I smiled. This woman was vastly underrated by her entire family. It was time to return to the room and report to Holmes what I had discovered tonight.

CHAPTER 22

Ghost!

made my way back to the East Tower, eventually managing to locate the spiral stone steps that led to the remote hall and our rooms. This area remained shrouded in obscurity, unlike other areas of the castle, with only oil-lit wall sconces and candles casting a dim glow. Considering this and its haunted reputation, I puzzled again why we had been placed there.

However I was eager to share what I had learned from Mrs McLaren and approached Holmes's room, at some distance down the hall from my own.

I knocked, but he did not answer. As I stood there listening, Mungo, our elderly attendant approached with a tray of water, whisky, and biscuits to tide us through the evening. 'Refreshments for you both, sir.'

I noted that his hands trembled, causing the glasses on the tray to rattle.

'Please bring them to my room. Mr Holmes appears to have retired.'

'Very good sir.' He began following me down the hall to my room. 'If I were you, I would go inside your room, sir, and remain there,' said he.

'One moment, Mungo,' I said. 'I saw a chamber pot in my room. Surely there is plumbing? I believe you pointed out the lavatory at the end of the hall. It is modernised, operable, is it not?'

We had reached my door, and Mungo stood there, with an unreadable expression.

'Do not go down there, sir, at any time during the night. During the day, yes, but not at night.'

'Why? Is it operable or is it not?' said I with some asperity.

'There is a ghost who often appears at night. It is a danger, sir. A servant fell down the steps nearby and broke his neck. Please do not ask me more.' The tray rattling grew louder.

'Give me that, please.' I relieved him of his tray before its contents were dashed to the floor. 'I do not believe in spirits, Mungo, save those that you have brought me to imbibe. Either the plumbing works, or it does not. Which is it?'

The old man hesitated, then answered with reluctance.

'It is built over a very old latrine from centuries past, sir. Just a long empty channel, several storeys deep, that is how they did it then.'

'But the laird has modernised the buildings. You have electric lighting, at least in some places. You mentioned modern plumbing earlier in the day.'

'When the workmen came to clear out the one in this

hall . . . down there,' Mungo indicated the end of our hallway past Holmes's rooms, 'to build the new facilities, they found . . .' he shuddered.

'Spare me the details, Mungo.'

'No, sir. They found what were thought to be human remains. More than one body, in fact.'

'My God! Recent?' I was beginning to think the McLaren estate was a veritable minefield of tragedy.

'Difficult to tell, because of, well, the condition, after time, in . . . you understand. But the bones were shattered, as if fallen from a great height. Fallen, pushed, we do not know. Imagine, sir!'

I inwardly cringed at the thought of such barbarity. Accident or murder, the image was horrifying. 'The child who disappeared from this hall, little Anne?' I asked. 'Could the remains have been hers? What was the state of the latrine at that time?'

''Twas not in use then. The long channel was covered over by a wooden lid, quite heavy, and this whole end of the hall boarded up. The police had a look, I think. But the idea was dismissed.'

'Dismissed? How?'

'I do not know, sir. Only that it was looked at, and left.'

'What is the current state of the plumbing? Why may I not use it if needed?'

'All is new, sir. The long channel has been blocked. The latest toilets have been installed in this hall, modern plumbing, even hot water!' He paused. 'And yes, sir, it works.'

'That is all I need to know.'

Mungo began edging away from me and towards the staircase. 'Will that be all, sir?'

I sighed. 'Thank you, Mungo.' With the tray of refreshments in one hand, I entered my room and closed the door. He called in after me.

'Please stay in, sir.'

I shook my head in annoyance. Taking stock of my room, I pushed a side table nearer the bed and lit two more candles there so that I would have enough light to read. Neither Verne nor Shelley appealed to my raw nerves, but perhaps Kingston's *Popular Sea Tales* would settle me nicely. Once in bed, however, I could not concentrate. Images of ghosts, bodies, missing children and, strangely, the lovely face of Isla McLaren, crowded my thoughts. I took another swallow of McLaren Top and extinguished the candles.

It was some hours later when I awoke. The wind had come up again and was dancing around the stone ramparts of the castle with an eerie howl. I could hear a flapping, as though curtains had become loose somewhere and were attempting flight. One of my windows rattled. I sighed. The whisky and overheated room, followed by all the water I had drunk were making their effects felt. I now had need of the plumbing.

I lit a candle and climbed down from the bed.

The fire had dwindled to embers and the room was freezing. Should I venture into the hall? I argued against it for convenience, and so pulled the chamber pot from under my bed. Holding the candle close, I noticed a crack in it,

253

and put it back. I did not believe in ghosts, after all, and as a doctor I had a high opinion of personal hygiene.

Throwing on both my dressing gown and my tweed jacket for warmth, I left my room, pulling the door shut behind me, and turned towards the darkened end where the latrine was located.

The candles all down the hall still glowed faintly, but the end of the hall faded into utter blackness. As I advanced towards this darkness I suddenly made out a glowing white shape that emerged into the black and seemed to hang suspended in the air. From this distance I gauged it to be the size of a small, slender adult. Vivid yet pale, it appeared to be hovering about two feet off the ground. A long dress floated around it, lifted as if by random breezes, the whole thing semi-transparent. There was a diffuse, moon-like orb where a face might be expected. In a languid gesture, the figure raised an arm and held a hand out in front of itself. The sound of the wind suddenly keened in the corridor, and half of the candlelit sconces went out all at once.

I found myself unable to move. As I stared at the apparition, two more candles suddenly went out, leaving the hall in darkness with only this glowing figure at the end.

I heard a sound, a low moan of anguish. It seemed to come from the thing itself. I felt a terrible rising in the back of my throat and a band constricting my chest.

I do not believe in ghosts, I told myself. I do *not* believe. And then the candle in my hand went out, as if blown by an unseen entity.

In a flash I was back in my room, locking the door

behind me. I lit four candles in rapid succession, threw two logs on the fire and stirred the embers until they took hold, and only then did I remove my jacket. I was quaking like the whisky glasses on Mungo's tray. I stood close to the light and the warmth, rubbing my hands in a fever to get them warm again.

I glanced in the mirror but, as earlier, saw little but smudges in the dim reflection. Of what use was such a mirror?

But more to the point, what had I just seen? Surely there was an explanation. I needed to talk to Holmes.

I took several deep breaths, willing myself to calm down. Holmes was asleep in the room down the hall. I would have to go out of my room and towards the darkness and the apparition – if it was still there – to reach him.

And then what would I do? Wake him to tell him I had seen a ghost, like a child running to its father?

It must have been the whisky clouding my brain. I had drunk far more than was my habit. This hallucination must have been the result of this overstimulation and fatigue. What I needed was sleep. I reluctantly made use of the room's 'facilities', then drew another blanket from a trunk placed at the foot of the bed, spread it over the thick pile already there, and crawled in to get warm.

I slept fitfully for some time, and then awoke with a start. It must have been several hours later as the fire had devoured the two logs and had once more succumbed to the cold draughts in my room. I opened my eyes. Only a faint orange glow came from between the tiles in the fireplace surround. The wind had died down and was silent. Was it the absence of noise that awoke me? I lit a candle and checked my pocket watch. It was three in the morning.

And then I heard it.

It was a terrible sound. A kind of gurgling, followed by the sound of strangulation or choking. A few seconds of silence, then a single keening sound. Then silence. I got up, put on my dressing gown and my coat once more over it. I tiptoed to my door and listened.

The high-pitched groan came again, off to the right. It was followed by more choking, not unlike the sounds I heard when I once witnessed a neighbour's dog choking on a chicken bone. Something or someone was in distress.

I felt in my coat pocket for my Webley, and for extra measure, jammed the knife from the shopkeeper into the other pocket. I took the candle, opened the door and stepped into the hall.

The tiny flame threw only a dim glow for a foot or two. The candles were all out, and at the end of the moonlit corridor the gloom faded into utter blackness. But there was no floating apparition.

I exhaled in relief. But then the choking sound came again. I froze. To my horror, something pale and white emerged from the blackness at the end of the hall. It was a larger figure than before. It floated about a foot and a half above the stone pavers and as I watched, it grew larger.

The thing was advancing towards me! I squinted through the darkness at the white, swaying form.

'Stay where you are!' I shouted, drawing the gun in my

right hand and holding the candle before me in an effort to see.

The apparition stopped moving. I blinked, trying to clear my vision. It wobbled slightly and then, from an alcove behind a pillar, removed a candle and held it aloft. I now discerned that the floating white shape was a nightshirt. Below this shirt were two thin, bare legs. And above it, a pale and wan face.

'Holmes?'

'Of course, Watson. Did you think me a phantom?'

'No. No, of course not.' I pocketed my revolver and hoped he had not seen it.

'What is the matter? You look terrified.'

'Were you—have you been in this hallway before? A few hours ago?'

'No.'

'I heard noises just now.'

'I have been made sick by the soup, Watson. Either the chef was careless or someone had creative thoughts about dispatching me.'

'Did Mungo tell you to stay away from that end of the hall?'

'He left me a note, which I disregarded. Why?'

A flood of relief washed over me followed immediately by another thought.

'Do you think someone poisoned your soup?'

'It is possible, Watson. But I had only one small spoonful before I detected something awry. It is at times beneficial to be a picky eater, although you could not have convinced those who raised me as a child of that fact.'

I shivered suddenly in the dank cold.

'Have you any food, Watson?'

'Yes, some biscuits.'

'Bring them and all your blankets to my room. You can stay on the large divan in the sitting area. It is near the fire. I can see you are shivering. You must be cold.'

'It is cold, yes. My fire has gutted out for the second time.'

'Mine lights well. Come.'

Twenty minutes later I had warmed up and was ensconced in blankets on a sofa near a roaring fire in Holmes's room. He had bolted the door, and to my surprise, stood a chair up against the latch to prevent entry.

'Really, Holmes, do you think that someone might try to break in?'

'Watson, until I can sort out this singular family, I think it best to stick together and remain on our guard. I have a feeling we will uncover more than one crime here, and if so, may encounter danger from unknown quarters. By the way, I managed to overhear your conversation with Mrs McLaren this evening.'

'What? How? We were quite alone in the Great Hall!'

'I was doing a bit of legwork on my own. Taking advantage of Laird Robert's absence I returned to his room for a brief search. I had a certain suspicion, and sure enough, hidden in a closet was "the laird's lug".'

'What is that?'

'Scots term for "the laird's ear". Inside the laird's bedchamber, there is a small garderobe secreted behind a hidden door which is made to look like a part of the wall. This small chamber contains a listening tube which feeds directly from another part of the castle, in this case, the Great Hall. Do not look so surprised, Watson, there is one in Edinburgh castle, and another at Muchalls. You and the lady were conversing there and I could hear everything you said as though I were standing next to you.'

'Devious! How did you stumble upon it?'

Holmes laughed. 'Stumble? You know my methods, Watson, I was looking for it. I wondered how the laird knew of our suspicions of Charles regarding the notes to Docteur Janvier. In any case, it is interesting that Fiona left all her worldly goods behind and that Coupe distributed them. I have begun to have a distinctly unfavourable view of that man.'

'This family and their retinue are full of surprises.'

'Yes, and there was more. Some of the laird's private correspondence revealed he is more interested in the phylloxera epidemic than he led us to believe. But perhaps most interesting of all, I found this!'

He strode over to an armoire and, reaching into the pocket of his waistcoat, pulled out a piece of jewellery. He held it in front of the fire and it glittered in warm tones, a small topaz drop earring, modest but quite beautiful. 'It was in the laird's bedroom, under a small table by the bed!'

'Whose, do you think?' I asked.

'What can you infer from this, Watson?'

'Holmes, I am too tired to play this game. Just tell me what you think, please.'

'Well, the earring is not gold but merely gold plated. You see the coating worn away, here. Therefore, not an expensive item. The type of gift a servant or perhaps a young clerk would give his betrothed. Note that the backing is bent. This earring came out by force. Its position under a table next to the bed would indicate either that it landed there either during a struggle, or more likely, in the throes of passion. The topaz stone, small and relatively inexpensive is nonetheless quite tasteful. Its dark amber colour would well suit a redhead.'

'Then Fiona's perhaps? But how could—'

'Here is the puzzle, Watson. Given the aggressive house-cleaning we know to have taken place directly after the laird and his family left for the South of France, it would have been found by the maids. No, the earring must have rolled under the table after that time. Therefore, it is likely the act occurred by someone using the room after the cleaning but before the family's return.'

'Fiona had purportedly eloped before then,' I reminded him.

'Very good, Watson, proceed.'

'That is what everyone believed. Everyone who did not know better.' The thought of a member of staff using the laird's bedroom for an affair was abhorrent to me. I suppose it was possible, but, a sudden thought intruded. 'Fiona's jewellery! Why would she have left it behind? But Coupe gave some trinkets to Gillian. Do you suppose . . .?'

'Bravo! But we need a few more facts in hand. Now rest your weary brain, Watson, for we have much to do

260

tomorrow. I hope Dr Fleming's final forensics report will arrive.'

'And I hope that we may put this sad case to rest, the sooner the better,' said I.

'Amen to that, my dear fellow.'

Holmes then blew out the candles, and retired to his bed, which stood behind a large folding screen, allowing us each a measure of privacy. Only minutes later I heard his faint snoring from across the room. I lay there awake a few minutes longer, wishing for his ease in dropping off to sleep as quickly as a child.

I watched for a while as the fire burned slowly in the grate and the wild winds came up once more to whistle around the castle walls. Were there listening tubes elsewhere in Braedern castle? What other entrapments lay in wait for the unwary here?

I would be happy to return to London and I endeavoured to bring my dear Mary's face into my imagination. Gazing at this vision of her sweet countenance, I fell at last into a deep, dreamless slumber.

CHAPTER 23

Alistair

he next morning was bright and cold. After a brief breakfast, served buffet style as was the custom in such places, we were guided to the South Wing, and the rooms of Alistair McLaren. My brief contact with him last night at dinner had left me with a distaste for both his sarcasm and his casual dismissiveness towards his wife.

In contrast to his brother's and father's spacious apartments, Alistair's rooms were crammed with books and scientific equipment of the type favoured by the mechanical engineer. A drafting table had been set up next to two of the largest windows I had seen in the estate, and he was bent over it, pencil and ruler in hand, when we entered.

A servant announced us and departed. After a moment he looked up, distracted.

'Oh, yes, you two. Come in and sit down. Have you had coffee? I shall ring.'

'We have had breakfast,' said Holmes, moving to stand beside him at the drafting table.

The man stepped away in annoyance. 'What is it you wish to see here?' he demanded.

'I do not know until I see it, Mr McLaren,' said Holmes smoothly. 'Ah, that looks like a new still design. That has, I believe, a longer neck than the ones your father showed us yesterday.'

Alistair's frown faded, and he stepped back to the table.

'Indeed it does! It prolongs the contact of the alcohol vapour with the copper as it passes through the still. A more delicate flavour can be the result.'

'A chemical reaction, then?' I asked. 'So that is the reason your stills are made of copper?'

'There are several reasons, Watson,' said Holmes. 'It affects the taste remarkably, in one respect by partly removing the sulphur compounds.'

'Precisely,' said Alistair, with the briefest flash of admiration towards my friend. 'You do not want your whisky to taste like rotten eggs, do you?'

I laughed.

'But a bit, aye, that you do want. It is little known to those who appreciate whisky, but the subtleties of flavour are the result of precise calibration, and are not always what one would suspect. I am known for my adjustments. Achieving the art, it all boils down to science really.' Alistair smiled at us. 'I have read of your methods, Mr Holmes, and they are not so very different from my own. Come, follow me to my office at the distillery and ask your questions there. It is more private and I can give you fifteen minutes.'

After a freezing ride downhill to the McLaren distillery, we were seated in Alistair McLaren's office located within the warren of stone buildings we had visited previously. It was a large airy space, lit through a window and skylight by the cold snowy white of a field outside. To my surprise, Holmes began the discussion with mention of Docteur Paul-Édouard Janvier, and the likelihood of British intervention in the wine industry debacle, a topic he had also raised with the laird.

'It is preposterous. Janvier is correct,' Alistair McLaren said. 'Seeding the phylloxera is impractical as a weapon. Slowing the research for a cure, however, that I might envision.'

'The plot to bomb Janvier's laboratory is said to have originated in Scotland.'

'Ha! Well, we have our reputation as hell raisers, do we not, Mr Holmes? But even so, it seems a futile gesture, in my view. Science will out, and that is that.'

'It is some people's opinion that the McLarens had a hand in it. Your family was conveniently in the area when the bomb went off. And the dynamite was manufactured in Scotland. The same kind, in fact, that you use here on the property.'

It was as if we had set off a small charge of said explosive directly under the younger McLaren. He stood up abruptly knocking his own chair over backwards. 'You will not be accusing me of this, will you, Mr Holmes? Because if you are, God help you! I shall pick you up and throw you straight through that window, and your little bulldog of a bodyguard along with you!'

I had risen to my feet without thinking and the two of us faced each other. Holmes had remained seated. He sighed.

'Mr McLaren, if I were to accuse any of the McLarens it would not be you. Your brother, on the other hand, might well be stupid enough to think it not only effective, but untraceable.'

Alistair McLaren paused. Then suddenly, he threw back his head and laughed. 'Aye, right you are there. Charles is an idiot. And he is constantly looking for ways to gain favour with our father.'

'But he already has the running of the distillery.'

'In name only. He is naught but a figurehead. Fancy dinners in London. Social appearances at the opera and such. But he can't even maintain the wife, that silly woman Catherine, to assist him with making his way in society. I am the one who runs the place. I am the one who has increased our production and serves now as master distiller. I am the one with taste, knowledge, and—'

'—and, by contrast, a very remarkable wife,' said Holmes.

Alistair's face darkened. 'Isla. Ach!'

'She is not, I presume, threatened by your temper and posturing, is she?'

Alistair McLaren paused. To his credit he took the insult in his stride. 'No. Nor I of her own. But the woman lacks a proper outlet. She is a steam engine trapped in the drawing room.'

'What do you mean by that?'

'I mean hers is an overactive mind. She is bored, and a woman bored is a danger. Her imagination runs wild.'

Holmes took out a cigarette and searched for matches.

'Not here, Mr Holmes. I allow no smoking.'

Holmes sighed and put his case away.

'Her imagination, you say? My impression was that your wife prides herself on her logic.'

'Ah, you noted that, did you?' Alistair smiled. 'For a woman, perhaps, she is logical. But she has not enough to occupy her. The womanly pastimes – she would sooner shoot a tiger than embroider a pillow. 'Tis a pity she were not born a man.'

'I presume her quickness of mind initially attracted you.'

'Have you never fallen in love, Mr Holmes? Intelligence in a woman can be an aphrodisiac. The mind plays tricks.'

'Hmm. She came to consult me in London, did you know?'

I started. Why on earth would Holmes reveal this?

Alistair shifted uncomfortably. 'Yes, of course I knew.' I did not believe him.

'Mr McLaren, who do you think killed that girl?'

'I have no idea. Nor do I care, frankly. Fiona's death, while sad, meant little to me. Many were taken with her, and the girl played upon this. Someone was jealous, I presume. Someone with a touch of madness evidently.'

'An interesting description. Does anyone come to mind?'

'No one in particular, no. Though I hope you catch the fellow, certainly. But one cannot discount Fiona's own role in her demise.'

'Do you mean to say she brought this upon herself?'

'That would be harsh. Let me simply say that she was one who craved attention and enjoyed creating drama about her.'

'I understand she was superstitious. Ghost stories and the like. She frightened the other servants?' prompted Holmes.

'Aye. The damned ghosts!'

'Do you believe in ghosts, Mr McLaren?'

'I do not. I am an educated man.'

'St Andrews, correct?'

'I am aware that you do your research, Mr Holmes.'

Holmes had moved to a bookshelf on a nearby wall and was perusing the books. He turned with a smile. 'As do you, sir. You are a wide-ranging reader.' He pulled a book bound in blue paper from the shelves and flipped through it. 'Hmmm. *The Third Annual Report of Her Majesty's Inspectors of Explosives, 1878.* I have read this. Some interesting developments since, wouldn't you say, Mr McLaren?'

'Indeed, Mr Nobel has—' he stopped suddenly. 'You already know that we make use of dynamite here.'

'Mr McLaren, you realize that if I connect a family member to the explosion at the Montpellier laboratory, that person will serve time.'

'Understood.' Alistair paused. 'You might want to know that Charles has tried several marginally legal endeavours regarding water rights and distribution, one of which involved an explosion to divert a stream, causing our father to spend a considerable sum on legal fees to bail him out.'

'Interesting. Then your father is not above buying the law, you say?' asked Holmes.

Alistair hesitated, then walked away from his drafting table and towards a sideboard, on which were arrayed the ubiquitous whisky bottles and glasses.

'A dram, perhaps?'

'No. The question remains, Mr McLaren.'

'Well, Mr Holmes. My father, like you, wishes for justice. But justice is not always served by the law. Surely you agree. That is, I believe, why he hired a *private* detective.'

'I am a consulting detective. I consult with the police. He is aware of the difference.'

'Then he surely expects to buy you, Mr Holmes. If he has not done so already.'

Holmes did not dignify this with an answer. But his tone became more sharp. 'Something puzzles me, Mr McLaren. Why did you see fit to bring up Charles and water disputes? As well as your father's questionable dealings. It is as though you are ready to throw both of your family members to the wolves.'

'I did not say Charles did anything wrong. Only that he might have done. And regarding my father, it is good that you know the kind of man you may be dealing with, that is all. Consider it a friendly warning.'

'I am not in need of protection, Mr McLaren,' said Holmes.

'Again, I would not go so far as to say I suspect Charles,' said Alistair. 'I simply do not like my brother. This is no secret. And so, Mr Holmes, it is for you to unravel the mystery, is it not? But do proceed with caution. The laird is used to having his way and once the mystery is solved, if the answer is not to his liking – well, you must comply, or watch your back.'

CHAPTER 24

Obfuscation

t last it was our prearranged time to meet with the instigator of this investigation, Mrs Isla McLaren. Why Holmes kept her for last, I could not fathom. With help from Mungo, we managed to locate her rooms in the South Tower.

Her warm and welcoming salon was appointed in warm reds with blue and gold accents, crowded by tall bookcases filled with gold tipped volumes, and accented with silk flowers in profusion. But it was books which dominated the suite, resting on most every surface, including the small table next to the lady.

Mrs McLaren the younger now regarded us calmly from a deep blue velvet armchair. The fire cast copper highlights in her hair and the light glinted off her gold spectacles, making it difficult to read her expression. She was truly a beautiful woman despite her studious exterior.

'The McLarens' fortunes, as you have noted, Mr Holmes, are on the rise. Despite Charles's shortcomings – and they are numerous – we have made inroads in the London market and a Royal Warrant seems within reach. And yet I fear for our future.'

'Why is that, Mrs McLaren?' asked Holmes, seating himself in a chair opposite hers.

'The family has an unfortunate reputation, one which has cast a darkness over the name, and one which we struggle to overcome.'

'There are indeed unusual features,' said Holmes, flashing me a look of subtle amusement. His humour could at times be said to be inappropriate.

'It is hardly a laughing matter, sir. There is what one might call an aura of tragedy. First the disappearance of baby Anne, when the brothers were quite small. A mystery that was sadly never solved. Then, later, the death of his wife, the Lady Elizabeth, followed more recently by Donal's unfortunate death at Khartoum, which sent the laird into a prolonged melancholy.'

'Of course, there is also Lady Elizabeth's ghost,' I supplied.

'And Donal's.' added Isla McLaren.

'Ah, I have not yet heard of that one,' Holmes drawled. His scorn for belief in the supernatural was in clear view.

'Donal's ghost was reportedly seen in and around the distillery.'

'His ghost, you say?' said Holmes with a smile.

'Yes. An angry one, reportedly. And with a death attributed to it in the distillery, an asphyxiation by carbon dioxide.'

'Why attribute this to a ghost? It is a very real danger,' said Holmes.

'The dead man had worked there daily for eighteen years. It was a mistake he would not have made. And the ghost had apparently been seen the night before in that very room.'

Holmes shrugged.

'Consequently,' Mrs McLaren continued, 'several of the older distillery men, all of them believers, deserted the company for other distilleries, one to Glenmorangie, one to Oban, and two as far as Islay. This was quite a loss as they had been with the family for many years, in one case for generations. And of course they took their expertise with them.'

'How did the family respond to this experienced man's accident?' asked Holmes.

Mrs McLaren shrugged. 'Well, following the death, the sightings of Donal's ghost stopped, the laird thereafter refused to discuss it. What you may find interesting is that none of the more recently hired war veterans abandoned their jobs, Mr Holmes. The new hires are a rough lot.'

'Indeed. So they were already in place. I am curious, how did your foreman, Cameron Coupe, take to their arrival?'

'Apparently he welcomed them, Mr Holmes. Cheap labour, if I may be so callous.'

Holmes sighed, and rose from his chair. He began to pace. 'The laird thinks contact between these men and Fiona was impossible due to various precautions. Would you concur?'

'I would. The laird has turned the castle into a fortress at night. At the distillery, the employee quarters are similarly secured. In my estimation this has been effective.'

'So it appears,' conceded Holmes.

Mrs McLaren kept her eyes fixed upon the detective as he moved about the room. 'I would have been more circumspect had I been given the selection of these men,' said she.

'Interesting. How so?' murmured Holmes from across the room, where he now stood admiring one of the bookshelves.

'You have toured the distillery, need you ask? A number of them are disturbed, impaired in such a way as to make them possibly unreliable.'

'Dangerous?'

'Many of the older employees have now left us as a result. The idea was promising, the execution less so.'

'The mental state of veterans is not always obvious, Mrs McLaren,' I offered. 'For example, I was much depressed upon my own return from war.'

Holmes glanced at me with approbation. He changed the subject abruptly.

'What of Lady McLaren, the laird's wife? You mentioned her story was part of the family's dark reputation.'

'Yes. Lady Elizabeth's death was never fully explained, and this earlier tragedy has cast further shadow upon us.'

He moved from one bookcase to another and asked, rather casually, over his shoulder, 'I know that the woman froze outside the castle and no one heard her cries for help. Do relate the particulars.'

'Mr Holmes, please sit down.' He seemed to ignore her and continued looking at the books, his back to her. She shrugged and briefly recounted the story of Lady McLaren's death by freezing, exactly as told to us by the groundsman and the laird.

'No one heard her attempts to re-enter the castle?' persisted Holmes.

'The bell malfunctioned.'

'It was examined?'

'Yes, Mr Holmes. There was a defect. The incident was ruled an accident. This was before I came to Braedern in any case. And since her death, her ghost is said to roam the hall near your rooms.'

'Why there, particularly?' Holmes now stood before a third bookcase, deliberately reading some of the spines.

Here Isla McLaren's faced darkened. 'I wager you have been told already, Mr Holmes. Stop, please. What is it that you find so interesting about my bookshelves?'

'Your books. Continue, please.'

'Holmes, really!' I exclaimed.

Mrs McLaren shrugged and gave up for the moment. 'You recall, Mr Holmes, that I am not a believer in ghosts. But this one story is hard to explain, among the many which I can easily discredit. That wing previously housed the nursery. And it was from there that the laird and lady's baby daughter disappeared one night.'

'Ah yes, we heard something of this,' I said.

Holmes continued his inventory of her books.

'When did this occur?'

'Some thirty years past.'

'Tell us what you know, please.'

'It is little spoken of. But from what I have discovered, Donal was six, Charles four, the daughter Anne was nearly three, and Alistair but an infant. One night, while the nurse slept, Anne simply disappeared. There was no evidence of a break-in, no struggle, and no one heard a thing. She simply vanished.'

'From her bed?'

'Apparently so.'

'The nurse slept where?'

'In an adjoining room. The other children were asleep when the nurse came to check on her at 2 a.m. and discovered the child missing.

Holmes turned from the bookcase to look at the lady. 'A kidnapping, perhaps? Was a ransom demanded?'

'None, and there was no explanation.'

'What kind of abduction could it be with no ransom?' I wondered aloud.

'One gone wrong. The child may have died. The kidnappers fallen out. Or it was a theft, pure and simple of a child for someone who wanted her,' suggested Holmes.

Mrs McLaren nodded. 'The poor Lady McLaren, who believed fervently in ghosts, was never the same afterwards, and lingered in the area frequently – in life, and some say she continued to do so after her own death.'

Holmes turned and now faced a smaller bookcase near her bedchamber. He began to peruse the books quickly, in a curious manner as though mentally cataloguing them at great speed. His thin fingers danced across the spines.

'All right, Mr Holmes, I have had enough.' She removed her spectacles and rubbed her eyes, clearly fatigued, though from the questions or Holmes's antics I could not determine.

He glanced up at her with a distracted smile, did a strange double take at her, then abruptly turned back to his inventory.

'Mr Holmes,' she repeated, with more firmness. 'I think of books as a window to a person's private self. The soul, perhaps. I have asked you twice to desist studying mine. Your actions are an intrusion.'

He seemed not to hear, and pulled a volume from the shelf. 'You have excellent taste. Ah! Goethe, in the original German. A fine evening's entertainment.' He opened the volume and thumbed the pages. 'But the title page has been torn out! Where did you acquire this?'

Isla replaced her spectacles. 'Why does it interest you? At a used bookseller, of course. Mr Holmes, you are transgressing. It is as if you went into my boudoir, opened the drawers there, and began rifling my undergarments.'

Holmes looked up in utter surprise at this. I felt my own face flush violently.

To his credit, Holmes closed the book and gently replaced it on the shelf. The lady approached, took the book back out again, and refiled it in its proper place an inch or two to the right.

He stepped back from her.

'You are not establishing rapport with your suspect, Mr Holmes,' she admonished. 'Although I would have preferred you consider me an ally. If you would kindly take a seat we shall continue. If not, I must ask you to leave.'

Holmes shrugged but duly sat and resumed our conversation, taking a pose so relaxed as to seem insolent. 'Very well,' he said. 'Let us return to the nursery which was in the East Wing. When was it modernised? Particularly the plumbing?'

Isla McLaren resumed her seat across from us.

'Shortly after the child's disappearance, the laird moved the other three children elsewhere, and much later, after Elizabeth's death, he finished the plumbing, and created the guest wing in which you now reside. And yet the Lady's ghost is said to remain. She is particularly vivid at night.'

'Yes, none of the servants will enter then, except Mungo, who is terrified.'

'They say she is an angry ghost, wanting to find her daughter, wanting to be "let in" – although whether to the house, or to the secret of Anne's disappearance is not clear. I will admit, this particular ghost gives even me pause.'

'Why? Have you seen it?'

'What does it matter? I am not a believer, Mr Holmes.'

'So much of your reporting is second hand, Mrs McLaren. "It is said", "I am told", and so on. I would like to hear something you have witnessed yourself, first hand. And so I ask you again, did you see the reported ghost in the East Wing? Or any others? As Shakespeare wrote "in the night, imagining some fear, how easy is a bush supposed a bear".'

'*A Midsummer Night's Dream*, of course. But comes the reply, "But all the story of the night told over, and all their minds transfigured so together." I played Hippolyta in a school production, Mr Holmes. Enough people have seen this ghost in the East Tower that attention must be paid. I myself did see a figure once, in the East Wing. But that is all. However, as I was about to relate, it is the idea of this "ghost" that gives me pause.'

'Why?'

'Let us assume, even though it has been seen by others, that it is an illusion. I can imagine no real advantage that such a devised haunting might confer, no motive for anyone to create or perpetuate such a myth. It is merely sad, and inconvenient. To the others, I can well ascribe some earthly motive. For example, I once caught Fiona impersonating a ghost, which I presume was to frighten Catherine from her husband's room. Fiona thought it a fine joke.'

'Fiona, you say. What about her friend, Gillian? No? Then you believe the ghosts of Braedern to be concoctions by someone with an interest in frightening others.'

'Did you not begin with such a theory yourself?'

Holmes did not reply directly. Instead he paused, taking in her apartment from his chair. 'But who is kept in line other than Catherine by such a device? Neither the laird nor either of his sons claim to believe in ghosts, Mrs McLaren.'

'True. And yet, you have noticed the rosemary every-where.'

'But not here,' I remarked with a smile which she returned.

'They could all do with a dose of rational thinking,' said

Mrs McLaren. 'Even the ones who present themselves as cool heads.'

'All of them, Mrs McLaren?'

She paused at this question. 'Judge for yourself, Mr Holmes. But often the man who thinks himself a paragon of logic is the most irrational and emotional of them all.' She held my friend's eyes.

'You speak of Alistair?' asked Holmes.

'Whom did you think?' she asked, with a sudden flash of anger. 'Good day, gentlemen.'

She stood, in a gesture of dismissal. Holmes and I arose and moved to the door. He turned to go, then paused, as if he had suddenly remembered something. Pulling a small shiny object from his pocket, he held up the earring that he had found in the laird's bedroom.

'Yours?' he asked.

'What?' Mrs McLaren approached, squinting for a closer look. 'Certainly not,' said she. 'Where did you find it?'

'Whose, then?'

'Tell me first where you found it.'

She stared at Holmes but he refused to answer. She turned to me with a smile, and with two strides, walked to where I was standing and boldly took me by the shoulders. She looked deeply into my eyes. I do not consider myself a cowardly man, but will admit I felt the sudden urge to run.

'Dr Watson will tell me, will you not? Was it when you were interviewing Charles? Cameron Coupe? The laird? Alistair? Ah yes, your eyes tell me what I need to know.

Thank you, Dr Watson.' She turned to Holmes. 'So, it was in the laird's room. Strange!'

Sherlock Holmes exhaled in frustration. 'I will not deny it. Now pray return the favour. Do you know to whom this earring belongs?'

'You did me no favour. And no, I do not know.'

Holmes held her gaze for a moment. 'But you have a theory which you will not divulge. Others beside yourself can read the truth in pupil dilation and changes in breathing, Mrs McLaren.'

I can only presume that is what she had just done with me.

'The earring is not mine, nor do I know whose it is. That is the truth, and that is all you will get. Quid pro quo. Good evening, gentlemen.'

I turned to go but Holmes turned back. 'Lying by omission is as shameful and dishonourable as lying outright. Perhaps more so.'

'Really?' she asked. This seemed to resonate with her deeply. Something in her demeanour changed. 'Perhaps I do this to protect you.'

'If you think Dr Watson and I are in need of your protection, madam, you are sadly deluded,' said Holmes. 'Good day.' Holmes strode out of the room with a level of anger that surprised me.

Just past the threshold I lingered with a nod to Mrs McLaren. 'Good day,' I said. 'Please forgive the—'

She slammed the door behind me.

When we were at last out of earshot, I put voice to my

thoughts. 'Holmes, what happened just now with Mrs McLaren? Perhaps she is withholding information, but I doubt she is a liar.'

'It is the same thing, Watson. There is something going on behind the scenes here. Something we cannot yet see . . . and Mrs Isla McLaren knows something. Her reasons for withholding are not clear to me, but I have sensed they were there from the moment we met.'

'What was so interesting on her bookshelves?'

'As she said, books are the "window to the soul".'

'I doubt you are interested in her soul, Holmes. That lady has a most peculiar effect upon you.'

'Enough, Watson. You are rendered useless in the face of beauty.'

'Then at least you admit she is beautiful.'

'Come, let us step outside for a cigarette.'

CHAPTER 25

Where There is Smoke

e removed ourselves to a sheltered porch outside the dining room, where, for the moment at least, we could be assured of no eavesdroppers. Holmes took out his cigarette case and began to smoke. We stared out at the blue-white expanse, and the brown knobs of the distillery buildings sticking up, snow-capped, down the hill from us. Without our coats, the winter chill was oppressive and I found myself shivering almost immediately.

Holmes inhaled slowly. 'Watson, these are deep waters. There are things about this case which defy logic.'

'Surely you do not suspect supernatural explanations?' I ventured.

'Of course not, Watson. You know me better than that.'

'I do, but I cannot fathom how all of these threads connect.'

'And yet I am sure they do. They must. It is as though there were some dark force behind it all. There are too

282

many deaths, too many mysteries which haunt these halls. If the culprit is a member of the McLaren family, motive, opportunity, and temperament do not seem to coincide, at least in the matter of poor Fiona Paisley. But clearly we have stumbled into a familial nest of intrigue.'

'What a terrible waste,' I remarked. 'In the presence of this much wealth and comfort, scrambling for prestige and power seems so pointless. There is enough to go around, one would think.'

'Never underestimate greed, Watson. Greed, jealousy, fear, and revenge are the four great motivators of crime. No one is immune.'

'Perhaps, although I do not believe I could ever act out of revenge.'

'I have often told myself the same thing, Watson, and yet if someone were to shoot you dead before my eyes, they would not live to gloat about it.'

I was as startled at this unprovoked expression of emotion from my taciturn friend, as if a gunshot had gone off next to us. I endeavoured not to show it. 'Well, that is comforting, Holmes,' I remarked. 'But it would hardly be revenge. What is that letter you are unfolding?'

'Something of interest. I found it when I stopped in to Alistair's rooms.'

He moved under a stone balustrade so that we could not be seen from any of the castle windows and handed the missive to me. It was addressed to 'M. McLaren' and read:

'Our year of plans has been thwarted. I have delivered the ice cream which you had commanded but our last confection met with warmth unexpected and therefore she melted before she could be fully enjoyed. If you wish further dessert items from me, you must contact me in the usual manner. But remember that each unique creation involves the raw materials from the special dairy cows of Scotland. It cannot be rushed. Better planning may furnish us a stronger outcome the next time.'

'What do you make of it, Watson?'

'I am confused. Does this refer to the frozen ice cream dessert?'

'The answer is no. But I know who wrote it.'

I said nothing. Eventually he would tell me. Patience.

'Come, Watson, observe. The writer is French. The "M." instead of "Mr" for "Monsieur" is the first indication, though not conclusive. The stationery is French, evidenced by the watermark here. The use of "commanded" instead of the more normal "ordered". *Commander* is French for "to order", as in goods or services. Also the reversal of "warmth unexpected" and "she melted". Obvious, no?'

'But the reference to the frozen . . . ice cream? Was a Frenchman involved in transporting the head?'

'No. And the French clues were only to test you, Watson. I happen to recognize the handwriting. It was Jean Vidocq's.'

'Holmes! Is *he* involved in the murder? The ice cream . . . *bombe*?'

'No, he refers to a bomb of a different sort, the bomb in Dr Janvier's laboratory. This letter is the last piece of evidence that confirms that Vidocq is causing the very threat to Dr Janvier he was hired to thwart – and at the same time gathering ammunition to blame the phylloxera fiasco on the McLarens.'

'But the special dairy cows of Scotland?'

'I wager that is code for the special dynamite produced in Scotland by Nobel.'

The wind had come up and the last fallen snow was being blown along the tops of the mounds along the ground.

'Holmes, this is most electrifying, but I am growing quite chilled. Do you have enough to have the police arrest Alistair, now? And can we not go in?'

'The walls have ears, remember, Watson? By the way, this letter was not written to Alistair.'

'But you found it in Alistair's rooms.'

'Yes. It was written to Charles. The pencil marks, you see? Those are mine. The faint imprint of the address from the envelope is visible when graphite is applied to the back of the letter. Look here.' He held out the letter to show me.

Faintly visible white beneath the graphite shading I could make out Charles's name.

'Well done, Holmes. But let us go in. I cannot feel my feet.'

Holmes smiled, looking off to the distance. 'As I suspected, Charles McLaren hired Vidocq to set the bomb off in Dr Janvier's laboratory. The hare-brained plot suits the older brother well.'

'But, stay a moment, Holmes. Mycroft told us that Vidocq is being paid by that man Reynaud, of the French government. So this now confirms that he is a double agent?'

'That, as you will recall, has been my working hypothesis from the start of this singular affair. Vidocq was hired by the French government to protect Dr Janvier from threats which they thought came from some British saboteur. And, indeed they did. Vidocq, well ahead of the government officials – note his reference to "our year of plans" not only knew who would be most interested in sabotaging the research for the phylloxera cure, but had already been solicited by Charles McLaren to offer his services. Now we have the missing link. This may even have occurred in London while Vidocq was there a year ago on the case with us involving the missing child and the stolen statue, remember? This theory of mine certainly fits all the facts.'

I began to stamp my feet to see if I could return feeling to them. 'Well, that is rather a poor showing on Vidocq's part. Profitable, I suppose, but hardly patriotic.'

Holmes smiled. 'You do not entirely understand, Watson,' he said. 'Presumably the French government has been made aware of Mr Charles McLaren's childish games through Jean Vidocq. For it is on the French side that Vidocq's allegiance, if he can be said to have any, must rest.'

'Do you think so? That Jean Vidocq is a patriot at heart?'

'No, but his government has more to offer him – money and honours if he plays his cards well.'

'I see it all now,' I said. 'The time and place of the bomb

were critical, no one was to be hurt! Charles must have had a great imagination to plot this out.'

'Not Charles, he lacks the long vision. Vidocq did it for him. But there is something else at work here. I sense a kind of *deus ex machina*, of a most evil nature.'

'Someone setting Charles on his path?'

Holmes shook his head, his expression grave. 'No. Someone who may have choreographed events to ensure we discover the connection.'

'Alistair? You found the letter in his room.'

'No. Someone seductive, someone with power over others, but hidden, and working behind the scenes.'

'What would be such a person's motive?' I asked.

'Who gets the business if Charles is exposed?'

'Alistair. But you do not think it was him.'

'I judge him both smarter, and yet less devious than either his father or older brother.'

'But that leaves who?'

Holmes stared at me. The answer was obvious.

'Isla McLaren,' I said reluctantly. 'But she is not so cold! I cannot believe it of her.'

'Really, Watson? I find her quite calculating.'

A sudden gust of wind blew a quantity of snow in our direction.

'Holmes, you know my thoughts about the lady. I cannot believe it of her.'

Holmes said nothing but blew some smoke into the freezing air.

'I am going inside,' I said, stubbing out my cigarette.

Within minutes we arrived at the door to Holmes's room. He unlocked it, but then paused abruptly at the threshold, holding up a hand.

'Now what, Holmes?' I asked tiredly.

'Someone has been in the room!' he whispered, blocking the doorway. His head swivelled as he took in the entire scene.

Peering from behind, I could discern nothing changed. 'How can you tell?'

'That Bible, for example, overlapped this table on the left lower corner. My jacket sleeve there was folded at the elbow. The intruder did not wish to – but ha!'

He rounded a corner to the niche wherein the bed was positioned and stood before it.

'Here he lies!'

Worried, I walked around the corner to join him. There lay Calum Moray, the groundskeeper's little son, asleep on the pristine coverlet.

As we watched he awoke suddenly and sat up, eyeing us in alarm.

'It is all right, young man,' said Holmes. 'Do you have something for me?'

The boy nodded and sprang from the bed.

'I set him on a few tasks, Watson,' said Holmes. Ignoring the fact that the child had fallen asleep, Holmes congratulated him with a clap on the back. 'An observant young man such as this shows much promise for police work. What have you got, Calum?'

Calum beamed. He stepped forward and from his pocket removed a small object and handed it to Holmes.

He took it and held it up to the light. It was the matching earring to the one Holmes had found on the floor in the laird's room! 'Excellent, my boy! Where did you find it?'

'Servants' quarters, sir. Old room of Fiona's that she shared with Gillian Andrews,' said the boy. Under Holmes's patient questioning, the boy then revealed that the earrings had been given to Gillian Andrews, the maid who had been Fiona's roommate, by Coupe. 'And Mr Coupe, he fancies her, he does. Gillian said so herself.'

'Mr Coupe fancies Gillian?' asked Holmes.

'Aye, sir. They meet up in strange places. It is like a game, she says. He gave her the earrings. And then she lost one,' said Calum.

Holmes thanked Calum and paid the boy a shilling.

'And there is more,' said the little boy.

'Do tell, young man,' said Holmes.

'Gillian is a ghost.'

I gasped. Not another murder, was my thought.

'Explain,' said Holmes, taking the boy gently by the shoulders.

'She puts white on her face and goes up to Charles McLaren's rooms,' said the child. 'Gillian likes to scare people. She can't scare me. But Lady Catherine . . .'

'Ah, I see, Calum. Thank you. Oh, and give me the key, please. The key you used to enter this room.'

'No key, sir. I—'

'Do you by chance have one of these, then?' Holmes removed a small lock-pick from his left cuff. At the boy's hesitation he smiled kindly. Calum nodded and pulled a

289

similar one from his own pocket. They smiled, rascals in collusion. Holmes replaced his lock-pick, gave Calum a second shilling and sent the boy off.

'A criminal in the making?' I wondered, after the door had closed.

'Or a detective. In any case, Watson, this earring is of little help. It appears that Coupe and the girl to whom he gave Fiona's jewellery then had a rendezvous in the laird's bedroom once the family had left for France.'

'What an extraordinarily brazen fellow, this Coupe,' said I.

'Yes! And Gillian as well, since Charles must have used her to keep his wife Catherine from his room. But the timing of Coupe's distribution of Fiona's jewellery may be telling.'

'Could he have written the note purporting to be hers about running away to get married?' I wondered. 'The one with the backwards lettering and all?'

'No. Do you recall I had him write some words for us during our interview? His penmanship was awkward at best. He would not be capable. But the timing of his distribution of Fiona's things tells me he knew rather sooner than others that she would not be returning.'

Just at that moment, a long, low moan sounded from the hallway outside the room.

'Did you hear that?' I asked.

Without answering, Holmes opened the door. We both looked out into the dim hallway. There was no one.

Holmes smiled. 'Perhaps another adventurous parlour maid,' he said, as we went back into the room and closed the door behind us.

I hoped so.

PART FIVE

THE DISTILLATION

'Revenge the sweetest morsel to the mouth that
ever was cooked in hell'
—Sir Walter Scott

CHAPTER 26

The Whisky Thief

ithin minutes of Calum's departure, Mungo arrived with a short note from the laird. It read:

'Mr Holmes, I must speak with you again. At 7 p.m. please ask to be directed to the maturation warehouse wherein we age the whisky. I need your findings to date on the case. You may ask me further questions at that time. This matter must be cleared by morning the day after tomorrow. The royal visit is that night and must not be tainted by an investigation.'

Holmes stood by the fire in his room, staring at the note with a frown. 'Ah, Watson, the man grows impatient.'

'Has the investigation been made public, do you think?'

'Not officially. Nevertheless, everyone, including the Royal Family, will have heard of the murder by now.'

'This meeting is in a remote area in the distillery. Might it be a trap of some sort?'

'He would have specified I come alone. But do bring your pistol in any case, Watson.'

At the appointed hour, with a map drawn by Alistair, we made our way alone through increasing snow flurries down the hill to the large warehouse where the casks sat ageing.

We entered the stone building through a creaking wooden door and soon found ourselves on a landing looking down into an enormous warehouse. Stretching off into the distance were casks of whisky stacked three high on long wooden trestles, held in place with heavy wooden blocks. My nostrils were assailed by the ripe smells of maturing whisky, dusty wood, cool winter air, and the sweet echoes of the American bourbon, port, and Madeira which had filled these casks prior to their use here. It was a pleasant smell – old, soft and mellow.

There was a fine layer of what looked like ash on the floor between the casks. Lanterns at either end of the room cast slanted, low yellow beams which reflected dully off the casks closest to the ends, but tailed off into darkness towards the middle of the chamber.

The oblong room extended into a T shape at a distance from the entrance, and at the intersection of the two long chambers was a raised platform on which a long trestle table had been set up. Standing on the platform was the laird, silent and unmoving. He appeared to be in a kind of reverie, staring at five very large casks, set up in a row against a wall at the back of the platform. Brighter lights installed above this platform cast a sharp-edged pool of light on this one area, highlighting the figure of the man and the five casks as though on a theatre stage, and casting black shadows under the table and casks. A single lantern sat on the trestle table, which was covered by a thin layer of dust.

We descended into the room, approached and stood near the table. The man did not move. 'Sir Robert?' said Holmes.

The laird started from his trance-like state. He turned to us and forced a sudden joviality.

'Ah, gentlemen. The reception will be held here. The tasting. The evening after next, representatives of the Royal Family will sit where you are standing. The Duke of Amberley. The Lord Chamberlain. And, if all goes well, a member of the Royal Family! It will all be decorated. Beautifully,' His voice faltered. 'As it was the night Donal left.'

'Your party for Donal took place right here, then?' said Holmes with sudden interest. 'I would like to ask you a few more questions about Donal's commission, and the night of his party.'

The laird's face darkened. 'What? Why? This cannot be related to Fiona's death. I have asked you here, Mr Holmes, to report to me on your inquiries. Here, well away from the castle. You have had ample time to discover—'

'Sir Robert, progress has indeed been made and I shall give you a report when I am ready to do so. But I ask that you remain patient just a short while longer. I would like to ask you about Donal's departure, the party, his commission, indeed everything about your late son.' Holmes altered his tone and became more gentle. 'Let us begin with the eve of Donal's departure for the army. Please tell me about that night.'

The laird hesitated and I feared he would refuse, but to my surprise he let out a long sigh, and said, 'I will humour you for the moment, Mr Holmes. But then you must humour me.' He took a second deep breath as a wave of emotion swept across his face. 'He stood right here,' said Sir Robert, indicating a spot adjacent to the special row of casks. 'My son, Donal. The table was here, just as it is now, but festooned with ribbons and flowers. June, it was. There was a fiddler, he stood there—' And as the laird pointed to a small area to the side of the table, his face softened as he travelled back in time to the night of the party. 'And the girls—'

'What girls?'

'Oh, the village girls. Three or four of them. They all wanted my son. He was much admired, a handsome boy.'

'And set to inherit the business,' said Holmes.

'Aye. The whisky was flowing. Silver quaiches lined the table. It was a bittersweet celebration, Donal and his friend set to leave for the army. I was already regretting the arrangements I had made for the posting, and yet I saw no other way to keep my boy from trouble. I had bought him, at rather great expense and considerable trouble, an officer's commission. But that night, the music . . .' The laird's voice faded as he remembered.

'Go on,' said Holmes, drawing closer to him.

'The party went on to the small hours. My wife Elizabeth grew tired and eventually I saw her to bed, closed up some accounts in my study, but then, seeing the light still on at the foot of the hill, came back. Everyone had gone but Donal and his friend, and oh yes, Cameron Coupe, there to close down the room and have a wee deoch an dorus.'

'One last drink, I see. You rode all the way down, it must have been the middle of the night, and it was only those three? What time was this?'

'Aye, just the three of them. It was one or two in the morning. I suggested Donal turn in as he had an early start but he wished to linger and said he would see me in the morning to say his goodbyes. That was the last I ever saw of my boy.'

Holmes once more looked around the room as if reliving the party of that long ago evening. 'Did he leave you a note explaining why he left early?'

'A short one. He could not face his mother for another painful goodbye. But she did not believe the note.'

'Why not?'

'Some silliness. Donal left behind a gift she had given him. A Celtic knife, a special one.'

'Describe the knife, please.'

The laird gave Holmes a sharp look. 'If this matters! It had, as I recall, a horn handle with silver filigree, and a big, amber-coloured jewel. A rather long blade for a jackknife, serrated on part of it. She said this knife had magic in it, and would "protect him against evil" but only if he were virtuous, otherwise it could bring him harm.'

Holmes glanced at me. That knife was in my pocket as we spoke, and we both knew it. He turned back to the laird.

'A knife with a kind of curse on it, then?' said Holmes. There was no trace of sarcasm in his tone, although I knew he did not believe.

'A blessing and a curse. She intended it, I suppose, to help keep Donal to his better nature. My wife, alas, was like that, ever since we lost Anne. Superstitious. Fearful.' He shook his head sadly. 'But she was sure he would never have left it.'

'Was the handwriting in the note your son's?'

'Unmistakably.'

'Do you still have it?'

The laird shook his head.

'And where is this "magic" knife now?' asked Holmes.

'Gone. I could not bear the effect it had on Elizabeth and so I gave it to my valet and told Elizabeth it was lost. It was a strange thing, however. My man swore it brought him bad luck and he sold it, I believe, in Aberdeen.'

Holmes mounted the raised platform and began to pace, his eyes raking over everything like searchlights. 'Where were the young men standing when last you saw them?'

'Right here.' The laird stood at one end of the table, near the single row of casks. 'I have not been in this room since Donal's death in Khartoum nearly four years ago now. I have sent in others to sample, I could not bear it, the memory of his last night is so strong. But now I must break the curse and turn this place once more into a room of celebration. When the royal party are here the night after next, I will give them a drink the likes of which they have never tasted before!' He tapped the nearest cask, inhaling deeply and seeming to take strength in the whisky-scented air.

Holmes paused at one end of the table. 'Laird Robert, who was Donal's friend?'

The laird turned sharply to him. 'Just a friend from Camford. I did not like the boy. It is irrelevant. He is dead now.'

'With respect, sir, it is not for you to decide what is relevant.'

'I have hired you to find my daughter's killer. Not to drill into the details of my late son and his friends.'

'It may well be relevant. I must know who your enemies are, Sir Robert. It is possible there is one lurking in history. Again, who was Donal's friend?'

'Ach, I wish he had never met the fellow. A troublemaker he was. I am convinced he set my boy wrong, inciting him into pub fights and the like, but Donal championed him to me, saying he would not go away unless I helped his friend too. I had to. Prison awaited my son if he did not go into the army.'

'Prison! What had they done?' I asked.

'Foolishness. Some time after University, 1876 it was,

they were travelling in France and got into a brawl with another young man. A broken nose and some broken pride. Unfortunately the nose belonged to a Duke's eldest son.'

'I see,' said I, trying to sound sympathetic.

'When I arranged for Donal, I presumed the other boy's family – they were very wealthy – would do the same. They declined, apparently having had enough of his trouble-making. I obliged and so you see, there would be no enemy there. Donal was to enter as a Guards officer, and he would ne'er see a day of fighting, was what I had planned for him.'

'And the other boy?' enquired Holmes, impatiently.

'The artillery, I believe, but – ah, you frown, Dr Watson. Dangerous, yes, but at least the post was as a junior officer. As it was he died not long after in El Obeid.'

'What was this boy's name?' asked Holmes in frustration.

But the laird seemed once more caught in his reverie. 'I remember the night was quite warm—' He turned to Holmes. 'August—'

'I thought you said this happened in June.'

'No, the name. August. August Bell Clarion.'

Holmes had his back to me. His body went suddenly rigid, his head tilted slightly to one side. There was some-thing in that posture that alarmed me. A critical fact had just been revealed, though I could not discern what it was. I expected a sharp question to follow, but it did not come.

There was a long pause. With a sharp intake of breath, Holmes looked around him, taking in the entire room and its contents again, as if he had just walked in and never seen it before. Whoever 'August Bell Clarion' was, he seemed to be known to my friend.

He turned back to the laird. 'Was this Clarion gone in the morning as well?'

The laird nodded.

Holmes frowned. 'What has been changed in the room since that night?'

'Nothing in this area. A new edition has been brought in over there,' He gestured down one of the aisles. 'But most of the casks in this building have been maturing in place for many years.'

'What are these barrels here, this row set out from the rest?' asked Holmes, indicating the five casks near the table where we now stood.

'They are casks, not barrels. How can this help us, Mr Holmes?'

'Nevertheless!'

'This row contains the tasting casks of our special edition, McLaren Garnet, taken at different times in the run, that is filled at different times during the distillation. Here our visitors are given a taste. This edition is matured in casks, port butts they are called, due to their size and because they previously contained port. It gives them a rich, nutty, sweet flavour, hard to describe but so easy to taste. It will be our crowning achievement.' He tapped the nearest one. 'They are all good. These five, filled at different times, are our tasters. 51 is my personal favourite. I shall serve from these tomorrow night. One will be opened to demonstrate the inside finish of the cask, one of our secrets.'

'Each cask tastes a little different?' I asked.

'Only to the educated taste,' said the laird. 'Later they will be combined in a single vat to unify the flavours before bottling.'

'So we have been told,' said Holmes. 'Was this special row set out in exactly this position, that night?' Holmes was eying the row, moving down along it with his sharp eyes taking in every detail.

'Yes, at my request. We have sampled them regularly, before and since. This whisky will be the making of McLaren Distilleries. One taste of McLaren Garnet and we will have our Royal Warrant.'

'When you sample them, who has drawn the liquid if not yourself?'

'Various people. Coupe of course, both my sons, and myself. Why?'

Holmes was at the row of casks now, walking down past them and staring at each with that eagle look of concentration. 'What are these . . . circles? Here, and here. Small round wooden plugs.'

'Surely you know, Mr Holmes and toy with me now. They are called "bung holes" and it is where we insert the valinch, or some call it the "whisky thief", and draw out a sample. You did not know? I will show you.'

He opened the plug on the nearest cask, and inserted a lengthy, slender pipe-like instrument of aged brass. Putting his mouth over one end, with a brief draw through the pipe, for that is what it was, he brought some liquid up. He took up a small glass, placed nearby for this purpose and deposited a half-inch of reddish amber liquid.

'Taste,' he directed my friend.

Holmes waved it away 'Thank you, no' he said crisply.

Before the laird could respond, I stepped forward to cover this awkward moment. 'I would be delighted,' I said, receiving the glass. I took a sip. I am no expert but the flavour was extraordinary. 'Very nice. Very nice, indeed!' I took another taste. Rich, flavourful. Warming.

'Aye, it is always best straight from the cask,' said the laird.

I turned to Holmes who had been standing to one side, but he was nowhere to be seen.

The laird saw my confused look and turned to see the faint glow of the lantern, just visible through the supports, in the shadows underneath the row of the five tasting casks. And there, in the very narrow space between the row of five casks and the wall, Holmes was on his hands and knees behind them, his magnifying glass out, searching the floor and the wall behind the casks. Bending down to see what he was doing, I noticed he had withdrawn a small pocketknife and was digging into a crevice in the floorboards.

'What are you doing?' cried the laird. 'Come out from there!'

There was no reply. He lunged forward but the area between the casks and the wall was too narrow for his broad and bulky frame and he could not follow where

Holmes, whippet thin and limber, had gone. I could not have fitted back there, myself.

'Mr Holmes!' the laird said. 'You try my patience exceedingly. What has this to do with Fiona?'

Holmes rose with difficulty from behind the casks and edged out from behind them towards me, pocketing his magnifying glass. His coat was streaked with dirt, his face a mask of concentration. In his right hand he held the small pocketknife, blade extended. He took a clean handkerchief, wiped his knife carefully upon it, examined the residue, folded both with deliberation and put them in his pocket. Only then did he look up at the laird. 'Sir, I can honestly say I do not yet know. But you must allow me to take the path I require.'

'Well let me inform you of my own "path", Mr Holmes. I have employed you to solve the murder of Fiona Paisley. I have seen little result. The night after next is the most important in the history of this distillery. I will not have it ruined by your presence.'

'I can assure you of complete discretion,' said Holmes smoothly. 'No one need know.'

I retrieved the laird's lantern from underneath the row of casks and replaced it on the table.

'I have been unable to keep the whole story from the public, Mr Holmes. The only possible way to defuse this scandal is to solve it before the royal visit.' His voice rose in pitch and volume as sweat began to pour from his brow. 'If the most renowned private detective in London cannot manage—'

'I am a consulting detective, sir. And you have yet to bring in the police.'

The laird's voice rose to a shout. 'Mr Holmes! Solve this case by noon the day after tomorrow. Otherwise, believe me, sir, there will be serious repercussions. I need not remind you that I am well connected in London. I can have you ruined and rotting in gaol. You look doubtful? Do not doubt it. Even your brother will be powerless to help you. You will have delivered your results and be gone before the royal visitors arrive. Is that understood?'

Holmes was about to make a stinging reply, and I put a hand to his arm, but we were interrupted by the sharp sound of a door banging open at the back of the room. Cameron Coupe was standing in the doorway, silhouetted against the bright gaslit courtyard immediately outside.

'Sir, I heard voices. Can I be of assistance?' he asked. Behind him loomed two distillery employees, including two burly men we had seen before, one with the ruined face. Their posture was distinctly threatening.

I wondered whether he had been listening behind that door.

'Thank you, no,' said the laird, altering his tone. 'But come with me to Building C for a moment, Mr Coupe. I need to understand the problem you are having with the temperature in the new mash tun.'

'It is indeed a puzzler, sir. We have been unable to stabilize the heating element. It is likely we will have to discard the batch. But I will show you, sir.'

The laird turned back to us with a scowl. 'You have

heard me, Mr Holmes. Be productive, or be gone.'

He departed the room, having worked himself up to an icy fury.

Holmes shook his head in disgust.

'You must admit that was not one of our better moments,' said I. 'What is it that you found there, Holmes?'

'I will know for sure when I analyse this. Back to the room!'

CHAPTER 27

Divide and Conquer

he moment we had closed the door to Holmes's room behind us, my friend set about muttering and fussing with some vials of liquid and a flame over near the window, using items he had packed for this purpose. He was examining the residue of what he had found in the warehouse but did not want to talk about it. I will admit to following the first part of this experiment with interest, but waves of exhaustion washed over me as his exploration proceeded.

Holmes was in the deep grip of what I call his 'professional enthusiasm' – which carried him forward with such a zeal that he defied all notions of human endurance. I, however, was not blessed with such a constitution and will admit I fell asleep, shortly after Holmes confirmed that what he had discovered under the casks was dried human blood.

The next morning, I was awakened by Holmes shaking my shoulder. I groaned and stirred, finding myself stiff. I had fallen asleep, fully dressed, on his divan, and he had clearly thrown some blankets over me. I had no recollection of any of it.

'Watson, wake up. You were still awake when I identified the blood? Ah, yes. Good! Unmistakably, there was violence done back in that warehouse. Some time ago from the looks of it, but the residue not thoroughly removed. I went back for a second look.'

'In the middle of the night, alone? You are mad, Holmes. You endanger yourself!' I shook my head, feeling it was swathed in a wad of cotton batting. 'Is there any coffee?'

'I have rung for breakfast to be brought to us here. We have more to discuss.'

Mungo arrived shortly after with a tray of breakfast which I took from him and closed the door.

'What a family! What a case! Watson, we are challenged to be our best.' My friend paced back and forth in front of the hearth, on fire himself despite his sleepless night. He stopped and turned to me, with what I recognized was more than a touch of manic energy.

'Have you not slept at all, Holmes?' I asked.

He waved his hand in the air dismissively. 'I have learned little else in the warehouse, Watson. But I remain puzzled by the ghost you said you saw the floating in our hallway. And so I returned to look into it further.'

'Did you see her? It?' I asked.

'No. But while you continued in the arms of Morpheus, I made a study at the end of the hall. There is a simple stage illusion called "Pepper's Ghost" with which I am

310

familiar and which could have created the illusion of the semi-transparent, moving figure you described. It would have required a live participant of course, which is another question. But this effect is not possible given the constraints of the room size and shape. There is no way to set up the mirrors and glass which are needed. Nor is there a way for these props to be so easily dismantled and spirited – if you will forgive the pun – away.'

I poured us both some coffee. 'And yet I am sure of what I saw, Holmes. Here, eat something.' I held out a plate of toast.

He waved it away. 'I believe you saw something. But we must leave this for the moment, and turn our attention to the late Donal McLaren. Something about the laird's story does not feel right. I am sure we have not been given the entire picture. If only we could find someone who knew Donal McLaren in the service. Few survived Khartoum, I recall.'

'No British did. Khartoum was chaos, Holmes. I know. I had a friend who served there.'

'A friend, you say?'

'An officer, yes. A Scotsman, Kenneth MacCauley. He served with Gordon but left Khartoum just before the massacre to meet up with the expedition sent to relieve them. It never reached them in time. But he knew everyone at Khartoum.'

'Where is this man now?'

'As a matter of fact, he is in Edinburgh. I visited him once there.' I helped myself to some smoked salmon and toast.

'Might he have any records, or any photographs perhaps of his regiment?'

'Why, indeed he does! One is framed over his fireplace. A fine-looking group of men, all of them lost. Tragic. Though I believe General Gordon could not have—'

'At last! We are rewarded with a bit of luck in this case. You must go there at once and retrieve your friend's photograph!'

'All right. But why?'

'There is something awry with this tale of Donal McLaren, something about his last night here at Braedern. There are missing pieces to this puzzle.'

I poured Holmes some coffee and placed it in his hand.

'What about Donal's friend, Holmes? That August fellow, the one who gave you pause?'

Holmes set down the coffee untouched, and continued to pace.

'Please, Watson, just do as I ask. It is vital to our case.'

'I am not comfortable leaving you alone in this place.'

'I give you my solemn pledge to take the utmost care. You must do this. It is of critical importance.'

Bravery was admirable, but Holmes's tendency to neglect his personal safety was a worry. I pressed him to keep my Webley with him at all times. 'Very well, Watson,' he conceded at last. 'But I will stop short of wearing a sprig of rosemary in my buttonhole!' I failed to find this funny.

My journey was tedious in the heavy snow, but by the late afternoon, a cab delivered me to the door of Mr and

Mrs Kenneth MacCauley in Inverleith Place in Edinburgh. I had wired ahead and was expected.

The elegant ex-soldier of my acquaintance, his impressive head of thick sandy hair intact, and his moustache of old still elaborately curled, greeted me with enthusiasm at his front door. Behind him stood his wife, a quiet, tiny woman with a warm smile and gentle demeanour. Before long the three of us were seated comfortably in his sitting room, and MacCauley rose, gently took the photograph from the wall, and placed it in my hands.

Faded very little, the crisp image revealed a virile, spirited group of perhaps twenty men, posed proudly on some steps in Khartoum. Scanning the faces, I looked for one which resembled the portrait of Donal that Holmes and I had seen in Sir Robert's bedroom. I saw none.

'There he is. That is Donal McLaren,' said MacCauley, pointing a thick finger at a very large, moustachioed man in the back row, towering above his neighbours. The man had a fearsome scowl. Judging by the daguerreotype I had seen in the laird's room, this was not Donal McLaren, though who it was, I could not say. 'Though truth be told, I did not care for the fellow,' continued MacCauley. 'The man had a streak of cruelty. But war brings out the worst in some of us.'

'And the best in others,' said I. 'Such as yourself, my dear fellow. Not everyone receives a Distinguished Conduct Medal.'

MacCauley flushed. 'Many were more deserving.'

Mrs MacCauley shook her head with a smile, and

313

approaching a small table near the fire, picked up the medal, now displayed in a polished wood and glass box and handed it to me. I admired it, and after another fifteen minutes of pleasant banter and reminiscences, I finally got around to asking MacCauley if I could borrow the photograph. 'The picture of Donal McLaren would be very useful to my friend Holmes in the case in which we are currently engaged,' I explained.

He grew immediately uncomfortable, looked away, at his wife, then down at his drink. Finally he said, 'I am so terribly sorry, old man. I just cannot part with it. It is, truly, my most treasured possession. Perhaps except for Jenny here.'

'I am not a possession, Kenneth,' said she, with a light touch and a pat on his arm. 'And yet I am yours.' He laughed and took her hand in his. The warmth between them touched my heart and I felt a pang of longing for my Mary.

I glanced again at the photograph. If I were an artist, I would try to sketch the man who was not Donal McLaren but who had taken his name. But I lacked the skill.

'Kenneth,' said the lady. 'Why not let Dr Watson have the photograph copied? There is a studio over by Inverleith Park where they do such things. Surely you could allow that?'

'Capital idea!' cried MacCauley.

But it had grown late and shops were closed. I was enjoined to stay the night at the MacCauleys' house, and get the photograph reproduced in the morning. Reluctantly

I agreed, and cabled Holmes, wondering if indeed word would reach him at remote Braedern. But to return without the photograph was unthinkable. I did not rest easy, despite my hosts' genial hospitality and a comfortable bed.

The next morning brought blue sky and a layer of ice over all of Edinburgh. Upon my early arrival at the photography atelier I was met with further delay. To copy the photograph was an arduous process. With no negative from which to strike a print, they would be obliged to light and photograph the print itself, very carefully to ensure the details of the faces would be captured. Anything less would not serve, and I left them with the admonition to take extreme care with the original. The process would take several hours. I left my friend MacCauley's precious possession with them and strolled out into the chilly streets, impatient and eager to return to Holmes.

As I wandered down Inverleith Street, I paused to buy a hot bridie from a street vendor. The smell of the Scottish meat pie reminded me pleasantly of some days spent in Edinburgh. It was then that I caught sight of a strange, foreboding edifice looming off to my right. It was Fettes College – where Holmes had gone as a youth! I stared up at the curious construction. It was an imposing building, complex with extravagant ornaments every-where – gargoyles, bartizans, gilded ironwork. It had a kind of French Gothic sensibility reminding me of châteaux of the Loire Valley, yet with other influences I could not name.

I had two hours and nothing to do. It was with a small

tremor of conscience that I turned my steps up the hill. I had no idea that my idle curiosity would turn out to be a journey into one of Holmes's darkest secrets.

CHAPTER 28

Fettes

ooking back now, it was an unusual path I chose. I approached the enormous main building and was further stuck by the strange moodiness of the place. It towered several storeys high with jagged spires and medieval turrets. Gargoyles peered down at me from a dark facade, and the entire edifice had a kind of frightening aspect. Or perhaps severe would be a better word. If black magic were legitimised as a scholarly pursuit, this might be its home. I approached and noticed a stone ribbon bearing the motto, 'Industria' and a large carving of a honeybee. How strange that Holmes or his family would have chosen such a place.

I walked around to the back of the building looking for a place to sit, and found a snowy park with a convenient bench. I brushed it with my gloved hand, set a newspaper down and took a seat. Nearby were a number of spirited boys, perhaps twelve to fifteen years of age, bundled against the cold and taking advantage of the break in the weather to pelt one another with snowballs. I was wondering idly what Holmes was like at this age when a short, stocky man in his mid-fifties, his white, wispy hair escaping a tweed cap, strolled by walking a small grey terrier dog. Glancing my way, he moved on, then suddenly stopped and turned back. He stared at me with a penetrating gaze that could paralyze a student. Despite myself, I stiffened in alarm.

'Dr Watson? Are you by chance Dr John H. Watson?' enquired the man. His accent was that of an educated Scotsman, his voice high pitched and piercing. I felt as though I were about to be quizzed on a chapter I had failed to read.

'Yes, I am he. Have we met, sir?'

He smiled. 'We have not, Doctor, but I feel as though I know you. You see, I read your story in *Beeton's Christmas Annual*. You are a friend of the detective Sherlock Holmes?'

'I am. But how do you know me, sir?'

'I saw your picture in *The Illustrated Police News*. Beeton's got you all wrong.'

I could hardly fathom it!

He stepped forward and offered me his hand. 'I am Dr Gordon Jennings, assistant headmaster,' the man continued and his lopsided smile dispelled the fearsome first impression. 'Of course you are wondering at my interest. I knew young Master Sherlock well in the brief time he attended Fettes. How happy I am to hear he is thriving and has found his metier, and a friend such as yourself. Come inside, please, have tea! We shall talk in my rooms.'

My delight was tempered by a vague sense of guilt at

the curiosity I felt. How might Holmes feel if he ever discovered this visit? But, I reasoned, this short excursion would make my time pass quickly. I glanced at my pocket watch. I had an hour and a half before the photograph would be ready.

We entered the grand structure that was the main building at Fettes, and arrived directly into an impressive hall, where an enormous fireplace, portraits of the founder, and various banners and awards were designed to impress the visitor. We faced a vast, imposing staircase with barley sugar bannisters leading to a landing that branched off to the left and right.

As I followed Dr Jennings up these stairs towards his private rooms, I asked about the unusual motto carved outside. Jennings explained, 'It is our school emblem, and part of the benefactor's coat of arms. Our motto is "Industria" – the busy bee. I remember Master Sherlock quite liked it.'

My host led the way down some long hallways, and an even longer stone corridor to a narrow circular staircase, and presently I found myself seated in his private quarters in the eastern wing of the school. It was comfortably furnished with two sagging armchairs near a cheerful fire. Scattered around were a profusion of books which spilled from crowded bookcases into dusty stacks scattered about the parquet floor, and an ink-stained standing desk. A tall, narrow window looked out on gothic ramparts. Dr Jennings called for tea, and launched without preamble into a reminiscence he seemed compelled to relate.

'It was 1870 and your friend was fifteen, perhaps sixteen years old. It was our first year as a school, and his last before University.

'Fettes, as you know, or perhaps you do not, Doctor, was originally conceived by its founder as a place for poor boys to get a good education. However, from the very start, we took in non-Foundation children as well. And most of these, like young Sherlock, were English and well to do. I cannot remember precisely from where he hailed, only that he was a paying student, who had been attending elsewhere, but that his parents wanted him moved for his last year before University.'

'Why, I wonder?'

'I do not remember why, only that it was regarded as being "for his own good". That is a sentiment often voiced where children were concerned.'

I nodded and he continued, poking at the fire as he did so.

'I need to give you some background about the school,' he said. 'Fettes was created in a kind of reaction to the prevailing notion of education at the time. Charity schools then were often rather punitive in nature, and as a result of their desire to *improve*, rather than *educate* their charges, the children who attended them usually ended up resentful, dishonest, and rebellious.'

'Any child would, I expect,' said I.

'But the emphasis at Fettes was to be on scholarship. Here, that meant the classics, rhetoric and history. Mathematics and science were given short shrift.'

'That is odd, given Holmes's temperament. I wonder, then, why his parents chose it for him,' I said.

He shrugged. 'The theory was to mould the "gentleman". Science and mathematics were considered crass, perhaps even a bit vulgar.'

'Vulgar? How strange! The very studies that save lives, build engines, and invent the future were considered low status?'

'Well, not fit for a true gentleman. You must have felt from time to time that men of science – such as yourself – are looked upon by some as, well, highly skilled tradesmen. Ah, tea has arrived.'

As a school prefect busied himself in setting out an antiquated tea service on a table by the window, my host got up and waved the young man away. 'Thank you, Peter, that will be all.' He then felt the temperature of the teapot with his fingertips, checked the colour, and laid out the cups himself. Outside the window behind him, a snow-tipped gargoyle leered down at the distant courtyard. The grey terrier dozed by the fire. I felt as though I had stepped back in time.

I pondered his last words. It was true even now that the work of a doctor was considered wet and dirty enough to garner disrespect from the upper classes – except, of course, when our expertise was urgently required. The detective's trade was even worse. It implied association with the crim-inal classes, and a certain kind of physicality that smacked of effort and sweat.

Despite this, Holmes retained the unmistakable deportment of a gentleman. Knowing him as I did, it was no affectation, but rather a deeply ingrained sense of who the man was. I took it for granted that Holmes had grown up with a certain level of privilege, although he never spoke of it, and his Spartan ways (except for a certain erratic vanity of dress) did not in any way speak of an expectation of luxury.

The old man finished his fussing and, retrieving two steaming cups of tea, returned to his chair opposite mine, placing one cup before me.

'A remarkable Souchong, try it. And yes, how very odd this anti-science attitude strikes us today in our second Age of Enlightenment, does it not?' he said.

I nodded and took a sip. The tea was smoky and excellent. 'Very good,' I said.

'And now to your friend. I remember his first day, distinctly. As assistant headmaster, it was my duty to greet new boys as they entered our school for the first time. Young Sherlock arrived late, two weeks into the autumn term.' The old man gave a little chuckle. 'He was immediately dubbed "Daddy Long Legs", a schoolboy sobriquet which he despised.'

This took me back to my own school days, hardly as distinguished, perhaps, where I had been tagged 'The Beagle.' I never liked it either.

'Incidentally, a gentleman, as defined by the school, was one who did not complain. And so Fettes wanted to wean all its boys from the notion that comfort was expected from life. It was a rigorous and physically challenging regime.

The day started before 7 a.m. with an ice-cold bath in the little tin tubs placed in each room.'

'In winter as well? That is not Spartan, it is barbaric.'

'Indeed. The tubs were filled at night in preparation for the morning. Sometimes a thin crust of ice would form on the water during the night, and when this happened, the boys were instructed to break the crust with their hair-brushes, and to get in and wash. It was a habit said to awaken and sharpen the senses.'

I little thought Holmes ever had need to 'sharpen his senses', but rather to dull them upon occasion, so acutely was he attuned to his surroundings.

'Physical fitness was important,' Jennings continued, 'and team sports were mandatory. It was thought that if the boys channelled their energy in this way and learned to compete in concert with others, that it would mitigate their natural aggressions and tendencies to violence or pranks. Solo sports such as tennis were discouraged as they were thought to lead to selfishness. However, boxing was a big part of the programme.'

'Holmes boxes to this day.'

Jennings smiled. 'How he came to it may interest you. Trouble arose because young Sherlock had no interest whatsoever in team sports, and refused to participate. Various punishments were attempted, but he was clever enough not to let on that isolation and library assignments were not the onerous task they would be for many, but rather a welcome distraction. When he was sent to the library on some ludicrous research task, he would appear to be disconsolate and contrite, but would secretly complete the challenge in a trice, and then spend the rest of the time researching matters of interest to him.'

'How do you know that?' I asked, fascinated.

'Because I was also the librarian and was tasked to supervise this "punishment". The school little realized that I sided with this recalcitrant rebel. I must say, however, that his choice of topics was idiosyncratic in the extreme. Railway developments, arcane details of criminal law, the geologic properties of soil in different areas of Britain, bloodstains, bodily decay after death – oh, and chemistry, a clear favourite. Those are a few that I recall.'

I laughed, thinking how Holmes appeared not to know or care that the earth revolved around the sun, but was nearly at the professional level in chemistry.

'I once went so far as to complete his assignment for him. I catalogued some obscure political data on the Plantagenet monarchy as he spent the time devouring the recent publications by Mendeleev and Meyer on their periodic table of the elements. He claimed it was the most exciting reading since English chemist John Newlands had discovered patterns in the weight of elements which seemed to remind him of the octaves in music.'

I smiled at this. 'There is a small laboratory in our sitting room in Baker Street,' I added, forgetting for the moment that I did not, at that precise time, live at 221B. I ventured another quick look at my watch. There was at least an hour more before the photograph would be ready.

'Sherlock excelled at his schoolwork, and after a very short time, several boys grew to resent his intellectual gifts, particularly since he took no pains to "hide his light," shall we say.'

I laughed.

But Jennings grew sombre. 'Funny now, perhaps, but it set off an incident that I will never forget.'

'What happened?'

'It was just prior to Christmas in 1870 and the boys were sitting their exams as well as preparing to return home for the holidays. Sherlock at fifteen was already a taciturn young man; I alone was privy to his witty flashes of humour. His time at Fettes was lonely, although perhaps I make too much of this. The truly introspective man does not require the boisterous companionship of his peers.'

'Agreed. But what is the story you wish to relate?'

'Well, as I said, it was the eve of departure for Christmas. The valises were packed and ready, and aligned outside each boy's door, awaiting a morning collection. Some of the boys had very early trains.

'Sherlock had duly placed his small valise at the door to his room but later discovered it missing. All the others were still in place.

'He immediately surmised the perpetrator and marched down the hall to confront one Master August Bell Clarion, who had been the ringleader of those who had tormented him since his arrival in September. Sherlock had made that arrogant bully look the fool on more than one occasion.'

August Bell Clarion! The name dealt me a solid blow. The very boy who had been the disreputable friend of Donal McLaren! Holmes had certainly reacted to the name.

Jennings pressed on. 'He also proved August had forged several other students' papers for a fee. In any case, that night he discovered his possessions strewn around, clothing ripped and his books set aflame in the small fireplace in the room. August and three other boys were lying in wait, having stupefied themselves on a bottle of whisky one of them had smuggled into the room to celebrate the end of exams. Being unused to the strong spirits, the boys were quite literally out of their heads.'

'Barbarians! But how do you know this?'

'It was witnessed by another student. Sherlock tried to rescue one of the books, which apparently meant a great deal to him, and unable to do so, turned on August Bell Clarion in a fury, pulling the bully off his bed where he stood crowing before his rapt audience in triumphant disorder. Down to the floor they went, fists and feet flailing.

'A battle ensued, four against one, and could have been a disaster had not the young pupil who had witnessed his entry into the room run to call for help.

'I was the one who answered the call, and separating the perpetrators from their victim, I then whisked Sherlock away to my rooms, where I attended to a sprained wrist and various minor injuries.'

'Ruffians!'

'I wrestled with myself on whether to wake the headmaster and inform the school, which was my responsibility, but something told me this would not be best for young Sherlock Holmes. He did not return home for Christmas as he did not want his family to see him in that state. He informed them that he wished to stay on to complete some chemistry experiments.

'I remember asking him if this was a suitable excuse that would not arouse suspicion. He said that not only would it *not* arouse suspicion, but if he told them the real reason, it would surprise them even less. You seem amused, Dr Watson.'

'Well, I do know that he survived his school days,' I smiled. 'But what of his family?'

'I never met them, but I was told they were eccentric. In any case, I returned with him to his dormitory after everyone had left. As we opened the door to his room, we confronted a shambles. It was only then that I saw a trace of emotion from Sherlock.

'In one corner of the room was an open violin case. The violin itself had been removed and smashed against the corner of the bed, and was lying in ruin upon his pillow. He approached it and picked up the pieces. If he did not shed actual tears, he did so inwardly I perceived, for I saw his shoulders shake.'

I felt a searing pain of sympathy for the child Holmes and regretted my moment of laughter earlier.

'What a shame. Did you ever hear him play?'

'Oh, yes. He practised in the chapel, in the middle of the night.'

The middle of the night!

'The reason was twofold. One was that the sound was insulated from where the pupils worked and slept, and the other was that the reverberations in that vaulted stone space were particularly felicitous to his music making, and he simply enjoyed the sounds it made there.

'There were those boys and members of the staff who thought Sherlock Holmes a cold-hearted automaton, but when I once heard him play, I knew otherwise. And after a time, and knowing what to look for, I noticed his kind sympathy towards younger boys, particularly those who were bullied.'

Ever the champion of the underdog, I mused. 'What happened when the boys returned from the holidays?'

'During the Christmas break, I had Sherlock's room changed for an empty one in the junior staff lodging, where one or two overflow students were housed. It was a mean little room, cold and with one small window which needed to be stuffed with a spare rag to keep out the draught, but it was private, and suited him perfectly. It had the added benefit of not receiving the cold baths daily, as it was up four flights of stairs and was frequently "forgotten." He thrived.'

'But what of this August Bell Clarion? You said there was a witness. There must have been repercussions?'

'The witness, Hemley, a junior boy, was disbelieved by the headmaster. August Bell Clarion's three accomplices told a well-rehearsed story confirming his version, and described your friend as drunkenly attacking Clarion with no provocation. Although Sherlock's and Hemley's stories matched and contradicted this, and the evidence of the opened suitcase was noted, August, or rather his parents, ultimately prevailed.'

'Against the evidence? How?'

'Come to the window, please.' I did so and the old man pointed to an imposing, modern brick building at the end of the courtyard. 'That is Clarion Hall, which went up the following year.'

'Then who was supposed to have beaten Holmes?'

'A fifth student, an enormous and obese half-foreign boy, was blamed for the attack and expelled. But what happened after that will interest you profoundly, Dr Watson. As I mentioned, young Sherlock healed quickly and he began pre-dawn workouts in the gymnasium to strengthen his injured wrist, and to develop stamina and flexibility following this attack. He took up boxing, and did so with a particular passion.'

I smiled. 'He does few things by half measure.'

'True. As always, when young Sherlock set his mind to learn a thing, he excelled at it. But he refrained from competing until near the end of the school year. He entered the school boxing competition at the very last moment. With apparent ease, he dispatched every one of his early opponents and qualified for the finals, facing, of course, the school champion—'

'Clarion!'

'Precisely. I can see by your smile that you well imagine the result. And you would not be wrong, Doctor. In June, a week before the end of term, Sherlock Holmes took first place in the boxing championship with a single knockout punch to Master August Bell Clarion, which broke that bully's jaw in two places, and kept him from the celebration for the those leaving for University.'

'That must have satisfied Holmes,' I remarked with a smile.

The old man looked hard at me. 'Yes and no. How well do you know your friend, Doctor? How do you think he felt about this?'

He was right of course. Holmes was not one to crow over victories. His satisfaction was generally of a more philosophical nature.

'In fact, Doctor Watson, he was immediately contrite and furious with himself for the extreme force he exerted on that critical punch. He felt he had lost control and told me he had been going only for points, not to break a jaw.'

'Were there any repercussions?'

'Fortunately young Sherlock had been accepted at Camford and was out of reach. The construction on Clarion Hall was halted in protest, but that was all.'

'But the building now stands.'

'It was completed later, in memory of a younger brother, Christian Clarion. That boy was even worse than his elder brother, and his parents had to make amends to the school and to send him on a round-the-world finishing tour. Rumour has it that he got into a brawl with another student in Florence, was tossed into the Arno and drowned.'

'I see. And what of the elder Clarion, Holmes's nemesis, August Bell?'

'Killed in service in Egypt several years ago, I have read.'

While I wish ill will to very few, this news, which corroborated the laird's story, was welcome.

'Well, Doctor Watson, does that give you useful insight

to your companion? I sense your kind sympathy for him and that is why I have been so forthcoming.'

'It has been most instructive. But there is one more thing. Mr Holmes left Camford early under some kind of cloud, I understand. Do you know anything of that time?'

Jennings sighed. 'Well, yes. Which is why I was so happy to read "A Study in Scarlet", Dr Watson. It seems Mr Holmes has at last found his place in the world.'

'But do you know the details of why he left Camford?'

'I will say only this. When I heard of Mr Holmes's troubles there I took it upon myself to travel south to appear as a character witness at his trial.'

'Trial!'

Jennings paused and regarded me carefully. Finally, he said, 'If Mr Holmes has not told you that story, then it is not for me to do so. There is another to whom you may wish to speak. An old woman who lives in the village of Atholmere. She is the grandmother of the victim in this case. I met her during the trial and was impressed by her wisdom. She, and she alone should give you the facts. Here is her name and address. It is two miles south of Aberdeen.' He took out a sheet of foolscap and wrote on it, handing me the page.

'Doctor Jennings, I thank you for your time. But I do feel I have been a little improper in learning what my friend may wish to have kept private. This further news—'

'Doctor Watson, that is your choice. But as his closest friend, you should know this one fact about Mr Sherlock Holmes. The Camford event was a scandal. And a very serious one!'

I paused, curious, but willed myself not to cross the invisible line.

Jennings waited, his eyes searching my face.

'The trial, there was a "victim", you said?' The words came out of my mouth unbidden. 'Then Sherlock Holmes—'

'Was himself the chief suspect.'

'For what, exactly?'

'Why, for murder, Dr Watson.'

CHAPTER 29

Thin Ice

n route back to Braedern, the perfectly reproduced photograph in hand, I pondered the
words of Gordon Jennings. Holmes had fallen
under suspicion for murder once since I had
known him, when a young policeman challenged how he
could possibly know the movements of the killer in a
certain blood-spattered room – unless he were the murderer
himself. Fortunately an intervention by the better-informed
Inspector Lestrade had prevailed, but not without some
difficulty.

But what had transpired at Camford? In any case, I could
not travel to Atholmere just then. Holmes had made it clear
that the photograph was an urgent priority, although I was
not sure why.

By the time I had taken the train to Aberdeen, and
another to Ballater, then hired a carriage, the afternoon
darkness had begun to descend around the forlorn castle.
The laird's deadline had been by noon this very day for

Holmes to have solved the case. While Holmes was not in the habit of bowing to such ultimatums, I wondered if the laird's threat carried any weight, and what progress my friend had made in my absence.

I proceeded to Holmes's room, and finding the door locked, knocked once. No answer. I knocked again 'Ye will nae find him there,' called Mungo, the old servant. He was standing at the other end of the hall, towels and linens in his arms.

'Where is he, then?'

'Do not know. Hiding, is my guess. He got a grand fright last night. And the laird is furious that he has had no report on Mr Holmes's work.'

'What do you mean a fright?'

'I think he saw a ghost. End of the hall here, just as I warned ye about. The Lady Elizabeth. She is not a friendly ghost. I am fairly certain, Doctor, that he was frighted near out of his wits.' Mungo seemed to enjoy the thought.

'Mr Holmes does not believe in ghosts, Mungo,' said I. 'Nor does he frighten easily. On whose account do you relate this tale?'

'We all heard the noises.'

'What noises?'

'The ghostly cries. Mr Holmes shouting.'

'And did you not run to see what it was?'

'Nary a soul will venture into this hallway at that hour, Dr Watson. I have told ye.'

'That is outrageous. Unlock this door for me, at once.'

The man hesitated, then complied.

The bed had not been slept in. But neither was there any sign of a struggle or mischief of any kind. 'Has anyone seen Mr Holmes since the events of last night?'

Mungo then said that Holmes had been seen talking to Isla McLaren in the morning. After a half an hour of searching the castle, I discovered Mrs McLaren in the library, seated on the sofa with a book. She looked up and smiled.

'Ah, at last. Close the door behind you, Doctor,' said she, calmly. In answer to my questions she replied that she understood Holmes had continued his investigations in and around the distillery and that he had last been seen several hours before. 'I hear there was some noise near your rooms last night. In the morning Mr Holmes questioned me closely about the late Lady McLaren's ghost, which is said to haunt that area. We discussed this, you must recall? He would not go so far as to say he had seen this ghost but that is what I surmised.' Mrs McLaren seemed almost amused as she related this information.

'Mr Holmes does not believe in ghosts,' said I.

She smiled in a way that irritated me in its complacency. 'Well, to be truthful, he seemed more angry about whatever transpired there last night than anything else.'

'Where is he now?'

The lady shrugged. She put down her book and rose. 'I do not know. The laird was looking for him earlier. I believe Mr Holmes said something about going into town. Shall we ask the servants?'

'Which town?'

'Ballater is the nearest. Perhaps he wished to send a cable. He received several last night.'

'One was from me. I am glad he received it.'

'Well, that is all, Dr Watson. I do not know where he is at present.'

There was a sudden commotion outside the room. The library doors were flung open and in rushed the groundsman, Ualan Moray, wet from the snow, and wild with panic.

'Dr Watson. Thank God!' He gasped and clutched his side, trying to breathe. 'Come at once! My missing son, Iain! Mr Holmes! The icehouse!'

'What icehouse?' said I.

'Down by the garden wall. Not used in winter,' said Isla McLaren, coming forward. 'Mr Moray, what has happened?'

The old man was out of breath and could barely string his words together. 'Mr Holmes – in danger – come!'

'Bring our coats to the Great Hall. Now!' cried the lady, and a servant dashed off. We both grasped Moray by an arm and took off at a run in that same direction. As we bundled into our coats in the Great Hall, we pressed Moray for more.

'My youngest, Calum, found Iain's knapsack buried in the snow down there this morning. I went and found the place unlocked but naebody there, so I brought Mr Holmes.'

'Unlocked, you say?' said Isla in alarm.

The servants brought the three of us lanterns and we dashed outside into freezing cold. The snow was coming down in a blizzard now and the greyish white swirls lit by our feeble lanterns disappeared into the darkness. 'Where is he now?' I cried. 'You said danger!'

Ualan Moray pointed down the hill in the direction of the small mound I had noted earlier. 'He is in the pit. The ladder is gone. Hurry!'

I had heard of icehouses on grand estates but never had occasion to enter one. They had deep caverns some several storeys deep in which ice was stored for summer use. They could be dangerous in the extreme.

'My God, Ualan!' said Isla. She took off down the hill and we slogged after her.

As we ran slipping and sliding down the incline, our voices threw clouds into the frigid air.

'Why did he go into the pit?' Mrs McLaren asked.

'Looking for my boy. He wanted mair light. I went to fetch a second lantern.'

'How long has he been in the ice?' I cried.

Next to me, Isla slid in the snow and she clutched my arm to keep from falling as we scrambled forward down the icy slope.

'Nae mair than twenty minutes,' said the old man.

The mound was some two hundred yards away. The air was so cold it seared my lungs with every breath. The new snow was powder and we slid and sunk in to our knees. Still we stumbled, sliding and unsteady. 'Mrs McLaren, you told me he went into town,' said I.

'That is what he told me!' she exclaimed. Was she lying? I glanced at her and nearly slipped on a tree stump, tumbling forward into a drift. The lady went down with me and one of the lanterns went out.

In a moment we were back on our feet, relit the lantern,

and pressed on, panting with the exertion. The icy air tore into my chest in waves of pain. We half ran, half tumbled and slid the last yards, at last arriving at the low white mound like a berm that projected up from the ground near the garden wall. We followed Moray to the other side of it, not visible from the castle.

From this side it was clear the small mound was a structure, like a child's playhouse, But the 'house' was sunk strangely into the earth, buried up to its eaves, with 'windows' which were opaque, and presumably just for effect, barely showing at the bottom. The door had three locks but all were open and the door stood ajar, the snow heavily trampled in front of it.

Moray tugged open the heavy door and we entered.

All was dark within, and I felt a chill even colder than the snow. Moray held his lantern aloft. Just visible was a concrete floor, and in the centre a deep, black pit, ten feet across. I moved to the edge and peered into the unfathomable depths. 'Holmes? Holmes!' I shouted.

There was no reply. My chest went tight. No sign of a lantern. His must have gone out.

'How deep is this?' I asked.

'Two storeys. But there will be ten feet of ice in there now.'

I looked frantically around for a ladder or any form of access. Mrs McLaren searched as well. There was nothing in the pit, nor on the walls.

'Where was the ladder when you left?' said I.

'Fastened to the edge. Here.' Moray indicated the strong hooks on the inside of the pit. 'Where it always rests.'

'Someone must have come in and taken it,' said the lady. She turned to Moray. 'You left the door unlocked?'

'Aye.' His voice caught in a sob.

I continued to stare down into the black chasm. 'Holmes?' I shouted again down into the void. There was no response. Where was he? Where was the light he had brought down with him?

'Was this here when you left?' asked Mrs McLaren. I turned to see her pointing to a large bucket. I had not noticed it before. It was empty, and near the edge of the pit.

Ualan Moray turned to it in surprise. 'No.'

A wavering, faint voice suddenly drifted up from below. 'Watson? Is that you?'

'Holmes!' A thrill of relief came over me.

'Bit chilly,' came the weakened voice.

'We are coming Holmes!' I shouted. 'Keep faith!'

I turned to the others. 'Moray, fetch a rope. And people to help. Quick, man. His life depends on it.' Moray took off at a run. I moved back to the edge of the pit. 'Holmes? Holmes? Can you hear me? The ladder was taken. Moray has gone for help. Are you all right?'

'I have found two bodies, Watson. Fiona is one. I cannot be sure of the second. But—'

'My God,' said Mrs McLaren.

'Are you all right?' I called down again.

Nothing.

'Holmes?'

'I shall get more help,' cried Isla McLaren, moving towards the door. 'In case Moray fails.'

'Be careful. There is treachery about.'

She shook her head as if I were foolish for saying so, and left at a run.

Alone in the chamber, I took Moray's single lantern and shone it around, searching for something, anything, to reach Holmes. There was nothing. I returned to the edge of the pit. I felt for my gun, and then remembered I had left it with Holmes.

'Holmes, try to keep talking.'

There was a long silence.

'Can you speak? Talk to me.' When a person freezes to death, sleep usually precedes it.

'Tea. Nice cup of,' came the weak voice.

'Very good idea. Holmes?' I had to keep him talking. 'I had a bit of an adventure in Edinburgh. I want to tell you about it.'

'Tell—'

'I have the picture. It is not Donal McLaren.'

'Ah—'

'But there is more, Holmes.' A second or two passed. 'Holmes?'

Silence.

'Keep talking, Holmes. It was a piquant tale,' I said. There was no reply. 'Holmes? A fascinating tale. Are you curious? Can you hear me?'

Silence for several seconds. Then at last, his voice, weaker than before.

'Bucket of water. Someone threw—'

Good God, he had been doused in water. The same person

who had taken the ladder must have done this as well. Holmes's clothes would be frozen solid. It was a miracle he was still alive. But he would not be for long if he could not be retrieved. I was torn. Would one or both of the others succeed in getting help in time? I knew only one thing. He could not be left here alone.

CHAPTER 30

Romeo and Juliet

y the grace of God Moray returned in time with a rope and four men. We found strong hooks on the walls and tied the ropes to them. I insisted on being first into the pit, one rope laced like a harness around my chest, a second in my hand, and a lantern gripped between my teeth.

It was a perilous descent but at last I stood on something solid, if terribly slick. I held up the lantern to send the feeble light around the pit. I quickly spotted the shadowy and macabre limbs of the two bodies Holmes had found, protruding upwards from the grey moonscape of the mounded ice. But where was Holmes?

I continued in a circle until I saw my poor friend, huddled over at one edge of the pit, and curled into a ball, his hands in tight fists. 'Holmes!' I cried out. He did not respond.

I lunged towards him and slipped on the treacherous surface, tumbling onto to the sharp edges of the ice rocks and bruising my ribs.

With difficulty I righted myself and clambered towards his unconscious form. I felt for a pulse. It was faint and his breathing was shallow. I managed to fasten my second rope around his waist and under his arms, and called up to the men above.

'Hurry,' I shouted. 'Raise him now! We are losing him!'

In the dim light of my lantern, I saw the rope tighten and his body began to lift from the ice, out of my hands and up into the darkness above me, silhouetted against the lantern light above. As he drew away from me I saw three pale faces lit from above peering down at us. Suddenly the depth of the coldness struck me in a wave of almost unimaginable pain. How had he endured nearly thirty minutes down here?

'We have him,' came a voice from above. Thank God.

Then I, too, was raised from the pit and once on solid ground, rushed to attend my friend, shivering myself as I did so. While the others pulled the two corpses from the pit, it was the live victim upon whom I concentrated. Holmes had indeed been doused with water, and in the brighter light of the rescuers' lanterns I saw that his clothes were eerily rigid, two thirds covered with a thin layer of crisp, new white ice. I wrapped him in blankets, listened to his faint heartbeat and began to help lash him to one of the sledges.

I stared down at the noble face, white and still. Had we pulled him out in time?

Meanwhile, the two frozen corpses, including the headless body of the poor lass, had been raised out by the others.

The second body, as one might have predicted, was Ualan's Moray's missing son, Iain.

I headed up the hill towards the castle with Holmes's still figure on the sledge beside me.

We were let into the kitchen area and quickly shown to a large room – a secondary food preparation room off the main kitchen which had an enormous fire at one end and an oven at the other. While I propped Holmes up in a chair near the fire and sent for fresh clothes from his room, two large oak tables in the centre of the room were cleared. There, the strongest servants, horrified but stalwart, placed the two bodies, which arrived shortly after we did.

Holmes was barely breathing. Under my direction, we moved him briefly into the pantry, and after my quick inspection for frostbite, dried him thoroughly and changed him into warm, fresh clothes brought down by Mungo. He remained unconscious during this, his right fist clenched like a rock, and I could not open it to examine his fingers for frostbite. I had to let it go and moved him back to the second kitchen.

His pulse gained strength as I enlisted the aid of two scullery maids to bring additional warm blankets and wrap him in them. I called for hot water bottles, tested their temperature, and placed one under each armpit, one on his stomach, another on his lap. Minutes later, I moved him back into the larger room, near, but not too close to the fire. We would have to be careful with this process because warming a frozen body too quickly could kill.

My doctor's bag having been brought down, I took his

temperature and listened to his heart. A fatal arrhythmia could occur at any time during the rewarming, and because of this, any sharp movement was to be avoided.

I called for warm brandy mixed with lemon and honey to start the warming from inside. To my relief, his eyes finally opened and I got him to take a few sips. That too would have to go slowly. His lips were blue and after a time, his body had begun to shake. That was a good sign.

At some time during this process, Isla McLaren had entered the room, and now stared down at my friend in grave concern. 'Dr Watson,' said she, 'Will he live?'

I nodded, willing it to be true. 'Very well then,' said she. 'The royal party has arrived for the dinner preceding the tasting. I will fetch the laird now, if he will break away.'

As she passed through the open door to the main kitchen I got a glimpse of servants rushing about with slabs of meat, bowls of fruit, platters of cakes. The festive preparations for the royal visit could not be in stranger contrast to our own gruesome task. I quickly closed the door behind her.

I glanced over at the stiffened remains of Fiona Paisley and Iain Moray. With a final look at Holmes, who was propped before the fire on two chairs and resting comfortably, I approached the two frozen bodies on the tables in the centre of the room.

They were both caught in strange, contorted positions resembling nothing so much as dead beetles – arms and legs oddly bent, some sticking up into the air. These positions related, I presumed, to how they had ultimately frozen on the uneven surface of the mounds of ice. The girl's headless corpse, white with frost as her head had been when presented on the platter, was perhaps even stranger than the boy's. Her back was arched, and arms extended, fists clenched. It was hard to think of this form as human.

The body of Iain Moray, on the other hand, was, like Holmes moments ago, covered in a white layer of thin, brittle, grey ice. This made him an eerie statue. His arms were extended forward and crooked, hands nearly touching, head tilted to one side, almost in a position of succour. He had once been a handsome lad, strong bodied, with a broad chest and shock of reddish blond hair, now frozen in a halo around his anguished face.

Already the frost and ice had begun to melt, leaving dark patches here and there on both corpses.

Ualan Moray stood over his son's body, weeping silently.

I became aware that a few of the kitchen staff were now huddled at the other end of the large room, eyes bulging in horror. Abruptly their gaze flew from the corpses to something over my shoulder. They screamed.

I whirled to see Holmes. Now standing, he was an emaciated, ghastly apparition. He had thrown the blankets and hot water bottles to the ground. With his white shirt hanging off his thin frame, his face a ghostly bluish pale, he was a fright.

'Watson!' he croaked. 'Clear this room!' I nodded at one of the servants and the room emptied, all save Ualan Moray, lingering in grief next to the body of his son.

'Sit down, Holmes,' I said. 'You are not at all well!'

He did not, and instead stepped forward to view the bodies. His legs buckled but I rushed forward and succeeded in catching him before he hit the flagstones. He was shivering now, deep, rocking tremors. He raised a trembling hand and looked at it with a strange dispassion, as though it were not part of him. It was shaking like the palsy.

'Devil take it!' He took a deep breath and willed the hand to stillness. 'Give me your glass, Watson! I need to examine the bodies.'

'Not yet. They will keep.' I picked up a warm blanket and threw it over his shoulders.

'No, they are melting as we dawdle. The glass, I say! And get me a pitcher of warm water!'

I had taken to carrying an extra magnifying glass at all times since our adventure with the *Twice Dead Missionary* some two years past in which a second lens had literally saved our lives, I handed him mine and he stumbled towards the contorted remains of Fiona Paisley. I placed a small pitcher of warm water nearby.

Holmes bent close over the body of the girl, peering through my lens at her arm, moving slowly down to the hand. By the other table, Ualan Moray had begun to keen over the body of his son. Holmes gave me a quick look, nodding towards the door, and I gently took Moray aside.

'Sir,' I whispered. 'Mr Holmes will find out what or who killed your boy. I promise. But he must work alone.'

The man turned to me with tears. 'My Iain,' he sobbed.

'Go to your other boy, Calum, Mr Moray. He will need

you now,' I said. Moray nodded, and allowed me to usher him out.

I turned then to watch my friend. Holmes, still trembling, had begun to circle Fiona's body, moving stiffly at first, leaning in to touch, pouring small amounts of warm water here and there upon the corpse, examining closely with the glass, fingering the frozen clothing. As usual, the exigencies of an exciting case inspired physical feats of endurance in Holmes beyond those which seemed humanly possible. Still shaking, he moved around the bodies – darting back and forth, quicker and quicker, precise and thorough, as in a macabre dance.

After a time he seemed satisfied. 'Take a look, Watson,' he directed. I followed him, casting my own medical eye on the corpses. He pointed at bruises on Fiona's wrists and forearms. But I saw no marks on the boy's.

Meanwhile, my concern grew for my friend. His lips were still blue, his body racked with convulsive shivers. 'Holmes,' I began. 'You risk going into shock. We must get you into a warm bath.'

'Later, Watson. These bodies will not wait.' He turned back to his examination. There was still no sign of the laird. Had I not been so preoccupied with Holmes, I might have dwelled on Sir Robert's curious absence.

But moments later the man himself, kilted and orna-mented, in full Highland dress, with lace cuffs, a jewelled dirk, and an ornate pistol tucked into his complex array, strode into the room, followed by Isla McLaren. Brushing past me and Holmes, he marched to the table where he cast his eyes over the frozen body of his daughter, took a quick glance at the boy's corpse, and with a soft gagging sound suddenly turned his back to us.

After several seconds he regained his composure turned to face my friend. 'What has happened here, Mr Holmes? How is it that Fiona, and this boy—'

'I am endeavouring to find out, Laird Robert,' said Holmes. 'I need time to examine these bodies. I want them moved to a cooler room.' He shivered violently. I picked up another blanket and put it on his shoulders.

If the laird noticed anything about Holmes's desperate condition, he did not remark upon it. 'Carry on, Mr Holmes,' he said coldly. He gestured an older servant to his side. 'See that Mr Holmes has what he needs. Block off the view from the other room, and warn everyone that if a word of this escapes the kitchen, the entire staff will be dismissed without reference.'

He turned to Holmes. 'The Royal family has arrived. I expect your full report this night upon their departure. Under no circumstances are you or Dr Watson to make an appearance. As far as they are concerned,' he closed his eyes for several seconds. 'none of this has happened.'

Isla stepped to him and took his hand. 'I shall remain, Father, and be your eyes and ears here.'

'It is not fit for a—' the laird began and then stopped himself. He seemed to realize that he was looking at the only member of his family who could handle the task. 'Isla, my gem. Yes, remain for now. You will miss the dinner and we will miss your presence. But you are right, it is for the best. But dress and join us at the warehouse promptly at eight for the tasting.'

She nodded. He then turned and exited abruptly.

Holmes had already returned to his examination of the bodies and was bent over Fiona's form with his glass when Mrs McLaren removed her winter coat and set her fur-trimmed hat upon a counter.

'He is remarkably recovered!' she said to me, watching my friend at his work. I thought I detected a brief look of admiration, but sensing my gaze she quickly shrugged it off.

Holmes looked up from peering closely at the girl's left hand. He gave Mrs McLaren his chilliest look, not difficult in his present condition. 'Two young people in the laird's employ lie dead here,' said he. 'And his dinner takes precedence.'

I wondered that he had not mentioned the laird's paternity.

'Well, one he already knew was dead,' said Mrs McLaren coldly, 'The other is not a complete surprise. Do carry on.'

'I intend to,' he remarked, through chattering teeth. 'Nothing, Mrs McLaren, will get in the way of my proceeding with this investigation, your father-in-law's peculiar priorities notwithstanding.'

'Do not judge so quickly, Mr Holmes. The future of the family rests on this evening. We already knew the girl was dead. Now, what have you discovered?'

He ignored the question. I glanced towards the closed door leading to the kitchen. Despite the laird's threat, I knew that every member of the household from the family principals to the lowest scullery maid would already be gossiping about the tragic tableau on view in this room.

'Mr Holmes?' Isla repeated. She moved closer to look at the bodies herself. 'Have you discovered anything?'

'The picture slowly emerges,' said he, cradling Fiona's frozen hand in his own and prying open the fingers. He shifted to one side to block our view of this.

'Do tell us, Mr Holmes,' said Isla McLaren.

'Ha!' he cried. He kept his back to us for a moment, then finally turned to face Mrs McLaren. 'Well yes, some things are quite clear,' said he. 'It appears that the girl died of a cerebral haemorrhage due to a flat, wide blow to the occipital region of the head, probably from a fall, and that her decapitation was post mortem. I received final confirmation in a wire from my forensic expert in Edinburgh last night. But before she died of this head injury, I see now that she struggled with someone. There are bruises here, on her wrists, and on the forearms as well.'

'Her killer!' exclaimed the lady. 'The fiend!'

'Patience. That is not the entire story. From the placement of the bruises, I deduce that the combatant, who was quite large – note the span of the fingers here – attempted to restrain rather than attack her, and was defending himself. Recall from the head that she bore no facial marks,' – and here he moved quickly down the torso – 'nor are there bruises elsewhere on the torso. No one struck this girl in anger.'

Mrs McLaren stepped forward to better see what he

had described. She was truly a remarkable woman to remain so cool in the presence of such gruesome evidence. 'Very well, then. But you said the blow to the head killed her?'

'Yes, here.' He pointed to the back of his own skull. 'It is likely that in the struggle, she fell backward upon the floor, as the fracture is wide and shallow, almost like a cracked eggshell. One can survive such a blow, but not always. The bleeding would have been internal and slow, death not immediate, although loss of consciousness, yes. Yes.'

'We did not notice this wound when we examined the head in France.' said I.

'True, because it was shallow. But unfortunately sufficient, and consistent with a fall backwards. Landing full force on a stone floor, for example.'

Holmes moved around to the other side of Fiona's body, indicating the next as though lecturing an anatomy class. 'From the splayed position of the limbs, here, the girl was thrown onto the ice insensible, and probably dead. The body froze in the position in which it landed. Still with the head attached, I might add.'

'How can you know that, Mr Holmes?' asked Mrs McLaren.

'From the angle of the neck, which froze canted back, obviously affected by the weight of the head which was still there at the time.'

At this point the lady was obliged to take a turn about the room before forcing herself to rejoin us. My admiration for her grew. 'Go on,' she said, having regained her composure. 'But why throw the body in the ice pit?'

'Exigency. The ground is frozen. Above ground risked discovery. There the body would remain preserved, without the attendant putrefaction. It was not a well-planned choice, but probably seemed a good temporary solution.'

'But what of Iain Moray, poor boy?' said she, now turning her attention to the young man's corpse.

'The boy's body tells another story entirely. He climbed down into the pit fully conscious, probably in an attempt to rescue the girl. It has already been established that Iain had taken to following Fiona. He no doubt saw her body being conveyed there, dropped his knapsack outside, which was later covered in snow, and entered. There are no bruises on his body so he did not encounter the perpetrator but perhaps waited until he had left. Or thought he had left.

'Iain Moray then climbed down the ladder into the pit and found Fiona, intact and dead from her head wound, though perhaps he hoped she was merely unconscious. We will never know that detail. Then someone, and my theory is that this was a second man, came and deliberately removed the ladder, leaving Iain trapped.'

'How can you know that?' Isla McLaren exclaimed.

I was happy, for once, not to be the one asking these questions.

'From the condition of his clothing. Note this thin, very brittle film of ice, so different from the frost on her clothing. He was then doused with water. That speaks of cruel intent, does it not?'

'The same fate meant for you,' I said.

'Iain was not so lucky,' admitted Holmes.

'Who could have done such a thing?' cried the lady. 'To either of you?'

'It is a murderous spirit, no doubt. Let me finish. Kindly note the position of his arms. The boy froze to death cradling something. No doubt he died holding the girl he loved.'

'But I thought his body was found some distance from hers?'

'Yes, and I shall get to that,' said Holmes. 'Iain froze to death, as I said, cradling her. But I believe someone, probably this second person, came later, separated the two, and sawed off the head of the girl with a serrated blade. As we have seen.' He shivered, though from the cold or a reaction to his own discovery I could not say.

'While still in the pit?'

'Possibly. Although it would have taken some time, and the perpetrator might have frozen to death himself while carrying out his heinous task.'

'And so someone retrieved the body, sawed off her . . . oh it is too horrible!' said Isla McLaren.

'In any case, my expert's assessment of the nature of the cut on the neck is that the head was already frozen when cut from the body. It also explains how her stiffened body lay propped up unusually on the ice as I found her, arms in the air – in the position in which they originally froze. The two bodies were thus separated and that is why I did not discover the boy's at first, but only later, as I struggled in the ice myself.'

'Remarkable, Holmes!' I exclaimed at this tour de force of logic.

Mrs McLaren nodded, then stepped away from Holmes for a second time, pale with the images created by this grotesque chain of events, and I rushed to steady her. She pushed me away.

'Dr Watson, I am not so weak,' said she. 'But thank you.' She took a deep breath and turned her focus on Holmes again. 'Have you any theories as to the perpetrator of this crime?'

Holmes stood back from the bodies and looked over the grotesque scene. 'There is a dark spirit at work here,' said he. 'But I feel certain that at least two hands were involved. The poor girl's death might have been an accident, and I lean strongly towards that theory, but what happened after was purely by design.'

'But what could have been the purpose?' Isla wondered.

Holmes glanced at me, but was silent.

'You may have discovered a method, but you seem no closer to a motive than before,' said she.

'We must begin with what we do know, Mrs McLaren, and that is a great deal. The beheading and the sending of this head are, I admit, puzzling. Whatever the motive was, it is twisted and cruel almost beyond comprehension. It harmed the laird, but it has also drawn attention to what I believe was the accidental killing of the girl. For that and other reasons I believe the killer and the sender were two different men.'

'Are you sure? Could it not be two aspects of the same

man? A Jekyll and Hyde perhaps?' said Mrs McLaren. She approached the body of the girl and reached out towards it.

'Do not touch! The person who beheaded Fiona and caused her head to be brought in on a plate has an unusual turn of mind, vindictive, angry, and obsessive. The act speaks of hatred, revenge, a wish to destroy.'

'Destroy whom?'

'Most probably your father-in-law.'

'Do you know who either of these two men is?'

'Yes, I do. I now know who killed Fiona.'

'Who?' cried Mrs McLaren.

'I shall tell your father-in-law at the earliest opportunity.'

'But the other? You said there was another?'

Holmes said nothing.

'When did you know the killer?' persisted Isla McLaren.

'Just now. The proof is here.' He patted the pocket of his jacket.

'What proof? Who?' asked the lady, approaching him. 'Not another earring!'

'No.' Holmes held his hand up to stop her. 'The laird will hear shortly. You will have to be patient, Mrs McLaren.'

The door to the kitchen opened as more hot tea and brandy were brought in, and in that brief moment I noted that beyond it the kitchen had grown more crowded and frenetic. Silver platters of prepared delicacies flew by on raised hands, smoked salmon, petits fours . . .

'You were asked to give me your results!' protested the lady.

'I shall report to the laird personally,' said Holmes. 'You

recall that someone attempted to kill me this very afternoon, and that person has not been found. Until that time, I must keep my silence.'

'No offence meant to you, Mrs McLaren,' I interjected. 'But we must be firm on this point.'

She hesitated, searching for a retort.

'If you leave now, you may be in time for dessert,' said Holmes, with a touch of sarcasm. 'This is an event not to be missed.'

The lady drew herself up in anger.

'The laird will send for you to make your report at the end of the evening,' she said.

She swept from the room without further words, leaving her hat on the counter. A servant slipped in immediately, retrieved it, and scurried after Mrs McLaren. I closed the door behind her, leaving us alone in the room.

I turned to my friend. To my surprise, his eyes had closed and he swayed, then sagged against the table. I rushed to take his arm. 'Holmes, I am concerned for your recovery. I insist you get into a warm bath at once.'

He nodded.

'Watson, you have not asked *what* it was that I found?'

'All right. If it will get us out of this room. Is there something?'

'Of course, Watson. I found *this* in Fiona's hand.' With a weak flourish, Holmes held up a small scrap into the light. 'A bit of fabric from a man's shirt. Torn in a struggle, no doubt, to the death.' He smiled in grim triumph. To him it was a prize.

I leaned in for a better look. 'Holmes!' I exclaimed. 'This is but a small bit of fabric and a button of a very common type. What are the chances of our finding the match?'

'I have already found it. Let us return to our room where there is more privacy.'

'And a warm bath,' said I. 'You are not yet out of danger.'

CHAPTER 31

Getting Warmer

oon afterwards, the door locked behind us, I sat on the divan in Holmes's room while he soaked in a copper tub behind a folded Japanese screen, and continued his story in what I felt was entirely inappropriate good cheer.

'Let me see if you can deduce where I found this torn shirt, Watson.'

'It is not the time for games. I want to know who tried to kill you in the icehouse. We did not think to look for footprints,' I said.

'*You* did not think. However, I noted that my rescuers trampled the snow beyond use.'

'You were unconscious!'

'Not quite. But back to the elusive torn shirt. Come now, humour me. After all, I nearly died.'

'Until I rescued you.'

'Yes, and thanks. But now I must amuse myself during this ridiculous process. Is there any more hot water in the kettle? I can tell you first that in the location I was searching, I found some broken glass, swept under a table, with shards still embedded in a small broom, so whatever transpired there happened relatively recently,' said he.

'Very well, broken glass. Perhaps someone dropped something. What location? And yes, there is a second pot, next to the first.'

'Ah, yes,' I heard the sounds of pouring water and a sigh of satisfaction. 'Now consider this. There were other signs of a struggle,' he said.

'Where *was* this, Holmes?'

'Patience. See if you can deduce. They were subtle, but there. A table by a chair, with a lamp that would normally be there for reading, now missing. That same table with a small dent where it had been knocked over. There was a stain on the carpet nearby with a distinctive odour. The broken lamp must have been kerosene, for the glass fragments carried that odour. And a curtain nearby, disturbed, with three hooks bent out of place, and then an attempt to restore them.'

'A fight, then, I suppose. It must have been frantic.' A sudden image of the sumptuous apartments of the family members swam before me. Bent curtain hooks and a kerosene lamp did not fit. 'Wait! From your description, it was not one of the sons. They all have gas and electric lights.'

'Excellent, Watson! Now consider the marks on her arms, the handprint revealing a man of considerable size and strength.'

'That is nearly every man on this estate, Holmes. Do not keep me guessing. Where was this torn shirt?'

'In the rooms belonging to Cameron Coupe. I examined them while you were gone.'

'Coupe! He killed her, then? My impression was that he had feelings for the girl.'

There was a long pause. I heard Holmes pouring in more water. He sighed. 'That impression was mine as well. But I am afraid he is Fiona's killer. In his closet I noted a shirt of a matching colour to the fragment in her hand, with a small piece of the collar torn away. There had been an attempt to mend it.'

I looked down at the small piece of cloth he had retrieved from the girl's hand. He had set it on a table.

'A match to this, then, Holmes?'

'I am sure of it. But, for what it is worth, I do not think Coupe intended to kill her. I think it far more likely that the girl, who was clearly intelligent, deduced the identity of her kidnapper and confronted him. In her rage, heightened further perhaps by a previous attraction, she assailed him. Remember, the pattern of bruising on the girl's arms, and nowhere else, conform more with someone attempting to restrain her rather than attack her. Her deduction, her fury, well, those traits would fit the various descriptions of the poor young woman.'

Once again I was struck with a kind of awe at my friend's ability to form a complete and complex narrative from seemingly unrelated fragments of evidence. A compliment at this juncture, however, might only serve to inflate his already considerable self-regard.

'Hmm,' said I. 'The head wound came from a fall, then?'

361

'Precisely. That is my reading of the event. Not a murder.'
It was as if he had been there.

I could not help myself. 'Astonishing, Holmes!' It was
then a second thought occurred. 'Then she attacked him?'
I wondered. 'In a sense, you blame the victim, then, Holmes?'

'No, Watson, not at all. Ultimately he will be found
responsible, and may hang. But I do not believe he acted
out of malice. It is far more likely to have been a tragic
accident.'

'But why would Coupe have thrown her body in the
icehouse?'

'Think, man! The ground is frozen. He could not easily
bury her or otherwise dispose of her – burning, for example,
would have produced a suspicious smell. He may have been
in a panic. Consider, it is a reasonable place to store a body
that would not be found for a very long time, if ever.
Perhaps he meant to retrieve it after the family had left for
the South of France.'

'Yes, that makes sense. Do you need more hot water?'

'No. The icehouse was not a terrible idea. Her body
would probably not have been found except for one thing.'

'What?'

'The act of throwing her body into the ice pit was
witnessed by two others.'

'Ah yes, the boy, Iain Moray.'

'Yes. But another as well.'

'I do not understand.'

'The person who beheaded the girl and sent the head to
the Hôtel du Cap could not have been Coupe. Such an

action would only draw attention to the death he was at such pains to conceal. Coupe also does not strike me as so sadistic or twisted. I do not think he killed the boy, either. It took a cold-blooded murderer to do away with Iain Moray in that fashion. If Coupe had seen Iain, or been involved in killing him, he would hardly have pointed us in that direction in his first interview. I am quite sure that he had no idea what became of the boy.'

I heard splashing from behind the screen.

'I see these points,' I said. 'But could Coupe have thrown the water on you today? Given that you were there, and had discovered the bodies?'

'It is possible, but I do not think so.'

'I sense an underlying animosity from the man,' said I.

Holmes sighed. 'He would benefit from discrediting us and having us leave, clearly. But I believe we seek a second person, who witnessed Coupe throwing Fiona's body in the ice pit, then watched Iain Moray enter. This second person then removed the ladder and threw water on the boy. This is a much darker spirit.'

'The same person who did so to you tonight!'

'Very likely. What still puzzles me is the motive for sending Fiona's head to France, Watson. It was clearly a message. But what that message was, I still cannot discern.'

'It could not have been a family member, because they were all in the South of France,' I said.

'No one is eliminated, Watson. The preparation for this deed transpired between Isla McLaren's visit to us in Baker Street, and their departure for France. Hand me a towel.

We will be late for the royal unveiling. It is something we must not miss, Watson.'

'I hardly think we will be admitted,' I said, handing him a towel over the top of the screen.

'Nevertheless, we shall go,' said Holmes, and I heard him rising from the bath. His movements sounded uncertain.

In spite of my earlier curiosity to view members of the royal family in close proximity, the evening had been too dramatic by far. Exhausted, I now had no wish to participate in these festivities, especially in light of Isla McLaren's words.

'Why must we go to this?'

'Because there is more to learn, Watson.' Holmes stepped from behind the screen attired in his purple dressing gown, rubbing his hair with a towel. He was somewhat restored, his colour now back to his usual pallor and not the deathly blue of an hour ago. But he was still shivering. I did not like it.

'Holmes, you are not recovered. You must rest!'

'Watson, you are totally convincing in the character of my personal physician, but I assure you, I am quite myself, or near enough. Let me see the photograph you brought back with you.'

'The photograph, yes, of course! In all the excitement I nearly forgot!' I went to my valise and retrieved it. As I did so, I was reminded of my visit to Fettes. There had not been time to relate this story. I considered doing so at that moment, but some instinct told me to wait. I handed him the photograph. 'Here, let me point out which one my friend identified as Donal McLaren.'

But Holmes was staring at the photograph in a kind of paralyzed horror. 'No need, Watson. It is this man here.' He pointed to the correct man and flung the photograph aside.

'Who is it?'

Holmes stood staring into space; the wheels were turning and I knew enough to wait. He turned with sudden resolve. 'Watson, hurry. We must not be late. Refresh yourself as I get dressed.'

'Who is that man?'

But Holmes was already pulling his clothing from the wardrobe. 'Make haste, Watson. We will speak of this later.'

'Could he be the one behind all of this?'

'Hardly! The man in that photograph is dead, Watson. Twice dead, apparently. It is August Bell Clarion.'

'Clarion! The man who was a friend to Donal?' And of course, Holmes's schoolboy nemesis. 'Holmes, while I was in Edinburgh—'

'Later, Watson. Hurry! Bring your Webley.'

'I left it with you!'

'Oh, yes,' said he. Removing it from a drawer, where he had evidently left it, he handed it to me. 'Do not look at me that way, my dear fellow. Had I been carrying it, it would be at the bottom of the icehouse now!'

I sighed and took it from him. 'My evening jacket is close-fitting. The gun will be visible in the pocket.'

'All the better.'

PART SIX

MATURATION

'Look back and smile on perils past'
—Sir Walter Scott

CHAPTER 32

The Angel's Share

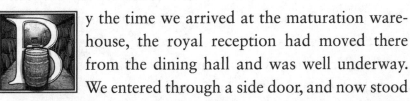y the time we arrived at the maturation ware-house, the royal reception had moved there from the dining hall and was well underway. We entered through a side door, and now stood on the landing of a short staircase leading down to the ground level. Raised as we were, and still in the shadows, we had an excellent view of the scene, while remaining largely hidden.

Illuminated by electric lighting, the table was set with two enormous candelabra, garlands and silver quaiches – the ornamental Scottish drinking vessels – with crystal decanters of whisky ready to pour. The liquids sparkled in the candlelight in jewel tones of amber, topaz and garnet. Two kilted bagpipers at either end of the dais were playing a loud and lively Scottish tune I did not recognize.

Centre stage, next to the row of casks we had seen earlier, dressed in full Highland finery with velvet jackets, kilts, sporrans, lace and decorative weaponry, the laird stood with sons Charles and Alistair on one side, and Cameron Coupe on the other. Coupe held in his hand the 'whisky thief' we had been shown earlier.

One of the five 'taster' casks had been pulled off its rack and now stood upended on the stage, a rope handle having been attached to the round end facing upwards, embellished for the occasion with a festive pine garland.

Seated at one end of this area were the two ladies of the family. In the little time since we had seen her, Isla McLaren had transformed herself. She was now dressed in wine-red velvet with subtle touches of emerald and pearl-encrusted Celtic jewels. She seemed remarkably serene, as if untouched by recent events. Catherine, attired in dark mustard silk and lace, and glittering with the family diamonds, sat stiffly opposite her on the dais. The entire family and its business, so it seemed, were on rather ostentatious display.

With their backs to us, seated in two rows placed in a semicircle facing the dais, was the royal party. As they turned to neighbouring companions, I recognized from newspaper engravings the Duke and Duchess of Amberley, wealthy Hanoverian relatives of the Queen. The Duke, I knew, had extensive influence over the agricultural interests of the Crown and owned property in the Highlands. Two other distinguished gentlemen I surmised were the Master of the Queen's Cellars, and the Lord Chamberlain. Several glittering ladies and another light-haired gentleman whom I could not quite see rounded out the front row.

A second row of courtiers sat behind these. Velvets, brocades and a great many jewels glittered on the women.

Many had touches of tartan in their sumptuous attire, a style the Queen encouraged at Balmoral.

I craned to get a better view of the man obscured from me in the front row. 'Is that Prince Arthur?' I whispered to Holmes, thinking it to be the Queen's son, a career military man a little older than myself. A small thrill of excitement passed through me, and I craned to get a better view, but Holmes tapped my arm sharply.

'Keep your eyes on Cameron Coupe,' whispered Holmes. I looked at the foreman. As I did, he seemed to feel our regard, looked up, squinted at us, and froze in what I took to be alarm.

Holmes offered him a little wave. I would swear the man blanched.

The music subsided and Laird Robert stepped forward. 'Welcome to the heart of our distillery, Your Highness, Your Lordship, Your Ladyship and esteemed members of the court. Here I would like to demonstrate a few of the secrets that make McLaren Whisky the pride of the Highlands. You are seated, of course, in our maturation warehouse, where through the years, the clear liquid of the raw spirits mature, taking on the warm, woody characteristics of the vessels in which they mellow, and flavoured as well by history. Take a deep breath, ladies and gentlemen, and inhale the scent of Scotland.'

The laird next introduced his family, then launched into a complicated description of the special barley, the special water, indeed all the details that went into a McLaren whisky. As he did so, Coupe looked away from us and struggled to focus on the laird.

The laird finally paused in his speech and turned to his foreman. 'And now, my chief distiller, Mr Cameron Coupe, will show you how we normally sample the whisky during maturation. We will then open the top of this specially prepared cask to reveal the secret that lends magic to the flavour of McLaren Garnet, and give you all a taste. Mr Coupe?'

Coupe stepped forward, with a respectful nod to the laird. But Charles stepped between them, and took the whisky thief from Coupe. 'As head of the distillery, allow me.' He elbowed Coupe aside and turned to the royal guests. Coupe said nothing but acquiesced without a word.

'Interesting,' whispered Holmes.

'Normally, honoured guests, we sample our whisky with the use of this instrument, called a whisky thief,' Charles said, and proceeded to draw a small dram from one of the four horizontally displayed tasting casks as the laird had done with us earlier, depositing a sample in a crystal glass.

Charles handed it to Prince Arthur, and all heads turned to watch. The royal personage, blocked from our view, apparently liked it. We heard a softly murmured approval followed by restrained applause from the group.

The laird removed the whisky thief from his son's hand and once again took centre stage. 'And now,' said he, 'I shall reveal another secret to our McLaren Garnet and then serve you all. Not only does maturing in port casks such as these lend flavour, but also crucial is the treatment of the interior of the cask. Here is one that has been opened at one end so that I may demonstrate. Mr Coupe? Open

up Number 51, and we shall serve from it for the group.'
He picked up a large silver ladle.

Coupe stepped forward to the upright cask. Charles,
feeling upstaged, moved in closer. 'We char the inside of
the cask,' he announced, 'which changes the flavour. Too
much and a burnt taste ensues, not enough and it is a little
too woody.'

But Coupe had taken on a strange posture. 'One moment,
Laird Robert. Something is not right—' he said, frowning
in concern at the cask. He bent down and rubbed at the
number with his hand. His fingers came away black. He
stared at them, then the cask, in confusion. 'The number
has been written over!' said he. 'It is—'

All the colour drained from his face. He rocked back on
his heels. 'Th—this is,' he stuttered. 'This is the wrong cask.
It is the wrong cask!'

Charles shouldered in to take a look. 'It is 51, taken
from over there! Oh, no, it is 59. A simple error. It matters
not a whit. They are all quite good, Coupe, step aside.'

But Coupe was gaping at the cask as though it had
turned into the head of Medusa.

Holmes moved forward a step and paused, like a pointer
on the hunt. What was all the fuss? I wondered. There was
a murmur of confusion from the crowd. Isla McLaren
stood up.

Evidently the laird was of the same mind as his son.
'Step aside, Mr Coupe! Charles is right, all of the casks are
good. Your Highness, Your Graces, the whisky varies slightly
throughout the run, although we do vat the entire run

before bottling for absolute consistency. But every cask is delicious and this is no exception. Open her up, Charles.'

'No,' said Coupe, swaying oddly. 'Do not.'

'Stand back, Mr Coupe,' said the laird sharply. 'Charles?'

Coupe stood back and froze, like a man facing a firing squad. Then a strange smile slowly spread across and distorted his face. It was as if he knew death was imminent, yet somehow welcomed it. A strangled laugh came from the back of his throat.

'Holmes, what is going on?' I whispered. I looked but he had moved from my side and, like a cat, had descended the steps silently. He was slinking along one edge of the oblong room, approaching the side of the dais. He glanced back at me, shook his head and held up a hand.

'Your Graces, gather round, please,' said Charles unctuously, 'so that you may see the inside of the cask.' As the royals and courtiers arose, he continued. 'Yes, do come closer.'

The honoured guests crowded around the cask. I watched Holmes and wondered what was going on. I craned my neck to see over the standing courtiers to the dais. 'That barrel is full, is it not? Might his Majesty need some gaiters when you pry it open?' intoned the Duke. The courtiers chuckled as though this had been the soul of wit.

'There is no danger of getting wet, sir,' said the laird, with a smile. 'We will not dismantle the cask, only lift this specially cut top from it. You see, the cask, once filled, loses a tiny amount to evaporation each year and the liquid will be some inches down from the top. That small loss is called "the Angel's Share".'

'Then there are some very happy angels, I suppose, if this whisky is as good as you say it is,' said the light-haired gentleman. It was indeed Prince Arthur. The prescribed chuckles were louder at this.

The laird took up a huge, ornate silver ladle in his hand. 'And now, at last, McLaren Garnet,' he said. On cue, Isla and Catherine rose and approached from either side with crystal whisky glasses ready to receive the precious liquid. All crowded in closer and for a moment Coupe was obscured.

Then suddenly I noticed that the man had moved to the edge of the crowded stage, sidling towards an exit opposite where I stood. Holmes was half way to that exit now, staying close to a back wall.

What the devil was going on?

Charles grasped the rope handle that had been added to the top of the cask, ready to pull out the cutaway top. He tugged, but it was wedged securely.

The laird turned to look for his foreman. 'Mr Coupe?'

On the stage, Charles shifted position for better leverage. 'I can open it, Father. The honour should be mine in any case. As director of the McLaren distillery I am proud to present—' and here he gave one mighty heave at the rope, then a second, and finally a third. The round cutaway at last came out with a popping sound. There was a pause as everyone stared down into the cask.

A sudden loud thud sounded as the heavy wooden top fell from Charles's hands to the floor. Catherine screamed and Isla's eyes widened in shock as a horrified gasp arose from the crowd. A lady in blue fainted dead away as the

Duke and Duchess recoiled in utter revulsion, the lady with a scream.

For floating in the deep amber liquid of the cask, the white, froglike face of a corpse bobbed to the surface, with dead bulging eyes and a wide-mouthed look of permanent surprise.

Even from the distance, I knew at once who it was. Young Donal McLaren. Preserved forever in alcohol.

'Holmes!' I cried in horror, thinking he may not have seen.

But there he was, dashing towards a side door where I just saw the flash of Coupe's velvet jacket as the man disappeared.

'See to the laird!' Holmes called to me over his shoulder as he ran after Coupe. I turned to see the laird slumped to the floor, leaning against the bottom of the cask.

Scream upon scream issued from the royal retinue. Chairs overturned and a flurry of silks and velvets and terrified faces rose in a tumult around me. Two of the courtiers flanked the Prince and all ran towards the doors. The Prince broke free and I got my first glimpse of him. He reached down to help Lady Catherine from the floor, and he and Isla raised her into a chair.

I had the sense of rushing into headwinds as I battled through the crowd to the cask and the fallen laird.

Standing transfixed were Charles and Alistair, and turning from Catherine, Isla McLaren.

The Prince was now being led away by the two courtiers.

I turned my attention to the laird. He lay still, head resting against the side of the upright cask.

'Sir Robert!' I said, reaching down to grasp his arm. He slipped off the side of the cask and downward with my touch, and a steward and I caught him and laid him out flat on the floor.

His face was bright red, his eyes rolled back into his head. It could well be a fatal stroke.

'Has he a private physician? Call him!' I cried, and a servant ran off. I would need help. I looked up to see only Isla McLaren now standing by my side, staring down at her father-in-law with concern. Past her the room was empty. The royal party had vanished faster than ghosts at a seance when the lamps were lit.

'How can I help?' said she.

'Get something to transport him back up to the castle.'

Charles and Alistair had no doubt followed their guests, perhaps in an attempt to calm them. Catherine was out cold, attended to now by two maids.

I felt the laird's neck for a pulse. It was shallow and racing. Alive, but for how long?

And where were Coupe and Holmes?

CHAPTER 33

Circles of Hell

hirty minutes later, most of the family were gathered in the library. There was still no sign of Holmes. We had the laird stretched out on a sofa and my medical bag was brought down from the room. Charles paced, distraught and impatient. 'Donal. My God, Donal!' He seemed more angry than shocked. Isla McLaren watched him dispassionately.

Alistair entered the room with the news that the royal party had all departed in haste. 'Who can blame them?' said he. 'And in case you are interested, Charles, your wife has been put to bed by her maid – with something to calm her nerves.' He moved to a sideboard and poured himself a whisky.

He held up the glass, smiled ruefully at the golden liquid, then downed it. 'We are finished.'

His own wife, standing at his side, nodded.

'Ridiculous!' exclaimed Charles. 'This is merely a setback!'

'You are an idiot,' said Isla McLaren. 'No one will ever touch a McLaren whisky again. Ghosts may frighten some, but an actual corpse sealed in one of our casks? There could be no better recipe for ruin.'

'She is right,' said Alistair. 'I have summoned the police. No way around it given our visitors.'

'That is unfortunate,' said Mrs McLaren.

'I will handle them when they arrive,' said Alistair. 'And the laird's doctor has been summoned as you asked, Doctor Watson.'

Meanwhile my patient showed no signs of regaining consciousness.

Charles had begun pacing in frantic despair.

'But our stock! What are we to do?' he cried.

'We will end up selling off the lot anonymously to be combined into some insipid Southern blend,' said Alistair bitterly. 'And then our doors will close. A fine finish after more than a hundred years.'

'Gentlemen, your brother lies pickled. Perhaps that should be your concern,' said Isla McLaren in a sharp tone.

'Donal's body has clearly been there for years,' said Alistair. 'No doubt since the night of his party. But who put him there?'

'Did you see Coupe? He knew what was in the cask,' said the lady.

But it occurred to me that with the exception of the laird, none of the family had expressed sadness or outrage at Donal's grisly fate. I looked around for Holmes and my worries increased.

A moan came from the laird. His eyes fluttered and I called for brandy. Isla McLaren had it in my hand instantly. He spluttered and choked as I held it to his lips. His eyes opened halfway and immediately squeezed shut again. His pulse was stronger.

'Sir?' I said. 'Sir Robert, can you hear me?'

Then he shouted, a terrible *cri de coeur*, 'Donal!'

In five more minutes I had him up and seated, with the family drawn around him in a grim circle. He sat pale and rigid, his eyes blinking as if seeing the world and everything in it for the first time. I was unsure of his level of awareness or whether he had sustained invisible damage. 'Sir Robert, can you hear me?' I tried to engage him, to get him to follow my moving finger with his eyes, but he was unresponsive. 'Can you tell me your full name, sir? Where are we? What is this room?'

He did not reply, merely repeating 'Donal' several times.

'What is his state, Doctor?' asked Isla McLaren. 'Can you do something?'

'I cannot yet tell. I am fearful of a stroke.'

Charles soon got up and paced nervously in front of the fire. Alistair slipped out of the room. His wife remained at the laird's side, attentive but at the same time remote – watching, listening, evaluating.

But slowly the patriarch seemed to rally. 'We . . . we . . . oh my God. How?' he slurred.

'Cameron Coupe had the skills and access to the unfilled casks, Father,' said Isla McLaren evenly. 'Clearly Donal was put into an empty cask the night of the party, or soon after, and it was later filled and has rested in the warehouse since. Which means he never went to India. Or the Sudan. Never served at Khartoum. And judging by what we saw tonight, Mr Coupe put him there.'

Mrs McLaren, it seemed to me, showed remarkable level-headedness given the sensational character of unfolding events.

The laird blinked at her. I am not sure he understood.

'How can you know what happened at the party, Isla? It was before your time here,' said Alistair, from in the doorway. He came in and stood before his father. 'No police, yet,' he added.

'The lady is correct,' said a sharp voice from behind Alistair. 'Her logic is sound.' Holmes stood at the door, dabbing at a cut on his forehead, his hair in disarray, his clothing torn.

'Holmes!' I cried.

'Mr Cameron Coupe is being held in the next room. He admits placing Donal's body in the cask. But he is not the murderer. Nor did he switch the casks to cause the events of tonight.'

'Someone else planned tonight? Not Coupe?' demanded Charles.

'No, of course not Coupe. Did you not see his reaction?' snapped his sister-in-law.

'Holmes, you said Coupe placed Donal into the cask! The murdering scoundrel!' exclaimed Alistair.

'I said nothing of the kind,' said Holmes with a school-master's asperity. 'He did hide the body, but as for the killing, Coupe was only a witness, or what we might term a principal in the second degree.' Noticing confusion in the room, he added, 'Donal was killed by another.'

'I say Coupe killed my brother!' shouted Charles.

Holmes had taken a position in front of the fireplace, holding his hands slightly behind him to warm them. 'Cameron Coupe says not. And I am inclined to believe him.'

Sir Robert stared up at Holmes. 'I do not understand.' His eyes focused, then went opaque, then grew sharp again. He was struggling for full consciousness.

Holmes turned to me. 'Is he compos mentis, Doctor?'

'I am not sure, Holmes. He is only intermittently lucid. He may have suffered a stroke.'

Holmes stared hard at the laird. 'Sir Robert? You are a strong man. I am going to presume you can hear and understand me. It is time that you learned some hard truths, sir. You wanted answers today. Well, I have a great many of them for you now.'

Holmes moved to one side of the fire and positioned himself in front of a large bookcase. He appeared to lean on it for support. I rose in some concern but he waved me off. Instead he took out his pipe and lit it, forcing everyone to wait. Charles snorted impatiently.

Holmes looked up and took in everyone in the room. He finally locked eyes with the laird. 'Sir Robert, I now know how both your son Donal and your daughter Fiona died, and at whose hands.'

'Daughter?' cried Charles. 'Fiona?'

Alistair laughed sharply. 'Oh, of course!' I turned to look at his wife. Isla McLaren was perfectly still, her face a mask. Had she known?

'Daughter?' said Charles again. His voice dropped to a whisper as the implication settled around him like a coal fog over London. 'Fiona was your daughter? Our sister?'

'We shall discuss Donal first,' said Holmes. 'I have examined the body. Donal McLaren was stabbed in the chest with a small, serrated knife blade. The body was well maintained in the high concentration of alcohol over all these years. Even as the percentage of alcohol declined due to evaporation, it was enough to preserve the corpse in near perfect condition. He was no doubt killed the night of his going away party and in view, or with the knowledge of, Cameron Coupe. Coupe then offered to hide the body for reasons he will have to explain to you. But he is prepared to do so.'

'Are you sure?' asked the laird. It was clearly an effort for him to speak.

'That the murder was the night of the party? Yes. When I visited your warehouse, Sir Robert, you noticed me examining the floorboards behind the row of casks set out as tasters. There I found some evidence of a long ago struggle, and a stain which I found suggestive. Using my pocketknife, I scraped a small sample from a crevice in the floorboards which in my room I later identified as blood. As Watson knows, I frequently carry with me the chemical means to make such an identification. As this area of the room was difficult to access it is likely to have remained more or less undisturbed since the time of Donal's departure celebration. It was probable that this dried residue dated from that time. Coupe only confirmed my theory.

'Next, the murderer. You mentioned that you arranged for Donal to have a safe posting to the Guards, but a less propitious placement for his friend in the artillery. I have two observations there.

'You were correct about this young man. The name August Bell Clarion is well known to me personally from school days. While this is hardly proof, I know it was well within his ken to commit such a murder in a sudden act of pique at Donal McLaren.'

'Why yes, of course!' I cried, thinking of what I had learned at Fettes – but had not had time to discuss.

Holmes threw me a puzzled look, but went on.

'As to motive and timing, consider this. Clarion was a violently jealous sort, easily provoked. Your son was hand-some, blessed with rich life prospects at the distillery, admired by women, and about to leave with a generous and relatively safe commission. Any one of these things could set off this vicious man, but in concert they offered a sure motive. I suspected that he was Donal's killer, and now we have proof in that Cameron Coupe witnessed the act and confirmed it. Your son was stabbed by Clarion on the night of the party.'

'But how did Donal's body end up in the cask?' asked the ever-practical Isla McLaren. 'And perhaps more perti-nent, how did that cask become singled out as the one to open tonight?'

'That you must all hear first-hand,' said Holmes. 'Bring him in.'

Coupe was dragged into the room by two burly servants, his hands bound behind him. He, too looked the worse for wear, his face bruised and bleeding. He was brought forward and now stood, pale and stoic before the laird.

'Cameron Coupe!' said the laird, as if seeing him, too, for the first time. 'I trusted you as I would trust my son.'

'Not so, my laird,' said Coupe softly. 'I was never family to you.'

'Why?' said the laird. 'Why do that to Donal? And to leave him there—'

'Ach!' Coupe's eyes filled with tears. 'I did not kill him, sir, but . . . there is not an excuse that will send me easy to my grave.'

'I thought better of you, Coupe,' said Isla McLaren. 'Why did you participate in this atrocity?'

'Mrs McLaren, if you please.' Holmes placed a hand on her sleeve and she recoiled in surprise. He turned to Coupe. 'Mr Coupe had plenty of reason to hate Donal McLaren. He had been promised the running of the distillery by the laird. Is that not so, Mr Coupe?'

At Coupe's sullen nod Holmes continued. 'But what happened that night to change things?' he asked.

'The laird announced that Donal would be given the running of the place upon his return,' said Coupe.

'Announced, you say, on that night?' asked Holmes.

'Yes,' said the laird. 'But to run it with you, Cameron Coupe, at his side. You and Donal were friends!'

'Nae, sir. You did not know your son,' said Coupe.

The laird looked poised to object but stopped before speaking. The weight of the room was against him. He sank back.

A silence ensued. Suddenly Isla McLaren's clear voice rang out. 'But if Donal died that night who wrote the letters from the wars?'

Holmes turned to her with a grim smile. 'Excellent question. August Bell Clarion was a master of forgery. I knew him at school, where he earned pocket money by writing papers for other pupils. More than once he caused trouble for others with this talent. He clearly took Donal's commission and proceeded in his place, using his name.'

'Then it was *his* bad behaviour that resulted in Donal – or who we thought was Donal – being sent into battle,' said Alistair.

'Correct.' Holmes turned to the laird. 'August Bell Clarion, posing as your son, was simply unable to keep his nature in check. His actions were dire enough to propel him out of the safety of the posting you had secured for Donal and onto the front line.' Holmes looked sharply at the laird whose face had crumbled with regret. 'Ah, I see you had a report of this event, whatever it was.'

The laird looked down, ashamed.

'And you believed it, sir. That tells me you knew your son's real character. Perhaps you were being generous in your earlier description to me, which truly has been of no help at all.'

'But we understood that Clarion died in battle in 1883,' said Isla McLaren.

'That was reported in the papers, yes,' said Holmes. 'Having some small history with the man myself, I investigated the report when I read of it. It was reliably corroborated. However, I now realize that whoever died in El Obeid on the ill-fated Hicks Expedition was not Clarion, but must have been some unfortunate soul whom the clever fiend induced to take his place.'

'I will kill this scoundrel,' swore the laird, rising unsteadily to his feet.

'Sit, Father,' said Alistair, taking the laird's arm and guiding him back to his chair.

'The war has done that for you, Sir Robert,' said Holmes. 'It was Clarion who served in Khartoum in the place of Donal, and he who died there. Watson has just returned from Edinburgh today with proof that Clarion was in Khartoum. He is pictured in a photograph of Gordon's men, identified by Watson's friend as Donal. No British survived the slaughter of the Mahdi's dervishes.'

The laird stared ahead, taking all this in with difficulty. 'But all the time, Donal was still here, in the—' The room was quiet, with only the sound of the crackling fire. A log fell further into the fire and sparks flew from it in Holmes's direction. He edged away slightly from the swirling embers, brushing at his trousers.

'But then what happened this evening, Mr Holmes?' Isla McLaren's cool voice cut through the silence. Alone amongst her family she seemed bent on stringing together a coherent narrative.

Holmes turned to the cowed foreman. 'Mr Coupe, here

is your one small chance at redemption. Explain what you saw eight years ago, and what transpired this evening, exactly as you did to me in the distillery some minutes ago.'

The man raised his handsome face up to the light and took a deep breath. 'The night of the party, I came upon Clarion and Donal. They were fighting. Some girl I think, or the commission. Clarion said you had bought him a death sentence.'

'I bought that boy a way out of gaol!' cried the laird. 'But my son?'

'Donal laughed at Clarion, and so the fiend snatched a knife – that self-same blade which had just been given to Donal by his mother Lady Elizabeth – and he stabbed his friend in the heart. I witnessed the whole thing. Clarion looked up and saw me. He recognized instantly that I was . . . that I did not—' Coupe looked down, ashamed.

'You were what?' asked Holmes.

'I was not so terribly shocked.'

'Perhaps relieved,' Holmes suggested quietly.

Coupe could not deny it. 'Clarion then came over and embraced me, wiping blood on my shirt and hands as he did so. He told me I was in with him now, and if I told what I saw he would implicate me, but if I cooperated he knew I would have the running of the distillery.' Coupe turned to the laird, eyes blazing. 'Then later, after Khartoum, once again you overlooked me and gave it to Charles.'

'But back to that night,' prompted Holmes. 'Clarion had you then, and he asked you to dispose of the body.'

'I told him I would take care of it. And I . . . I—'

'You hid the body in one of the casks being filled shortly after. That took some doing, but you were trained as a cooper. You noted the number. It was 59, I believe,' said Holmes.

'I did. God forgive me. It seemed a fitting end for Donal McLaren,' said Coupe.

'Donal was your friend!' roared the laird, rising to his feet and swaying there, his arms raised as if to throttle Cameron Coupe. He stepped forward, but stumbled and was caught again by Alistair.

'Sir,' said Coupe, 'your Donal was not the man you took him to be. 'Twas he and not Charles who bombed a neighbour's distillery not so long before he left.'

'I am no cowardly bomber, Father, how could you think so?' said Charles.

'Ha,' said Alistair, 'that is exactly what you are. Montpellier, Charles? I happen to know your idiot plan with that Frenchman, Jean Vidocq, to blow up Dr Janvier's laboratory. I have the letter proving it.'

Sir Robert turned to face Charles. 'Is that true?'

'Not precisely,' corrected Holmes. '*I* now have the letter in my possession. It is my opinion that the bomb was intended for a deserted laboratory, and at lunchtime, virtually ensuring no one would be there. A gesture rather than a terrorist plot. Am I right, Charles?'

Charles looked from Holmes to his father in helpless guilt. 'I was doing what any businessman would do. Protecting our investment. Advancing our cause. No one was to be hurt. We planned it most carefully . . . I thought you would be proud—'

Sir Robert's gaze lingered for a moment on Charles, then he turned to Holmes, focusing his red-rimmed, penetrating stare on my friend. 'I hired you to find a killer and instead you destroy my family.'

'I have no desire to destroy anyone,' said Holmes. 'Only to reveal the truth.'

The laird turned on Cameron Coupe with sudden ferocity. 'And you! You vile beast! Liar! You betray my trust and besmirch my dead son's reputation—'

Coupe looked around the room in defiance.

'Sir Robert, you have not yet heard the worst of Donal,' said he. 'Little Anne! When Donal was six years old. She was only three when she vanished. Her brother Donal threw her down the medieval cistern at the end of the nursery hall. Four storeys down to an unimaginable end.'

A collective gasp echoed throughout the room. Even Holmes looked surprised at this.

'No!' shouted the laird, staggering back. 'Say it is not so!'

Coupe choked out the next words with difficulty. 'He told me so himself! Bragged of it, even.'

The laird shook his head in bewilderment and horror. 'Anne!'

Charles stepped forward in a new show of bravado. 'Father! Do you not remember? I tried to tell you, but you did not believe me.'

The laird turned to Charles, aghast. 'You were four. You could barely speak.'

'But I saw it. I saw Donal do it,' said Charles.

'And you have stayed silent ever since?' asked Isla McLaren. 'Why?'

Charles looked ashamed. 'Donal told me he would do the same to me if I told.'

'Your son Donal was a monster, sir,' said Coupe. 'I will admit that thinking of him in the cask, though I did not kill him myself, gave me no small pleasure over the years. This whole family is cursed!' Coupe suddenly spat at the laird's feet. Years of pent-up hatred found their release in this moment.

Holmes nodded to me and I gently but firmly led the laird back to his chair and sat him down. The older man was shaking, with rage or shock I was not sure. His pupils were pinpoints.

'I will now relate what happened to Fiona, at least most of it,' said Holmes quietly. 'There is one small detail that eludes me.'

'My God,' mumbled Charles. 'Our sister.'

'Mr Holmes! Tell us what you have found!' said Isla McLaren.

'Your plan was ill-conceived from the start, Laird Robert,' said Holmes. 'Fiona had an admirer who kept his feelings secret. That was Cameron Coupe, was it not?' Here he turned to the foreman, whose face revealed the truth of that statement. 'Perhaps you can imagine just how painful this made your assignment to him, Sir Robert. And yet he carried it out. Tell us why, Mr Coupe.'

The man still stood, hands bound behind him. He seemed to have shrunk in grief and guilt. And yet he retained a flame of righteousness. 'It is true. I loved Fiona,' said Cameron Coupe. 'You asked, Mr Holmes, if she might have wandered into the distillery, met with some of the workers. I made sure that did not happen, though I had to be much on my guard as she was an adventurous girl. But I could do nothing about what went on in the castle. I knew that there, she had been sorely used. Charles had taken advantage and would soon discard her, like so much rubbish. It is his way.'

'You know nothing of this, Coupe!' shouted Charles.

'I knew why the laird wished to discourage all the attention. I naively thought it would work. And that she might – I do not know – be humbled, or made sensible. And then, perhaps I could—'

'You might comfort her? And thus gain her favour?' exclaimed Isla McLaren. 'My God, you men think the world of yourselves!'

Coupe was white with shame. 'You are right, Mrs McLaren. But oh, how smart that girl was. Even though the other servants teased her when she came back without a hair on her head, how they goaded her, making her think it was ghosts, all the time that clever girl was thinking, thinking. And then she found, in my room, I stupidly kept—'

'You *kept what*?' asked the laird.

Holmes nodded to Coupe.

'I kept her hair. Foolish, but—'

'You imbecile!' cried the laird.

'When she discovered it, she knew at once it was I who had done the deed,' said Coupe. 'She attacked me! I tried to talk to her, to explain, but she was in a rage. She flew at me and we struggled. I was being so careful, but she was wild. I took her arms to stop her but she wrenched away, and she fell. She fell and hit the back of her head and then she was still.'

Coupe turned slowly to face Holmes. 'But how, sir, how did you know?'

'I examined your rooms earlier and found evidence of a struggle, and the torn shirt which you attempted to repair. And then, upon examining her body tonight, I found a matching piece of this torn shirt clutched in her hand. You are careless, Coupe, with your crimes.'

A silence fell over the room.

A single tear coursed down the face of the disgraced foreman. 'She was dead, sir, and no one unhappier than myself.'

'But what then?' cried the laird. 'How did her body come to be found in the icehouse, and her head delivered to the South of France?'

Coupe hung his head, unable to speak.

'I can answer the first part,' said Holmes. He turned to Coupe, repeating what he had told me earlier. 'The ground was frozen and so you could not bury her. There was no easy place to hide her body above ground where it would not be found. You had to act quickly. And so, the idea came to you to use the icehouse, which once filled, is not accessed in the winter. This must have been, in your mind, only a temporary measure. Am I right, Mr Coupe?'

'Yes, sir. It is as if you witnessed my every move.'

'Just as you thought of the cask of whisky ten years past. You thought. You thought—' stammered the laird.

Cameron Coupe looked down at the ground, filled with remorse.

'But you have two more things to tell us, Mr Coupe,' said Holmes. 'First, why and how was Fiona's head delivered to the Grand Hôtel du Cap?'

Coupe opened his mouth to speak, and stopped suddenly at the explosive retort of a gunshot. He looked down in utter surprise to see a bloom of crimson appear on his chest.

The laird had drawn what I had taken to be only an ornamental pistol from the front of his velvet dress jacket, and had fired point blank at Cameron Coupe.

'Sir Robert!' cried Holmes, and leapt upon the man, wrenching the gun away.

Coupe staggered back and fell.

Holmes confronted the laird, his face terrible with anger. I rushed to Coupe's side. Everyone else in the room was motionless, pinned by shock.

Coupe lay bleeding on the floor. 'Release his hands,' I cried. Alistair did so as I knelt beside the fallen man, took a pillow from the sofa and pressed on it to staunch the wound. My doctor's bag was already in the room and without a word, Isla McLaren brought it to me.

The laird stood blinking at his wounded employee. I glanced up to see him sink to his knees with a moan. Alistair helped him into a chair, placing a hand on his shoulder to restrain him if needed. He nodded at Holmes.

Choking back his fury, Holmes knelt beside me. 'Watson?'

I shook my head. The prognosis was dire. The bullet had entered Coupe's upper left chest between the heart and the shoulder. If it had hit the subclavian artery he would have less than two minutes to live. But if it had missed that critical vessel, there was a chance. I pressed hard on the wound.

'Coupe. Coupe!' cried Holmes, turning to the prostate man. 'Can you speak?' But Coupe was insensible.

Holmes leapt to his feet, and growled in frustration. 'That was a foolhardy move, Sir Robert. I knew Coupe was the culprit in Fiona's death, before I entered this room. But still we do not yet know how the head was sent to the South of France, nor how the cask came to be the one opened tonight. I am quite sure that this man, culpable as he was in other respects, is not personally responsible for all these things. He had more to tell us.'

'One might almost think the ghost of August Bell Clarion has been at work,' said Charles.

'There are no ghosts,' said Isla.

'No, there are no ghosts. And Clarion is dead,' said Holmes. 'I am sure of it.'

Given my friend's history with August Bell Clarion I could well appreciate his thoroughness in this matter.

'Then who switched the casks?' asked Isla.

'I had hoped Coupe would have a theory. Now we may never hear it, nor how Fiona's head travelled to the Grand Hôtel du Cap. Both were perpetrated by someone who wished to destroy the McLaren family,' said Holmes.

'Perhaps just a madman,' said Charles.

'No,' said Holmes. 'This is far too planned, too carefully orchestrated. This family has a knack for seeding resentment. Look to someone on the property.'

A groan arose from Cameron Coupe, as Holmes said these words. Holmes turned to him eagerly, but the man was beyond words. Holmes sighed in frustration.

'I must attend to this bullet wound urgently,' said I. 'And the laird also needs care. Get me some men to transport them to a place I can see to them! I will need boiled water and clean sheets.' A servant was called in and dispatched at a run.

'That man killed Fiona,' cried Charles, pointing to Coupe. 'No matter what he says, I think he cut off her head and took it down south. He will rot in gaol!'

'No,' said Holmes. 'Her death was an accident. And no, he did not send the head. He was away at a meeting of master distillers at the time when he would have to have done that. It was not Coupe.'

'One of the workers, then?' suggested Isla.

Alistair stepped forward. 'Yes, one of the workers must have been involved. There is one, a badly disfigured man, who works closely with Mr Coupe. That is, I saw them frequently in company. A remarkably ill-tempered individual, whom I recommended we let go. But Charles would not have it.'

'It is not up to you to run this company,' said Charles. 'It is up to me. I am the master of the McLaren Distillery. And things will be very different from this day forward.'

'You are master of nothing now,' struck in Isla quietly. 'The McLaren Distillery is finished. You will be lucky to avoid gaol yourself.'

'My wife is correct,' said Alistair. 'I have you for planning the bombing in Montpellier. As Isla says, gaol awaits. Come, Mr Holmes. Let me point out this man to you.'

CHAPTER 34

The Missing Man

olmes hesitated as I took him aside and pressed my revolver into his hand once again. 'Very well, Watson. But learn what you can from Cameron Coupe. At any cost.' A violent wind had come up and as servants brought their coats, and more joined at Alistair's behest, I will admit to worrying about Holmes's physical state. But he would hear no objection, that was clear.

He and Alistair departed with three servants into the whirling snow. I turned my attention back to my patients. The laird was not in immediate danger and I ordered his valet to attend to him, adding strict instructions about pupil dilation and breathing and what to do if he regained consciousness. This allowed me to focus my attention on Coupe, who was still unconscious and declining rapidly. I needed to remove the bullet, and stop any internal bleeding.

A second pair of hands would be helpful in what I was about to do, but it could not wait. We quickly moved Coupe to a guest bedroom nearby on the ground floor. Hot water and clean sheets arrived, and I took from my bag the few surgical instruments that I carried.

As I made my preparations, the door was flung open and Isla peeked in. 'The laird's personal physician has arrived, are you in need of assistance?'

'Send him in,' I cried, grateful for this small bit of good fortune.

I poured boiling water over the instruments and was scrubbing my own hands in another vessel when a stout woman with blonde braids ringing her broad face rushed into the room, accompanied by a bony young man who resembled a scarecrow.

'Madam, please!' I cried. But Isla followed them in.

'Dr Watson, this is Dr MacLeish and her assistant, Geordie,' said Isla. 'And this is Dr Watson, former army surgeon.'

Dr MacLeish was a woman! And a remarkable doctor, I was soon to discover.

'How long since he was shot?' she asked, moving to the bedside, and looking down at the handsome, pale face.

'Twenty minutes.'

'Ach, Cameron Coupe. Shame! Best distillery man in the county.' I did not disabuse her of the notion. Without being asked, she began to scrub her hands.

With no need of instruction, the two of them nimbly assisted me as I set up a makeshift surgical theatre in the room. The patient was draped in clean sheets, and Dr MacLeish had called for even more boiling water and applied herself to sterilizing my instruments, adding a few of her own.

I nodded my approval. 'Thank God. Not every doctor subscribes to the germ theory.' I bent to examine the wound more closely. The patient had gone into shock. We would have to work quickly

'Thank Joseph Lister, not God,' she said with a wry smile. 'Well, I guess him, too. I will take all the help I can get.'

Cameron Coupe's pallor, sheen and rapid heart rate indicated shock, and I feared he was near death. I quickly finished washing. 'Let us proceed,' I said. Doctor MacLeish tied on a pristine white apron over her ample form, and faced me, her hands in the air to dry.

'I certainly respect a war-trained surgeon,' said she, peering sharply at me. 'But you look as though you have been awake for three days straight, Doctor. I am glad to be here to assist you, sir.'

At my hesitation, she added simply, 'I took a surgical degree in America. Edinburgh has not yet caught up to the idea of ladies with blood on their hands. But be assured, Doctor, I can help you.' Behind her, Isla nodded silently to me. I wondered briefly at this, but let it pass.

In thirty minutes the two of us had the bullet out and the damage repaired as best we could. Doctor MacLeish was more competent than many battle-trained men, and was adept at clamping off bleeding vessels, freeing me to discover the bullet and remove it with minimal damage. I knew that Coupe had received his best chance at survival, though he had lost a lot of blood, and was not out of danger.

We departed from the room, leaving Dr MacLeish's

gangly assistant, Geordie, to watch over the patient. Charles McLaren was instructing a large, imposing footman to keep watch outside the door to make sure Cameron Coupe 'did not escape'. The irony was poignant, as it would be a miracle if the man survived the night. Coupe knew more than he had been able to tell us, and while it was highly unlikely that he would regain consciousness, young Geordie promised to fetch me promptly if he did.

I briefly visited the laird in his rooms before retiring. The man was still unconscious, and resting peacefully. But his face was that of a man aged ten years in a single evening. A full recovery would be a miracle. Dr MacLeish concurred. She said she would remain with him through the night.

Finally free to help Holmes, I ran to his room, hoping to find him there. The door was ajar but the room was empty and freezing cold. Disappointed, I closed the door and busied myself by resurrecting a healthy blaze in the grate. A wave of exhaustion swept over me.

The discovery of Donal's body floating in that cask was certainly one of the grislier moments of our adventures to date. But perhaps even more disturbing was the thought of what had transpired with little Anne some thirty years prior, at the end of the very hallway in which we were housed.

I could not wait to be gone from this place.

In the meantime, the temperature had dropped well below freezing and I grew concerned about Holmes down at the distillery after his earlier misadventure in the icehouse. But I was not to worry long, for soon afterwards the door clicked open and there stood Holmes, snow dusting his shoulders and dishevelled hair. He was pale as candle wax, and from his defeated posture, I knew at once he had not been successful.

'The bird has flown, Watson. A man called Jowe Lammas was involved, without a doubt, though his motive eludes me. Disfigured in the Afghan wars. Gone some twelve hours ago. The trail is covered by snow, and is now cold in every sense of the word.'

'Joey Lammas? A singular name. Is he the man we saw in the distillery with the laird?'

'Yes. One eye, facial scarring. But it is "Jowe."' He pronounced it 'jow – way'. 'A Scottish word, apparently. But long gone.'

Holmes stood swaying in the doorway as the energy left his body. I judged him to be on the brink of collapse, and ushered him to the sofa. I removed his coat, and threw a blanket over his shoulders. He stared at the flames, unable to speak for several minutes.

'Coupe?' he asked, finally, his voice a near whisper.

'I removed the bullet. The laird's personal physician arrived in time to help and is attending to Coupe and the laird. Coupe's chances are slim.'

'A double loss, then. I fear he was our only source to untangle the final strands of this web.'

'But what of this man Lammas? Fled, you say?'

Holmes's investigation in the workers' dormitory had only added to the puzzle. This Jowe Lammas, the man seen often in Coupe's company, had vanished apparently after having murdered a fellow workman, Seamus Marchand, with a knife. Other workers confirmed that Lammas had indeed been the facially disfigured man we had noticed on our first visit to the distillery, who had separated the two fighting men. He had a fearsome reputation, prone to violence whenever he was called up to restore order, providing Coupe was not present.

Lammas had made no effort to conceal the evidence of his crime; bloodstains and the murder weapon had been left behind, as had gin bottles, gambling stubs and chewing tobacco beneath his bed.

'A common thug, then,' I exclaimed.

Holmes sighed. 'It would appear so.'

Holmes reckoned that it had been either Lammas or Marchand who removed the ladder and threw water down upon him. But why, or at whose behest?

'That puzzle remains,' said he, 'as does the reason for Lammas and Marchand switching the casks for this evening, thus exposing Coupe.'

'It was them, do you think?

'It is the only thing I learned for certain. They were seen in the area of the maturation warehouse late this afternoon with no reason to be there.' Holmes shook his head ruefully.

'But how would Lammas know about Donal's body in the cask?'

'That is the question, Watson. We have presumed that only Clarion and Coupe knew of the ghastly interment. This leaves two possibilities. Either Coupe was so hell-bent on revenge at the time that he was sloppy, and was seen, or there was yet another party involved.'

'What about this August Bell Clarion fellow? Might he be somewhere, somehow still in the picture?' I asked.

Holmes sighed. 'I think not. I had a theory before I found Marchand's body and the suggestive detritus left by Lammas. But it appears I was wrong.'

'What theory, Holmes?'

He did not reply, but leaned back on the sofa and sighed.

'I am inclined to think it was Lammas or Marchand who brought the head down to the Grand Hôtel du Cap,' said Holmes.

'But why? Initiated by them, or by some other?'

'I wish I could say. Increasingly Cameron Coupe seems to be the answer. I had discounted this, but perhaps I have misjudged the man. And if he does not recover, we shall have no way to find out.'

'Did you encounter the police? Alistair said they had been summoned?'

Holmes closed his eyes. 'Regrettably. The local man, Gerald, an "inspector" in name only, is an idiot. We spoke briefly of the icehouse bodies, and he ignored my findings entirely. His conclusion was that the two young people had probably killed each other!'

'What a fool! I recall Mrs McLaren describing him to us in Baker Street.'

'Yes. Alistair had the good sense to throw Gerald and his even more obtuse young constable off the property without even mentioning Donal's body in the cask. He then wired the regional lawmen in Aberdeen. They will be out in the morning. God willing there is an intelligent man on the force there.'

At this point exhaustion overcame us both. Things felt perilously out of control, and it was with great unease that we both retired. Once again, I chose to remain on the sofa in Holmes's room, our door secured against any unwanted entry. I slept restlessly, but had I any foreknowledge of what would transpire in the morning, I might not have slept at all.

CHAPTER 35

You Must Change Your Thoughts

he next morning dawned even colder than the preceding days. I found that Coupe had survived the night, but had not regained consciousness. He clung to life upon a slender thread. The laird's condition had not changed and Dr MacLeish split her time tending to both patients. I could do nothing more in service of either man, and so I joined Holmes for breakfast in the dining room. We were alone. It was early and the rest of the household must have chosen to dine privately, for which I could hardly blame them.

Holmes would not touch food, but after his third cup of coffee began pacing nervously by the windows that overlooked the distillery. It was now fully shrouded in snow. Long icicles had formed in the night and hung outside the tops of the tall windows like glistening daggers.

The detective was distraught, angry, his mind evidently churning.

I ventured to interrupt his thoughts. 'I have packed my things, Holmes. Coupe is in good hands but I hold little hope for him. Both he and the laird are now being seen to by Dr MacLeish. There is really nothing for me to do here, medically speaking.'

There was no answer.

'I understand the police are due in from Aberdeen this morning. Surely they will find your results remarkable. And then, I hope, we might leave.'

Still no reply. Holmes was now unmoving, staring out of the window with his back to me. There was a long pause.

'I have failed, Watson,' said Holmes suddenly. 'Failed in the most miserably botched investigation of my career.'

'How can you say that, Holmes? You may have missed this Lammas fellow, but look what you accomplished! You have shed light on not one but several crimes stretching back years.'

'But not the one mystery that most disturbs me,' said Holmes. 'Not the one I was actually hired to solve.'

'That is not true! You have unmasked that poor girl's killer. The family now knows exactly how Fiona died. You have found the missing boy. Your investigation has brought to light little Anne's murder and the bombing of Dr Janvier's laboratory. As a result of your work here, Charles McLaren, Jean Vidocq, Cameron Coupe – all three of these men will now answer for their very serious crimes. And the laird himself, while perhaps not legally culpable, has received a punishment one might say is suited to his hubris.'

Holmes stopped pacing and faced me. 'I take no satisfaction

in that! And Charles McLaren and Vidocq, I fear, will both escape prosecution. You wait and see, Watson.'

'Holmes, you well know that justice has been served. Charles has lost his business, and Jean Vidocq at the very least will never again be consulted by the French government after this. Cameron Coupe has received the harshest punishment of all. Surely you can take pride in the remarkable investigative work you have done here.'

I held out a plate of toast to him. He ignored it. His stubbornness had begun to irritate me. 'Holmes!'

'You sound as though you were handing out second place in a schoolboy poetry contest to someone who can't spell,' he spat. 'It is a failure, plain and simple. This Lammas—' He paused. He stopped pacing and cocked his head in a manner I well recognized. 'Lammas.'

'Holmes? This Lammas?'

He would not reply but stood deep in thought.

'They – or you – will find him, Holmes. The man is so disfigured he cannot move freely without notice. Eat something. You must regain your strength. Do not underestimate the challenges of yesterday.'

But Holmes remained at the window, his back to me.

'Alistair McLaren has put out word on Lammas to the police, although I have little faith they will accomplish the simplest of tasks,' he said in a strange voice.'He has likely put a great deal of distance between us already.'

'The net will be cast wider. He will be found. Now sit down, Holmes. You try my patience exceedingly!'

Holmes took a deep breath as if he had had a sudden

idea, and turned to face me. I did not at all like the look I saw on his face. It was as though a spider had suddenly crawled out from underneath his breakfast plate.

'What do you know about August Bell Clarion?' he said sharply.

'What?'

'Your remark in the library. When I mentioned that August Bell Clarion was known to me personally. You said "Yes, of course!" As I have never spoken of him to you, how is it that you seem so familiar?' asked Holmes.

There were times when his remarkable attention to detail could strain our friendship. I will admit to a pang of guilt, however, about my visit to Fettes. 'Holmes, you are exhausted, as am I. Let us finish our business here. Give your testimony to the Aberdeen policemen and let us be on our way.'

'Tell me now.'

I sighed. 'Very well. I had meant to tell you earlier but we have been somewhat occupied.' I smiled, hoping to defuse my friend's anger. It had no effect. 'While I waited for the photograph to be copied in Edinburgh, I was in the neighbourhood of Fettes, and, having nothing better to do, I decided to walk around the grounds. I had read of it, of course, and you mentioned—'

'You decided to "follow in my footsteps"?'

'Nothing so premeditated, Holmes, I assure you. Idle curiosity, that is all. It is an interesting building. I thought to have a closer look to pass the time. But while I was on the grounds, a gentleman apparently recognized me and approached me.'

'Recognized you?' said Holmes, incredulous.

'Yes, as Doctor John Watson, from an engraving.'

'That Beeton's picture looked nothing like you.' He was referring to a sloppy artist's rendering purporting to show the two of us in the first published account of our adventures, in the *Beeton's Christmas Annual*.

'No, from *The Illustrated Police News*,' I said. 'In any case, he said he knew you. He was very happy, in fact, to learn of your success and that you had found your metier.'

'What gentleman?'

'An older man. He invited me to tea, Holmes. A Dr Jennings.'

'Gordon Jennings! You took tea with Gordon Jennings?'

'Steady on, Holmes. This was not my idea. He was friendly and forthcoming. And he – well, he told me a story.'

Holmes grew very still. 'Stop right there.'

'There was no harm done, Holmes. I did not prompt this story. And I was very sorry to hear of the incident.'

Holmes was staring at me in a way that I liked not at all. I had the sudden sensation that I was standing in the centre of a deep lake and on very thin ice. My friend was an extraordinarily private man. Even though I had not solicited this information it was, nonetheless, not meant for my ears and I knew it. I would need to be careful.

'I am sorry, Holmes.'

'*What* incident?'

There would be no escaping. 'At Christmas. August Bell Clarion was a fellow student who had grown jealous of you, apparently, and he and some friends attacked you and destroyed some things. Your violin—'

Holmes regarded me with a kind of cold fury. I became aware of the feeling of my heart beating.

'—and the subsequent revenge you took upon him via the boxing match.' I attempted a smile. 'Well done, I should say!'

'I do not exact revenge,' said Holmes. 'I needed to stop him. That was all.'

'Yes, well, I gather you did, for a time?'

'What do you mean?'

'Really, it is nothing.'

'Watson, what do you mean?'

'All right. Professor Jennings hinted that there was more to the story, later, at university,' I said.

Holmes stared at me. Had I not known the man to be the soul of honour I might have sensed the threat of physical violence. I continued, but with trepidation.

'I stopped him, of course. I let the subject drop.'

Holmes exhaled sharply.

'See here, I am sorry, Holmes. But I did not solicit this information.' I looked at my friend. He was terrifyingly still and I could not recognize the expression that distorted his face. It was a kind of incredulous fury.

The reaction seemed extreme. But of course the fatigue and horrors of the previous day would have unhinged a lesser man. Guilt at my indiscretion shifted to concern for him.

'You begin to worry me, Holmes. Sit down.'

'You should leave,' he said softly.

'What? You are not yourself. Come, sit down and let me take your pulse.'

411

Holmes stepped away, then turned his back on me to stare out the window again. It was clear his mind was churning. But to what purpose? He sighed as though having made a decision, and turned back to face me.

'Watson, you have overstepped the bounds of our friendship.'

'You are overreacting! Holmes, you have had a terrible shock—'

'Go back to London. Go home to Mary where you belong.'

'I shall do nothing of the sort. I will see these men from Aberdeen with you. And you will return with me.'

'No. Leave at once. If you value this friendship, if you value my feelings for you in any way, then you must leave immediately. Before I do something irrevocable.'

I had never seen such an expression on my friend's face.

'Well this is rather irrevocable right now, I would say—'

'Watson! Remove yourself from my sight. I cannot stand to look at you!'

It was useless to argue with him in this state. I rose from the table, and as I did so, a flare of anger welled up inside me. I suddenly felt the aggrieved party. I flung my napkin down.

'Holmes! You wrong me. And after all this time together!'

'Leave!' he cried and turned away to face outside the window. His voice dropped to a whisper. 'Leave me.'

A short while later I found myself en route to Aberdeen where I would catch an express via Edinburgh to London.

The horrors that Holmes and I had uncovered in Braedern were so numerous, and so ghastly that I could scarcely fathom them. But even beyond these was the shock of Holmes's words to me this morning.

A mixture of anger, fatigue and sadness made clear thinking impossible and I attempted to sleep during the journey, if only to escape my deep distress. I was of no use to anyone in this state, least of all to myself. But rest would not come.

I closed my eyes, and the passing Highland snowscape was replaced by a series of vivid tableaux of my time with Holmes, racing together across the moors of Dartmoor, long train journeys spent in companionable silence, laughter at shared stories in Baker Street, the faces of sundry clients, lit alternately by terror, anguish, surprise and gratitude.

And here my mind stopped manufacturing these images and an ineffable sadness overcame me, replaced by a white-hot surge of anger, blocking out all of these others with the image of Holmes's grimace of fury this morning. Even allowing for his mercurial temperament, the unfairness of his rage, his misplaced resentment over what had been mere friendly curiosity on my part, his callous dismissal of years of friendship struck me to the core. I could hardly bear it. My novel lay unread upon my lap.

Exhausted and dispirited, I disembarked in Aberdeen. I consulted the schedules for the quickest route back to London, and thought briefly of cabling Mary. But she had written that she was away herself for a few days, and the thought of returning to an empty house held little appeal.

Perhaps I should stop over for a day or two in Edinburgh to sort out my thoughts and to jot down notes on this case while it was fresh in my mind.

As I pondered this in a restaurant at the station, it occurred to me that my hurt and anger were misplaced. Holmes had been under tremendous strain. Surely his rejection of me was not a personal attack and I began to regret not staying to temper his interactions with the police.

But I could not return now; he would not allow it. In slightly calmer spirits, I vowed to attempt a reconciliation after a week or two had elapsed.

Fortified by this plan as well as a good meal, I bought a ticket for Edinburgh. As I sat waiting for the train, I was distracted by a young couple sitting near me. I could not help but overhear their conversation.

'St Andrews will take you back, Richard, once they realize their mistake,' said the girl. 'You are destined to be one of their most famous graduates.'

'I shall never graduate now, Polly,' said the boy. 'And our parents! What they will say?'

'They will support you, Mother at least. And eventually Father will come around.'

'They will disown me.'

There was a pause. 'I will get us some tea. Wait here. You must change your thoughts, Richard.' She got up to seek refreshments and I took the opportunity to glance at the young man. He watched after her with tears in his eyes. He then slumped forward and buried his head in his hands.

I turned away, saddened by the young man's plight.

Holmes, too, had left university under some cloud, I remembered. The words of Jennings at Fettes echoed in my mind. Camford. A trial. And an old woman best equipped to tell me the details.

I reached into my pocket for the scrap of paper on which Jennings had written down her name. Mrs Simpson in the village of Atholmere. Two miles south of Aberdeen.

I looked up. The boy and girl had moved away. Holmes would never approve of what I was about to do. But I was angry enough – and curious enough – to ignore the thought.

What had happened to him at Camford? And if it involved this August Bell Clarion, might it not relate to the case at hand?

This thought banished any reservations I had. I went to the ticket office, and exchanged my ticket for a local. One that stopped at Atholmere.

CHAPTER 36

The Ghost of Atholmere

t was 4 p.m. and dark when I arrived at the small village of Atholmere. Narrow, hilly streets wound circuitously, their rough cobblestones slippery in the chill dampness that hung over the town in a miasma of grey. The yellow glow of gaslight and candles cast small rectangles of light out into the gloom, and a lone fiddle played a mournful Celtic melody in the distance.

As I made my way to the designated address, I found my already despondent mood affected by my surroundings to a degree that surprised me. Perhaps my fatigue made me vulnerable to melancholy, or perhaps some long buried ancestral memory was at play.

While I had no living relatives to query, I remembered being told as a child that I had Scots ancestry. But it mattered little now, as the history I was bent on unearthing applied to my friend only. In the back of my mind, I had a strong intuition that there might be some relation to our current case, perhaps through this August Bell Clarion fellow. At the very least, it might offer an insight into my estranged friend.

At last I arrived at a small house near the top of a hill. From this vantage point one could look out at the loch, stretching off in a greenish black into the distance. In the dim light it appeared to be endless and still, an eerie sight, and one that filled me with an inexplicable dread.

I knocked on the door. It was opened presently by a small child, a girl of perhaps ten, in such poor and patched garments that she looked like a street urchin. But on closer look, she was clean and well fed, the patches were sewn with care, and she had the rosy cheeks of health. No orphan, then, but more likely a very poor, yet very loved child.

She stared at me in frank and intelligent appraisal.

'Aye?'

'Hello,' said I. 'My name is Dr John Watson. I am a friend of Mr Sherlock Holmes. I am here to meet the lady of the house, Mrs Agnes Simpson. Is she in?'

She seemed to recognize our names. 'Wait here,' said she without pretence of politeness.

A few moments later I stood warming my hands at a small but welcome fire in a cramped and cosy parlour upstairs. The room was a hodgepodge of castoffs, dark wood furniture which did not match, crocheted antimacassars, dingy paintings of dramatic Scottish landscapes, and a set of curved Indian knives on the wall. Next to one very worn chair was a pile of books which stretched from the floor to the top of the armrest. Several family portraits stood atop an old upright piano. The room, like the girl's clothes, spoke of genteel poverty but also care and attention.

I became aware that I was being watched and turned to see a woman in her seventies standing in the doorway. Dressed in the fashion of fifty years earlier, in a long serge gown of deep blue with lace at the collar, and her silver hair draped over her ears in loops, she stared at me with the same piercing eyes as the little girl.

Mrs Agnes Simpson had once been a great beauty, that was clear. Still graceful and charming, she radiated a warm serenity. 'Dr Watson, it is, then,' said she. 'Your work with Mr Holmes precedes you here in Atholmere. I have read "A Study in Scarlet", and you are just as I imagined.'

I smiled and bowed politely. 'Mrs Simpson,' said I. 'I am honoured. I hope my visit is not inconvenient.'

'Doctor, I have been very much hoping to meet you.' She smiled. 'I see this surprises you. Sit down and let us talk.'

Moments later we sat facing each other before the fire. She asked the child to fetch tea. I wanted to launch urgently into my questions as Holmes would have done, but instinct told me to adhere to decorum. I waited as the girl served the tea, placing a plate of shortbread between us, before withdrawing into the shadows. The candles near us and the meagre fire gave off a soft light which did not penetrate the dark corners of the room.

'Well, Dr Watson,' she began. 'When I read your account of Mr Sherlock Holmes, his singular gifts, and his profession, I was much moved, and happy that he had found a friend such as yourself. But I was also consumed with questions. You see, I knew of him as a young man, during his student days.'

'Yes, that is why I am here, ma'am. Dr Gordon Jennings of Fettes suggested I speak to you about what transpired at Camford.'

'Did he? You are curious then, about your friend?' I hesitated and she peered at me with sudden interest. 'Where is he, at this moment?'

'Elsewhere. He—we are on a case. That is why I have come. I am not sure, but I suspect the family we are investigating are perhaps haunted by something in the past. There was a son, a friend of August Bell Clarion.'

She started at the name.

'You know this Clarion, then?' I asked.

'Yes.' She shifted uneasily and carefully pulled up a tartan lap rug. She tucked it around her legs, shifting to stare at the fire. Finally, she turned to me with a searching gaze. 'Before I tell you the story, Dr Watson, I must confirm something. You are a remarkable spinner of tales. Is Sherlock Holmes the white knight you portray?'

I felt myself colouring. 'I may alter names and places and summarize, but regarding Mr Holmes, I write the truth, Mrs Simpson. He is a man of honour. He lives for his work, and in the service of justice.'

She nodded, smiling.

'He does not think of himself as any kind of hero, however,' I added.

She smiled. 'Truly? No vanity, then?'

'Well, no hubris, at least. Vanity, well . . .'

419

She laughed. 'You confirm my picture of the young man that I knew.'

'I am not here to pry, Mrs Simpson, but—'

She smiled at this. 'Of course not. Let me ask you something else if I may. Mr Sherlock Holmes is still a very private man, is he not? Ah, your face gives me your answer. And yet you love your friend. That is why you are here.'

I had begun to feel quite warm in the little room. I was sitting too close to the fire and shifted my position on the couch. I felt a bead of perspiration on my brow and wiped it quickly.

'I would do anything to protect him, Mrs Simpson. Our present case is puzzling in the extreme, and has proven quite dangerous. What happened at Camford?'

'Do you know of Charlotte Simpson?'

'No, ma'am, I have not heard the name.'

'Charlotte was my granddaughter.'

'Was?'

'She died some years ago. At the age of nineteen.'

'I am sorry to hear it. May I ask how?'

Here the lady paused and replaced her teacup in its saucer. She stared at me with piercing eyes.

'Some say she was murdered. And some say she was murdered by Mr Sherlock Holmes.'

CHAPTER 37

Charlotte

put my teacup down, my hands having grown suddenly unsteady. Her words echoed those of Dr Jennings. That is not possible,' I said.

'Oh Dr Watson, I know that he did not murder my Charlotte. My granddaughter, God rest her soul, was found hanging from a ceiling fixture in the salon of a house where she rented a room. The police ruled her death a suicide at the inquest, but many think this was a result of cruel treatment by Sherlock Holmes.'

'He is not a cruel man,' I said. 'He can be insensitive at times, but—'

The old lady smiled at me. 'I know.'

'How on earth could he be suspected of causing a suicide?'

'They had formed a close friendship and he broke things off with her just before her death. Charlotte was vulnerable to spells of melancholy, you see.'

'But what of the evidence? Did Charlotte leave a suicide note?'

'Apparently, and the police took it. It has since vanished.'

I glanced at my teacup and left it on the table. My mind was reeling.

'Are you familiar with a man called Orville St John?' asked Mrs Simpson. 'Ah, I see that you are. Yes, the man with the missing tongue. Have you met Mr St John?'

'Yes, but I understand little. Please continue.'

She paused. 'Let me begin. Evidence against your friend, Sherlock Holmes regarding Charlotte's death was compelling but circumstantial, and insufficient to convict. He got off with being expelled from Camford. But many believed in his guilt.'

As the fire nearby burned low, this woman began a tale that I would be hard pressed to relate verbatim. I will admit to waves of emotion upon hearing it, and begged leave to take out a small writing pad and make notes, lest I forget any part of it. This, then, is what I learned.

Charlotte Simpson was Agnes Simpson's granddaughter. Charlotte had been a pupil at Briar Rose, a school for girls near Fettes in Edinburgh, and had shown an astonishing aptitude for mathematics, science, and history. A precocious reader as a child, quiet and reserved by nature, she also displayed a prodigious musical talent. Had she been a man, and had she lived, the aged Mrs Simpson related, she would most certainly have been a scientist, a doctor, or a university professor. There was no limit to her intellect.

As she spoke, the lady's face took on a faraway look, her features softening. 'Charlotte could have had the world at her feet. But—'

Her voice broke and her eyes filled with tears. She quickly looked down at her cup of tea. She took a deep breath and resumed, her voice back to its prior crisp tone.

'Charlotte was hampered by one serious flaw. It runs in our family – her father, my son Philip, suffered severely from it, as did my own father. Myself to a lesser degree. That flaw was a melancholy nature, marked by periods of deep depression. It is a fearsome disadvantage, particularly at a young age, when the black dog can seem permanent and insurmountable. Later, if one is lucky, one can learn to muzzle the dog, and one finds one's personal remedies. I have done so, as have others in our line.'

I wondered briefly at this lady's words. I was tempted to ask what her personal 'remedies' were. Apparently my thoughts were as transparent to Mrs Simpson as they were to Holmes, and she smiled. 'Reading, work, and helping others. That is what fortifies me. You might suggest these to your friend, though as to the latter, he is already doing so. It was clear from Charlotte's letters to me that she and her young friend Sherlock Holmes had this in common.'

'Please tell me what happened. These letters? May I see them?' I asked. If there were letters written by this young lady that would shed light on her relationship with my friend, I was seized with a sudden intense desire to read them.

'You will read them shortly, Dr Watson. First I must give you the background. And eventually we will come to the events of 1875.'

I sat back, grasping at patience.

'You mentioned August Bell Clarion,' said she.

'Why, yes! I know little more than that he and Holmes met at Fettes and both went on to Camford. But he was a monster in the making by all accounts.'

The lady smiled, but her eyes held great sadness. 'Indeed. It is interesting that you use that word. August Bell Clarion was the grandson of my brother, and second cousin to Charlotte. And yes, he also attended Camford with Mr Holmes.'

Something unpleasant shifted in the pit of my stomach. 'He is dead, I understand.'

'Yes. Killed in the Sudan some time ago at El Obeid, shortly after joining the military, apparently. The family received word of his death but no details. And now to the tale regarding the terrible events at Camford.'

I decided against recounting what I had discovered about Clarion's fate at Khartoum, and sat poised with pen in hand.

'As you know,' she began, 'women still, to this day may not graduate from our finer universities although they may attend classes. In 1875, even this was quite the exception. But my granddaughter Charlotte was granted the rare privilege to sit in on some of the lectures at Camford. This was only at the individual lecturer's discretion, provided she sat quietly in the back, and did not speak or distract others.

'Chemistry was her passion and that lecturer would not allow her in. This led to an action she later regretted, but also to her friendship with Sherlock Holmes. To understand what happened between them, you must first read these.' She turned to the girl. 'The letters, Aline.'

Mrs Simpson stood and nodded to the young girl who dashed up the stairs and returned carrying a faded, decorative candy box, which she placed on a table before me. It was about 8 by 10 inches and the words 'Finest chocolates' was barely legible in gilded letters, surrounded by a wreath of flowers.

'Open it,' she said. 'I will leave you to this and return in a little while.'

She and the girl left the room. I moved my chair closer to the fire and the gas lamp near it and opened the box. Inside was a stack of letters. A few were on plain white stationery, written in black ink. I recognized my friend's handwriting, and they were addressed to Miss Charlotte Simpson. But the majority were on delicate tan stationery written in an unusual brown ink with a graceful hand. These were from Charlotte to her grandmother. The letters were arranged chronologically.

Charlotte's letters were articulate, witty, and personal. As I read them I heard the voice of an admirable young woman, well read and curious, a bit rebellious but passionate about learning above all. I was struck with sadness, knowing her tragic end.

The first to her grandmother related her thrill at being accepted to attend classes at Camford. She described in detail her inspiration from the science classes, but also her excitement about the cultural resources – the art galleries, the museums, and the concerts, all part of the constellation of a great university.

Her male colleagues' reactions to her ranged from

grudging acceptance to outright hostility. 'But mostly, Grandmamma, they simply disdain me,' she wrote. 'Fortunately I do not care. I am determined to be a chemist.' I had no doubt that she would have achieved her goal.

She mentioned her annoying cousin August Bell Clarion and his insistent attempts to spend time with her, in the company of his handsome friend Orville St John. 'It is almost as though August covets me himself, despite our family ties, and yet he seems to press his friend upon me as well. I suspect he would love to see us fall in love, only to ruin it. Oh, yes, August is a monster, I am convinced. But fear not, Grandmamma, I have no desire to pair up with anyone, even though August's latest candidate, Mr Orville St John, is very handsome and well spoken. This young man professes to admire my intelligence, though I perceive his ardour would diminish were I to actually sit beside him in some class.

'In any case, Mr Orville St John is overly solicitous and, in the final analysis, not intelligent enough,' she wrote. 'Nor am I sure I would ever want a husband!'

A second letter related that Mr St John had taken to sending flowers and gifts of food to her meagre lodgings in the town. 'I am afraid he somehow feels himself encouraged and I must put a stop to that! Peanut says I should make myself unattractive but I think she simply wants to see what I look like with my hair a mess and an ugly dress, the imp! The direct approach is best and I shall let him down this weekend, at the very latest. It is kindest in the long run.'

I wondered who 'Peanut' might be and deduced a young female friend or relative.

Shortly after that letter came a sharp turn in her narrative.

'Disaster, Grandmamma! My hubris has ruined all. The lecturer in the organic chemistry class I so desired refused to let me attend, and so I disguised myself as a boy, thinking to sit in the back, but I was discovered. One of the boys pulled off my cap and the game was up. Only it is not a game to me, and I am bereft. Two other lecturers have now banned me from attending their classes as well, in solidarity with the first!

'I find myself in a pit, Grandmamma, wondering if life will ever offer up its riches to me, or if I am destined to be only someone's wife, someone's mother, with no science or intellectual challenge in my future. Oh – I am not criticising your choices. You had even fewer chances and have sharpened your mind through reading. But after my intoxicating taste of university life – oh, it is all too bleak. I am in despair and have spent two days in bed.'

A short note followed. 'Grandmamma, please be assured that I am recovering. Yes, the black dog we both know came upon me, but I am resourceful and resilient, as you have taught me. I hope to write to you soon with good news.'

In the following letter she mentioned another young man, whom she did not immediately name. He was not as obviously attractive as Mr St John. 'He is perhaps too thin and intense to be thought handsome. But it is his mind that I find intriguing. He has a chilly exterior but underneath is a kind spirit. And here is the good news I had hoped to convey. This young man has agreed to bring me books and classroom notes since he is in several of the classes from which I have been barred. This is no small thing, Grandmamma. We are meeting in secret, and he risks expulsion if we are thought to be too much alone together or intimate. The school is very strict on such matters.'

Of course, this 'young man' was Sherlock Holmes.

'He is most business-like and proper,' Charlotte wrote later, 'and devoid of any hint of flirtation, but I adore his courtesy and sly sense of humour. He has dark grey eyes with a touch of green, the colour of the sea under a storm. And there is something quite thrilling about the way his mind works.'

She continued by recounting details of his clever machinations to supply her with needed materials, and began teasingly to refer to 'Sherpa Holmes' for his willingness to traverse dangerous territory, carry copious baggage – not only class notes but many books as well. 'He responds to every request, Grandmamma, while maintaining a remarkably unruffled equilibrium. You see, I read the books you sent. I particularly loved the Marcus Aurelius, and I shared it with him.

'I suppose other young women might desire to awaken emotion in him, but I understand that his detachment is probably a cover for a deeply emotional nature, and comes at a high cost. I respect that and do not push. We connect so completely on scholarly matters, I would never dare to risk that which is so precious to me.'

I paused at that letter. I had come to the same conclusion about Holmes's nature myself, but that was after living with the man. That a nineteen-year-old girl with limited contact understood Holmes so completely was startling. But then, women have often surprised me in this way.

At this point in the chronology, Holmes's notes to Charlotte began and soon became frequent. I will not recount them here as most were nothing but plans about where and when to meet and discussions of chemistry. His tone was pleasant but always formal and the notes quite brief.

However, a late one caught my attention. It read: 'Miss Simpson, as it is raining and quite frigid, we should surely meet indoors. I know a small pub nearby where I am friendly with the proprietor and we may be assured of privacy in a back room. Perhaps there I can assist you with your chemical conundrums and we may discuss the assign-ment at our leisure. In addition, they serve a much-admired Sunday roast. Will you join me at four o'clock this Sunday?'

Charlotte wrote to her grandmother on the Monday following: 'Grandmamma, something wonderful has happened. Mr Holmes invited me to dinner and we spent four very lovely hours together yesterday at a private room in The Spotted Dragon. Now, do not be alarmed. It was innocent, yet I sense that the tectonic plates in his world have shifted ever so slightly. He did or said nothing that could be construed as romantic. And yet I am quite, well nearly, confident that his eyes lingered just a moment longer on mine. And our hands touched briefly. I cannot be assured it was not an accident, but still. Do not worry, Grandmamma. All is proper and you can remain assured of my integrity.'

Their following notes remained formal and succinct and Charlotte did not indicate anything further until two weeks later.

'Grandmamma. It is nearly Christmas and I cannot wait to see you and talk of university and reading and life. I have exciting news, although I will admit it is a slender thread. Yesterday was my last meeting with Mr Holmes before the holidays, and I presented him with a fruitcake and a long cravat which I knitted for him against the cold. He was surprised and seemed embarrassed. For a moment I thought it was because he had nothing for me, but I expected nothing, he has been the soul of generosity throughout the term and it is I who owe him.

'But to my surprise he pulled from his satchel a package wrapped in silver paper. It contained the most beautiful scarf I have ever seen. It is French chiffon, a delicate electric blue with very particular red, peach, and cream flowers, and very long and sheer. The colours are perfect for me, and those I most favour. He must have taken notice of this. So few men see colour, and when I complimented him on his artistic choice, he mentioned that his grandmother was the sister of the artist Vernet.

'I will admit, dear Grandmamma, that on impulse, I kissed his cheek and he turned as red as the roses on the scarf. It was funny! But do not worry, things went no further. I shall discuss this with you at length at Christmas.'

The letters stopped, presumably for the holidays, then resumed in January. It was shortly thereafter that another disaster befell poor Charlotte.

'Grandmamma, cousin August has once again inserted himself into my life. Somehow he has discovered my connection to Mr Holmes, whom he describes as a freakish hermit who has been ostracised at school for blowing up the chemistry laboratory. I happen to know he did not blow up the laboratory, but only a small part of it. August says no one will share a room with Mr Holmes, which I am certain suits him just as well.

'But August discovered a letter I had written to Mr Holmes, and while you and I know that this is perfectly innocent, August says he will not fail to make the case that Mr Holmes has been inappropriate, and has been taking advantage of me. This even at the expense of my reputation!

'Grandmamma, I ask you, how could this fiend be related to us? Apparently he and Mr Holmes have been sworn enemies since both attended Fettes. I had no idea. But my instinct to keep my activities with Sherlock Holmes a secret was correct. My friend will now face expulsion, and all because of me. I never mention August to anyone because frankly I am ashamed of my kinship with that awful young man. Oh, what shall I do?

'Can you help me, please? Have a word with August's father, perhaps? Though I fear nothing will stop this villain. I do not hesitate to call him that. Frankly, Grandmamma, I feel a chill each time he is near and make sure never to be alone with him. The horror! Please, please do what you can.'

Several days passed. Then came this letter from Charlotte. 'It is in the deepest despair that I take up my pen today. Forgive my terseness, for I have not the energy to offer much. I received an angry, well, no, a cold letter from Mr Sherlock Holmes yesterday, severing all ties. He has been suspended from university for fraternizing with me, with expulsion threatened. Mr Holmes writes that had he known of my relation with August, he would have taken care, and could have averted this disaster. How, I do not know. But he further chides me for keeping this from him and writes "this deception was unworthy, and hardly the basis for the kind of friendship you so clearly desire. You will not be seeing me again."

'My reply to him was returned unopened. August has done his work.

'Mr Holmes is right to put distance between us. I feel our friendship was doomed from the start. What I do not know is if he has been lied to by August, who is capable of saying just anything, or if he simply despises me for keeping my family relationship to his nemesis a secret. Truly I do not know! But who knows what August has told him? If Mr Holmes thinks me duplicitous, I simply cannot bear it. I meant no harm, only to shield him from one who hurts nearly everyone he touches. I am bereft. Not only have I lost my university connections, but my dearest friend, for that is what Mr Holmes has been to me. Pity me, Grandmamma, I fear I am finished.'

There were no more letters.

The candle next to me had burned low as I set this last letter down. The sense of loss was palpable. It was a terribly sad fork in the road for two young people, I thought, knowing the future of both. A small noise nearby caused me to look up. The little girl had re-entered the room and now regarded me steadily. 'You are crying,' she said.

'Of course not,' said I, rubbing my eyes. 'Just eye strain from so much reading.'

She nodded sagely and fetched her grandmother.

'Where is Sherlock Holmes's note to Charlotte?' I asked the lady. 'The one that caused her so much grief? Shouldn't it be here? And her suicide note?' I asked.

'Charlotte's suicide note was taken by the police. And as for Sherlock Holmes's letter to Charlotte, it was here, at one time,' said the old lady. 'I believe Peanut took it. And probably still has it. Everyone in our family thought Charlotte killed herself as a direct result of his last letter. Everyone but me, that is.'

'Who is Peanut? What did the letter say?'

'Peanut was a younger cousin, who idolized Charlotte. They were very close. As to the letter, it was curt, and as she described. I could see why it would have pained her deeply. But it was understandable, given the circumstances.'

'But why did the family immediately think of suicide?' I asked.

'Well, the family inferred, and I think this originated with August, that Mr Holmes had taken advantage of Charlotte, and had relations with her. He said that Mr Holmes destroyed her honour, perhaps with a false promise of marriage.'

'It would be far out of character for him,' I said.

'And for Charlotte as well. But people love to gossip and believe the worst in others,' said the lady.

'Mrs Simpson, I must ask you something. What happened to Charlotte's early suitor, Mr Orville St John? In London, not long ago, he attempted to kill Mr Holmes three times.'

Mrs Simpson paled. 'He tried to kill Mr Holmes? It was my understanding that the unfortunate Mr St John had a successful business and marriage. I was told he had put that terrible affair behind him,' said she.

'But what was the terrible affair? And is it connected to Charlotte's death?'

The lady sighed. 'Yes. And it is a grim tale,' she said. 'You are aware of Mr St John's heinous accident?'

'Only that the poor man is missing his tongue.'

'Did you know that Mr Holmes and he were involved in a bloody boxing match in a pub only minutes before this tragedy befell him?'

'No, I did not!' said I.

'The details were related to me by August, which of course means they are not completely reliable. However, everything that took place in the pub is a matter of public record. Here, then, is Mr St John's sad story.'

CHAPTER 38

Golden Bear and Silver Tongue

s Mrs Simpson began to relate this second part of the tale, young Aline tended to the fire and brought us hot whisky-laced tea. The damp Scottish air had seeped in and around our legs and I shivered. The gas lamps and candles sent flickering lights on the walls and I could not dispel the oppressive feeling of tragedy which had begun to pervade the room.

Mrs Simpson began. 'The Golden Bear was one of the pubs favoured by students at Camford. Apparently, your friend did not regularly frequent pubs, nor drink to excess, but I can presume he was at that moment attempting to drown his sorrow at the loss of his friendship with Charlotte.'

'But he broke it off with her himself,' I exclaimed.

'Dr Watson, you are not so far from your college days to forget how black and white the world is to young people. No doubt Mr Holmes himself felt very betrayed. At that moment he did not know of her death, only that he had rather precipitously broken things off with her, and he was probably filled with regret. In any case, he was drinking heavily.

'And so your despairing friend sat at the Golden Bear drinking alone and in very dark spirits, when August and Orville entered. Mr St John had just been told of Charlotte's death by August, who placed the blame squarely on Mr Holmes's "mistreatment". He made Orville St John believe that Sherlock Holmes had destroyed her honour, leading to her suicide. Orville was devastated by this news.

'And now, suddenly sitting before him, was the culprit! Orville and Sherlock came to blows and the drunken student crowd was apparently titillated by the action and began shouting for a match. The situation threatened to turn deadly.'

'My God! Were the police called?' I asked.

'No. It was the pub's policy to refrain from calling the police.'

'Why?'

'The Golden Bear attracted many students from the university. They were a boisterous crowd, young and fearless, and they drank heavily to relieve the pressures of their education and family expectations. Fisticuffs and even more violent mayhem were not unheard of. And so the owner devised a kind of protocol in place to handle such moments. It had served beautifully until that night.'

'What protocol?'

'There was a secret back room known as the "steam room." It was set up as an impromptu boxing arena. Students

436

would have a go at each other and bets were placed, but the fights were broken up before any real harm. It was an illegal practice but tacitly allowed by the community. It kept many a window unbroken and gave the students a relatively harmless and very contained outlet for their aggressions.'

'I see,' said I, thinking I might have benefited from such an arrangement myself upon occasion as a younger man. And perhaps even now, recalling the hard right I had once dealt to Holmes's French rival Vidocq.

'Well, both your friend and Orville St John were recognized as members of the boxing team, and the crowd apparently screamed for a match. I am told your friend resisted but the crowd closed ranks and forced the issue. The proprietor later told the police that had he known the degree of animosity between the combatants, he would never have allowed the match.'

As Mrs Simpson continued her story, I felt a chill running down my spine that was unaffected by the warm fire now burning in her grate. I glanced up and saw the small girl, still in the shadows in one corner of the room. Her eyes gleamed with interest as she listened to the tale.

'The child?' said I, nodding in the girl's direction.

'Aline knows,' said she, and turned back to her story. 'This match grew serious and bloody quite quickly. My great-nephew August related to me that your friend was far more skilled than his rival Orville St John, and that St John appeared to be so blinded by rage against Mr Holmes that his furious attack grew out of control. Mr Holmes easily got the best of him.

'Orville and August had many friends in the audience, and your friend apparently none – no, Dr Watson, not a one – and while the cheering began one sided against Mr Holmes, your friend's skill and gentlemanly fair play won admiration and eventually the favour of the crowd.'

I could well imagine this.

'St John found himself downed repeatedly, and to his great embarrassment, each time was helped back up by Mr Holmes who remained courteous throughout.'

'Seeing that his friend was losing, August said he then stepped in to break up the fight but as the two combatants were drawn to opposite sides of the room by several students each, St John broke free and in some kind of fit, drew a knife from his pocket, and attempted to stab your friend in the back! But young Mr Holmes sensed this and side-stepped it, managing easily to remove the knife from Orville's hand.

'The crowd, shocked by St John's cowardly act, now cheered Mr Holmes. My great-nephew and two others restrained St John. That young man, realizing he was phys-ically beaten and that the tide of public opinion had turned against him, then pulled out his greatest weapon.

'You may not know that Orville St John was known at Camford as "The Silver Tongue". A remarkable debater, he was so skilled at rhetoric, and so dynamic and persuasive a speaker, that – coupled with his tall and handsome demeanour – he was said to possess the power to separate a starving man from a banquet, or to part the sea at his command.

'He began with an apology to Sherlock Holmes for the knife attack, painting himself as a man overcome with grief. He appealed to the decency and fair play of the crowd. As he felt their judgement soften, he explained his mad act. Orville St John implied that Sherlock Holmes had kicked his dog—'

'That is preposterous,' I said.

'Yes, well apparently your friend had been bitten severely the year before by another student's dog, but in any case, he continued by saying that this "monster" Sherlock Holmes had since done something far worse. He had so deceived a young lady, that this sweet young girl, barely nineteen, had killed herself over it!

'Sherlock Holmes fell back at this. He did not know until that moment of Charlotte's death. August then stepped forward to tell everyone that he had found the body and the suicide note which blamed Sherlock Holmes.

'The drunken crowd went mad, and fell upon your friend, who at this point was so stunned by the news that he could barely defend himself. He somehow escaped into a back alley, running for his life.

'Where he went from there, no one knows. He was not seen at his lodgings that night or the next day. Although the police reported that later that night someone of his description attempted to enter the house where Charlotte died, but was prevented by the police who had cordoned off the area pending their investigation.'

Of course he went there, I thought. He would have tried to learn the truth. 'Do you know if he succeeded in getting in eventually?' I asked.

'I am not sure. Buoyed by an apparent win, Orville and August were toasted by the crowd, but the victory was a bitter and empty one, for the grieving Orville St John could not bear to linger. He, too, was bereft at the death of the young woman he loved, and was not in his right mind. Despite the pleadings of August, Orville St John left the pub only minutes later.

'After ten minutes or so, August Bell Clarion also left the pub alone claiming he needed to find and comfort his friend. As Holmes and St John did before him, August left by the back door which led down the alley.'

Mrs Simpson turned to the girl. 'Aline, now you must leave us, dear.' As soon as the child had gone, she continued, in a hushed voice. 'While the events at the pub have been corroborated, from here on out, we must rely entirely on the testimony of my great-nephew, whom I know to have been a duplicitous man.

'Three streets away, he says he discovered the unconscious form of his friend Orville St John lying senseless on the pavement, face down, a pool of blood forming around his head. Turning his friend over, August discovered a horror that made him retch in the street. St John's tongue had been cut from its moorings with his own knife, and forced down his throat; he was near death from shock and loss of blood.

'August said he next grabbed a hot coal from a chestnut peddler, and cauterised the wound, saving St John's life, and then summoned help. St John was removed immediately to the hospital where doctors managed pull him back from the brink. When he finally regained his senses the next day, only August Bell Clarion, who had never left his side, was in the room. My great-nephew had been sleeping in a chair next to the bed and he related the following to the police and to the family.

'When St John awoke and discovered his ghastly situation, he attempted to jump out of the window of the third floor room where he had been placed. But August was able to stop him. The police arrived to question the traumatised young man, but St John was unable to help. He had been struck on the back of the head in the alley and had not seen his attacker. But he believed with certainty that Holmes was the culprit.'

My stomach turned at this tale, the horror of this attack affecting even my war hardened sensibilities. And yet I knew with equal certainty that it could not have been Sherlock Holmes who did the deed.

Mrs Simpson continued: 'Mr Holmes was finally found a day and a half later. He had been wandering alone in the countryside, with no witnesses, had not eaten or slept, and appeared shocked at the news of Orville St John's catastrophe.

'Of course he was suspected of the crime and arrested, thus thwarting any investigation he might have done on his own into the incident. His involvement could not be proved, however, and some small bits of evidence, gathered I believe by his own brother, then a rising young barrister in London, ultimately cast doubt on Sherlock's guilt.'

'Mycroft! What evidence?'

'The pattern of blood on August's coat, the testimony of the chestnut seller on the description of the man who attacked St John from behind. These saved the day, although, various pieces of evidence including the coat later vanished from the police station and the chestnut seller recanted his story. August had done his work.'

'I wonder how he got the man to recant?' I asked.

The lady eyed me sharply. 'Do you know the story of Clarion Hall, at Fettes?'

'Oh yes, of course. I presume, then, that his parents bought his freedom.'

She nodded. 'It appears so. But Sherlock Holmes was also freed. Character witnesses included the assistant head-master from Fettes, an influential tutor at Camford, and a fellow student, Victor Trevor.'

'And the tutor?'

'Mathematician. I forget; an Irish name. But I believe the rest you know.'

I sat there, stunned for some minutes. Mrs Simpson watched me with a sad but peaceful regard. Eventually I found my voice.

'I know for certain that Sherlock Holmes did not do this to Orville St John. He would never do such a thing.' said I.

'Drunk and overcome with grief, as he was supposed to have been, it was suggested that—'

'No. Never.'

Mrs Simpson nodded, and was silent for a long time. A deadly calm settled over me. I now knew the origin of St

John's vendetta and that it went far beyond his own horrible maiming to the death of a very special young woman. I resolved to do something, somehow to bring this terrible tale to a conclusion, and to clear my friend's name once and for all. I wondered, however, why St John's rage against my friend had lain dormant for so long, and was only recently revived.

'Mrs Simpson, since you do not believe that Charlotte killed herself over Sherlock Holmes, what do you think happened?'

'I think she was murdered.'

'But by whom?'

Mrs Simpson did not reply, but looked at me pointedly. Finally she said, 'As to disbelieving her suicide, I am in the minority. It is true she was deeply upset. But I did not think her as fragile as all that. It is my belief, that with a few wise words, those two . . . well, at least Charlotte, might have . . . oh, it is no use speculating. Your Mr Holmes, I understand, has remained a bachelor.'

'Yes,' I said. 'He abjures any notion of romance as being detrimental to his work.'

'He has not grown to despise women, I hope?'

'Not at all. He is the soul of courtesy and respect. Kindness, even. But it is my belief that he does not fully understand them, and, well, he is not forthcoming on the subject.'

'Pity. This sad conflagration was a triple tragedy in a sense. Charlotte, Orville St John, and even your Mr Holmes was not unscathed.'

I stood up, distraught and feeling the need for action. I was not sure that anything I had learned would help our current case. Instead, I felt only that I had further transgressed my friend's privacy, along with a vague sense of unease about leaving him alone at Braedern. I decided to return, no matter what he might say about it.

'Mrs Simpson, I am grateful for your time and hospitality and frankness. I must leave you now. I am still not sure what to make of this story. Perhaps if I saw his note to her. Or this suicide note—'

'Yes, well, for some time Peanut carried with her Mr Holmes's note to Charlotte. It became an obsession. I hope she is over it and threw it out long ago.'

Could there be another enemy to Holmes, lying dormant somewhere, now a grown woman?

'Who is "Peanut"?' I asked. 'And where is she now?'

Mrs Simpson sighed. 'She was Charlotte's younger cousin, twelve at the time. She even resembled her idol in both temperament and looks, though with darker hair. Spent every spare moment with her. Intelligent, too, and—'

'But what became of "Peanut"?' I cried, an urgency rising within me.

Mrs Simpson continued at her own pace. 'She was devastated at the death. She was the first to find the body, in fact. They made her give her account at the trial, young as she was.'

I had to find this girl. 'Did she, too, blame Holmes?'

'Yes. Children, even clever ones, think simplistically. But she was, and I presume still is, a rational girl.'

444

'Where is she now?' I had grabbed my coat and was putting it on. Aline stood by with my muffler.

'I do not know, exactly. She married into wealth and moved away. We have lost touch. Poor little Peanut.' Mrs Simpson picked up an old daguerreotype of a child. Smiling down at it, she said, 'Of course no one calls her that anymore. She is all grown up and goes by her married name.'

Mrs Simpson held up the daguerreotype. It was a beautiful child's face, familiar somehow. The wind howled suddenly and the trees brushed against the house. I shuddered.

'What is her name now?' I asked, already knowing the answer.

'Isla McLaren,' said she. 'Ah, but you grow pale, Dr Watson. May I get you some brandy before you leave?'

PART SEVEN

THE POUR

'I am not omniscient but I know a lot'
—Goethe, *Faust*, First part

CHAPTER 39

The Lady

t was close to midnight when I arrived back at Braedern. I had missed most of the train connections and was forced to arrange private transportation at considerable expense and what felt like perilous delay. But mad visions of the tale I had been told, Isla McLaren's relationship to a ghost from Holmes's past, and an insight into his aversion to this same young woman whirled in my brain. Is it not possible that ghosts are actually subtle ideas, just out of reach of our consciousness, tickling our minds with possibilities but vanishing just as we may try to label them?

In some way, Isla McLaren must have reminded Holmes of Charlotte Simpson. I am postulating that this was not on the level of consciousness, but enough to set off an extreme and painful reaction. That his masterful brain would not have made the connection was telling. This ghost was well hidden to my friend.

Perhaps he had been right about one thing all along. She could be a very real danger to him.

By the time I arrived, the castle was dark and Mungo let me in. The old man was surprised to see me. 'I thought you had returned to London, Dr Watson,' said he. 'I apologize but we have cleared your room and removed the bedding for airing. But I can—'

'Later!' I cried. 'Where is Mr Holmes?'

Mungo had no idea, and when he refused to accompany me to the East Tower and Holmes's room, I barked out, 'Damn it man, there are no ghosts! But there are real people who may be in danger!'

He offered me the keys, but would not go.

I found myself alone in our hallway, now nearly pitch black with only one light flickering feebly. I made my way to his room and unlocked the door. It was empty and cold. I felt in my pocket for the reassuring presence of my Webley and the knife. Holmes was formidable in combat but unarmed. Regret and fear filled my veins with ice. How stupidly angry had I been to leave my friend in this place? And where was he now?

I retraced my steps to the main hall and ran to Isla McLaren's room. It, too, was vacant. I felt panic rising in my gorge. It was she who had initially wanted Holmes to come to Braedern.

Alistair McLaren was next. I awakened him from a sound sleep. He did not know where his wife, or indeed anyone in the family was, except his father, who was resting comfortably under the supervision of Dr MacLeish.

The man responded to my alarm with a shrug. 'It is my opinion, Dr Watson, that the ghosts have played out their hand in this family. It is left to a few of us to pick up the pieces.' I asked after Holmes's whereabouts and he replied, 'I have no idea. Your friend seemed inclined to persist, despite the rest of us being more than willing to leave the final stones unturned. He was not to be dissuaded, however. The last I understood was that he sought out more information on the various buildings in the distillery, though what he could hope to find at this time I cannot imagine.'

'And your wife?'

'It is nearly midnight, Doctor. Presumably she is sleeping.'

'She is not in her room.'

Alistair's one eyebrow shot up. 'You checked? Then she is probably reading in the library. Good night, Dr Watson.'

But she was not there, either, and I returned to Holmes's room with a sick feeling. Should I await him there? I was not easy with that thought. I paced the room, looking for any indication of his whereabouts. And it was then that I saw it.

A note, scrawled hastily on a slip of paper, lay upon the desk. It read. 'Sherlock Holmes, I have information you seek. Meet me at Building C, the mash tun at midnight.' It had been written in Charlotte's unusual shade of golden brown ink. This had to be from Isla McLaren with revenge on her mind. It was just past midnight now. I wasted not a second longer. My friend was in danger and I knew it with a cold certainty.

I ran from Holmes's room into the hallway. The single

remaining lamp which had been flickering earlier was now out and the hall was shrouded in darkness. I went back for a candle, then emerged a second time into the hall.

I felt a sudden chill draught, and turned.

There, at the end of the hall, floated the eerie, glowing female figure I had seen on our first night at Braedern. My spine went rigid. The transparent figure emitted a high-pitched, keening wail. I could not move. Her diaphanous lace dressing gown, lit from within, blew softly in billows around her pale feet. The moon-like globe of her face bore features this time, barely distinguishable and wavering as if several feet underwater.

The figure was semi-transparent. It could not be a trick of the light. Holmes had said there was no room to create a stage magic illusion there.

'You are not real,' I called out. I could hear the quaver in my voice.

The figure continued to glimmer as I watched, and now she appeared to smile and nod. What did this mean? Suddenly one arm extended, pointing off to the right, in the direction of the distillery. Her other hand waved in that direction as if exhorting me to go there. The ghost quivered and her luminescence grew stronger. She was trying to tell me something. Something I already knew. I tore myself from looking at this apparition, and ran from her, down the hall, down the stairs and towards the front door of the castle. Holmes was at the distillery. In Building C.

After a perilous descent down the steep icy hill, I tore over ice-slicked cobblestones between the buildings of the distillery towards Building C, the one that housed the new mash tun. I fell, tearing the knee of my trousers. The heavy door was ajar and I entered the building into an anteroom which led into the main area. Over near a set of controls I saw a body sprawled on the floor. Rushing to it I discovered a workman, with bulging eyes and swollen tongue, apparently dead by strangulation. In his hand was a sheet of paper attached to a board, some kind of record of temperatures. I moved on.

I came to the cavernous room where the grains were soaked and raked in that huge, heated cast iron vat, the 'mash tun', turning into a hot, slimy soup. It was that same enormous vat where we had seen the men arguing at the controls.

It was dimly lit here. The metal grillwork flooring over the concrete made a silent approach difficult. I advanced cautiously. The mash tun was at the other end of the room. The vat itself extended up from the floor, some ten or fifteen feet. A metal staircase led to a platform near the top of the gigantic vessel.

At first I saw no one but heard the soft murmur of voices against the mechanical hiss and clank of the steam engine which drove the rakes circulating in the mash tun. I started to light a match but thought better of it. I inched my way silently towards the voices, careful to hide behind various pieces of equipment.

There he was!

In the dim light I made out Holmes, above me on the platform, unmoving and focused intently on something before him. He was very near the opening in the metal canopy which covered the vat. This yawning and treacherous opening was protected only by a narrow iron railing. The warm, churning liquid below gave off a cloud of steam which billowed around his backlit figure. The air reeked of wet grain.

I carefully ascended a staircase off to one side and emerging on the same platform, but across the room from him, I hid behind a boiler. Peering around it, I discovered the subject of his gaze. If what I had just seen in the hall had frightened me just a little, this sent ice through my veins.

A ghostly female figure faced him from the other side of the cauldron of bubbling liquid, terrible in her deathly aspect.

This apparition was brighter than the one I had just seen. White as porcelain, her hair, face and arms were aglow. The electric light on the wall behind the figure shone through the diaphanous fabric of her filmy dress and she seemed to shimmer in the darkness. The pale hair was dressed in a style of twenty years ago, blonde but tinged with white.

But it was the face that chilled my blood. Backlit and in shadow, it was terrible, with lips of frost and a deep hollowed blackness around the eyes. It bore a look of quiet fury. I had thought to find Isla McLaren. But instead—

Circling her bare, blue-white neck the clear mark of a ligature was visible.

Holmes was mesmerized. He stared at the figure, unmoving.

'Holmes!' I called out. But my voice did not carry over the noise of the engine. Or, he did not seem to heed me.

'Charlotte?' he said softly.

The apparition slowly raised her right arm and pointed at Holmes. Her voice was hoarse, low pitched, and strange. 'Sherlock Holmes. Murderer. Confess.'

I stepped out from behind the boiler and moved closer to where Holmes stood. I hoped the apparition would not notice me in the dim light. I called out again, just above a whisper, 'Holmes!'

But whatever it was that faced Holmes heard me. 'Silence!' the creature shouted in my direction.

Holmes did not move. 'That is her voice.' I was not sure whether he was speaking to me, or to himself.

'Confess!' intoned the apparition.

I stepped closer. I took the gun from my pocket and held it at my side. This was Isla McLaren. No matter what it looked like, it had to be Isla McLaren. But—

'If you are the ghost of Charlotte Simpson then you know Sherlock Holmes would never kill her—kill you. He is not that kind of man,' I called out.

Holmes turned to me in surprise. 'Watson! When did you—stand back, Doctor! Put that gun away.'

'You cannot kill me, Doctor Watson. I am already dead!' said the apparition with a bitter laugh, spreading her arms wide, daring me.

Holmes moved closer to me. 'Put it away, I say,' he said softly.

'Holmes, you do not believe this, do you?' I whispered. 'You do not believe this is Charlotte?'

He looked at me in utter surprise, then recovered and

moved to stand between the ghost and me. He turned his back on her. His voice dropped to a whisper. 'Do it, Watson. Please. No matter what happens. Just put the gun away.'

Reluctantly, I replaced the gun in my pocket. He turned back to face the spectre.

'Confess,' said the ghost, her voice terrible. 'I want to hear you say it. You killed me, Sherlock Holmes.'

'I did not kill you.'

'You made me a promise. And then you cruelly abandoned me.'

'I made you no promise.'

'Say my name.'

My friend paused.

The man for whom empirical evidence ruled all would not believe this was a ghost. Would he?

'Say my name!'

'Why should I believe you?' said Holmes. It was as though he wanted to.

But it was Isla. It must be. And yet it did not quite look like her. 'Because you gave me this.'

She reached into her voluminous white dress and withdrew a faded scarf, blue with pink, coral and red roses. It was six feet long, French chiffon, and appeared to be shredded in places. Holmes rocked backward in surprise. He squinted in the dim light. 'Where did you get that?' His voice was muted, full of wonder.

'You gave it to me. Do you not remember? Wrapped in silver paper as we stood under the elm tree in the courtyard in front of the Green Pelican Inn. It was snowing. You had

chosen a combination of my favourite colours and I complimented you on this.'

Holmes did not move.

'Then we went inside. We stood by the fireplace. I said
I had never met a man like you. And you were uncomfortable. Do you remember what we said?'

Holmes shuddered. 'Please, no,' he said softly.

'We had been studying Todhunter's book, *The*—'

'—*History of Probability*, yes,' said Holmes with difficulty.

'See, you do remember. And I told you that the laws of
chance said I was not likely to find anyone like you ever
again. And you, so very confident, started to agree. But
then you suddenly caught my meaning. And you said no,
that I would surely find someone better suited—'

'Stop!' Holmes cried. He swallowed and took a step back
as if struck. He seemed to shrink before my eyes, the vital
energy draining from his body. 'How—how can you know
this?'

'Because I was there. Say my name.'

Holmes was silent.

I wanted to speak but could not find my voice. The
muffled sounds of the engine and the enormous rake droned
steadily on. I became aware that the room was very warm
from the steam arising from the tank.

'Say it,' said the ghost.

'Charlotte,' said Holmes. 'Charlotte Simpson.'

'I had feelings for you,' the ghost continued. 'But not long
after this, you wrote me that horrible letter. It was a knife
in my heart. As surely as if you had plunged it in yourself.'

Holmes looked stricken. 'I was brusque. I—'

'Did you love me?'

'I felt betrayed.'

'Betrayed?'

'I had told you of my troubles with August Bell Clarion. You were his second cousin. You hid the relationship. Lying by omission—'

'—is as shameful and dishonourable as lying outright. Or so you feel.'

The same words Holmes had said to Isla during our interview.

'I thought he must have put you up to this,' whispered Holmes.

'You thought I would participate? That I was like my cousin August?'

'You underestimated him. He was insidious.'

'Holmes!' I whispered.

He ignored me.

'But how could you think Charlotte was so easily swayed? How could you think that of her—of me?' she corrected.

'I was young,' he said. 'Inexperienced. And I—'

'I ask you again. Did you love me?'

Holmes paused.

'Did you love me? Did you love Charlotte?'

'In the only way I could,' he said.

The ghost regarded him sadly.

'But if you were Charlotte, you would know that,' said Holmes.

'But how? *How* did you love me?' she said.

There was a long silence. Holmes could not bring himself to speak. Finally he looked down at the floor, his face torn in anguish. 'That shall remain between us,' he said in a choked voice.

The ghost waivered, unsure. Holmes rubbed his eyes. With effort, he took a deep breath and regained his poise. He drew himself up tall. 'And now it is my turn.' He glared at the female figure standing before him, and abruptly his voice sharpened into its normal tone. 'Where did you get the scarf, Mrs McLaren?'

The woman facing us across the vat stood very still. My hand found my gun and rested on it. There was a silence.

Slowly, the pale figure reached up and pulled off the white-tinged, golden-haired wig to reveal dark auburn tresses. The rim of where the white makeup ended and her own skin colour began was visible at her hairline. She removed a handkerchief from her sleeve and rubbed off the ghostly paint, then took the familiar pair of small gold glasses from her pocket and placed them on her face.

And there she was, Mrs Isla McLaren. It had been a remarkable disguise. Even though I knew it must be her, she had made me doubt it. I raised the gun and aimed it at her.

'I am glad you confirm you had feelings for my cousin, Mr Holmes,' said Isla McLaren in her own, natural voice.

'Your cousin?' said Holmes.

'Isla McLaren is the young girl you may have known as Peanut.' I said.

Holmes looked at me, startled as though he had forgotten

I was there. He nodded, and turned back to the lady. 'Ah, yes, of course. The resemblance is not something I would normally miss.'

'Our own ghosts are hard to see, Holmes,' said I.

He smiled ruefully. 'Ah, so you are Peanut! You were but a child! Charlotte spoke of you but we never met.'

'Twelve at the time she died. I was the person who found her.'

Mrs Isla McLaren fingered the scarf around her neck. Silence, except for the soft cacophony of the dripping condensation from the mash tun, the splash of the rakes, and the faint huffs and clanks of the engine. Steam continued to rise into the room.

'Mrs McLaren, I will ask you again. Where did you get the scarf?'

'She was hanging from it when I walked into the room.'

Holmes closed his eyes and pressed his fingers to his forehead, blinking back emotion. 'Yes, I know. But it disappeared from the evidence room during the investigation. When did it come into your possession?'

'I received it in the post, shortly before I came to you in London' said she. Then, turning to me, 'Put down your gun, Dr Watson. I mean your friend no harm.'

I did not believe it for a moment. 'Holmes, I would not—'

'Watson!' Reluctantly I lowered my gun. 'In the post? From whom?' he continued.

'Anonymous, but the writer identified himself as a retired policeman who worked on that investigation. He said he had proof that your letter caused her to hang herself.'

'And you came to London for what reason? Retribution?'

'Not exactly. You and I are much alike, Mr Holmes. I wanted to take the measure of the man. I believe in drawing my own conclusions, just as you do.'

'And your conclusion?'

'The jury is still out.'

Holmes turned to me thoughtfully. 'Interesting. Watson, remember our visitor Mr Orville St John? He of the missing tongue?'

'Of course.'

'You recall our brief conversation in sign language? He told me that he had received a letter as well. The writer said he had proof that it was I who cut out his tongue so long ago.'

He turned back to Mrs McLaren. 'I am fortunate that you are more circumspect. I somehow think that you might have succeeded where he failed. It is as if August Bell Clarion were still alive, playing the game as he always has. Sending you and Orville St John to do his own dirty work, is that not so, Mrs McLaren?'

He paused but she did not reply.

'Let me see the scarf.'

She hesitated. He held out his hand to receive it.

Isla McLaren then slowly lifted it from around her neck and held out the scarf with both hands, as if it were a banner. Lit from behind by one of the electric lights on the walls, it glowed in beautiful, if faded colours. It was wrinkled, though, and badly shredded in places. She walked towards us. We remained near the open panel. The steam had begun to make my eyes water, and I blinked to clear them.

I did not trust this woman and kept a firm grasp on my pistol.

Holmes hesitated before taking the scarf. The memories it must hold for him, I thought, feeling pain for his loss.

He took it from her, handling the fragile fabric with care. Then he held it up and gently shook it out. I watched as he forcibly distanced himself from the memory and once more became a man of cold science.

He pulled a magnifying glass from his pocket. 'Hold this fabric up, Watson, extended here, against the light.' His voice was brisk. Too brisk, I thought.

I reluctantly pocketed the gun, keeping an eye on Isla McLaren and did as he asked. He leaned in to examine the scarf minutely, with the dispassionate but intense regard of a laboratory technician.

After a moment he stood back and waved his hand dismissively.

'She did not die from hanging. The marks tell the story. I can prove it. Stand closer, Watson. Here.'

I hesitated. This did not sound like a good idea.

'It is all right, Watson. Come over here.'

I did so and he took the scarf from my hands and made a circle of it in the centre. He then moved behind me, looped this over my head and drew it uncomfortably tight round my neck. I gagged and my hands went instinctively to grasp at the scarf.

'You see.' said Holmes, letting it loosen only slightly. 'She was strangled manually, not hanged. It happened like this. Her killer came from behind most likely. You saw where

Watson's hands naturally went. Keep them there, Doctor, as I remove the scarf.'

He unwound it from my neck and held it up to the light. 'See these raking tears here, near the centre? They were made by her hands as the killer—'

He paused, words escaping him suddenly. He cleared his throat, blinking rapidly. But he took a deep breath and willed the scientist back to life.

'As the killer tightened the scarf. Charlotte, she . . . she struggled to break free, and clawed at this part here, near the middle.'

He then pulled the scarf through his hands to one end. 'Yet at this end, you see the marks of the knot for the noose? We know that her hands were not tied, as you testified, Mrs McLaren, and the court papers showed. In an official hanging, the hands are secured because instinct compels one to fight the knot. If she were alive when hanged, the shredding from her nails would have been here—' he pointed to an area closer to one of the ends, 'rather than where they are.'

He dropped his hands, and the scarf dangled limply from them. His face was a blank, devoid of all expression. 'She was strangled by someone, then hanged to make it look like a suicide.'

Isla McLaren and I could not move.

As if a switch were pulled on an electric light the full visualization of the crime swept over Holmes. He swallowed, blinking back tears. No one was more surprised at this than Holmes himself. He put his hand to his eyes, embarrassed. I took the scarf from him and both Mrs McLaren and I turned from Holmes to give him a moment of privacy.

'How did you know my nickname?' Isla McLaren asked me in a choked voice.

'I just came from your grandmother in Atholmere,' I said.

She nodded. I gently folded the scarf into a small square and handed it to her.

'Bravo, Mr Holmes,' said Isla McLaren. 'I believe you are right. And you know that August was upstairs in her room when I found her in the sitting room,' said Isla.

'I do,' said Holmes. 'I read the notes of the trial again and again. How is it that you were not mentioned by name?'

'My parents kept my name from the transcript. Do you not remember the reference to "a local child"?'

'Yes. I attempted in vain to discover this "local child". I was blocked from any investigation I attempted.'

'August came downstairs minutes after I found Charlotte hanging. He told me he had found her suicide note.'

'Which he no doubt forged. His special gift,' said Holmes. 'He forged the elopement note from Fiona as well. And the anonymous policeman's to you. And to Orville St John. But this note, ah this note! You were standing by the body. August Bell Clarion came downstairs from her room and told you he had just found Charlotte's suicide note?'

'He had it in his hand.'

'Did you wonder why it was upstairs and not near the body?'

'I presumed she wrote it and left it on her desk,' said the lady.

'Tell me exactly what happened.'

'He would not let me see it. I grabbed it but he pulled it away, out of my hand.'

'Then how do you know what it was?'

'I saw her handwriting. And her special brown ink. The . . .' Isla McLaren was rocked by a sudden memory. 'Oh my God, the ink!' A sob escaped her and she covered her mouth in anguish. 'I . . . later noticed a brown ink stain on my hands!'

'Either he had just written it,' said Holmes. 'Or your hands were wet.'

'It was *waterproof* ink. Therefore it must have still been wet. He killed her, then went upstairs.' she cried.

' . . . and wrote the note, minutes before you arrived. He was writing it as you were with Charlotte,' said Holmes. 'I suspected August killed her but could not get access to prove it. Together we now have the proof.'

'What a shame this monster eluded a trial,' I said. 'Death at Khartoum is almost too easy an end for him.'

'It is not over yet,' said Holmes. 'He feigned his death once in El Obeid. I now believe he was able to do so a second time. August Bell Clarion lives and I will find and stop him at all costs.'

'He lives?' I could not believe it.

'Yes. And he has been here all along. Scarred beyond recognition, and having returned here because Cameron Coupe, complicit in Donal's death, would be forced to offer him sanctuary. We have seen him.'

'My God!' I said. 'But you say we have seen him?'

'Here?' asked Isla

'Yes. I missed him, Mrs McLaren, and so did you. It is Jowe Lammas, Coupe's right hand man.'

'My God!' said Isla. 'Lammas! Lammas is the month of August.'

Holmes nodded. 'And "Jowe" is a Scots dialect word for—'

'— the peal of a bell. Oh, my God!' she cried.

'He was here, but he has fled,' said my friend, the curtain of exhaustion once again settling over him. 'I have searched everywhere on the property, with the help of Moray and little Calum and Alistair, and men they trust. But I believe the man we know as August Bell Clarion has not gone far. I feel it. And I am certain he will strike again.'

'Perhaps sooner than you think, Sherlock Holmes,' said a voice from the darkness behind us.

CHAPTER 40

A Wash

 mirthless, terrible laugh sounded from behind an adjacent boiler to our right. We turned to see a grotesque figure emerge from behind the equipment. He was towering, muscular, and with a face that looked like it had emerged from the depths of hell – one eye gone, a jagged scar, a slab of meat for a face, red and veined and like the devil himself. He laughed again, a peculiar high-pitched sound. It was Jowe Lammas. Or—

'August Bell Clarion,' said Sherlock Holmes. 'You are looking well.'

With a feint to the right, Clarion lunged suddenly and grabbed Isla by the wrist, yanking her to him. He held her tightly, pinning one arm to her side, and then brutally grabbed the other and twisted it behind her back. She screamed in pain.

'Quiet, little cousin,' said the heinous figure in a hoarse whisper. He wrapped one enormous arm around her neck and squeezed. 'Or I will snap this little stem.'

In the instant, without a word and entirely on instinct, Holmes and I separated from each other and now faced the man from either side. He immediately shifted Isla to block my angle on him.

'Ah yes, Dr Watson, you are the one with the gun,' said he. 'You may not wish to shoot through this young lady, even though she has been enjoying impersonating a ghost. You are not quite transparent after all, my dear.' He twisted her arm some more and she cried out in pain. 'Nor are you dead yet, Isla.'

'Fiend. You killed sweet Charlotte! Our own cousin!' she spat.

'Well, yes, though it was her own fault,' said Clarion. 'Did you know you very much resemble her? Lovely little things, both of you.' He gave her neck a squeeze and she gagged. I heard Holmes's sharp intake of breath near me.

He regarded Holmes with a fierce concentration. 'Here is what I would like you to do, gentlemen. Dr Watson, throw your gun into that mash. Go on, do it.'

I glanced at the opening over the mash tun into the grey, swirling soup below. It was at least five or six feet deep, maybe more. I would never retrieve it. Another scream from Isla McLaren as he twisted her arm, and Holmes nodded to me to release the gun. As I did and Clarion watched me, I saw Holmes move slightly in my peripheral vision.

The gun sailed through the opening and made a small splash in the swirling mash. 'Very good,' said August Bell Clarion. Retaining a stranglehold on Isla, he released her other arm and withdrew a Webley of his own from his pocket, training it on Holmes. He began to laugh. It was a strange coughing sound, mirthless and frightening.

'Worried about this young lady?' he wheezed.

Holmes shrugged. 'Not particularly. I see you have risen from the dead. Twice,' he added casually.

'I knew it would take more than once to fool the "great" Sherlock Holmes,' said Clarion.

'Your first "death" at El Obeid was rather more convincing.'

'Indeed, my substitute did die. Gruesomely, I understand. The second time I had to make more clever arrangements.'

Holmes nodded. 'I have sensed your subtle hand, Clarion. But clearly you did not escape unscathed.' He passed a hand over his own cheek.

A grimace passed over the ruined face of August Bell Clarion. 'There was an interesting way of extracting information among the tribe which snared me after Khartoum. I was lucky to escape with my life. But they released me when they finally understood I was helpful to their cause.'

'You betrayed Gordon at Khartoum!' I exclaimed.

August Bell Clarion shrugged but did not answer.

'You then returned to Scotland and blackmailed Coupe, who was party to your murder of Donal McLaren, to hire and promote you,' said Holmes. 'How then did you become involved in the Fiona case? It was you, was it not, who sent the head to the South of France?' remarked Holmes. 'I presume you used an intermediary, probably Seamus Marchand, the man who later helped you switch the casks. And who paid for his loyalty to you in blood. Your fingerprints are all over this series of events.'

August Bell Clarion smiled and it was a tear rent through the spidery scars of his reddened face. 'Back in form, Sherlock Holmes. Exactly right. But how did I become involved, you ask? I walked in on the little scuffle between Coupe and Fiona. Or rather the end of it. The rest you can imagine. Although it took you some time.'

'But why send the head?'

August Bell Clarion laughed. 'You have not figured that out?'

'You resented the laird for the army post he arranged for you—'

'He gave me a death warrant, not a gift. I was happy to repay him. But no, that was not it.'

Holmes paused. I looked about for something, anything I could use against this monster. He was intent on my friend, and at that moment, held all the cards. My hand stole to my pocket. The knife! That cursed artefact, reputed to kill the evil and protect the good. I felt its reassuring cold handle. Just a thing. Nothing magic. A thing. But perhaps a useful one.

'But to send a man his daughter's head on a plate – that is going rather far, even for you,' Holmes continued. 'You must have had something in mind.'

Clarion smiled, savouring the moment. 'It really had little to do with him. Although Fiona being his issue did add a certain piquancy to it. You still do not understand, do you? Where is the brilliant reasoner your chronicler portrays, Mr Sherlock Holmes?'

Holmes said nothing. The sound of condensation dripping,

the rhythmic clanking and whoosh of the nearby steam engine, and the splash of the rakes churning incessantly in the huge vat below us filled the void. Holmes remained puzzled, I could read it in his posture.

'Consider this. First I sent Orville and Isla after you but both failed in their mission.'

'Of course,' said Holmes. 'Orville St John said he had recently received a letter proving it was I who cut out his tongue. I presume you impersonated a policeman on paper in that missive.'

Clarion laughed. 'Yes, indeed.'

'Forgery is your gift. I have not forgotten.' said Holmes. 'So you thought to incite St John to murderous revenge. It almost worked. You, of course, cut out his tongue yourself. Mutilated your own best friend.'

August Bell Clarion smiled. Half of his face cooperated. The other half crumpled like wet newspaper. 'Friends are there to be used. Besides, he argued with me too much. Take note, Dr Watson. But poor Orville. He never saw me coming. I knocked him out first, of course. But so difficult! The tongue is a very strong muscle, you know. You would have been sent up for that if it were not for your interfering brother Mycroft,' said Clarion.

The silver tongue. The champion public speaker who had just turned a crowd against Sherlock Holmes. It was a near perfect frame.

Isla McLaren struggled, and grunted in pain.

'Be still, little one,' said Clarion. 'Yes, the letter you received was written by me as well.'

Holmes nodded. 'Of course! From this same mysterious policeman. I will wager he had "proof" that I caused your cousin's death, and sent you the scarf. Is that right Mrs McLaren?'

Isla struggled to reply but Clarion tightened his grip and she made small choking sounds.

'A miscalculation, Clarion,' said Holmes. 'Mrs McLaren did not entirely take the bait. No, she wanted to see for herself.'

The lady, unable to answer, moved her head almost imperceptibly in a nod.

'But the question of Fiona's head remains,' said Holmes. 'Why did you send it to the hotel?'

August Bell Clarion laughed loudly. 'I am surprised! You have never been accused of false modesty, Mr Sherlock Holmes. How could you miss this? It was all about you. I knew you would come to Braedern when you heard of it. It was just the *outré* touch to attract you, like the proverbial moth to the flame.'

I had been right. The head had been sent to the Grand Hôtel du Cap for no other reason than to lure Sherlock Holmes to the Highlands. If we managed to live through this, I would surely remind him of it.

'But you had no way of knowing I would be there!' said Holmes.

'It did not matter. You would come when you heard of it. That you were there was just a bit of luck!'

Isla McLaren had begun to slump, presumably in considerable pain from Clarion's grip. Her eyes were half closed. Was she suffocating?

'Mrs McLaren!' I cried. Clarion ignored me.

'I suspected you from the start,' said Holmes. 'I had your death at El Obeid investigated one more time, and confirmed. But when I saw your photograph at Khartoum as Donal McLaren, I knew.'

He had, of course, said the opposite to me. August Bell Clarion's gaze shifted to my face. Once again his face creased in the horrific smile.

'Poor Doctor Watson, you have been left out of the game,' said he. 'Sherlock Holmes was never much of a friend to anyone. Have you not figured that out?' He turned to Isla McLaren. 'He really did crush your cousin Charlotte's dreams, you know. A cold, cold man. He is incapable of love.'

My hand tightened around the fabled knife. Perhaps if I could get closer.

Mrs McLaren continued to struggle but could not move in his grip.

'Oh, but you think he is capable of love, Isla? Shall we see?' Clarion glanced my way.

'August Bell Clarion,' said Holmes quickly. 'Your fight is with me. Let them go.'

Without warning, and still with his grip on the girl, Clarion swung his gun to point at me. Mrs McLaren screamed. I ducked but the sound of a shot echoed in the cavernous room. I felt a sharp sting in the outside of my shoulder near my old wound, and turned to look at it. Just as blood appeared on my shirt, a wall of pain hit me and I sank to my knees.

Holmes was immediately at my side.

'Watson!' He bent down and grasped my forearms, his face close to mine. 'Watson! Tell me you are all right!'

My arm throbbed. But I still had sensation in it. I moved my hand to make sure.

'Just a graze,' I whispered. 'A wild shot.'

'Make it be more,' he whispered back, leaning in to apparently examine the wound. 'Oh, my God!' he cried.

Blocked by Holmes, I reached down with my good arm into my trousers pocket and found the jewelled hunting knife. I thrust it into his hand. He pocketed it as I groaned and fell backward, pretending to lose consciousness.

Through half closed eyes, I witnessed the following. August Bell Clarion stared at us in rapt fascination. Holmes leapt to his feet.

'You have killed John Watson!' he cried in thoroughly believable anguish.

Suddenly Isla McLaren trod on Clarion's instep with every ounce of force she could. 'Fiend!' she cried as her sharp heel hammered into his arch. He screamed and dropped the gun. Holmes dived for it.

Clarion flung Isla to the side where she slammed into an iron pillar with a sickening thud, and dropped to the floor. Blood gushed from her forehead. Abandoning my pretence, I was on my feet and at the lady's side in a moment. She looked up at me in confusion and fear. Conscious, at least.

'Watson!' came a strangled cry from over my shoulder.

Clarion had fallen upon Holmes and the two of them

rolled on the platform, struggling for the gun. Next to them loomed the opening into the bubbling mash below.

Before I could respond, August Bell Clarion had Holmes pinned against the railing blocking the opening to the mash tun. The fiend slammed a knee into Holmes chest, and I heard the crack of a rib. Holmes cried out in pain. I ran to help my friend and the two of us struggled mightily with Clarion at the edge of the opening.

But both of us were hurt, and my right arm was virtually useless. The villain was a whirling dervish of hatred and fury. He punched me hard in my wounded shoulder and the shock of pain sent me reeling. As I stumbled back, Holmes leapt onto Clarion, but the fiend twisted, and in a paroxysm of hatred, delivered a second stunning blow to the chest, then grasped Holmes by the shirt and lifted him up, tipping him backwards over the railing. Time slowed as I watched in horror as Holmes fell backward into the steaming mash.

I heard the terrible noise of a splash and rushed to the edge and peered down. In the split second of this distraction I felt myself grabbed and hoisted into the air.

Then I too, was flung down into the vat, and went under, into the mushy liquid. So hot! My God, the burning—

I surfaced, gasping, my feet sliding as I struggled to stand in the soup. The liquid was viscous and slimy. I retched as I inhaled the steamy, odoriferous air. The heat! Agony.

'Look out!' cried Holmes and I turned and in the dim light, saw the whirling tines of the rake nearly upon me. I would be pulled under and drowned – but Holmes grabbed me by the collar and yanked me away from the slow moving but inexorable blades. We moved as far from them as possible. The liquid was up to our chests, and it was hard to move on the slippery bottom which seemed to be on a slant towards the centre. A wave of dizziness swept over me.

Holmes's face was bright red, and he was saying something but the sounds were muffled, distorted. I rubbed my ears trying to clear them.

My skin was on fire. We had minutes – or perhaps seconds – before losing consciousness.

'The rakes!' Holmes was pointing, and I followed his gesture to see that the tines of the giant mechanical rake had rotated clockwise and continued to revolve, slowly and relentlessly across the surface of the vat. They were now approaching the ladder. In a moment of apparent insanity, Holmes splashed towards them, positioning himself right under the opening, and flattened himself against the wall of the tank. Clarion could not see him from there. In horror I watched as the rake drew closer to Holmes.

'Holmes! Move away from there! I shouted.

I heard a laugh and looked up. August Bell Clarion was peering in. I had the vague sensation of a shadow behind him.

Holmes gave me a quick wave and then let out a cry.

The rakes were nearly upon him! They were close, too close! 'Holmes!' I cried.

Clarion, eager to witness the demise of Holmes, leaned in through the opening.

Holmes let out a blood-curdling scream, and the villain leaned in further. Suddenly he pitched forward, pushed from behind. I got a quick glimpse of Isla behind him as he tumbled down, his voice piercing the air with his own scream of panic.

The huge body tumbled down, just as Holmes slid out of reach of the machinery. Clarion landed directly on the turning rakes. They squealed and moaned, the tines digging into his body, carrying him down into the steaming mash, his hands flailing wildly just above the surface.

'Quick Watson, the heat, we must get out,' said Holmes. The rakes suddenly ground to a halt. Clarion's body had become entangled under the surface and they were jammed.

Holmes and I clambered over the rake and towards the ladder. My friend propelled me up first as Isla reached down to help me, my wounded shoulder making the climb difficult. As I neared the top I looked down to see Holmes wavering at the foot of the ladder, half in and half out of the mash. His face was terrible; his eyes were shining grey marbles in a bright crimson grimace. He swayed, blinking.

'Holmes,' I cried.

And then as I watched, a huge white hand flashed upwards from the steaming mash and grabbed Holmes by the neck, pulling him backward and down. With a strangled cry he went under.

'Holmes!' I attempted to back down the ladder but Isla had an iron grip on my collar and stopped me.

I turned to see the two men floundering and struggling in the grey soupy liquid, primordial creatures battling to the death. As Clarion pulled himself free, the rakes resumed their relentless journey and the splashing figures veered, flailing wildly, from the path. They went under, surfaced, and went under again.

I heard Isla McLaren's voice shouting but I could not make out the words.

Suddenly there was the sound of metal grinding on metal and the rakes came to a stop.

But where was Holmes?

The surface of the mash, swirling from the rakes and the men battling to the death grew still and deadly calm.

'Holmes!' I cried.

Suddenly there was a flurry of splashing liquid and a figure, covered completely in the slurry, raised above the surface, brandishing the knife, the fabled knife. Was it Holmes?

The dripping arm came down and splashed the surface of the mash, then came up again, and again. A stain of pink bloomed in the surrounding liquid. There was a wild splashing nearby, and then stillness.

But who had been stabbed? I wrenched free from Isla McLaren's grasp and leapt from the top of the ladder and back down into the mash.

The knife-wielding figure stood and faced me, only shoulders and head visible, covered with the greyish stuff.

'It is over, Watson,' said the familiar voice, slurred and hesitant. Thank God, it was Sherlock Holmes. Then the great man passed out, and sank backward into the liquid.

I caught him and for a moment we both went under. I

was aware only of grasping his jacket, and his own hand grasping my arm. Then overwhelming heat, and then blackness.

I came to some minutes later, lying on a hard surface with the sensation of something soft and freezing cold on my neck and wrists, and strong draughts blowing on my hot, wet clothes. I opened my eyes and all was a blur. Turning my head I made out Holmes's prone figure next to mine. We were lying on the metal platform near the mash tun.

Isla McLaren's face swam before mine. 'Dr Watson!'

Then everything went black again.

I later learned what had transpired. August Bell Clarion escaped from being trapped in the rakes and attacked Holmes, who managed to disable him by stabbing him with the jack-knife. Clarion fell once more, mortally wounded and was, at last, fatally trapped by the rakes. He suffered a heinous death from stabbing, heat and blood loss, and ultimately suffocation as the rakes pinned him just below the surface.

Isla had sounded the alarm and almost immediately two men, including the groundskeeper Ualan Moray, arrived in time to turn off the machine and fish Holmes and me out of the deadly vat before we drowned or died of heatstroke. More help came in the form of Alistair, who had eventually begun to worry about his wife and had arrived on the scene with several men in tow.

Snow was applied to our necks, wrists and bodies to bring out temperature back to normal. Although dangerously near death from hyperthermia, we were alive only because the heating unit and temperature gauge in the mash tun had been faulty. Had it been working as usual we would have been boiled alive.

Alistair directed others in the unenviable task of removing the remains of August Bell Clarion from the mash tun. By luck, the skilled Doctor MacLeish was still on the property. Holmes and I were transported to the castle and attended to through the night by the good doctor and her assistant.

Two days passed, and Holmes and I recovered with cooling baths and rest. My shoulder needed nothing more than a few stitches but I will admit to a great exhaustion, and welcomed a small amount of morphine, though Holmes refused. Instead he dealt with the Aberdeen and London authorities who arrived to gather the bodies of August Bell Clarion and Donal McLaren and take statements from everyone involved. I was dimly aware that Holmes exchanged several cables with Mycroft.

It was very early the third morning that we were recovered enough to depart Braedern, which the newspapers, in the wake of the multiple tragedies, were now referring to as 'cursed Elsinore'. None of the family was in evidence as our luggage was loaded, but as we settled into a carriage the boy Calum Moray ran up. He carried a small package and handed it up to Holmes. 'From Mrs McLaren,' he said, shyly.

Holmes untied the package. It was the small Goethe book he had remarked upon in Isla's room. He opened it and the frontspiece page, previously missing, fluttered out.

He quickly replaced it but I saw his own familiar handwriting in an inscription. I knew at once it must have been his gift to Charlotte.

He thanked the boy, and we departed.

Holmes closed his eyes as the carriage drew us over the snowy hill and away from Braedern Castle and the doomed McLaren Distillery. I looked back at the forlorn and windswept buildings and the castle, rising like a jagged, black dinosaur from the snowy hill. I was never so happy to leave a place in my life.

CHAPTER 41

221B

t was a full week after our return to London that I managed a visit to 221B. The snow in London had persisted and the Christmas season with its attendant noise and jollity was hard upon us, turning every shop window and street corner into a postcard illustration. I found it a welcome antidote to the darkness and drama we had faced in Scotland, yet I knew it was a season that little comforted my friend.

It would be another two weeks before the case involving a goose and a stolen jewel would distract his feverish mind, and I had heard from Mrs Hudson that aside from a small mystery involving a pickled brain stolen from Bart's collection, a matter he solved in three hours, Holmes had had little to occupy him.

As I ascended the stairs at 221B, I felt a prickle of concern. I could never be precisely sure which version of Holmes would greet me when I arrived at our former shared lodgings. But a lively Paganini violin piece floated down from his rooms, giving me hope.

He must have noted my approach, for Holmes stopped playing and threw open the door. 'Watson!' he cried. 'You have come at the perfect moment!' To my surprise, he was well rested and sleek, wearing his finest waistcoat, though topped with his blue dressing gown.

Setting down his violin, he embraced me in an unusual display of warmth. Behind him a crackling fire burned cheerily and some pine boughs and candles on the mantle had displaced the usual clutter. On the dining table, a generous display of cakes and sandwiches had been laid out by Mrs Hudson. I felt suddenly that I had wandered into some alternate 221B.

'Holmes,' I said. 'I am delighted to see you thus. What is your news?'

He had barely recounted his small triumph with the stolen brain when, to my complete surprise, Mrs Hudson announced that Mrs Isla McLaren had arrived for a visit. She swept into the room, festively attired in a gown of pine green and Christmas red with her usual touches of tartan trim. Taking in the newly cosy ambience with a smile, she greeted Holmes warmly. Pretending polite indifference which fooled no one, he invited her to sit and take tea.

For the next hour, this fine lady sat before the fire with us, during which time the three of us cleared up most, if not all of the remaining mysteries of the dramatic events at Braedern.

Cameron Coupe, she related, had survived his terrible

injury and to our great surprise, was being looked after by the laird, who saw past the man's more bizarre actions to the loyalty beneath the surface. Puzzling to me, but perhaps Coupe was the son the laird deserved, I thought. I wondered what their future held.

The eldest son, Charles, had been charged with arranging the bombing down in Montpellier but somehow had escaped on a technicality, and while free of gaol, was so disrespected in his field that he would never be allowed near a distillery again. Catherine had left him and returned to her family. The McLaren plant was closed, presumably for ever, and the castle had been put up for sale.

'What of the ghost of the Lady Elizabeth McLaren?' I asked.

Isla looked uncomfortable. To my surprise, so did Holmes.

'I think I saw her,' I admitted. 'The first night we were there. And then again.'

Holmes would not meet my eyes.

'Mr Holmes did as well,' said Mrs McLaren. 'Did you not, Mr Holmes? You were shouting at something the night Dr Watson was gone.'

'A trick of the light, that is all.'

Isla held his gaze then shrugged. 'How curious. Well in any case, you should know that Anne's remains were found, exactly where one might expect, and have been given a proper burial, Mr Holmes. The apparition of Mrs McLaren has not been seen since.'

Holmes murmured his approval, then handed Mrs

McLaren a small volume of Scottish poetry. 'From Hatchards, in return for the Goethe,' said he. 'Note the inner rhyme schemes in these early Scottish sonnets. You may wish to challenge yourself further.'

'Thank you, but . . .' She looked puzzled.

'Really, Mrs McLaren. Your secret was out when I noticed the collection of poetry in your room, the inks and pens on your desk, and the fact that no one else saw the sonnet you described having arrived in the basket upon Fiona's return.'

But of course! The sonnet sent back with Fiona had been penned by Isla, no doubt to attract Holmes with the puzzle! It had almost worked.

'Nicely done, Mr Holmes,' said the lady.

'Frankly, no one else seemed capable. What I wonder about, however, is the one you wrote to Dr Paul-Édouard Janvier in Montpellier.'

I had completely forgotten. Janvier had told us the last of the three threatening notes he received was in rhyme!

'That was yours as well, was it not?'

Isla flushed and nodded. 'I regret writing that.'

'What was your motive?'

'Charles asked me for the favour. It was a distracting challenge. I never thought for a moment he would make good on the threat.'

A woman bored is a danger, her own husband had said. All too true, in Isla McLaren's case.

'You should apply your gifts with more discretion in the future,' said Holmes.

'I shall keep that in mind,' said she. 'But I have come for more than a social visit, Mr Holmes. I have something I know will interest you.'

The lady took from her handbag a large brown envelope, and from it withdrew a series of grotesque, fading photographs. Moving the refreshments aside, she spread them out on our dining table. Against the background of holiday cheer and domestic comforts, we found ourselves drawn in a tight circle, peering at the sordid tableau.

For there were the police photographs of the scene of the late Charlotte Simpson's death. Strangely, in that room, they had the effect of a death mask thrust into the centre of a child's party.

Holmes studied them. 'The pillows,' he said, finally. 'They are not as you described.'

'True,' said Isla.

There was a sofa in the picture, near where the body of a young woman hung from a ceiling light. Every pillow was in its proper place. But, as Isla pointed out, these pillows had not been so when she had arrived on the scene. Instead, they had been spread around as if from a struggle.

'Had I seen these photographs, I would have deduced the obvious,' she said.

Holmes stared at the photos, a grave expression on his pale face. 'Yes, as would I. August Bell Clarion was wise to stage the scene to eliminate any sign of the struggle which you did not register at the time. It is no wonder that everyone from the police to the family accepted the theory that the poor girl . . .' his voice trailed off.

'That she killed herself, yes,' said Isla McLaren.

'She was capable of it,' said Holmes. 'I knew it. And I believe you knew it as well. It was what drove you to rush to her on that day.'

The lady was silent.

'I am afraid I rebuffed you unkindly, madam,' said Holmes. 'For that I apologize. Your resemblance to Charlotte was, well, somehow I must have seen . . .

But not observed, I thought.

'You need not apologize,' said she. 'I, on the other hand saw a decent, if somewhat rude young man, with perhaps too much conceit about his own intellectual gifts. That fit exactly with the Sherlock Holmes my cousin described so long ago.'

'She thought me rude and conceited?'

Mrs McLaren just stared at him. 'And loved you in spite of it.'

Holmes cleared his throat and pointedly returned to studying the photographs.

'You did not notice the pillows awry when you first got there?' he queried.

'I did not. Remember that I was but twelve years old and had walked in on the scene of my dear cousin's death. My only thought was to try to save her, because to my self-obsessed child's eyes, she could not possibly have thought to leave me in this way.'

'And she did not,' I said. 'I doubt she would have left either of you in this way.'

For several long minutes Holmes flipped through the

other photographs, studying them with care, and then finally set them down. Mrs McLaren gathered them up and replaced them in the brown envelope, which she tucked inside her handbag.

For a full minute the three of us sat there in silence. Holmes closed his eyes, and was lost in his thoughts. I saw through his stoicism to his deep pain.

Isla McLaren regarded my friend. A look of concern passed over her and she glanced at me.

'Holmes,' I said gently. 'It is time to release this ghost.'

His eyes sprang open and he rose to his feet. 'Mrs McLaren. It is good to see you looking so seasonal! And I note that you have a business engagement here in London. I have no doubt that it will go well for you.'

She rose. 'But how did you—never mind. It is true. Alistair and I are being courted by both Dewar and Buchanan. They both wish us to manage one or more distilleries in the Highlands and it is up to us to choose. Our talents, apparently, fit well with their needs.'

'That is excellent news,' I exclaimed, happy that Isla and Alistair McLaren, at least, had survived the debacle of Braedern.

Holmes abruptly turned to the door. He had heard something that Mrs McLaren and I had not.

'Ah, another old friend arrives, Watson! It is an embarrassment of riches,' he said with that sardonic humour of old.

'Then I shall leave you, sir,' said the lady. She began to gather her things.

At that moment Mrs Hudson knocked and entered. 'Monsieur Jean Vidocq to see you, Mr Holmes. Shall I send him—'

'No need, Mrs Hudson,' said Holmes. 'He already arrives.'

Behind our landlady, a tall, top-hatted figure was just visible bounding up the stairs. *'Bonjour mes amis!'* boomed the handsome Frenchman, appearing over Mrs Hudson's shoulder.

The good woman cocked an eyebrow at his presumption but let him pass.

He strode into the room, took in Isla McLaren with a frankly admiring glance, walked right up to her, and reached for her hand. She extended it coolly and he kissed it with the flourish of the born courtier.

'Enchanté, Madame,' said he. 'You are Scottish, I perceive.'

'Ça, c'est bien évident.' she replied in perfect French. *That is perfectly clear.* Even I understood her jibe. 'Excuse me.'

She withdrew her hand and with a small wave and an amused smile to Holmes and me, took her leave. A faint whiff of perfume lingered in the air behind her.

'Ah, the Scottish heather,' said Jean Vidocq, savouring it. 'And a touch of lavender. Mmmm. *Douce. Très douce.'*

'What do you want, Vidocq?' said Holmes.

Vidocq took in the room, the refreshments, the decorations, and Holmes's perfect grooming. 'I see you are at last developing the taste for the finer things in life,' said he, with a pointed glance at the doorway through which Mrs McLaren had just passed.

'Unlike yourself, I do not consider the conquest of married ladies to be an appropriate use of my skills,' said Holmes.

'*Alors*, it is a skill which it is doubtful you possess, *cher ami!*' smiled Vidocq. 'Will you offer me a libation? I have travelled far. And I bear news for you.'

Holmes sat down in the large basket chair and steepled his hands. He yawned. 'Enlighten me on this one point, Vidocq. How is it that you are not in prison?'

This question intrigued me as well, and I was eager to hear the response. I went to the sideboard and offered him a whisky.

'A good French brandy for me, please,' said Vidocq. 'If you have any. But none of your vile English pastries.'

I poured him one, and a whisky each for Holmes and me. I happily took a piece of one of Mrs Hudson's delicious fruitcakes. What do the French know of cake?

'The news, Vidocq, the news,' prompted Holmes. 'Oh, and by the way, my brother Mycroft expressed a certain satisfaction with my uncovering of Charles McLaren's involvement, and your, shall we say, help with the little matter of the bomb at Dr Janvier's laboratory. Although I understand a Monsieur Reynaud of the French government was less than pleased with your adventurous ways.'

'Ah, it is nothing. Thanks to you I have had some little problem in extricating myself from this small bombing incident – you know perfectly well I would not harm a soul – but at last, it was done,' said the Frenchman. He took a sip from his drink and savoured it. 'And very good, *oui,* because yet another misfortune was directed to Dr Janvier which I was able to prevent.'

'Another commission, or a real threat, this time?' asked Holmes.

'Oh, very real! A consortium of Germans and Belgians. But easily handled,' he waived away an imaginary swarm of flies. 'I am well paid for this. A medal will be forthcoming, next month, I believe.'

Holmes barked out a laugh. 'You should consider a career as a bareback rider in the circus, Vidocq,' he said. 'Charles McLaren is facing a stiff penalty, if not gaol, for his part in the planning. Although "intention" is all that can be proved. And his father, although ruined, retains enough assets to buy his freedom.'

'It is ever so. A rather weak link, that blustering idiot Charles,' said Vidocq. 'A beautiful wife, however.'

'Women will be your undoing, Vidocq.'

'Yes, it is probably true. But not yours, Holmes. Have you never reconsidered your position in that respect? Think of all that you are missing.'

'Oh, I have most definitely given the matter all the attention it deserves,' said Holmes. I glanced at him but he refused to meet my gaze, instead staring intently into his whisky glass.

I believe it was on that very day, and perhaps at that very moment that Sherlock Holmes truly did put his ghosts to rest, for I never heard mention of Charlotte or the troubles at Camford again. Perhaps he vanquished these memories to some locked and remote place in what he called his brain-attic where they would never again see the light of day.

I on the other hand, have not those powers of will. To this day, I wonder about the pale figure I saw not once but twice in the hallway of the East Tower. And the strange knife which fulfilled its promise of protection. I would not go so far to say I believe in the supernatural, but I might, after this singular adventure, be somewhat less eager to ridicule those who do.

'Watson!' Holmes interrupted my ruminations. A smile spread slowly across his face, and he raised his glass. 'It has been a remarkable journey! Let us toast to whatever spirits continue to move us to our higher selves,' said he, eyes shining.

I raised my glass to join him in a toast to that fine senti-ment, and so did Jean Vidocq. 'To whatever spirits!' I said.

For annotations with interesting
facts about the people, places,
and things in this novel, visit
www.macbird.com/unquiet-spirits/notes

Acknowledgements

First a salute to Sir Arthur Conan Doyle, who is my first and best writing teacher and favourite writer among many. I fell in love with Sherlock Holmes and Dr Watson at age ten and have remained in love ever since.

Greatest thanks go to my husband Alan Kay for his unflagging generosity, enthusiasm and good humour throughout this long process. It would not be possible without you, bear.

I had a great deal of help along the way, but none more surprising and welcome than the eleventh hour incisive editorial comments of the esteemed Nicholas Meyer, who is not only my personal hero for his brilliant Holmes trilogy starting with *The Seven Percent Solution*, but also one of my favorite movie directors. Nick's generous notes made me laugh, cringe, and polish like crazy. Thank you, Nick.

Tough love offered by my writer's group colleagues 'The Oxnardians', Harley, Patty, Matt, Jamie, JB, Linda, Bob, Craig and John improved this tale, as did key criticism from the insightful Lynn Hightower, with nuanced editorial comments and cheerleading from Dennis Palumbo, Chris Simpson, Ramona Long, and Nancy Seid.

A special salute to the remarkable Sherlockian, Leah Cummins Guinn for her skilled research and commentary. I knew if I made you laugh, we were good. Thank you as well as to renowned Holmesian expert Catherine Cooke, good friend and curator of the Sherlock Holmes collection in London, for an early read and comments. Ailsa Campbell, from her desk in the Scottish Highlands, gently guided me to 'mair' accurate dialect (and other things) at a key juncture.

Dana Cameron and Carla Kaessinger Coupe's contribution spawned a certain intriguing character in this novel; ladies you know who I mean, and I thank you for this vote of confidence/challenge!

Of course there was a certain 'please don't throw me in the briar patch' element to researching the whisky business and my partner in crime here was the generous, delightful, world-renowned whisky expert Charles MacLean, who sports a Doyle-worthy moustache and knows everything and everyone in that world. Charlie also accompanied me on a fascinating visit to the deliciously gothic Fettes, which is not only Holmes's alma mater, but also James Bond's and the model for Hogwarts. I didn't know that when I selected it.

A helpful stay in Islay at Loch Gorm House was facilitated by Fiona Doyle (possibly a distant relative of Sir Arthur) and input from Adam Hannett of Bruichladdich and Jim McEwan 'The Cask Whisperer', as well as Audrey McPherson at Royal Lochnagar in the Highlands lent more than a bit of flavour. Scottish Holmesian Barry Young kindly provided research materials.

Thanks to Les Klinger for his unfailing Sherlockian cheer and moral support. Thanks to my wonderful agent Linda Langton, whose enthusiasm has meant so much. And to David Roth for early encouragement, and mystery legend Otto Penzler whose enthusiasm for my first novel gave me wings.

Appreciation to Dottie, Jane, Sara and Megan for extending the reach on the first book, and a special thank you also to Dr David Reuben, Rose, and Helen, you know why. A late visit to curator Emilia Kingham at the University College London Pathology Collections was gruesomely informative and also fun. A conversation about ghosts with medium Ann Treherne of the Conan Doyle Center in Edinburgh was an eye opener.

A salute to the wise and brilliant Lee Shasky, who sadly passed during the writing of this book, and whom I forgot to mention in my acknowledgments last time. Her wise words and generous spirit live on.

Finally, thanks to friends and extended family who graciously excused my absence and preoccupation for the many, many months this took, and especially to the wonderful staff at HarperCollins including Georgie Cauthery and David Brawn, who has made the journey possible . . . and also a pleasure.

I raise a glass of good single malt to you all.

Holmes and Watson return
in DEVIL'S DUE